T0082942

ONLY FOOLS DENY
WOMEN'S
EMPOWERMENT

LEON DUPLAN

authorHOUSE®

AuthorHouse™
1663 Liberty Drive
Bloomington, IN 47403
www.authorhouse.com
Phone: 1 (800) 839-8640

© 2017 Leon Duplan. All rights reserved.

No part of this book may be reproduced, stored in a retrieval system, or transmitted by any means without the written permission of the author.

Published by AuthorHouse 10/30/2017

ISBN: 978-1-5462-1398-7 (sc)
ISBN: 978-1-5462-1397-0 (e)

Library of Congress Control Number: 2017916296

Print information available on the last page.

Any people depicted in stock imagery provided by Thinkstock are models, and such images are being used for illustrative purposes only. Certain stock imagery © Thinkstock.

This book is printed on acid-free paper.

Because of the dynamic nature of the Internet, any web addresses or links contained in this book may have changed since publication and may no longer be valid. The views expressed in this work are solely those of the author and do not necessarily reflect the views of the publisher, and the publisher hereby disclaims any responsibility for them.

To my wife, sons and grandsons for the their love.

To God for giving me the inspiration for writing this book.

*To my parents for teaching me to treat
women with respect and dignity.*

CONTENTS

CHAPTER 1

It was a sunny morning when Richard Solaris arrived in his office at eight-thirty on Monday May 16, 2010. He had been delighted with the final weekend gathering with all his family except his father, who now lived in Los Angeles. Parking his car in the reserved space for vice presidents, Richard walked through the employees' entrance to find a group watching the news on a small portable TV. Prompted by his curiosity, he approached to greet them. Spotting him, they rose from their seats so he could hear the news that had struck the world, the death of Pope Leon XVII and preparations for his funeral.

John Harris, the local news reporter, commented that Phillip Mattberger, better known as Pope Leon XVII, was born on June 23, 1925, in Salzburg, Austria, and had died at noon last Sunday, May 15, 2010, in Rome due to respiratory arrest and several cardiovascular, pulmonary, and hepatic afflictions he had suffered for a long time and that had become more severe in the ten days prior to his death. Mattberger's pontifical term had been short, lasting only twelve years, beginning on September 24, 1998, when the cardinals gathered in conclave and designated him as Pope. His papacy ended on May 15, 2010, with his death.

The Pope had made multiple trips outside Rome, visiting different countries on several continents such as Mexico, a country he had visited five times that had always offered him a special love. During his pontifical period, he was awarded various prizes, winning the respect and admiration of not only the Catholic community, but also of hierarchs of other religions, such as Jewish leaders. His pontifical term was traditionally conservative, refusing to eliminate the celibacy of priests, to allow women into the priesthood, and prohibiting certain methods of birth control. At this moment, a great desire arose to know who would be his successor and if he would make reforms or adopt the same policies as his predecessor.

Meanwhile, as preparations for his funeral got under way, millions of people had congregated at the entrance to the Basilica de San Pedro, waiting to give the Pope their last tributes. Leaders throughout the entire world—in government, private and ecclesiastic sectors—continued to confirm their attendance at his funeral. The Pope's body would remain on display for three days so the people who loved him could pay their last respects. On the day following his funeral, in the same Basilica de San Pedro, the College of Cardinals would meet, and all cardinals would remain there until the new Pope was elected.

Unexpectedly, John Harris interrupted his news of the Pope to announce the disappearance of the vehicle in which Cardinal Leonardo Ponti and two bishops were traveling to attend the Pope's funeral. Harris said the cardinal had left his residence and in his vehicle with two bishops. The residence was close to the Basilica de San Pedro, and they should have arrived in five minutes. Two hours had passed, and nobody seemed to know of their whereabouts. Worries arose that something serious had happened to them. Several calls were made to their personal cell phones with no response. Their phones seemed to be out of service. Cardinal Leonardo Ponti was widely recognized as a principal prospect for being election as the next Pope. "Any clues regarding these disappearances will be deeply appreciated. Please stayed tuned to this channel until we can give you further information," John Harris said.

Continuing with his news, John Harris referred to the terrorist attacks that had taken place the previous Sunday night in Shanghai and New Delhi. Two car bombs had exploded, killing and wounding several people. The entire world was profoundly concerned about such attacks that had become more frequent. In the majority of cases, the victims were innocent people. Police from around the world had united to fight against these terrorists, offering large rewards for the capture of the attackers. In spite of their efforts, the results until now were unsatisfactory.

After watching the news for several minutes, Richard apologized, saying he had a very busy day ahead. Upon leaving, he picked up some documents from his desk for the meeting with his area directors that was held every Monday. Walking toward the conference room, he noticed his boss's private office open, so he assumed Joseph Blumekron had not arrived yet.

Richard Solaris was thirty-four years old, six feet tall, with a slim but athletic build. After he graduated from college in industrial engineering eight years ago, Richard began to work for a major transnational insurance company in Mexico City. Starting as the treasurer assistant manager of the treasurer's department, and rose in the ranks to become CFO of the company, a position he still held today.

When Richard was about to enter the conference room, he received a call on his cell phone. The caller ID showed it was from Alice, his secretary. Annoyed, he recalled his instruction to her not to transfer calls while he was in the conference room.

Alice had worked as his secretary for the previous five years and knew her boss well. Before had could scold her for transferring the call, she apologized, stating that upon her arrival at the office, she had found in her voice mail a message from Mr. Sosa, who had left a phone number for Richard to call him back. Comparing the number with the one received from his father, she saw that all the numbers matched except for the final digit, so could sense this was a delicate matter that required his immediate intervention. Furthermore, from the tone of voice in the message, she assumed it was an emergency.

Richard dialed the phone number immediately. The individual who answered sounded extremely nervous. Knowing it was Richard who had called, Sosa introduced himself, saying he was the manager of the condominium where his father lived and that Richard had met him two years ago when he had visited. At that moment, Richard remembered Sosa. He was tall with slightly gray hair, chubby, about fifty-five years old, divorced, with an unmistakable Cuban accent.

Sosa thanked Richard for calling him back so promptly. Then, stammering, he said he had some news regarding his father. Richard prayed that he would get straight to the point and was becoming extremely nervous.

Sosa breathed deeply and apologized, saying he was the bearer of bad news. His father's body had been found dead that morning on a pathway at the back garden of his condo. The reason was yet unknown, although it was supposed he had committed suicide.

Richard could not believe what he was hearing, and nearly shouting, he asked how it had happened. Sosa answered he was sorry he had little information, but no one seemed to know what had really happened. The purpose of his call was to inform Richard that a neighbor had called the police, who would arrive shortly, so he suggested he board the first flight available to Los Angeles. Sosa said he was in no position to provide further information about his father. Richard thanked him for his call, then said he would make immediate arrangements for the trip and would hope to arrive around six p.m. He said he would see Sosa soon.

"I will be waiting for you," Sosa said.

Hanging up his phone, Richard felt he would faint. Tears started to flow from his eyes. He could not understand how this tragedy could have occurred. It had hardly been two days since he had talked with his father by phone, and he had showed no sign of taking his own life.

Trying to hide his feelings, Richard left the conference room. Arriving in his office, he told Alice about the death of his beloved father.

Alice executed his orders. First, she canceled his engagements for the workweek. Then she informed Mr. Blumekron about what had occurred. As well, she put Richard on the line with his wife and then called the airline to make reservations for the next flight to Los Angeles. Later, she sent apologies to the directors, explaining why Richard had exited the conference room so quickly and without giving any explanation. Finally, she contacted to Joseph, Richard's driver, asking him to come up to the office and receive instructions from his boss.

Less than three minutes passed before Richard was speaking with his wife, Evelyn. Knowing that her husband never called at that time of the day, Evelyn asked Richard with a worried voice if everything was well. Richard answered it was not and immediately told Evelyn the news that had received from Sosa of his father's death. He explained to Evelyn that no one seemed to know the real cause of his death. He was surprised that his father had passed away so unexpectedly. As she could imagine, they required his presence and he had to travel to Los Angeles immediately. That was all he could tell her at the moment. Richard asked Evelyn to prepare his luggage for three or four days, as well as to have his passport and visa that he kept in the upper drawer of his desk ready. Joseph was on his way to pick them up and bring them back to the office. Richard promised to keep her posted on everything. He excused himself for having to cut the call short as he had other things to do before his departure. When was about to hang up on Evelyn, Richard said he had forgotten to tell her not to mention anything to his sister, Monica, until he could talk with her because he knew how she would react. Thanking Evelyn for her support and understanding, Richard expressed his love to his wife and ended the call. Unable to breathe, Evelyn replied in a low tone of voice that she loved him as well.

Ten minutes later, Alice was notifying Richard that his flight reservation was for 1:30 p.m. He was to pick up the ticket at the airport two hours prior to departure. She also said that Joseph was waiting for him outside his office. Richard told Alice to let him in.

Joseph found Richard with a bunch of papers on top of his desk. Giving instructions, Richard told Joseph he needed him to go to his home; retrieve his passport, visa, and luggage that his wife had prepared for him; and bring them back to the office immediately as he was in a hurry to go the airport and pick up his reserved ticket.

Joseph left the office in a rush. It took him almost an hour and a half to pick up the requested documents and luggage and return to the office. He told Alice he would wait for his boss in the parking garage, ready to take him to the airport.

Walking inside her boss office and glancing up from her notes Alice apologized to Richard, saying she felt bad for not offering him her condolences for his father's death, but as he knew, the day had been so busy and she had completely forgotten to do it. Richard understood perfectly what she meant and answered was fully aware of how busy they were, but anyhow, he really appreciated about her concern for his father.

Putting his jacket on and straightening his tie, Richard picked up his belongings and left the office in a hurry. The elevator was not at his floor, so he raced down the stairs, jumping them two at a time, until he reached the basement, where Joseph was waiting for him.

CHAPTER 2

Following Richard's instructions, Joseph drove him straight to the airport in the black Audi A-8 the company had assigned for his personal use. They had little time to get there.

On their way to the airport, Richard told Joseph that he was going to make a confession that required Joseph's maximum discretion. After making Joseph promise not to reveal it to anyone, Richard commented that his father had passed away in Los Angeles under abnormal conditions as there were signs he might have committed suicide. Joseph paused before answering. He refused to accept that Richard's father had committed suicide. He had had the privilege of serving him as a driver while both of them worked for the Ministry of Foreign Affairs. His presence of mind and equanimity were always astonishing, so Joseph refused to believe it. Thanking Joseph for his sincerity, Richard said he agreed, although they had to find out more information.

Looking at Richard in the rearview mirror, Joseph could see him close his eyes. He refrained from uttering another word, leaving Richard to concentrate on his deepest thoughts. Avoiding intense traffic the best he could, Joseph arrived at the airport in forty-three minutes. After retrieving the luggage from the trunk, he handed it to Richard with his passport and visa and asked if he should park the car. Thinking for a moment, Richard responded it would be better if he returned to the office in case Alice needed him. Thanking Joseph, he dismissed him. Watching him disappear among the many automobiles, Richard considered how lucky was to have a driver like Joseph.

Carrying his luggage, Richard arrived at the airline's front desk. Showing his passport and visa, he requested the reserved tickets and a boarding pass that he paid with his credit card. After completing his registration, he went up to the restaurant on the second level where he had a cup of coffee and some pastries.

Boarding the plane, Richard felt great relief. All the stress that had arisen in the past hours was reflected in his weariness. Shutting his eyes, he attempted get some sleep. Unable to sleep, though, he directed his thoughts to events in his lifetime as he had experienced arriving at his destiny. He would be submitted to a police interrogation, so he was gearing up to confront the authorities.

Richard's first thoughts were directed to early stages of his life, such as a childhood birthday when his parents, sister, friends, and relatives gathered to celebrate him, hugging him, congratulating him, and urging him to blow out the candles and eat a piece of cake. His mind then went to the day of his professional examination, his graduation as an industrial engineer, his wedding with Evelyn, and the birth of his two sons, all memorable events of his lifetime at which his parents were always present.

Then he remembered wise advice he had received from his father, such as when, at the request of a friend, Richard had embarked on a new business venture, investing most of his savings and ending up losing it all. At that time, his father said to him, "Richard, life presents to us challenges, threats, and opportunities. Some lead to success and others to failure. Although it is hard to understand, failures become a lesson, so learn from them and do not to repeat those mistakes. Just consider yourself lucky that when you lose your savings, you were not married. Otherwise, everything would have been more difficult for you. In order to restore you financially, I propose that you live with us, as food will always be on your table. However, my suggestion is to reflect on this unfortunate incident and apply it as a valuable lesson for the future. Then take my advice and never invest more than thirty percent of your assets in a business, either from your own money or a loan. As you become more successful, people will always be encouraging you to invest more with false promises."

Richard recalled his father's proven strength and integrity. Over three decades, he had held important positions in the public sector. His vocation as a politician was highly recognized, his last position being the Undersecretary Minister of Foreign Affairs.

Richard's reminiscences took him to his father's dedication to his family. Despite the demands of his work, he always found time for his family. Richard thought of his father as being conservative. Without being absolutely austere, he still never pursued great luxuries. An example was his father's dresser. It held a small number of suits that his father regarded as sufficient to be well dressed. None of them were from prestige designers, and in most cases, he had bought the fabric that he then brought to a cheap custom tailor. Their house was spacious but would never be considered a grand mansion. Like his father, his mother never put on fashionable jewelry, and her attire was rotated and combined wisely so that it consistently looked new. The allowance Richard and his sister received was generous but never exaggerated, and when needing an additional amount, they were asked about its purpose. Absorbed in his thoughts, Richard smiled, knowing that his father was a responsible, moderate, and overall honest person.

However, Richard's smile suddenly vanished when he remembered his mother's death, which had occurred on July 29, 2007, one week prior to his father's retirement after having finished a thirty-year term of service in the public administration. Everything fell apart when his mother went to a local supermarket two blocks from their house for the weekly groceries as she did every Wednesday. Knowing the store owner well, she paid for her groceries in advance, which a messenger later delivered to their home. On that day, as his mother paid for her groceries, two hooded persons with foreign accents, that later the cashier identified as women voices, came inside the store and took money from the cash register and from his mother's handbag. Threatening both with guns they were told to obey their instructions and hand over the money without resistance. However, even the money was handle without resistance one of the robbers started to shoot her gun, injuring the cashier in one arm, who instantly hid behind the counter. But the shots killed Richard's mother, who was unable to find a place to hide and was hit by two bullets, causing her immediate death. Richard recalled this tragedy with sadness and resentment toward his father, who refused to publish the event in the newspaper and never made any intent to capture the criminals even while having the means to do it.

Regrettably, after that incident, Richard's father changed completely from being a cheerful and sociable man. He fell into a deep depression that lasted fourteen month, causing Richard and his sister's life to be a living hell. His father hardly wanted to leave his bed, bathe, or shave, and in his continuous delirium, he blamed himself for his wife's death. His mental state was unstable, swinging suddenly from depression to lucidity Richard was sure which was worse. When his father was lucid, shouted angrily, forcing everyone to leave him alone. Luckily, after intensive psychiatric treatments and the care of their domestic assistant, Romy, in the month of September of 2008 Richard's father finally recovered from his depression. Seeing him healed some of his friends invited him to come back to the public administration. Even so, their attempts failed, as Richard's father expressed his desire of start a new business in the tourism field.

Richard relived the moment when his father met with him and his sister, Monica to inform them his psychiatrist had advised him to move away from his mother's memories. Therefore, following his instructions he intended to work in the tourism industry, but in the United States instead of Mexico, taking only Romy to serve as his domestic helper. Some friends in Los Angeles, California, had also offered to help and guide him when asked. His departure was expected at the end of the month, depending on the time it took to legalize Romy's migration papers. The news impacted Richard and Monica greatly. Knowing their father was a man of firm decisions, they opted to support him. To end the conversation, their father mentioned that this business represented for him a new challenge of life with an opportunity to travel around the world at reduced rates, a dream he had always had since childhood.

Monica understood her father's reasoning, except for why he wanted to execute his plan in the United States instead of Mexico, where they all lived. His response left them astonished. He said he didn't want to become a burden to them, as well as he didn't want them to look at him with pity. For that reason, he had determined to go away from them for some time. Monica burst into tears and replied he would never be a burden to them. Richard intervened to end the discussion, saying to his father that if it was not possible to dissuade him, all they could do was to offer their support whenever he needed it. Richard recalled the moment when his father stood up and, with tears in his eyes, hugged them and kissed them on the cheeks.

Richard had to recognize that from that moment on, his father's life took a 360-degree turn, as his dedication to the new business was full time. Whenever Richard spoke to his father, he was always working on agency affairs. His trips to foreign countries became more frequent with more extended stays. While in Mexico and when his stay was no longer than two or three days, he preferred to stay in a downtown hotel to attend to his business issues instead of going to their house. All these circumstances created distance in the family. Richard recalled with sadness when one time a friend of his told him that his father was in Mexico, but his father had never notified Richard. When he reproached his father, he received an answer like, "Look, son, I am a grown man who does not need nanny to take guardianship of me." His answer hurt Richard deeply, causing an even greater distance between them.

From then on, Richard's father's life became a mystery. The economic resources that his father once treated with extreme caution now flowed lavishly, allowing him to buy a luxury condo in Los Angeles with a price upwards of two million dollars, as well as expensive imported furniture of not less than five thousand dollars.

Richard vividly recalled the occasion when he claims his father about this ostentation, as he had always been a conservative man. In response, his father stated, "I have reached sixty-five years of age, and I want to enjoy life. Death searches for us every day, and we will never know when it will come for us. Fortunately, the agency has turned out to be successful, and my profits have allowed me to buy all these luxuries."

Richard was never convinced by this response, knowing full well that a travel agency in operation for only two years was unable to generate the profits his father now alluded to that would allow him to buy an expensive condominium where he lived. Furthermore, Richard was aware that the retirement income his father received from his government work would never allow the kind of life that his father had carried out. Richard's reflections raised the following question for him: Were the resources utilized to buy his expensive condo and furniture connected nexus with his father's death?

Richard's memories took him back to the time when his father was visiting Mexico for a family reunion. He was euphoric due to consuming several glasses of wine and explained to his children to what he ascribed the success of his agency. According to him, he had made contact with several religious organizations, primarily in the Eastern Hemisphere, rendering them the services of organizing social and cultural events for their conventions when they were in the United States. These VIP clients were used to moving around in extreme luxury without concern for costs, as most of their expenses were paid directly by the religious organizations to which they belonged. These services required coordination with travel agencies in other places, demanding that he travel continuously abroad, which caused constant absences from Los Angeles.

Suddenly a flashback came to Richard, the scene when he had met some of the people his father worked with. A return from a business trip from San Francisco, California, allowed a stop in Los Angeles to see his father. Identified by the security guard as Gerald Solaris's son, Richard was permitted to go inside his father's condo. Utilizing the key his father had given to him, he took the elevator to the tenth floor.

When the elevator doors opened, he found his father was not alone. Several voices were coming from the dining room. Approaching cautiously, Richard saw four people besides his father seated around the dining table. Everyone had notebooks and pens, and in the center of the table sat a large teapot used to refill their cups when needed. While his father spoke, the others' faces showed panic.

Attempting to avoid noise that would make him noticed, Richard was able to quickly review of the people at the table. He first noticed they all had different nationalities. One for sure was Jewish, probably a rabbi, since he wore curls that flowed out of a black hat, and his left wrist showed a magnificent gold watch full of diamonds. The other was an Indian since he wore a turban on his head with a pendant in front, displaying a splendid emerald of great size. The other two he identified as an Arab and an Asian, both dressed elegantly in fashionable tailored suits of fine cashmere with dark ties. The one he identified as the Arab wore several necklaces of precious gems around his neck. Not to be outdone, the Asian wore two golden chains with turquoise gems

To better hear the conversation, Richard moved closer to the table. At that moment, his father raised his head. Looking in the direction of his father's glances, all the guests turned around to look at Richard, showing fear in their expressions. Taking in their reactions, his father calmed them down, saying this was his son, Richard, who had come to see him. After the guests heard who he was, the panic on their faces disappeared. They greeted him amiably and invited to take a seat in the living room.

Richard recognized during the introductions that he hadn't paid attention to their names or high ecclesiastical positions. His attention was focused on the clothes and the expensive jewelry they pompously exhibited. Considering the way they dressed, Richard wondered to himself, *How can those priests afford such expensive jewelry when in their communities they preach humility?* Richard also recalled the when he glanced toward his father, he saw him wearing a cheap watch and his golden wedding ring.

As all of those present spoke perfect English, the conversation was carried on in that language without complications. Richard recalled the moment he was about to leave and all of them insisted he stay, saying their work was not important and could wait. Still, knowing his visit was inopportune, he apologized and let them know he had just stopped briefly to greet his father. Looking at his watch, he said it was time for him to leave as he had invited a client to dine at seven o'clock and did not want to be late. Without pressing Richard anymore, the group members mentioned all of them had a tight friendship with his father, whom they had known for several years. To end the conversation, they invited Richard to visit their respective countries, words that to Richard sounded more like a pleasantry than being sincere.

Coming back from his memories, Richard came to reality when he heard the voice of a flight attendant instructing the passengers to put their seats in an upright position, fasten their seat belts, and close their tables. Obeying her commands, Richard realized how his reminiscences had shortened the trip.

Arriving at the John Wayne Airport in Los Angeles, Richard hurried to the immigration line for foreign individuals, presented his passport and visa, responded to the questions, collected his baggage, and moved through customs without further complications.

A few minutes later and after picking up his rental car, Richard took Highway 405, which led him straight to his father's condo located in Marina del Rey.

The gate for visitors was different from the gate for condo owners. Visitors and employees needed to show the security guards their identifications while condo owners opened the other gate just by pressing the remote control installed in their auto. Richard drove to the visitor's gate, and straight off, a security guard came to his car. Richard explained that Mr. Martin Sosa was expecting his visit. The guard opened the gate, giving Richard instructions on where to park his car and find Mr. Sosa.

CHAPTER 3

While Richard drove his car to the residential area, he decided to do a quick physical inspection of the place. Without question, if the place was not paradise, surely it was very close to it.

The complex had three towers of twelve luxury floors each, following a state-of-the-art design of extreme elegance. The building facades were covered with a green Carrara marble, displaying ample crystal windows from which terraces of tile and porcelain protruded. All of them overlooked the marina, where one could enjoy the magnificent views of many different-sized anchored yachts.

Beautiful blooming gardens, carefully tended by expert landscapers, decorated trails that led to the condos. Aside the trails were fountains spurting water and forming impressive waterfalls that flowed into small lakes. The rear gardens were carefully planned with a nice diversity of colorful blossoms and leafy trees, creating a regal and romantic feeling when someone walked under their exquisite shades. At the end of the garden was the pool area, with an interior heated swimming pool, Jacuzzi, and sauna, as well as ample comfortable dressing rooms separated by showers for men and women.

Adjacent to the pool area was a large building fully outfitted with a gymnasium, two tennis courts, and a squash court. Next to that was another small building with a paved floor used for basketball and soccer practice.

Leaving aside his inspection, Richard returned to reality. Leaving his car parked where the security guard instructed, he hurried to meet with Mr. Sosa. While walking, Richard saw a silhouette approaching him that he immediately recognized. Sosa looked thinner than when Richard had met him two years ago. Sosa seemed worried when greeting Richard, saying it always was a pleasure to see him again, although he regretted the circumstances. He asked Richard how his flight was, Richard responded that his flight was excellent, but he immediately returned to his point of interest and asked Sosa if there was further news about his father's death. Shaking his head, Sosa responded, "Unfortunately, everything still remains the same Mr. Solaris."

Sosa informed Richard that the police had taken up an inspection of his father's apartment and were questioning several people. Romy, his father's domestic assistant, was weeping all the time and anxiously waiting for Richard's arrival. Richard hardly remembered Romy, but intrigued, asked if Sosa knew what she had said to the police. Sosa responded that that was impossible to know, as each interrogation was strictly personal, and no one could be present when another individual was being interviewed. Richard understood and asked Sosa what their next step was. Sosa answered that he was afraid Richard had to speak with the police, so he would introduce him to Lieutenant Samuel Lewis, the person in charge of the investigation.

Going inside Sosa's office, Richard found Romy. She was in the reception room, heartbroken. Seated in an armchair, she could not stop weeping. Her irritated eyes showed her pain. Seeing Richard walking into the room, Romy rose from her seat and, sobbing, said she could not understand what had happened last Saturday; when she had left him, he looked perfectly healthy. Richard tried to calm Romy, saying they had ignored many things, but getting upset was not the solution, so he promised to confront the matter together, and until everything was cleared up, she could count on his support. Thanking Mr. Solaris, Romy dried her tears with his handkerchief. Seeing her calmed Richard excuse himself, saying had to leave as Lieutenant Lewis was waiting for him.

Instructing Richard to close the door, Lewis invited him to sit down. Apologizing for conversing in English, he explained that his Spanish was bad, and even though he had taken several years of Spanish in high school, lack of practice had made him forget it. On the other hand, his English was excellent, enabling Richard to understand him.

Lieutenant Samuel Lewis was nearly thirty-eight years old, with six feet tall, and robust complexion. He had worked on the homicide squad of the Los Angeles Police Department for more than fifteen years. His résumé confirmed him to be a faultless, incorruptible man with an extensive ability to resolve difficult cases.

Rising from his seat, Lewis looked for an ashtray where he could throw his cigarette butt. Without finding one, he threw it into the wastebasket, making sure it was full extinguished. Thanking Sosa for bringing Richard in, Lewis asked Sosa to leave him alone with Mr. Solaris. Without complaining, Sosa left the room, saying he would be outside in case he was needed.

Lewis asked Richard if he could call him by his first name because he despised the use of last names or professional titles. In return, Richard could simply call him Sam. Richard smiled in a sign of acceptance.

To start the conversation, Sam said it was his understanding that Sosa had given Richard some information regarding his father's death. Richard answered that his information was scarce, that all he knew was that his father's body had been found dead on a pathway at the back garden, leading them to suppose he had committed suicide. Also, a neighbor had called the police, who will arrive shortly. As well, had being requested to take the first plane available to Los Angeles because his presence was required. That was all he knew so far.

Lewis smiled and said to Richard it was true that at the beginning, they thought his father had committed suicide, but going further into the investigation, they found he had been assassinated. Hearing that word, Richard felt a tremor in his legs. However, making an effort to demonstrate strength, he asked Sam what basis he had to establish his presumption. Arriving after the neighbor's call, Sosa had provided Lewis with keys to begin the inspection of the apartment. "In that examination were found facts that led me to consider your father had not committed suicide. I must say my conclusions are solely my own. However, my fifteen years' experience as a detective leads me to believe I am not mistaken. The results of the autopsy should confirm his opinion."

Richard asked Sam what facts he was referring to.

Responding, Sam said, "In the first place, I never found a note or written statement from your father, as is customary with a suicide. Broadly, people who commit suicide leave a note behind to exonerate third parties. Second, the dining room window from where your father was supposed to have jump is too high off the floor, and although I searched to find a stool he might have climbed onto, I never find one, leading me to conclude that someone loaded his body and later threw it out the window. Third, the pathway where his body was found its inadequate, as there are too many trees aside. In general, the suicide tends to avoid trees, as they are scared to pass over them, and although in some cases they might mitigate the fall, sometimes trees can cause serious pains before dying. Fourth, your father still wear eye glasses. Broadly, the suicide removes them before jumping to avoid seeing the site in which he intends to land, but overall experiments a freaking fear that the crystals might go inside his eyes. Fifth, his personal calendar showed the names and dates of future meetings, leading me to conclude he had never thought of ending his life. Sixth, all traces of your father were erased. I never found fingerprints of either your father or other persons, leading me to believe the perpetrator cleaned them to prevent being identified. Seventh, there are other spots more suitable to jump from, such as the living room terrace, where without great effort, anyone can climb the wall and jump off, avoiding passing over the trees. Eighth, in his dressing room was a traveling bag with several pieces of clothing on top, forcing me to assume he was coming from a trip and had not unpacked yet. After interrogating, Mr. Sosa, I found your father was steady, walking several times during the workweek, including last Friday, when he walked toward the gym to exercise, changing my opinion such that he was not coming from a trip but was preparing his luggage to travel soon."

Richard thought these points sounded logical and compelling, so he asked if they had someone in mind who could have committed the crime. As far as he could recall, his father had no enemies. Shaking his head, Sam responded that at that moment, they had no one in mind, guiding them to see every person as a suspect.

Lewis proposed that Richard meet him in his office in three hours for a thorough interrogation, saying a long and painful night lay ahead of him. As have to go to morgue and identified his father's body. But to make his night less painful, he would instruct him in the steps to follow, and if questions arose, he should let him know so he could explain them better. Convinced by the detective's sincere words, Richard thanked Lewis.

By Lewis Richard was aware his father's body had been transferred to the morgue in an ambulance two hours earlier, where he was required to identify it. Once he identified the body, it would be submitted to an autopsy, by which the forensic doctor would determine the exact time and actual cause of his death. The outcomes of the autopsy would be turned over to Lewis in a time not to exceed three to four hours.

"Any questions so far?" asked Lewis. Richard responded that everything was clear.

Lewis asked Richard if he had plans for where his father's body would be buried because, if were to cremate the body in Los Angeles, everything would be easier, but if he planned to bury his father in Mexico, he would be required to acquire several permits and authorizations, which could take him longer time, Richard responded that at the moment, he had not thought about this issue. He had to consult on the matter with his sister and wife and together make the decisions.

Sam's question made Richard realize his sister, Monica, had not been informed about their father's death. Apologizing to Lewis, he dialed her cell number. Nobody answered, so he left a message on her voice mail requesting her to call him back immediately.

Getting up from his chair, Lewis left the office to locate Sosa, who was waiting in the reception room. Lewis requested that he find Detective Miguel Rodriguez, who had stayed parked in the patrol car. Knowing his services were required, Rodriguez hurried to attend to the call of his boss.

At the age of twenty-four, Miguel Rodriguez was one of the youngest men in the homicide squad of the Los Angeles Police Department. Coming from Hispanic ancestry, he was a United States citizen now. His parents spoke Spanish with him at home, so he would not forget it. Since childhood, Miguel had dreamed of belonging to the homicide squad. His dream came true when, at the age of twenty-two, he was accepted into the division. His goal in life was now one day to be like his boss, Lieutenant Samuel Lewis.

Going inside Sosa's office, Miguel Rodriguez found Lewis waiting for him. He received instructions from his boss to take Mr. Solaris to the morgue, as was required, to identify his father's body. When they finished, Rodriguez was to bring Mr. Solaris back to the office for an interrogation. Lewis proposed that Richard leave his car parked where it was and go with Rodriguez in the patrol car, as Miguel knew the routes better and could drive him to the morgue faster. Without objection, Richard agreed.

Leaving the office, Richard saw that Romy was no longer in the reception room. He then walked faster to reach the patrol car, where Rodriguez was patiently waiting for him.

Along with the way to the morgue, Rodriguez started a conversation when he was interrupted by the ring of Richard cell phone. His caller ID showed the name of his sister, Monica.

After greeting Richard, Monica said she had received his message in her voice mail asking her to call him back. Thanking Monica for her quick response, Richard said he needed to talk with her urgently, saying he was at that moment in Los Angeles. Monica asked if he was with their father.

Seeking the best way to tell his sister the bad news without hurting her too much, Richard said his father had suffered a terrible accident the previous day. The fall had fractured his skull. The doctors had done what was possible to save him, but they had failed. Monica became pale before asking Richard if he was insinuating that their dad had passed away. Without being evasive, Richard responded with the distressing truth.

Richard heard Monica explode in hysteria. When she recovered her breath, she said she hoped Richard was joking and that her dad was in good health. Richard said he wished he could say that, but the truth was their father had passed away yesterday. Right away, Monica said she was taking the first plane to Los Angeles. Richard tried to calm his sister, saying it was not a wise decision to come. He was taking care of problems as they arose. He promised to keep her posted on everything and that they would make the decisions together. "Don't you think that's best?" Richard asked. Monica was not convinced but agreed to Richard's demands, requesting he not forget to keep her posted. Promising he wouldn't, Richard ended the call with his sister.

Richard turned off his cell phone. The lie he had told Monica made him feel really bad; however, anything was better than telling Monica their father had been assassinated, recognizing that her reaction to the truth would not have been a slight attack of hysteria but rather her schizophrenia problem would have come back.

Without any commentary on what he had overheard, Rodriguez drove straight to the morgue. Arriving there, Richard was introduced to the forensic doctor, who conducted them to the basement where closed shelves kept the drained bodies. Walking through a narrow corridor, the forensic doctor suddenly stopped in front of shelf 456 B. Opening the door, he confirmed the label coincided with Gerald Solaris's name, then removed the body to present it to Richard.

Rodriguez watched the forensic movements and approached Richard to ask if was ready to confront the moment. Richard, who was on the verge of vomiting at the smell of chloroform that infused the place, made efforts to restore himself. Looking at Rodriguez, he said was ready.

The sheet from the top part of the body, reveal only the face. The disfiguration caused by the fall still kept the unmistakable gaze of his father. Recognizing the body, Richard left the room hastily. Rodriguez and the forensic doctor could hardly hear when Richard pronounced in an almost inaudible voice that the body belonged to his father.

Rodriguez ran after Richard before he could reach the forensic doctor's office. Seeing him so pale and on the verge fainting, he helped Richard to walk and offered him a cup of coffee. Richard, attempting to hold in his reaction, thanked Rodriguez and accepted the offer of coffee.

Going over to the coffee maker, Rodriguez inserted several coins. In a moment, two cups of coffee were dispatched, one for Richard and the other for him.

Coming back with the two cups of coffee, Rodriguez found Richard waiting for him. Walking into the forensic doctor's office, Rodriguez heard him say the results of the autopsy would be ready in about four hours and turned to Lewis in the police station. The doctor then excused himself and exited the room, saying he had a busy day in front of him.

Patiently, Rodriguez waited until Richard finished his coffee. Rodriguez picked up both empty cups and threw them into the wastebasket, then subtly asked Richard if was ready to go the police station where Lieutenant Lewis was waiting for them. Wiping his mouth with a napkin, Richard replied he was ready and followed Rodriguez into the patrol car.

CHAPTER 4

The size of Lieutenant Lewis's office was less than one hundred square feet. His furniture was totally austere and consisted of an old, small writing desk with three chairs in front of it. Behind the desk was a bookcase full of books, properly organized. Lewis was examining some papers and smoking a cigarette when Richard and Rodriguez entered the office. Showing courtesy, Lewis offered them a seat and something to drink. Richard rejected the drink saying had one cup of coffee at the forensics office and for him that was enough, not to Rodriguez that standing up excuse himself and leaving the office said he will go to pick another cup of coffee.

To begin the conversation, Lewis said he had gotten a call from the forensic doctor telling him how bravely Richard has behaved when he was needed to identify his father's body. Richard smiled and said the doctor must have been joking because he never imagined that moment could be so hard. Sam replied that he thought the doctor's words were sincere, since most people, when it comes to identifying the body of a dead relative, suffered fainting, attacks of hysteria, or vomiting, and Richard didn't fall into one of those categories. Richard felt relieved and thanked Lewis.

Lewis was anxious, so he asked if Richard was ready to start the interrogation. Richard answered yes he was, and Lewis said he could commence by giving his father's general information.

Richard start saying his father, Gerald Solaris, was born in Mexico City on October 5, 1945, and graduated as a lawyer from the University of Mexico in 1972. Being working at the Ministry of Foreign Affairs, was paid a scholarship to study international laws at Harvard University in 1981. In 1970, Gerald met Richard's mother, Claudia, who was five years younger. Five years later, they married. During their marriage, Claudia gave birth to two children. One was him, Richard, born in 1976, graduated as an industrial engineer, and married with two children, currently helding the position of CFO of a transnational insurance company in Mexico City. The other child was Monica, his sister, born in 1978 and at this moment taking care of her household. She was married with two children, and her husband was a retailer of domestic products.

Richard's father, the only son in his family, was educated in a religious environment in Catholic schools. When his father decided to be a lawyer, his grandparents were disappointed, for to them it would have been a blessing if he had followed the career of a priest. Being Legionaries of Christ, his paternal grandparents gathered every Tuesday and Thursday with other married couples to practice and teach the Bible. His paternal grandfather was a very generous man and donated significant amounts of money to charitable institutions for the poor. After attending Sunday mass, Richard's sister, Monica, and he always received a gift from his grandfather, a practice that was stopped when his father mentioned they already had too many toys. Richard's maternal grandfather was a prominent owner of a local newspaper and a religious devotee of the Opus Dei.

Both their maternal and paternal families were very well connected people. Significant figures from the governmental, private, and ecclesiastical sectors attended Richard's parents' wedding. Their religious nuptials took place in the Metropolitan Cathedral of Mexico City, and offering mass was the prime archbishop. The President of Mexico and other politicians were witnesses to their civil marriage.

His father's work started with a small law firm in 1968, where he eventually reached a supervisory position. In 1972, he went to work for the legal department at the Secretariat of Commerce, where he remained for five years. At his maternal grandfather's request, he went to work at the Secretariat of Foreign Affairs in 1977, starting as assistant manager of the Department of Foreign Affairs. For his efficient work of thirty years, he climbed several positions until reaching Undersecretary of Foreign Affairs, a position in which stayed until his retirement. Richard's father was to turn sixty-five years old in five months. His intention was to celebrate his birthday in a hotel in Mexico City, inviting several friends from the governmental, private, and ecclesiastic sectors. Lewis frown and thanked

Richard for the information. Then he said that this information led him to various conclusions, such as that his father was educated in a religious environment; that he had excellent relations with the governmental, private, and ecclesiastical sectors; and that maybe his political position in which stand could generate some enemies for him.

Lewis then asked Richard if he could remember some facts of his father's life that could be relevant to the case. Richard briefly described what he had remembered on the airplane traveling to Los Angeles. Lewis's face changed color while listening. Stopping Richard, Lewis said that in his opinion, they were confronting a puzzle for which the pieces did not fit. The changes in his father's life were intriguing, as at first, he was totally austere, and then he started to live with great ostentation. Also, why did he refuse to capture his mother's killers when he had the means to do so? Why did he blame himself for his wife's death, later taking him into a deep depression? Who were those strange personages with different nationalities, wearing expensive jewels and visiting his father that night in his condo? What was his father saying that made them express panic in their faces? Where did his father get the resources to buy that expensive condo and furniture? Richard said he had asked himself the same questions without finding answers.

In the next three hours, Richard was submitted to a thorough interrogation. Richard had to think fast to reply to several questions. Lastly, Lewis asked him if he could recall the names of the persons who were at his father's condo that night two years ago. Richard apologized for not answering the question, saying that when his father introduced him, he had not paid attention to their names or positions because his mind was focused on the jewelry and attire they wore. Lewis then went in another direction and asked Richard if he felt comfortable reproducing the image of one of them. Richard humbly replied that in his youth, they considered him a good drawer of physiognomy. Pleased with that answer, Lewis said to Richard, "But before we do the picture, I need you to tell me what you know of Romy, your father's domestic assistant." Sipping his coffee, Lewis asked Richard to start with her general information.

Romy Choweski was fifteen years of age when the Russian invasion made her flee Czechoslovakia, her native land. Being rescued from a concentration camp, she was sent to Mexico where her aunt, Isabel Pawa took good care of her. At the age of twenty-one, she was able to legalize her immigration status, a requirement to become a Mexican citizen.

Romy started to work in her aunt's employment agency, which provided domestic workers for residential houses, being the same that Richard's mother used when required to employ those services. Romy's excellent references made her the ideal candidate to take care of the work that his mother demanded. Since the first interview, Romy had had good chemistry with his mother, who immediately hired her to work for them. Her respectful and friendly treatment made his parents love her as another member of the family.

Romy's role during his father's depression was crucial to his recovery. As a reward for her care, his father took Romy to live with him in the United States to serve him as a domestic assistant. At first, Romy worked full time, but due to his father's frequent absences from Los Angeles, she asked to work only four days a week. Her work days were Monday, Wednesday, Friday, and Saturday, starting at nine a.m. and ending at six p.m. On Tuesdays and Thursdays, she taught Spanish to a group of American children, and on Sundays, her day off, she took a breather. Without any objections, his father granted Romy all her requests.

Richard knew that Romy lived alone in a rented house, although he did not know the exact address. He said the distance to his father's house was great, hence the decision to finance a vehicle for her transportation. At the moment, that was all Richard could remember about Romy.

Lewis asked Richard if Romy had any other relatives or friends besides her aunt Isabel. Thinking for a moment, Richard answered that he knew Isabel Pawa was born in Poland and had married an Englishman named Howard Preston. They gave birth to a pretty red-haired girl named Leslie, better known by the nickname of Howie. Besides them, he did not remember anyone else.

"Do you know why they call their daughter Howie?" asked Lewis.

"Not really, but I suppose it's in reference to her father's name, which was Howard, and Howie sounded good to them."

Sipping his coffee several times, Lewis asked Richard if he knew what Romy's main hobbies were. Romy loved to collect stamp impressions. Most of her money was spent on purchase stamps, as she felt proud of her collection. Every stamp they received at home from different parts of the world was given to Romy. Also, she loved to play classical music and go see Western movies in which the hero ended up wedding his lover. Also, she enjoyed practicing martial arts, which she believed was an essential tool to defend herself from attacks by men. Lewis paused, then asked Richard if Romy had been married or had a boyfriend. Richard responded that he believed Romy had hated men since the violations she and her mother had suffered as prisoners in the Russian concentration camp.

Taking notes, Lewis looked at Richard straight in the eyes and asked if he knew of someone who wanted to harm his father, either his person or reputation. Richard answered that he had asked the same question of himself without anyone coming to his mind.

Suddenly, there was a knock at the door, making Lewis rise from his chair. Opening the door, he saw Miguel coming back with his cup of coffee. Inviting him to a seat, Lewis said he was glad Miguel could join them for the interrogation. Looking at Miguel, Lewis asked him to tell Richard what Sosa had told them that morning.

"Richard, this morning we received a call from Sosa informing us the dissapearance of the security guard on duty the day your father died. First it was thought that the guard had forgotten to punch his time card when he left that Sunday night. Sosa called the guard's wife, who seemed ignorant of her husband's whereabouts. "This seems strange, making us believe his missing is linked to your father's death."

"I think will second that motion," Richard said with a worried voice.

Lewis also showed Richard his father's personal calendar, where he had written dates for his next appointments. "Richard," Lewis said, "take some time to look at his calendar and see if something draws your attention."

Taking the book, Richard began to study it. Quickly his attention was drawn to the annotations his father had made eight days prior to his death. On May 7 and 8 were written the words "seriously ill"; on May 9 and 10, "need hospitalization"; on May 11 and 12, the word "stable"; and finally on May 13 and 14 were the words "extreme gravity."

Lewis then asked Richard if he knew if his father suffered from a disease.

"Not that I am aware of. My father was a healthy person who loved to exercise," Richard responded.

"Then it seems to me he was monitoring the illness of a relative or acquaintance, don't you think?" Lewis asked.

"That could be, but it's hard to be sure."

"Is there anything else on the calendar that caught your attention?"

"Yes, on July 29, the day my mother died, my father wrote the words 'Fix and attend mass.'"

Seeing the interrogation was not leading to positive results, Lewis picked up the calendar and rose from his seat. In a strong tone of voice, he asked Richard where he was last Sunday. Calmly, Richard answered he was in Mexico with his sister, Monica. Her husband had thrown a barbecue party with other couples. He had arrived before three p.m. and had departed after nine p.m. And if Lewis needed a witness, he could call his sister or the other couples, who were also invited, to verify his statement. Seeing Richard was getting upset, Lewis calmed him down by saying that was not necessary at the moment. Thanking Richard for his patience, the detective said that last question ended the interrogation.

Miguel, who had listened to Richard's interrogation without uttering a word, suddenly said he had other things to do and exited the room. Lewis signaled Richard to follow him. Walking at a fast pace, they crossed a large corridor and arrived at a door with a sign that said, "For authorized personnel only." Lewis inserted his identification card and opened the door. Richard saw a seated man with glasses, who was working on a computer. When the man saw them, he rose from his seat to greet them.

David Curtis was twenty-seven years old, tall, and blond, with downcast eyes and a friendly glance. He had worked for the department almost six years. He was experienced in the reproduction of spoken pictures when they were required to identify a person.

After introducing Richard to David, Lewis let him know they needed his services to reproduce the spoken image of a person. "David will guide you in the reproduction of the picture we need to make. Take your time, and when you're finished, bring it to my office," Lewis said.

David led Richard to a seat in front of a large screen, explaining that the projection he would witness in the display was precisely what he had experienced in his computer. David's work consisted of presenting several faces, and Richard was to select the one who in his impression was more similar to the individual they needed to reproduce. After choosing the face, he would then proceed to modify the eyes, nose, or mouth, adding or eliminating a mustache or beard, putting on glasses, or whatever was needed. The process was repeated as many times as needed until he finally approved of the reproduction. Richard was made aware that the reproduction picture was to serve other police entities to identify that person, so Richard should take his time, be patient, and never feel desperate. "Any questions?" David asked.

"None so far," Richard responded.

Following David's instructions, Richard closed his eyes and tried to concentrate on the face they wanted to recreate. His mind flew to the moment when he met the strange personages that were that night visiting his father in his Los Angeles condo. Searching for several faces he stopped when saw clearly the image of the Jewish rabbi. There was no doubt, Richard knew he was making the right selection as this was the man with whom he had spoken longer and remembered him better.

Working for several hours, David made multiple changes in the face selected until finally, Richard exclaimed fervently that the similarity was unmistakable. David became excited at his statement too. Nevertheless, he advised Richard to take the time, close his eyes once more, and search for the face's expression. "Once you place the face, open your eyes quickly and look again at the picture to see if indeed it coincides with this image. Remember when I said the reproduction would assist other police entities in finding this person? Well, it is true."

Following David's suggestion, Richard saw the picture again until he said he had no doubt that the reproduction was excellent, and anyone who needed to find him would instantly recognize him.

Richard yawned. The weariness of the day was overwhelming. All his body hurt, so when David said he needed to deliver the picture to Lieutenant Lewis, Richard proposed to do it personally. David rejected the offer, saying delivering the picture was part of his job, and Lewis had requested him to do it personally. After picking up the picture, David put it in an envelope and walked toward Lewis's office, followed by Richard. After leaving the envelope for Lewis, David left the room but not before he received Richard's congratulations and thanks for his excellent work.

Suddenly, Lewis's phone rang. The call lasted more than ten minutes.

When he hung up, he offered a seat and asked his opinion about David Curtis's work. Richard responded he was struck by the way Curtis had guided him to make the spoken picture. His ability to interpret instructions were fantastic, making the reproduction go faster and more accurate. Delighted with his response, Lewis mentioned that was why Curtis was considered the best man in the reproduction of spoken pictures. His work had become an essential tool when is needed to find a person.

Opening the envelope, Lewis extracted the spoken picture Curtis had given him. A quick look was enough for him to exclaim there was no question the person was a Jewish rabbi. Putting the picture in the scanner, Lewis emailed the reproduction to the other police agencies so that they could search for him immediately. "If I am not mistaken, it won't be too long before we receive good news," Lewis said.

Lewis told Richard that while he was with Curtis, he had received the forensic doctor's report. The outcome of the autopsy coincided with his judgment that his father had not committed suicide but had been assassinated. So that Richard could understand, Lewis read the important parts of his report, skipping details that weren't relevant.

"As is customary for this kind of report," began Lewis, "he starts by describing the generals of the dead person. In this instance, he says, 'Name Gerald Solaris, sex male, age between 64 and 67 years, 6.05 feet tall and weight close to 210 pounds.'" The second section related personal characteristics, which at that moment Lewis preferred to skip. "The third part refers to the point we are interested in. It says the cause of death was lipothymia that occurred on Sunday night, May 15, 2010, between 21:15 and 21:30. This was proven by application of cooling tests and signs of dehydration in the eyes and mucous. Lipothymia," he explained, "comes about when the person suffers a respiratory attack due to the absence of Ioxygen. The doctor found in your father's throat an imperceptible puncture, probably caused by a needle from a shot containing thallium nitrate. Then he states the nitrates changed, the hemoglobin transforming the oxygen in the blood into methaemoglobin, which is a form of hemoglobin containing ferric iron. That decreases the ability to bind with oxygen, leading the individual first to a lack of Ioxygen and later to a respiratory attack. In death from lipothymia, the palms of the hands and the lips display a purple color, and in Gerald Solaris's case, they were like that. Likewise, the report says both of his wrists had swelled, making him suppose the victim had fought, offering resistance to his aggressor before dying. The damage caused by the fall of his body is keyed out in another chapter, which at this moment we'll skip. As beside be to technicians, results are very impressive. To conclude his report, the doctor states the cause of death was lipothymia due to the insertion of a needle in the throat containing the injection of thallium nitrate, leading your father first to the absence of Ioxygen and subsequently to a respiratory attack. As well, he ensures that when the body was cast out the dining room window, he was already dead. Now our job consists of finding who the person who perpetrated such atrocities is," Lewis pronounced.

Leaving the report on his desk, Lewis regarded Richard, who looked tired and sleepless. Looking at his watch, he saw it was almost two o'clock in the morning. Considering Richard had had a heavy night, Lewis proposed that Rodriguez could take him to the nearest hotel, where he could rest and sleep. Tomorrow at nine a.m., Rodriguez would be picking him up because Lewis wanted him to be present at the time they visited his father's travel agency.

Lewis dozed on a sofa in a room adjacent to his office when his cell phone rang. Looking at his watch, he saw it was three o'clock in the morning. His caller ID showed an unidentified individual. Unsure, Lewis answered it. He recognized Richard's voice, which immediately apologized for waking him up, saying he had remembered the Jew's name who had been with him the night he visited his father. He preferred to tell Lewis before could forget it. "The name was Jacob for sure." Where he was not sure was the last name, which could have been Kravitz or Levitz. Saying that, he hung up the phone before Lewis could reply to him.

Still half asleep and without standing, Lewis took a pen from the pocket of his suit and wrote in his calendar the probable names that Richard had provided. Yawning and stretching his arms, he walked straight to the coffee maker, where he prepared a cup of coffee that would wake him up faster. While sipping his coffee, Lewis wondered if it was possible that an international organization could be behind Mr. Solaris's murder. Silently, he examined his notepad and, stubbing his cigarette in the ashtray, thought must find a way to prove he was not wrong in his statement.

"Are you okay, mate?" asked Rodriguez as he entered Lewis's office.

Slowly Sam raised his head. The dim light obscured his expression. "Sorry, Miguel. I apologize, but I didn't hear you come in." His voice sounded weak, as if something seriously worried him.

"You don't look too good, Sam. Have problems?" asked Rodriguez.

"No, Miguel, I am fine, just a little tired. All right, Miguel, I must confess to you I am worried that behind the murder of Mr. Solaris is an international organization, but how can I prove it?"

"It's strange, but I've been thinking the same thing," Rodriguez responded. "In any case, this is not a matter to discuss today. I advise you to go home, take a refreshing shower, and sleep for a while."

"I will gladly follow your advice, but not at this moment. I still have work to do that can't wait until tomorrow."

"Sam, Sam, Sam" Rodriguez leaned into the light to see his boss's face. With a broad smile, he said, "One of these days, I'll be blamed for your death."

"Very kind of you, Miguel. I am honored to know that after I am gone, you can take my place."

"You know damn well I don't have your skills and experience."

"Perhaps not at this moment, but everything is a matter of time. Remember, Miguel, that practice makes the master."

Finishing his cigarette, Sam crushed the butt into the ashtray. Then he said to Miguel, "All right, buddy, follow me. We still have work to do."

CHAPTER 5

At nine a.m. sharp, Rodriguez was picking up Richard at the front door of his hotel. As he fastened his seat belt in the car, Rodriguez asked if he had had a good rest. Richard answered that everything that was living made him extremely nervous, and last night he could not sleep well just thinking about who could be his father's killer. In spite of his efforts, no one had come to mind.

Rodriguez slapped Richard on the shoulder, saying, "Don't worry, Mr. Solaris, Lieutenant Lewis and I won't lay off until we see this murderer captured and appropriately punished." Richard was pleased with his reply and thanked him, saying he was right and he himself instead should stay calm.

Upon their arrival at the travel agency, Lewis waited for them at the building's entry door. Under his arm he carried a search warrant, authorizing him to inspect the company.

Richard, who had ignored where the agency was, had imagined by his father's comments that the company was of great size. The reality was the opposite. The agency was located on the second level of a building in poor condition. On that day, its elevator was out of order for repairs. Upset, the three men started to go up the stairs that led to the second level.

The outside windows of the stairs were sealed with paint and covered with blinds, leaving the sun with no possibility of penetration. Walking through a dark corridor, they came upon a hidden office in a remote corner with the sign for Liberty Travel Agency. Opening the door carefully, they found a small reception room with an empty desk. Without seeing anyone nearby, Sam tapped on the door. A bent man of approximately seventy years opened the door and with a friendly smile received them, saying his name was Arthur Whitney and asking what he could do to serve them.

Lewis showed his badge and said he was Lieutenant Samuel Lewis of the homicide squad of the Los Angeles Police Department, and the other men with him were Detective Miguel Rodriguez of the same institution and Mr. Richard Solaris, son of Mr. Gerald Solaris and the owner of that travel agency.

Lewis waited for Arthur to recover his breath. After a moment of silence, he said, "Mr. Whitney, we have a search warrant authorizing us to inspect the travel office."

Hearing those words, Arthur became pale, but regaining his composure, he opened the door to allow them inside. After shutting the door, Arthur said, "Please follow me, gentlemen. I want introduce you to Mr. Robert Laris, who, besides being the agency's accountant in the absence of Mr. Solaris, is the proper individual to speak with."

Richard was utterly disappointed when they walked inside. He found an open space of less than 150 square feet, sparely furnished with an old, small writing desk with a laptop and phone on it, which Richard thought belonged to Mr. Whitney. On the right side at the back corner of the room were three small cubicles. The one on the left seemed to be the smallest in size, probably used as a file room, where an attractive young lady, perhaps the receptionist whose desk was outside, flipped through several dossiers. Seeing them, she smiled. The other two cubicles were of a similar size, one maybe belonging to his father and the other to the accountant. Richard concluded that the personnel they had seen were the only ones working for the agency. Intrigued, he wondered how his father could have generated profits from this agency to buy his expensive condominium. As always, his question remained without an answer.

When introduced to Robert Laris, Lewis showed his badge and the search warrant. After examining the order, Laris agreed and stated he had no objection, and they could immediately make the inspection. However, he was surprised to see the homicide squad of the Los Angeles police was required for this.

Understanding his comment, Lewis explained to Laris why they were involved. "Perhaps you don't know, Mr. Laris, but Mr. Solaris was found dead last Sunday night on a pathway at the back garden of his condo. The initial thought was he had committed suicide but it has become apparent he was assassinated." Laris and Whitney were mute and petrified at his words. The first to react was Laris, who asked if they knew who had committed the crime. Shaking his head, Lewis answered that at that moment they didn't but anticipated, with their help, to find who had done it. Laris immediately replied they were mere employees who knew nothing about what happened in Mr. Gerald Solaris's private life. Lewis smiled and said, "Be prepared because at the end of this week, you will be called in for an interrogation. Rodriguez will give you the address and time at which you will need to attend."

Without waiting for answers, Lewis started to give orders for the search, telling Laris they needed the accounting records such as financial statements and invoices from when the agency had begun until that day. Every text file was to be handed directly to Detective Rodriguez, who, after reviewing them, would continue to shut and seal every drawer in the desks and file cabinets. As of that moment, it was strictly forbidden for anyone to transfer or use the documents without Lewis's authorization. The violation of his orders would result in jail. "Is that clear?" Lewis asked.

Laris and Whitney listened carefully to his instructions and simultaneously replied, "Yes sir, we do understand."

Laris made Arthur Whitney responsible for telling Adele about the documents they needed. "Tell Adele to assist them and to stop any work she is doing right now." Adele, who was still working in the file room and was not aware of what was taking place. Nevertheless, still was curious when saw Rodriguez standing at the side of his boss. "Adele," Arthur said, "this gentleman requires some documents. Stop what you're doing and get those documents ready in less than ten minutes."

Rodriguez had not stopped looking at Adele and, smiling, said, "And don't take one minute more, please."

Obtaining the list of documents, Adele proceeded to find them in their respective files. Digging through file cabinets, she searched for every document, slamming drawers. In less than the time required, Adele was handling Arthur a full expandable file that covered the list. Arthur flipped through the documents and headed to find Rodriguez, who stood waiting for them. Taking the material from Arthur, Robert Laris made a quick inspection of them and handed the whole bunch to Lewis, who immediately turned away, saying it was necessary to detail each document. "Once the list is ready, we will review every document together, and if everything seems correct, I will sign them off as received," Lewis said. Following instructions, Laris proceeded to list every document. When finished, he called Lewis so they could review every report together. Giving his approval, Lewis signed them off as received.

Laris suggested working in Mr. Solaris's office. He said no one would bother them there, and they could freely talk. Sam and Richard agreed, collected the documents, and followed Laris, who, rising from his seat, started to walk toward the private office of Mr. Solaris.

Richard found his father's office scarcely furnished with only an executive desk with three chairs in front of it. Behind it was a bookcase full of volumes with several papers on top, which Richard thought his father must have been using at that moment. On top of his desk sat a family picture with his father and mother seated and his sister and him standing behind, hugging them. Richard recalled that moment. It was on his father's birthday, that his father had hired a professional photographer to take that picture. His memories made Richard almost cry. Seeing Laris they were comfortably seated, and with no further requests, left the room.

No one took his father's chair. Sam and Richard sat in front of his father's desk. To start the examination, Lewis opened a binder with the financial statements. Extracting the last one corresponding to the month of April, he removed the staples and separated the balance sheet. Going over it, he found the company's capital totaled $78,755 dollars, coming from Mr. Solaris's initial contribution of $50,000.00 and the added earnings from previous years and the present one. Looking at Richard, Sam asked him if he thought the profits shown in the statements were sufficient to buy his father's expensive condo. Richard answered they could hardly buy a cheap used car, raising the mystery of how his father had gotten the resources to buy it.

Reviewing the other items in the balance sheet quickly and realizing none was significant, Lewis closed the balance sheet and restapled it. Shutting the binder, he collected the other documents over the desk and signaled Richard to follow him.

Laris was helping Rodriguez to seal drawers when Lewis called him. Taking out his notes, Lewis asked Laris if the profits shown in the financial statements were the only ones earned by the agency or if there were others. He also asked if at some point Mr. Solaris had made withdrawals or transfers of funds to his personal account. He warned Laris that if he lied, he could go to jail. Laris was upset at the threat and, facing Lewis, answered with a firm voice. The profits shown in the statements were the only ones, reflecting every cent generated by the agency in its two years of operation. Also, he assured Lewis that since he had started to work for the agency, Mr. Solaris had never made any withdrawals or transfers of funds to his personal account nor had he paid dividends to himself from the agency funds. Thanking Laris, Lewis said that was the exact response that he had expected to hear from him.

Breathing deeply, Lewis asked Laris why on the assets side of the balance sheet he had found an item called "Other Investments in Companies." "Can you tell me the significance of this?" Laris explained Mr. Solaris made purchases of shares in the stock market. However, during the time that they held the shares, they never increased in value. On the contrary, when they were sold, they lost money. The loss was also reflected in the financial statements.

Changing the subject, Lewis asked Miguel to gather all the invoices of the agency since the beginning of the agency to the last one issued that day. He needed them listed and classified in chronological order, detailing in each the name of the client, the address, total amounts, and type of service provided. "When you're finished, bring the list to the office so I can go over it," Lewis said.

Lewis said to Richard they should leave because other things waited for them. On the street, Lewis looked for a place where they could eat. Across the street was a little cafeteria that advertised delicious deli sandwiches. He and Richard walked to it. They sat at the counter. Sam ordered a large ham and cheese sandwich with a Coke. Richard ordered the same. "Never mind. This is on me," Lewis said when Richard tried to pay.

Richard was about to take the last bite of his sandwich when Sam interrupted him, asking him if he knew what he was going to do with his father's body. Richard answered that if the decision were his, he would choose to cremate his body in Los Angeles and have the ashes sent to Mexico, where they would be deposited in the family crypt. But as he had promised his family they would make the decision together, he would ask his sister and wife and accept what they decided. Sam suggested Richard call them now and over what they had decided. Dialing his sister's number, Richard waited for two rings before Monica answered. His sister and Evelyn had discussed the subject of his father's remains and decided that they would agree to what was best for Richard himself. Thanking his sister for her understanding, he said the best thing for him would be to cremate his father's body in Los Angeles and then take the ashes to Mexico. With Monica expressing no complaints, Richard ended the call.

Hearing Richard's conversation with his sister, Lewis congratulated him, stating it was the best decision they could make. Offering Richard his help, he said the forensic doctor who performed the autopsy on his father's body was his friend and would gladly assist him with his father's funeral arrangements. Richard thanked Lewis for his offer.

CHAPTER 6

That same afternoon, Sam Lewis met with his director, Donald Myers to keep him posted on the latest developments. Listening silently to the detective, Donald drank from a glass of water before said he agreed that Lewis was facing a big dilemma. Even recognizing that Lewis's investigation was thoroughly done, Donald was not sure to involve the Transnational Intelligence Police Agency, (TIPA), feeling was a discredit for his institution, if they find out they were wrong, when supposedly they assumed Mr. Solaris had been assassinated by an international organization, and the truth was had been killed by a sole individual. However, recognizing Lewis's skill and experience in solving difficult cases, Donald was willing to take the risk and authorized the detective to call them.

Lewis was pleased with his boss's response, promising Donald he would not regret his decision. He said he would try to find a way Raymond Sullivan, director of the TIPA could help them without compromising their institution. Wishing him luck, Donald smiled and hoped Sam was correct.

Donald's phone suddenly rang, and he answered it. He told Sam Rodriguez was waiting for him in his office. "Tell him I'll be with him in a minute," Lewis replied.

Sam found Rodriguez seated in front of his desk in his office. Miguel respectfully stood up when Sam entered. To begin the conversation, Rodriguez said his work was complete, and he had found the agency had filed all the invoices on the computer. At Sam's request, they listed them in chronological order, detailing names of clients, addresses, amounts, and types of service provided. Thanking Miguel for his work, Sam said he would review them later.

Rodriguez asked where Richard was. Sam responded that he had sent him to the morgue to see Dr. Cussac, who was to help him with his father's funeral arrangements. Rodriguez intervened for Richard defense, saying every problem lay on his shoulders. Sam agreed but said he considered Richard capable of figuring out any problem he faced. "Notwithstanding, if he fails to do it, don't you think he can count on us to support him?"

Rodriguez was pleased with his boss's response and smiled, saying, "Damn, you are right, Sam. You know, Sam, I really like this guy."

Rodriguez was silent for a while before asking Sam if the thought had crossed his mind that Richard Solaris could be involved in his father's death. Sam answered that he used the American principle that no one should be considered guilty until guilt was proven, instead of the Mexican principle that considers everyone is guilty until innocence is proven. "Does that answer your question?"

"I guess it does. Thank you, Sam," Rodriguez replied with a big smile.

Miguel left, and Sam sat at his desk. He began to review what Miguel had brought to him. Taking the list of invoices out of the envelope, he searched in the clients column, trying to find one name that could be similar to the name of the Jewish rabbi or at least a hint to determine an overseas address where the rabbi could be found. Discouraged when he did not find one, he lighted a cigarette and began to think about his next step.

Finishing his cigarette, Sam threw the butt into an ashtray and moved to his computer. He started to compose a report for Raymond Sullivan on the relevant facts of his investigation. Before beginning to write, he decided to create an index, which he thought would make it easier for Raymond to find the data. Labeling each document, he first introduced the spoken picture of the Jew, ending with copies of the forensic doctor's report on the autopsy, the list of invoices that Rodriguez had made, and Gerald Solaris's personal calendar. Finished, Sam asked himself if Raymond would be capable of figuring out this puzzle with the limited information that he provided. As for himself, at that moment, Sam did not think many pieces of the puzzle fit together.

Seven years had passed since Raymond Sullivan had left the homicide squad of the Los Angeles Police Department to go to work for the Transnational Intelligence Police Agency. At the age of forty-nine, Raymond had been called by Clark Robinson, CEO of that institution, who offered him the position of general director. The location of his office was now Lexington City in the state of Virginia. Sam Lewis attributed many of his skills to the teachings of and experience with Sullivan when they had worked together. When Raymond left the Los Angeles Police Department, Lewis felt a great emptiness in his heart. Besides considering Raymond a great boss that he admired and respected, they had also become close friends. This case offered the opportunity to work with him once more, only increasing Lewis's excitement.

Sam called Raymond at his private number. Raymond was in the middle of a meeting when his phone rang. Recognizing the caller ID, he immediately answered. Apologizing, he said was in a meeting but would call him back. Sam agreed, and Raymond hung up the phone.

In less than ten minutes, Sullivan called Sam back. After their greetings, Raymond asked Sam if he still worked for the police department. Sam responded he still did. Raymond said, "As you know, the doors of our institution are always open for you when you decide to come and work for us." Thanking Raymond, Sam said that for the moment, he was pleased with his present work and had no intention of changing jobs.

Disappointed, Raymond asked Sam what he could do for him as he supposed his call had another purpose other than to greet him. Sam agreed and stated the purpose of his call was to inform him about a case he thought his agency should be involved in. "What leads you to believe that?" Raymond asked.

In less than fifty minutes, Sam had explained the relevant facts of his investigation. He passed over some details that could be read later in the report he would send via fax or email. After Sam finished, Raymond said, "I must agree with you that the evidence leads me to also believe that the intervention of our institution is required. Nevertheless, before I give my final approval, I need to analyze the whole report in detail." He promised to read it that night if Sam sent him the report in less than an hour via fax or email. "Does it sound reasonable to you if I give my response by tomorrow before noon? I first will need to discuss the case with the responsible agent."

Sam agreed and requested another favor of Raymond, to keep the information strictly confidential until he definitively decided if he would take or refuse the case, as he had promised Donald Myers not to compromise their institution if was not involved an international orgnization. "You can count on me for that," Raymond responded. Sam thanked Raymond and ended the conversation.

Later that night, Raymond Sullivan was seated in his office reading Lewis's report. Raymond underlined paragraphs he considered relevant in yellow. At about three o'clock in the morning, he closed the report and stood up. The weariness of the day was reflected in intensive back pain. He rubbed his eyes and tried to alleviate the pain. He did arm and leg stretches and some sit-ups. The physical exertion made him feel better, leading his thoughts to the strategy that would follow. Without question, the case was difficult and required an experienced person. Closing his eyes, he started to go over the names of some potential candidates. He stopped at one. Of course, there was no question the best candidate for this case was Albert Colliere. Early in the morning, he would speak with him.

Tall and bulky with a pale face, full dark hair with some gray visible, and midnight-blue eyes, Albert Collier was without a doubt the image of a leader at the institution. Aged forty-nine, he had never married. He had a doctorate in criminology from the University of Lyons in France and had worked for INTERPOL for twenty years. His transfer to TIPA was thanks to the intervention of an American senator, who invited him to be part of the institution. In the organizational chart of the company, Colliere appeared at the same level as the directors. His excellent work led him to be nominated for ten consecutive years as the best detective at the institution. For him, the only important thing in life was his work. Every member of his squad, including Sullivan, admired and honored him for his accomplishments and experience. In his long career as a detective, he had solved every one of his cases, all except the one in which France's Secretary of State and other members of his staff died in a plane crash while they were traveling to a meeting of the European Union. The cause of the accident was determined to be pilot error. However, Albert was never convinced by that verdict, as he had found the pilot belonged to the French air force and had been awarded the Medal of Merit for his flight skills. That fact led him to wonder how a pilot with that experience could crash a plane against a mountain at such a low altitude.

At 7:30 a.m., Raymond's secretary was calling Albert, requesting he come to Raymond's office. In spite of knowing Sullivan for a long time and being of similar age, Albert always showed deference to his boss and never spoked to him in family terms. Raymond had encouraged him to do so, but despite his boss's insistence, he never did.

Meeting in Raymond's office, Albert listened attentively while Sullivan read him Lewis's report. When Raymond was finished, he said he had to agree with Lieutenant Lewis, who believed an international organization was behind Mr. Solaris's murder. However, to better support his point of view, he needed to collect more evidence, so he had requested more time to analyze the case. Recalling his promise to Lieutenant Lewis to treat the case with strict confidentiality, Raymond suggested Albert be discreet and not involve anyone else unless he got his authorization. Colliere promised discretion. He rose out of his seat and before leaving and proceeded to collect the information on top of Sullivan's desk Raymond requested that they meet in his office before noon. Looking at his watch, Colliere agreed.

In his office, Colliere read Lewis's report. A low lamp illuminated his computer, showing a reflection off his cup of chocolate. "There must be a clue hidden in here," Albert said to himself. The week had been exhausting for him. He had been working two crimes at the same time, and now one more was added. Leaving aside his tiredness, he tried to concentrate in his new assignment.

Expert at quick reading, Colliere proceeded to analyze the report in detail, stopping only to study the paragraphs Sullivan had underlined in yellow. Finished with his reading, he moved on to scan every document and organize his files. Examining the Jew's spoken picture, Albert learned his name was Jacob, but his unknown last name could be Kravitz or Levitz. Typing the name of Jacob Kravitz into the computer, he added the correlative data that he considered to be relevant, such as if he was high in the hierarchy of the Jewish church and his age between fifty-five and sixty years. Instantly the computer showed three possible candidates with that name; however, none of them matched the correlative data.

Without despairing, Colliere substituted the last name of Kravitz for Levitz and left the correlative data the same. This time, the computer said Jacob Levitz was a Jewish rabbi, aged fifty-nine years, a widower, and currently living in Jerusalem. Satisfied with that answer, Colliere printed a copy for Sullivan.

Before noon, Albert was seated in Sullivan's office, waiting for him. Sullivan's secretary said the boss would be there in five minutes, as he was busy in another boardroom talking to some people. When Sullivan arrived, he apologized for the delay. Looking at Albert, he said he could tell by his face the detective had encountered something of interest. Albert agreed and said he thought he had found the man they were looking for. Sullivan asked Albert to show him his findings. After explaining the procedures he followed and the results, Sullivan mumbled for a moment, looked at the printed picture, and said, "What I understand, Albert, is that the man we need to find is named Jacob Levitz, aged fifty-nine years, a widower, and presently living in Jerusalem."

"Exactly, sir. You are correct," Albert replied.

Sullivan was anxious to know what the next steps would be. Thinking fast, Albert responded he should first call Lieutenant Lewis and tell him they had accepted the case. Then, if Sullivan agreed, he could travel tonight to Jerusalem and see if could find Jacob Levitz. Knowing Albert was a man of action, Sullivan gave his immediate agreement, saying his secretary would take care of his tickets for a flight that night to Jerusalem.

Leaving the office in a rush, Colliere went home to pack his luggage. Back in the office, he dictated letters to his secretary, that took note of his pending tasks On his way to the cab, Albert found Raymond approaching him in the hallway. He had come to wish him luck and to say goodbye. Raymond reminded Albert not to forget to keep him posted on every event. Albert promised to do so.

CHAPTER 7

A t 8:30 p.m., Albert Colliere was standing in line at the Alitalia counter. The airline manager took personal care of his tickets when he saw his badge. His first stop would be the city of Rome. From there he was to take another flight directly to Jerusalem.

After eighteen hours of exhausting travel, Albert finally arrived at the Ben Gurion International Airport in Tel Aviv. As they landed, the flight attended provided the time in Jerusalem. Looking at his watch, Colliere saw it was seven hours behind, so he adjusted it to Israeli time. The night had settled on Jerusalem, and he needed to find a place where pass the night.

Finished with his immigration and customs proceedings, Colliere looked for a car rental agency, becoming discouraged when he found there were no cars available at the agency. Hauling his luggage, he went out to the street to look for a cab. Fortunately he saw a young man waving his hands and addressing him. Walking toward him, Colliere found the young man spoke perfect English and gently offered him a cab that was parked across the street. Without delay, Colliere picked up his luggage and walked toward the spot where the driver said the cab was parked. After putting his luggage in the trunk, the young man apologized, saying the airport forbid taxi drivers to park in front of the door unless they had a passenger aboard. Colliere told the taxi driver he needed to find a place to spend the night. The driver responded he knew of a nice hotel. Without another choice, Colliere accepted the recommendation.

For more than an hour, Albert was driven along unknown routes. At long last, when the taxi stopped in front of a hotel and feeling relief, Albert asked the driver where he was. The driver answered they were near the rural road that led to Jericho. Leaving his passenger inside the cab, the driver went to see if the hotel had rooms available. Alone and in complete darkness, Albert felt an intense fear. Watching through the passenger window for anyone approaching, he unhooked his gun in case he needed to defend himself. To his relief, a few minutes later, the driver came with news the hotel had rooms available.

Stepping out of the cab, Albert gathered his luggage and paid the driver plus a generous tip. The driver said his name was Isaac Chelminsky, and he spoke Yiddish, Hebrew, and English fluently. He was licensed to be an authorized translator as well as being owner of the taxi. On the back of the business card was his personal phone number where Albert could call him at any time and he would pick him up wherever he was. His rate per hour was twenty American dollars for eight hours of services, including translation services. If that time was exceeded, his rate increased by fifty percent. Emitting a big smile, Albert thought that without question, Isaac knew how to promote his business. Then, looking at the young fellow who stood at his side, he said, "All right, Isaac, you are hired. Come and pick me up tomorrow morning at eight at this same hotel. By the way, my name is Albert Colliere." Waving his hand, Isaac said goodbye. Taking the wheel, Isaac promptly disappeared.

At six o'clock the next morning, Albert woke up. His stomach demanded something to eat. Eighteen hours had gone by without a meal. The dinner on the plane was a hard, dry sandwich that was impossible to eat. Exiting the room, he looked for a place to have breakfast. Walking through the hotel, he found it was old but kept in good shape. The lobby was pleasant and seemed to have been recently remodeled with new furniture. At the front desk was a young lady with a sweet smile who when asked what he needed. Albert said he was looking for a place to have breakfast. Looking at the clock on the wall, the young receptionist answered the hotel had a small restaurant, but it was not open until seven a.m., so he should wait for another fifteen minutes. Annoyed, he went to a chair in the lobby and waited for the restaurant to open.

In the restaurant, Albert was disappointed to find a lack of variety on the menu. The full breakfast included only a plate of fruit, cucumber salad with some tomato pieces, and a cup of coffee or tea. Finishing the breakfast, he went to his room and picked up his luggage. At the front desk, he paid his bill and then proceeded to walk toward the street and wait for Isaac's arrival. To his surprise, he found Isaac already waiting for him at the hotel entrance.

In the cab, Isaac asked if Albert had had a full rest and if the room met his expectations. Albert just responded everything was fine, as the rooms were good-sized and clean, and the bathroom had a bathtub with shower. Pleased with his response, Isaac asked where he should he drive him.

Albert said he was trying to find a rabbi named Jacob Levitz. Logic told him the best place to find him was in a synagogue. Taking the picture from his pocket, he showed it to Isaac, expecting he might recognize him. After studying it, Isaac apologized, saying the face was not familiar to him, but he supposed he was a rabbi based on his picture.

Isaac suggested Albert first go to the Menachem Tzion Synagogue on Ha-Yehudim Street at the north of Hurva. That temple was popular with Jews, and perhaps somebody there would recognize the picture. The other option was the Great Synagogue, where for sure someone would know Jacob Levitz or at least provide the information they needed to find him. Albert accepted his suggestions, and Isaac drove first to the Menachem Tzion Synagogue. Using Isaac as a translator, Albert showed Jacob's picture to the responsible person at the synagogue, who, after studying the picture, denied ever seeing him. Frustrated, Colliere picked up the picture, thanked him for his help, said goodbye, and asked Isaac to drive him to the other church.

The location of the Great Synagogue was in Old Jerusalem, a few blocks from the Wailing Wall. Its outer facade showed an austere temple. The church was built on four pillars, each of them sixty-three feet in height by twenty-eight inches in width. The interior included separate seats for men from women. Walking through a large, dark corridor lighted only with wax lights, they came to the main altar, where a rabbi makes his prayers. On the left side of the altar was a small separate room, which Isaac explained to Albert was the Beth Midrash, used for the Torah study.

Standing patiently, they waited until the rabbi ended his prayers. When he finally did and proceeded to exit the main altar, Isaac approached him. Speaking in Hebrew, he explained to the rabbi they were trying to find someone. Isaac showed the picture to the rabbi, and his face lit up. Emitting a big grin, he said, "Of course I know Jacob Levitz. He is a rabbi highly recognized for this temple. Unfortunately, at the moment he is not here, but maybe with luck, you can find him at his house." Isaac paused to translate what the rabbi had said for Colliere, who quickly tore a piece of paper from his notebook and handed it to Isaac, requesting the rabbi write the address down.

Without further complications, Isaac drove to the address. Arriving, they saw a man leaving the house. His features matched those of the picture perfectly. Without thinking twice, Albert stepped out of the cab and greeted Jacob by his name, asking him to stop. Hearing his name, Jacob stopped and turned around. Colliere showed his police badge and introduced himself, then asked Jacob if he could question him. Jacob calmly asked, "What can I do for you?"

Getting straight to the point, Colliere asked Jacob how close his relationship with Gerald Solaris was. Hearing that name, Jacob became nervous but controlled his emotions. He responded that before he answered the question, he would like to know the reason the TIPA was involved. Understanding his concern, Colliere explained that last Sunday, the body of Gerald Solaris was found dead on a pathway at the back garden of his condo in Los Angeles. At first they thought he had committed suicide, but the autopsy revealed he had been assassinated. The time of death was last Sunday night between 9:15 and 9:30. "Does that answer your question?" asked Colliere. Jacob's face was pale, and stammering, he asked if they knew who had committed the murder. Albert responded that at the moment it was unknown, although he expected to find the criminal with his help.

Jacob breathed intensively before stating in a low voice that his relationship with Gerald Solaris was strictly from work. "We both were owners of travel agencies. Mr. Solaris had his in the United States, and mine was in Israel. Several years ago, we worked together to organize events for our respective clients, but I don't know much about his recent life." Laughing sarcastically, Albert mentioned that Jacob had a record of entries to the United States, the last one being twenty-six days ago at the Los Angeles International Airport. "So tell me, Jacob, if your visit was not to see Mr. Solaris, what was the purpose of your trip?" he asked.

Jacob stayed mute and did not reply. Patiently, Albert waited for his answer. Knowing he would lie, the detective chose to move in another direction and asked Jacob if it was true he had told Mr. Solaris's son, Richard, on the night he had visited his father that he had maintained a close relationship with his father for several years.

"I can't remember saying that to Richard," Jacob responded.

"I also think your memory is down to remember names of the persons that were with you that night when Richard Solaris visited his father in his Los Angeles condo two years ago, or am I wrong?"

Jacob firmly replied he could not think of their names. "You have not seen any of them again?" asked Albert. Jacob replied that was correct.

Hugely disappointed with his interrogation and seeing it was not leading to better results, Albert decided to end the questioning. Warning Jacob that if he had withheld information or lied to him, the next time his followers would be watching him behind bars. Jacob understood what he meant but chose to remain silent. Losing patience, Albert gave Jacob his business card, saying that on the back was written his personal phone number where he could call him at any time in case his memory was refreshed. When Albert dismissed Jacob, he said, "And don't forget the next victim could be you." Understanding the meaning of his words, Jacob did not respond.

When Jacob saw the detective stepping into the cab, he went to find a phone booth. Isaac made a U-turn and stopped the cab to follow Jacob at a discreet distance. In the telephone booth, Jacob inserted several coins and called the operator to make international calls. After giving the operator the number and name of Liu Wong Yen in Shanghai, China, he waited for several minutes until he was told no one answered at that number. Inserting more coins, Jacob called the operator again and this time gave the number for Hemant per Rai Shah in New Delhi, India. After a wait of several minutes, was informed Hemant per Rai Shah was unable to take the call, but another person on the line had accepted it. Accepting the call, Jacob spoke quickly to his interlocutor, expressing his desire to speak with Hemant per Rai Shah. After a pause, the person on the other end of the line answered that was not possible since his uncle had died three days ago when a car bomb exploded while he was getting into his car with other three persons, the latter only getting injured. Jacob remembered the incident. He had heard it on the news but never imagined one of the victims would be his friend Hemant. Offering condolences, Jacob gave thanks for the information and hung up the telephone.

Jacob felt a strong dizziness when he dialed the operator, requesting to speak with Mohammed Mussain in Arabia. The phone was picked up on the first ring. The operator informed Jacob that Mr. Mussain was on the line.

"Hello, Mohammed, is Jacob who speaks."

"Jacob, what is wrong?" answered Mohammed. Speaking quickly, Jacob told Mohammed everything he knew, including about Hemant's and Gerald Solaris's deaths. "Is Liu aware of this?" Mohammed interrupted.

"Nobody besides you knows. I tried to reach Liu on his telephone, but no one answered. Maybe by now he is dead too. I heard on the news that another car bomb was blown up in Shanghai, killing and wounding several people. If this comes to be true, then three deaths are unlikely coincidental." Jacob's face showed desperation, and he begged Mohammed to call Liu. "Maybe you will be luckier than I and can find him," said Jacob finally.

Mohammed proposed to meet later and discuss the issue. "If you agree, Jacob, we can meet tomorrow and have breakfast at seven a.m. in the restaurant of the Hotel Excelsior in Rome. I likewise promise to attempt to reach Liu and see if he can join us, as three brains can think better than a single one. The three of us will make a plan that can help us solve our troubles. Do you agree with my idea?"

"You can count on me," Jacob responded

To end the conversation Mohammed told Jacob he should try to calm down as the stress harmed his health. Jacob mumbled but did not clearly respond.

When his conversation with Mohammed was over, Jacob walked to his home. After a wait of two hours, Albert saw Jacob leaving the house, carrying a suitcase under his arm. In the street was a cab waiting for Jacob. Albert told Isaac to follow him. Having followed the cab for thirty minutes, Isaac finally said there was no doubt the taxi was leading them to the Ben Gurion Airport.

Albert called Raymond to update him about the recent events. So Isaac couldn't hear, Albert spoke in a low voice when he informed Raymond he had found Jacob Levitz, who became extremely nervous when informed of

Gerald Solaris's death and began lying to him. "When we were finished, he ran straight to a phone booth where he made several calls that I suppose were outside of Israel. Right now, Jacob Levitz is leading me to the Ben Gurion Airport. He is carrying a small suitcase, making me suppose his trip will be out of Israel."

Raymond interrupted Albert to say, "Find out the flight number, airline, and destination, and when you know it, call me back immediately."

Arriving at the airport, Albert dismissed Isaac, paying him triple the rate for his services. After Isaac thanked him, Albert walked inside the airport. Watching Jacob at a discreet distance, he saw him approaching the counter for Israel Airline Flight 464 with the destination of Rome. Albert called Raymond and updated him on his findings. Raymond instructed him to buy a ticket immediately on the same flight and to follow Jacob without being noticed. A few minutes later, Albert was in line at the same counter Jacob had been at before. Showing his badge to the airline manager, he bought a ticket in first class and requested the authorization to board the plane before other passengers did. The manager agreed without objection.

Trying not to lose Jacob's trail, Albert looked for a place to eat, being utterly disappointed when he found the restaurant at the airport was full of people and have to wait a long time. On the way to boarding the plane, he stopped in a shop to buy a magazine. As Albert boarded the aircraft, the pilot and flight attendant welcomed him and led him to his seat. When Jacob and the other passengers boarded the plane, Albert was comfortably seated, reading the magazine that covered his face.

CHAPTER 8

Rosemary, the receptionist, looked up from her work and saw Richard, who stood watching her in the main door of the morgue. The young secretary without a doubt was attractive, even when wearing a black tailored jacket and skirt that made her look severe. Making an inward smile at Richard, she asked what she could do for him. Richard answered it was a private affair, but he supposed she could tell Doctor Cussac that the detective Samuel Lewis had referred him. "Oh! Then I guess it must be an important matter," she said, offering Richard a seat to wait.

Rosemary walked through a long hallway, stopped at a door, and without knocking went inside. Doctor Lee Cussac was behind his desk working on his computer and making several calls. Knowing he hated to be interrupted while working, Rosemary apologized, stating that in the reception room was a gentleman who said he had been sent by Detective Samuel Lewis and wanted to speak with him. Doctor Cussac knew who Rosemary was referring to. He had just hung up with Detective Lewis, who explained to him in detail what Richard required.

Following the instructions, Rosemary led Richard to Cussac's office, this time knocking at the door and waiting for his response to proceed inside. Receiving Richard with a smile, the doctor offered him a seat and said he was expecting his visit as Lieutenant Lewis had talked to him, explaining his needs. Apologizing, Richard stated he did not want to bother him knowing how busy he always was, but Lieutenant Lewis had insisted he come.

"I am glad he did," Cussac said. "The lieutenant has done me many favors, and now it's my opportunity to return some of them."

Considering the painful memories the office brought up in Richard, Cussac apologized, saying he was sorry for the awful moments that he had made him go through yesterday. Richard did not rebut his apology.

Cussac explained to Richard what the whole process consisted of. The first thing to do was to receive the original of his father's death certificate and a transcript of the autopsy report. Second, he was to fill out and sign the forms authorizing the removal of the body from the morgue. Third, arrangements should be made for his father's funeral and cremation of his body. "Unfortunately," the doctor said, "the crematory closes at three o'clock, and we will have to wait until tomorrow. Still, I suggest we can reserve a time for your father's cremation." Richard at once agreed.

Cussac called the crematorium. The employee who answered said the only time available for cremation the next day was at ten a.m. as the early shift was already taken. Without Richard showing any objection, Cussac confirmed and reserve the time.

With the reservation for the cremation made, Cussac dialed the number for the funeral home and was transferred to the manager. Briefly, Cussac explained to the manager that a friend of his was making arrangements for his father's funeral and wanted to know the best plan for him. The manager stated it was best if could meet personally with him and show the plans they had. He would be in the morgue in about thirty minutes. After a wait of forty-five minutes, Rosemary finally announced the funeral manager's arrival. Rosemary led him to Cussac's office.

The funeral manager explained to Richard several funeral services the agency provided. Richard thought for a while before determining what plan would be most convenient for his needs. He selected a plan that included pickup of his father's body from the morgue before nine a.m., placing it in a wooden casket previously chosen by him and transferred to the crematory. Ending with cremation and the delivery of ashes in an urn selected from a pamphlet. The agency was to be responsible for all permits and the required cremation procedures, but Richard was required to be present at the time of cremation. Accepting all the terms, Richard signed the contract and paid for the services with his credit card.

While the manager was filling out the forms, Cussac's phone rang. Talking for several minutes, he then passed the phone to Richard, saying it was Lieutenant Lewis, who wanted to speak with him.

After greeting him, Richard informed Sam he had concluded the arrangements for his father's cremation. The time was scheduled for tomorrow at ten a.m. at the Torrance Crematory. Lewis congratulated Richard, then said he had another purpose for his call, which he imagined was not very pleasant. Richard at once responded, "What do we have now, Sam?"

Sam explained to Richard that they did not know how, but the press was aware of his father's death. A newspaper cover story said that his father was a recognized official of the Mexican government who had retired after thirty years of service. After his retirement, he had moved to Los Angeles, California, where he bought an expensive condominium in Marina del Rey, exceeding two million dollars in value, and for which he had paid cash. This past Monday morning, his body was found dead on a trail at the back garden of his condominium. The police had at first said he had committed suicide, but after the investigation, it turned out he had been assassinated. The crime appeared to be associated with money laundering or dirty business conducted by mobs abroad.

Richard was alarmed when he heard the news report and immediately asked Sam for his advice. Sam suggested he call his wife and sister immediately, telling them the whole truth. It was better for them to know his version than that of the Mexican media. Richard agreed and hung up the phone. He first called his sister. After explaining to Monica for forty-five minutes the reasons he had to lie to her, she refused to accept his excuses, saying she was sufficiently mature to know her father had died by assassination rather than suicide. Richard preferred not to argue with his sister and agreed with her.

Ending his conversation with Monica, Richard called his wife, Evelyn, who had the same reaction as Monica's—anger at his not telling her the truth. However, after understanding her husband's intention to protect them from getting involved in the matter, she did not complain anymore. Feeling that her husband was undergoing tremendous stress, she offered her help.

Richard replied a great help would be if she could call his boss, Mr. Blumekron, and tell him the truth. "Say at this moment I am too busy, but when I get some relief from the arrangements of my father's funeral, I promise to call and inform him of the events with more detail."

Thanking her for her understanding, he informed Evelyn of his plans to return to Mexico the next day when the funeral was over. First, though, he needed to speak with Mr Sosa about several matters. Later he was to pick up his automobile he had left parked at the condo and return it to the airport. As he ignored the time that would take him to fill his commitments, he preferred to take a cab when arrived to Mexico and not to bother his wife going to pick him up at the airport. Promising Evelyn he would let her know his flight schedule when returning, he ended the call by sending her a kiss.

Cussac waited until Richard finished his calls. The general manager had left, and Cussac approached to show Richard on a map the exact site where the cremation was to take place. "To relieve you from some work, I can take care of the early steps at the morgue to make sure your father's body is transferred correctly to the crematory," Cussac said. Thanking him for his valuable assistance, Richard requested a last favor, to call a taxi that could take him to a hotel near the crematorium. "If you wait ten minutes," said Cussac, "I can personally help you with that, as the crematory is on the way to my house."

After driving forty minutes through excessive traffic, they finally arrived at the Royal Holiday Hotel, which was within walking distance from the crematorium. Before Richard dismissed Doctor Cussac, he expressed his gratitude, stating that he hoped one day they could correspond further. Giving him his business card, Richard invited him to visit Mexico City, saying he could stay at his home. Cussac took the card and put it inside his pocket. Thanking Richard, he said he would consider his offer for his next vacation.

In the hotel, Richard was received by the bellboy, who accompanied him to the front desk. Finishing with his registration, he took the elevator that led to his room. After taking a shower, Richard felt much better. Looking at his watch, he estimated the time in Mexico City was past five o'clock With luck, he still could find Mr. Blumekron in the office.

He dialed Blumekron's private number, and it was he who answered. Skipping some details, Richard told his boss the whole story, who listened to him without interruption. When he finished, Blumekron reminded Richard that Jacinto Meraz, their attorney, could advise him better on these issues. Richard thanked Blumekron for his advice but said at the moment he had not faced any trouble, but he promised if something emerged, he would first call Meraz.

Carrying on with their conversation, Richard told Blumekron of his plans to come back to Mexico the next night after the cremation was over. Blumekron replied there was no need to rush as Alice was taking charge of his pending appointments, and besides that, tomorrow he was flying Vancouver to meet with some bankers, so he would be out of the office for the whole week. "Feel free to take three days off and put your thoughts in order." Thanking his boss, Richard stated that maybe he would take the time.

The distance to the crematory was short, so Richard decided to walk instead of hail a taxi. Sharp at nine o'clock in the next morning Richard was standing at the entry doorway of the crematory, waiting for the arrival of the ambulance that carried his father's body. Upon arrival, the body was immediately transported to the cremation furnaces. To fulfill his commitment, Richard waited until the cremation was over. Closing his eyes, he prayed for his father. When the cremation was finished, Richard was he to receive his father's ashes at the counter desk in the selected urn in twenty minutes.

When Richard received the ashes, he felt a strong nausea. He took a seat in the small waiting room. While resting, he saw two familiar figures approaching him. He immediately recognized one as Lieutenant Samuel Lewis and the other as his inseparable companion Miguel Rodriguez. They had come to extend their condolences. Inviting them to sit, Richard expressed his gratitude for their presence. They asked Richard if everything had gone well at the cremation, and he responded that thanks to their and Doctor Cussac's help, everything went fine.

Sam said he was glad they could help him. However, he had come not only to convey their condolences but also to update him on what was going on with the case. "Knowing of your intention to return to Mexico tonight, we informed our superiors. They had no objections but told us to advise you that your father's case was transferred to the Transnational Intelligence Police Agency. This change does not prevent us from helping you when needed, though." Leaving the urn on the table, Richard raised himself from his chair to hug his friends. Laughing, he said he never could have conceived of having two Los Angeles cops as his buddies. Sam responded in bad Spanish but using familiar terms *"Tu serles mi bueno, amigo."*

Watching them step inside the van and disappear made Richard feel a terrible loneliness and sadness. Going to the counter, he requested information about a chapel where he could pray. In the chapel, Richard walked toward the altar and kneeled down in front of the image of Jesus Christ. Praying for his father, he asked the Lord for clemency and pardon. Leaving the chapel, Richard felt a large ease. On the way back to the crematorium, a middle-aged man approached Richard to ask if he needed a cab. Responding affirmatively, Richard walked with the driver toward the crematorium entrance where a taxi was parked.

CHAPTER 9

Richard showed the security guard his identification and was
allowed entrance. Sosa had been advised of his arrival. As Richard
was leaving the taxi, Sosa approached him to say, "Mr. Solaris, we
thought you had forgotten us and were by now in Mexico." Apologizing
for not calling him earlier, Richard said the authorizations and procedures
had taken longer than he expected. "Don't feel bad, Mr. Solaris. I am just
joking, as everybody knows what you can expect when having to deal with
the police," Sosa said.

Richard expressed to Sosa his desire to return to Mexico that night.
He had come just to pick up his car and inform him of his decision
that regarding his father's condo, they would have to wait for another
occasion because he needed discuss the matter with his sister. Richard
suddenly remembered Romy and asked Sosa what he knew about her.
Sosa responded she had come that morning to deliver an envelope to him.
Richard put it in the pocket of his suit.

Richard informed Sosa the police were going to carry on with their
investigation, so he asked him to be helpful and try to make their task
easier. "Don't forget to keep me posted on everything, and if they request
my presence, call me and I will get the first available flight. If by any chance
you incur some expenses, pay them and charge it to me. I will try to refund
you quickly. Here is my business card. You'll find my cell phone number
there. Call me at any time." Paying attention to Richard's instructions,
Sosa smiled and responded Richard should not worry, as he would be
watching after everything.

Sosa approached Richard and whispered in his ear, "Mr. Solaris, we
heard in the news your father was assassinated. Is that right?"

Richard thought a moment before he responded, "Maybe it is true, but no one can be sure until the investigation ends. Let's leave the police to do their work. Don't you think so?" Sosa smiled and agreed.

Richard remembered the disappearance of the security guard who was on duty the day his father passed away and asked Sosa if he knew anything about their whereabouts. Sosa apologized and said he still was missing, but he had found out the guard used to drink a lot and go out with ladies, something that, to be honest, he had ignored.

Sosa remembered another envelope that had been delivered in the daily mail that morning to his father's address. Richard put that envelope in the pocket of his suit as well, saying he would read both when he was on the plane. Thanking Sosa for his attentions and services, Richard went to pick up his car. Starting the engine, he stopped at the gate to thank the guard on duty. Recognizing Richard, the guard greeted him. While driving to the airport, he could not cease thinking of the events that he recently had lived through.

At the airport, Richard returned the rental car to the agency. At the counter, he showed the airline employee his passport to purchase his first-class ticket to Mexico. His flight was to leave in three hours, so he had time to call Evelyn and inform her of his estimated time of arrival. The waiting room for first-class passengers had trays with light snacks and deli sandwiches, as well as coffee and tea. Richard felt tired and decided to skip the meal and instead find a comfortable seat. Reclining his head, he fell into a deep sleep. When he awoke, it was almost time to board the plane, so he quickly grabbed a sandwich and a cup of coffee that he could eat and drink quickly.

Only two passengers wearing a suit and tie were boarding the plane, and Richard was one of them. To feel more comfortable, he removed his tie and stuck it inside the pocket of his suit. Looking out the window, he saw everything was in complete darkness. Turning on his reading lamp, he remembered the envelopes Sosa had given him. By random he took out first the one from Romy. Opening the envelope, he found a letter written by Romy in which she expressed grief for his father's death and requesting him to call to discuss her status. *Poor Romy,* Richard thought. *Possibly she wants come back to Mexico and work for us, or perhaps she has decided to stay in the United States and is looking for severance or a reference letter.* Whatever she decides is not a high priority for me at this moment.

Returning the letter to his pocket, Richard felt the other envelope Sosa had given him. He took it out and saw there was no return address. Supposing it was a promotional pamphlet, he thought he would tear it up, but an impulse made him stop, and he decided to open it. To his surprise, he found a bank account statement with a location in the Cayman Islands. Looking at the balance, Richard almost fainted when saw that his father had deposited nearly eighteen million dollars into the account. Regaining his breath, he looked again at the statement. *Yes, Richard* said to himself, *there is no doubt my father deposited that amount into this institution.* Immediately a question arose of how his father could have gotten that amount when the profits of the travel agency seemed to be small and his retirement funds from the government would never have reached that amount. Looking for answers, Richard felt an intense headache. Asking the flight attendant for aspirin, he took two and reclined in his seat. He closed his eyes, and soon the fatigue of the day overtook him in a profound sleep.

CHAPTER 10

Arriving in Rome, Jacob went directly to the Excelsior Hotel. He had made a reservation by phone for two rooms. After registering, he received the keys to his room and then walked toward the elevator. Colliere was on the verge of doing the same but stopped when he thought he would lose Jacob's trail. Performing a fast inspection of the hotel layout, he found that both elevators and the guest stairs opened to the lobby, so he decided to choose that location as his point of observation.

Carrying his luggage, Colliere found a seat on a comfortable couch in the lobby. Reclining his head, he fell into a deep slumber. At two o'clock in the morning, Colliere was awakened by the hotel's security guard, instructing him to leave or take a room, saying that the lobby was not a place to sleep for free. Colliere whipped out his badge from his pocket. The guard apologized and offered his cooperation.

At 7:25 in the morning, Jacob came down the guest elevator. Covering his face with a magazine, Colliere saw him go into the restaurant. The hostess took him to a table far from the entryway. Colliere saw that most of the tables were still empty and his presence would be easily noticed, so he opted to stay outside.

At 7:35 a.m., another person with Arab features joined Jacob at his table. Colliere decided to make his entrance at this time. Eluding the hostess, he sat at a table close by with his back to Jacob. Waiting for the right moment, Colliere rose from his seat and, without being noticed, took digital pictures of both people with his digital camera.

Returning to his seat, Colliere heard Jacob say to Mohammed that a TIPA agent by the name of Albert Colliere had found him yesterday and had started to question him about his relationship with Gerald Solaris.

After finding out Gerald Solaris had died by assassination, he chose to lie to the agent, saying his relationship with Solaris was only work related. "He did not believe me because he threatened me, telling me I would go to jail if I had lied or withheld information from him. His investigation will surely continue until he finds the whole truth."

Mohammed listened to Jacob's story without interruption and then said he had also tried to reach Liu on his phone without getting an answer, making him suppose Jacob was right when he said Liu was also dead from the car bomb explosion in Shanghai that killed and injured several people. "Jacob, are you aware that if Gerald, Mussain, and Liu are dead, we are the sole survivors? Don't you think we are in danger too?" asked Mohammed.

Jacob's face turned pale before he said he knew that, but what could they do? Mohammed responded that last night, he could not sleep, and the solution came to him—they should go to Mexico and meet with Richard, Gerald's son, and tell him everything they knew about his father's activities and the role he performed for the organization. Perhaps after knowing everything, he would join them and help them. "What do you think of my idea?"

"You can count on me," Jacob responded.

Colliere listened and recorded their conversation. He knew the recording would allow him to hear the tape several times until could understand the meaning of every word. What worried him was ignoring what Gerald Solaris's activities were and the role he performed for that organization. Paying his check to the waiter, Colliere walked toward the hotel lobby. In less than an hour, he saw both Jacob and Mohammed coming down the guest elevator. Hauling their luggage they make a brief stop at the front desk, and paid their bills, then walked out onto the street and requested a taxi from the porter. Carrying his own luggage, Colliere ran to grab another taxi, offering the driver a generous tip to follow them.

Arriving at the airport, Colliere stayed at a prudent distance, watching the pair go to the Ali Italia Airline counter and buy first-class tickets to Mexico. Immediately, he called Sullivan on his cell phone to inform him of his findings. Sullivan asked Colliere if he knew what Gerald Solaris's activities were and the role he had performed in the organization. Colliere responded he had asked himself that same question. Expressing satisfaction with Colliere's work, Sullivan requested of him a last favor—if he would watch them get on the plane to Mexico and call him back to inform him. He did not have to follow them. Sullivan suggested Colliere take the day off and tour Rome, which he said was a beautiful city. Hanging up, Albert laughed, knowing well that Rome was not a city to be seen in only one day.

Following his boss's instructions, Albert watched Jacob and Mohammed board the plane to Mexico. After informing Sullivan of their flight number and airline, he was released from his duties.

Albert thought it was a good idea to follow Sullivan's suggestion, so he decided to tour Rome. Although he had been to Rome several times, his visits were always work related, and he had never been there as a tourist. To begin his tour, he chartered a taxi that took him first to the Coliseum and then the Basilica de San Pedro and the Sistine Chapel. At noon he bought an ice cream that he ate in front of the Trevi Fountain, into which he threw several coins and made three wishes. As darkness fell, he took a taxi to the Hotel Excelsior, where this time he registered for a room. After taking a fresh shower, he reserved by phone his flight back to Washington. Having gone to bed early, he woke up at six o'clock in the morning. Opening the window, he breathed in the fresh air of the morning and thought Rome would be a pleasant place for his retirement.

After hanging up with Colliere, Sullivan called Sam Lewis to update him on the recent events in the investigation. Raymond asked Sam if he had any idea of what activities Gerald Solaris performed in the organization. Sam responded he had not the slightest idea. Raymond mentioned to Sam that Richard should be advised that Jacob and Mohammed might possibly visit him. "Tell him to listen carefully to what they have to say. Likewise, he should ask for important information about his father but not offer them information that could compromise our investigation. Keep me posted. . . . Oh! I nearly forgot. Send my regards to Donald Myers and his wife, Katy, whom I have not seen in a long time," Raymond said when finishing talking to Sam.

CHAPTER 11

rriving at the Mexico City airport, Richard hailed a cab to his house. Evelyn and his two sons were waiting impatiently for him. When he opened the door, the two kids climbed up to embrace and kiss their father. Betty, less prudent than Tony, asked Richard if he had brought them gifts. Evelyn, who was watching the scene, said their father had been very busy and was unable to get them gifts. After showing frustration in their faces, the two kids started to chat with their father, telling him of their adventures while he was gone. After listening to them for several minutes, Evelyn intervened to remind them that tomorrow was a school day, and they needed to wake up early. Obeying their mother's commands, the two kids said good night and kissed their father.

Alone in the bedroom, Richard asked Evelyn about the news about his father. Evelyn responded they were saying his father was involved with the mob, who had killed him. Facing Evelyn, Richard said, "What they say may be true."

Evelyn begged Richard to forget what was happening for a while and instead focus on getting some rest. "Tomorrow will be another day," Evelyn said, giving Richard a kiss and turning the lights off so he could go to sleep.

Even after closing his eyes, Richard could not sleep. Through his mind ran the huge amount of money his father had deposited in that bank. There was no doubt that his father had no longer been an honorable person. The profits of the travel agency and his retirement fund from the government were insufficient to allow any person to live the way his father had. For a moment, Richard thought he was living a nightmare and that when he woke up the next day, everything would vanish and return to normal.

Fatigued, Richard fell asleep. He woke up at five o'clock in the morning with a strong chill throughout his body. Turning on his side bed lamp, he tried walk to the bathroom, but the feeling that he could tumble made him return to bed. Evelyn, watching Richard, asked if was feeling well. Richard replied that his head hurt and he probably had a fever. Leaping out of bed, Evelyn went to find a thermometer, which she inserted into Richard's mouth. The reading showed Richard has a high fever, so Evelyn suggested calling the doctor right away. Richard stopped her and requested she give him a couple of aspirin and put the ice bag on his head and wait to see how he felt. If by seven in the morning he was not feeling better, he would allow her to call the doctor. Obeying his instructions, Evelyn waited until seven. Seeing her husband was getting worse, she proceeded to ring the doctor. The call was picked up by the doctor's voice mail where Evelyn said her husband was sick and required urgent care.

Despite her urgent message, the doctor did not appear at their home until nine o clock. Examining Richard, he diagnosed the fever was due to the flu he contracted during his trip to Los Angeles. As a remedy, he prescribed to remain in bed for three days and take expectorant. While the doctor wrote the prescription, Richard said that his work was important, and he needed go to the office and take care of some works that left unfinished. The doctor responded that if he desired to be well soon, he should follow his instructions and rest in bed for three days, reminding him that relapses were always worse. Also, he recommended that Richard quiet down, leave the stress aside, and forget about his other activities, as none of them were more important than his health.

For the next two days, Richard remained in bed, doing nothing. On the third day, as the doctor had predicted, he started to feel much better. Having slept until eleven a.m., he decided to shave and shower. Lying on the bed, he began to make phone calls and dictate letters to Alice. Taking his medicine regularly made him sleep all night. Nevertheless, on the fourth day of his illness, Richard woke up at five o'clock in the morning trembling. Suddenly he remembered that two years ago, his father had left for him in a sealed envelope a letter with instructions not to open it until his death. Richard kept it under lock and key in a file in his office desk. Richard could no longer sleep. He was anxious to go to his office and open the envelope to read the missive.

At six a.m., his alarm clock sounded. Once he silenced it, Richard headed to the bathroom where he showered and shaved. Twenty minutes later, he found his wife under the blankets. Leaning over her, he kissed her and said goodbye. Evelyn, still dazed, asked Richard where he was going so early. He replied that he had suddenly remembered some things he had left in the office and need to attend. Since he could not sleep any longer, he preferred to take charge of them, but he promised Evelyn he would be home early. Evelyn reminded him of what the physician had mentioned about relapses and that he should consider his health first and then other matters. Richard leaned in to kiss her on the forehead and said he would stick to her advice.

CHAPTER 12

Without traffic, the time from his home to the office was twenty minutes. Arriving there, Richard opened the gate with his remote control. Picking up his briefcase he had left in the rear seat, he gently closed the door of his automobile. The security guard arrived at his post and asked Richard if he had been out of town as he had not been seen in the office for the last week. Richard responded he had first has traveled to Los Angeles and later was sick in bed, but today he was feeling much better and had decided to arrive early and take care of some works that left without finished. Facing Richard, the guard asked if he needed him to open his office, as he knew Alice had the keys for the office but still had not made it to work. Richard thanked the guard and followed him.

After turning on the lights to the room, the guard opened the office and left. Immediately Richard walked to his desk and pulled open the upper drawer with the file with the envelope inside. Being comfortably seated, Richard examined the envelope, recognizing his father's handwriting. The envelope read, "Do not open this envelope until my death." Using his letter opener, he opened the envelope and extracted the letter from it, then started to read.

Dear Richard:

When you open this letter, I will no longer be alive. Foremost, I must start by expressing to God my gratitude, who blessed me by giving your mother to me as a wife and you and Monica as my children. As we know, your mother was the mainstay in our family that we lost when she passed away. Her death took me into a deep depression, as I blamed myself for her death. During my childhood, your grandparents educated me under religious and moral principles, which I kept until the year 2005. I broke them later due to several circumstances and the threat that made me belong to an organization that only brought to me suffering and remorse for the remainder of my lifetime. God knows exactly what I mean and humbly request His pardon and clemency.

Richard, as you read this letter, many answers to your inquiries will be provided; however, other questions will arise, which I recommend forgetting. When you are finished reading this letter, please follow my instructions thoroughly, as any mistake can carry you to terrible consequences.

Everything started during the middle of December 2005, when I needed to travel to Frankfurt, Germany, and attend to matters as the Director of Foreign Affairs. During my stay in that city, I was invited to serve as the representative of the Mexican government at a reception offered by the German embassy. At that event, I encountered an extremely attractive woman named Gwen, who spoke perfect English and invited me to visit her offices the following day. Having finished my work, I accepted her invitation, so she picked me up on the following day at the entrance of my hotel.

In the journey to her offices, she mentioned to me that being eighteen years of age, she had married a prominent businessman eighteen years older than her, the owner of the most important aluminum factory in Germany. Their marriage had lasted only one year, as her husband passed away when he suffered a heart attack.

As is common in such cases, I expressed my condolences on his death, saying how hard it must have been for her to lose him so soon. The answer surprised me when she said his death had been a blessing for her. Seeing the astonishment in my face, she explained to me her marriage had been hell because her husband enjoyed mistreating and denigrating her in front of people. With his demise, she had obtained her freedom. Designated as the only heir of his whole fortune, she inherited the aluminum factory, several properties, and a huge number of bank accounts. But even though this fortune would allow her to relish life without economic problems, she adopted the determination to sell some properties and withdraw significant amounts of money from the bank accounts to invest them in an institution that had as its purpose the defense of women against the mistreatment and discrimination of men. Pursuing her objective, she made a partnership arrangement with a North American researcher named Susan Myers, PhD. Joining forces, they formed an organization that they named as INPOWER.

Understanding her reasoning, I congratulated her on her noble project, stating my repulsion to those men who used their strength to abuse and discriminate against women. I trust that my commentary pleased her as she smiled at me.

For the next fifty minutes, she drove various routes on highways unknown to me at speeds over 200 miles per hour. Lowering her speed, she took a local road that, although narrow, was well paved. The route was fenced in by mountains and tall trees and went to a small valley, at bottom of which was an esplanade with an airport and several buildings. I asked Gwen to whom they belonged. She answered they were part of her development. She explained that the airport had two runways; one was for their personal use and the other was to land small planes such as a Lear or Falcon. It was outfitted with a modern radar system capable of tracing strange objects that approached from several miles distant, making it impossible for any pilot to land without the prior authorization of the flight controllers. The buildings were used as a headquarters for the people who worked for her in the development.

The buildings I had before seen in the distance came into clearer focus. The ground was level and spread over several thousands of acres, surrounded by enormous fences about twenty feet high. Each corner had turrets with guards inside, quick to snap their weapons up at any intruder who dared to enter without their permission. Just imagine a feudal castle.

Before we reached the front entrance, Gwen stopped her car and used a radio to notify the security guard of our arrival. She took from the glove compartment her identity tag that she put into a reader and typed in her secret code. We waited until the first door opened to allow our entry. After we passed through the door, it closed to leave us trapped in a room in total darkness. Gwen lowered her window and loudly pronounced her name in a microphone that recognized her voice. The room lit up. Once the system corroborated her identity tag, password, and voice identification, another door opened, leading us to a narrow tunnel that, once illuminated, disconnected the alarms to admit us to the exit doorway.

Exiting the tunnel, we came upon three paths. Gwen took the one on the right, driving her car toward a building that without a doubt was the tallest and nicest of the development. After descending a ramp, we arrived at the basement floor, where she parked the car in a space reserved for directors. Walking through a long corridor, we arrived at some private elevators. Gwen used her key to press the button that led us to the requested level.

The doorways of the elevator opened on the seventh story, revealing the offices of the main directors. Most of them were twenty-five by twenty-five in size, though others seemed to be smaller, maybe fifteen by fifteen. All of them were nicely decorated. Gwen flipped the switch to her office and we entered, shutting the door behind us. The view from her window looked out on a nice interior garden below with tall trees, carefully decorated by expert landscapers. Pulling together some papers from her desk, she asked me to follow her. Using the stairs, we arrived at the third level, where we found the auditorium. The auditorium had the capability to comfortably accommodate more than 500 people, divided into two sections of 250 each. On the same floor were two small conference rooms for twelve persons each. Each of these rooms was furnished with a rectangular table, twelve armchairs surrounding the table, and in the left-hand corner attached to the wall, a bookcase holding a gigantic television screen. In one of those small rooms, Gwen introduced me to the four people you met that night in my Los Angeles condo.

Gwen waited and then rose up from her seat to bid us to enjoy a light snack consisting of pastries, coffee, and tea, which most of us declined.

Instead of going back to her seat, Gwen walked to the bookcase embedded in the wall. She pressed a hidden button hidden in the back and moved the Rembrandt painting to the left, revealing a safe. Opening it, she extracted several boxes with videocassettes that she put into player and projected onto the gigantic TV screen. Regrettably, Richard, I am unable to disclose the contents of those videos, which to me seemed very impressive and shocking.

When the videos were finished, Gwen turned the TV set off and said everything I'd seen was extremely confidential and should never be revealed to anyone else, as her organization would be in peril. She told me that all work they performed in their organization was done in conformity to a strategic plan. To indicate the truth of what she said, she mentioned our encounter was not just a coincidence but was part of a plan in which they had bugged my home and business phones and set up cameras to learn all my tastes, habits and customs. By these means, they knew the number of kids I had, what schools they attended, what religion we professed, and in what ways and at what times we did our daily activities, as well as understood the excellent relations they knew I had with the governmental, private and ecclesiastical sectors. The results of their monitoring led them to selecting me as the fifth male member of their organization, once structured only for females. Without giving me the opportunity to refuse, Gwen rose from her seat and was followed by the other members. They started to clap as a sign of welcome to a newcomer to their organization.

Finishing the applause, Gwen said to me that everyone in that room received payment for their services. The amount was three million dollars per year, and it was paid up front. The process would repeat every year as long as I stayed in their organization. The money would be deposited directly into my personal account, and I could make withdrawals without restrictions. In addition, they remarked, there was another account also in my name that belonged to their organization, from which I was allowed to make unlimited withdrawals with the only condition being that I explain the reason for the expense. The initial balance of that account was 150 million dollars. They also recommended I open both accounts in the same bank, with a preference for a certain paradise location to facilitate the transactions.

Richard, now you know the source I used to buy my condo and the other minor expenses, which I would have gladly returned if I could have held to the straight life I learned from my parents. The withdrawals from my personal account were rather modest as I always kept in mind to save the funds for the benefit of you and Monica.

To avoid problems with the IRS, I declared these funds properly every year. You will find my tax returns for all these years hidden in a fake drawer of my desk at the travel agency. To access them, you'll have to remove the top drawer and slide the lateral side to your right. The deeds to my two properties and an old watch that belonged to your great-grandfather are also there, which you can take as part of his inheritance.

Now pay attention, Richard, to the following instructions. The two accounts were opened in the Stanley Bank of the Cayman Islands. The number of my personal account is 090706543, and the other account I used for expenses belonging to Gwen's organization has the number 090072139. Close both accounts and open new ones in your name. Jenny Hawkins is reachable at the following number: toll free 1 855 345-1344. She will help you to follow the procedures properly. Be prepared, as she will first require you to properly identify yourself. Once you have sent your identification via fax or email, she will require you to answer five easy questions: *"What was my favorite pet's name?"; "What is my favorite book?"; "From which university did I get my law degree?"; "What was my mother's maiden name?"; and "What was my father's main activity?"* As you can see, all are easy questions to which you know the answers.

Once you have identified yourself and answered the questions to her satisfaction, you will ask Jenny to give you the balances from both accounts. First transfer the entire amount of my personal account to the new account you open in your name, dividing half of it with your sister, Monica, allowing her the decision to keep the money there or transfer it to another bank of her preference. In order to ease the transfer of the expense account funds, I previously had signed a non-negotiable check to Jenny for which you are the named beneficiary. Jenny only needs to fill the check with the amount you will mention to her. Remind Jenny to endorse the check, writing the number of your new account on the back. This procedure will deposit the money instantly and enable you to make immediate withdrawals. Once you hold the funds in your account, ask Jenny to buy for you a money order in the whole amount and to help you establish an electronic transfer to the Mossler Bank of Zurich, as they have received instructions on what to do when they receive the funds. Richard, don't forget to ask Jenny for a receipt for the transaction to exempt you from any responsibility.

Finally, I must say that everything I did wrong was to protect you and our family. Perhaps one day you'll understand what I mean. Richard, as a last favor, please forget this letter ever existed. God only knows if one day will gather again the entire family. Now, before I say my last goodbye, remind Monica how much I love you both. Kisses and hugs from your father.

Gerald Solaris.

Richard remained unmoving for several minutes. Without a doubt the letter answered many of his questions. However, others had emerged, such as, What was the purpose of bringing his father into the organization? What was his work in order to receive such a high payment? What caused his father to blame himself for his mother's death? What did his father fear that led him to ask he forget the letter? What was the content of those videos that he refused to disclose? What was the purpose of the expense account, and why was the amount so high?

Without answers to his questions, Richard chose to leave them aside and focused on pursuing his father's instructions. Foremost, he dialed the indicated number and asked the operator if he could speak with Miss Jenny Hawkins. Once he was identified to Jenny, she asked Richard, as his father had anticipated, to send her his identification card and answer some questions. Following the procedure, Richard send his ID by email and answer her questions. Then he express to Jenny his need to cancel both of his father's accounts and to open new ones in his name. While Jenny proceeded to make the cancellations and fill out the new forms and contracts, she asked Richard about his father. She knew that when Richard called, his father would no longer be alive. Surprised at her question, Richard replied that his death had been unexpected and had been very painful for the whole family. Expressing condolences to Richard, she refrained from uttering further commentary and concentrated on her work.

When Jenny finished filling out the forms and contracts, she informed Richard he could go ahead and make the transfers. At that instant the thought crossed Richard's mind of what would happen to him if those funds were illegal or came from laundered money or dirty businesses. Despite his concern, Richard took the risk and accepted the transactions. The balance of his father's personal account was immediately transferred to his new account.

Richard intended to split the amount in half with his sister, but he thought it would be better to speak to her first and know her decision. When he reminded Jenny about the check his father had previously signed and for which he was the beneficiary, Jenny answered she had at hand the check that could be filled with the amount required at any moment. She notified Richard that the balance of the account was at that moment one hundred thirty-five million, four hundred fifty thousand, and eight dollars.

He authorized Jenny to fill the check out with that same amount, endorse the back of the check, and write the number of his new account so that the deposit was immediate as he was intending to make withdrawals. As she completed the transaction, Richard made another request of Jenny, to buy for him a money order in that same amount and transfer it electronically to the Mossler Bank in Zurich. Richard could hardly believe how easily these transactions were made by just following his phone instructions. Perhaps Jenny was doing all this as a last favor to his father.

When Richard was notified that the money transfer to the Mossler Bank was completed, he felt great relief. Remembering his father's instructions, he asked Jenny to scan the receipt and email it to him, even if the original would be sent later by messenger. Finished with his father's commands, Richard congratulated Jenny on her efficiency and thanked her for her willingness to perform these services.

CHAPTER 13

Richard's intercom rang. Alice was calling to say Lieutenant Samuel Lewis was on line two. Richard took the call and remembered that in their last meeting they have talked in familiar terms. Yet at the moment, he preferred to be more formal and said, "Hello, Lieutenant Lewis. I was about to call you."

In reply, Lewis said, "Hello, Richard. Did I catch you at a busy moment? How has your family assimilated the news of your father's death?"

"The news is terrible. They want to link my father with the mob, which for me is hard to believe," Richard replied.

"True or false, the statement is just a rumor and should not be taken seriously," Sam responded.

Richard agreed but not really convinced by Sam's words. Then he said his father had left him a letter with instructions not to open it until his death. In the letter, he found information that he thought was relevant to the investigation. However, he felt uncomfortable talking about it by phone. What was Sam's suggestion?

Without taking Richard's words seriously, Sam asked Richard to pay attention. "Richard," he said. Jacob was found. Gathering with other person they express their desire of come to Mexico and meet with you. The purpose is to talk about your father. The agent saw them yesterday boarding a plane to Mexico, so probably by today, you might be hearing from them. Richard, while you meet with them, be careful. Don't talk too much. It's better that you listen and try to collect information from them. Never make any comments that can compromise our investigation. At the end of your meeting, call me with the results. I wish you luck, Richard," said Sam and hung up the phone.

Richard was on the verge of returning his father's letter to his files when he received the call from Sam. Notified of the men's possible visit, he preferred to keep the letter in the pocket of his suit. While working on other matters, he received a call from Alice, who announced she had on line two a person who refused to provide his name. Richard knew to whom Alice was referring and accepted the call.

Introducing himself by name, Jacob reminded Richard about when they had met two years ago in his father's condo in Los Angeles. Apologizing for not calling him before, he said it was not until two days ago that he became aware of his father's death. At that moment, he was in Mexico City for a brief stop, but he intended to return to his country tonight. He did not want to lose the opportunity to offer his condolences on Richard's father's death personally. So if he could receive him in a moment, he would like to speak with him about his father.

Richard suggested the meeting take place at a small restaurant close to his office at eleven a.m. when there were few customers and no one would bother them. Accepting his suggestion, Jacob took note of the address.

Richard arrived at the restaurant before the scheduled time. As he had anticipated, the restaurant lacked clientele at that time of the day. In a corner right by the window, Richard saw two people talking at a table. He instantly recognized them as Jacob and the Arab. Neither of them wore their cultural attire and expensive jewelry. They both simply wore elegant black suits with blue ties. Waving their hands, they invited Richard to join them at their table. To show respect, they stood up and introduced themselves, saying their names loudly. Paying attention this time, Richard said he remembered them both, as Mohammed was also there the night he visited his father's condo. Jacob agreed and Mohammed smiled, saying he remembered him too.

Once seated, Jacob started the conversation, saying they both had come to offer their personal condolences on his father's death and to know if it was true that his father had died by assassination. Richard was ready to respond when the waiter made his appearance to take their orders. Jacob and Mohammed ordered tea while Richard preferred to take a cup of coffee. After the waiter left, Richard renewed the conversation, saying that unfortunately the statement was true, even though the police had first thought he committed suicide. But later the results of the autopsy revealed he had been assassinated. The autopsy report revealed the cause of death was a shot of thallium nitrate into his body. As far as Richard knew, his father had no enemies who would want to kill him

Mohammed frowned, and Jacob rubbed his beard before asking Richard if at any time he had heard his father mention the name of Gwen Swayze. Richard thought a moment and then answered he had never heard the name until this morning when, reading his father letter, he became aware of her existence. Richard suddenly exclaimed with excitement, "Hey, then you must be the people that my father mentioned in his letter who were present when he watched the videos." Jacob did not deny it. "Then you must know the content of those videos?" Richard asked.

Pausing, Jacob said, "Yes, Richard, but before I answer your question, I would like to know what your father said in his letter."

Richard was prepared to confront this moment and had safely kept the letter inside the pocket of his suit. Questioning himself if it was a wise decision to show the letter, he took the risk and took it from his pocket and handed it to Jacob. Richard said the letter was written in Spanish, but if they allowed him, he could translate it for them. Jacob mentioned that would not be necessary since, even though he and Mohammed did not speak Spanish well, they were nevertheless assiduous readers of Mexican history, which they preferred to read in the original language.

Moving to another table, both read the letter simultaneously and in perfect silence. Finishing up, their faces showed astonishment. Lowering their voices, they began to converse in a foreign language incomprehensible to Richard. The discussion lasted several minutes before they come back to the table where Richard remained seated.

Richard asked Jacob what their impression of the letter was. In response, Jacob said everything his father had stated was true, and Richard should believe that what his father did, good or bad, was intended to protect him and his family. "We don't have the right to involve you in this matter and put your family at risk. So following your father's recommendation, it is much safer for you to forget this letter ever existed."

Richard sipped his lukewarm coffee, then replied that he would gladly follow their advice. Still, he felt the letter was tied to his father's death and would not rest until he could see his father's killer properly punished and in jail.

Adjusting his glasses, Jacob responded, "Richard, our visit has two purposes. The first was to offer our personal condolences on your father's death. The second is to request your help, but after reading your father's letter, we have no right to involve you in this matter, so Mohammed proposes we leave you immediately."

Seeing them rising from their seats, Richard exclaimed, stammering, "Hey, please . . . please wait . . . err . . . wait. Please don't go." Holding Jacob by the sleeve, Richard made him return to his seat. Showing despair, Richard begged, "OK, but before you go, I want to know the kind of service my father rendered to your organization, the purpose of the funds for expenses, and finally the content of those videos. I think I at least deserve responses to those three things."

Looking at Mohammed, Jacob started to address his partner in an unintelligible language to Richard. Finally, Jacob said to Richard, "We're sorry, but we are unable to answer your questions. Mohammed insists that we leave. However, after discussing it, we have determined to tell you briefly something in regard to the content of the videos if you promise to us that after hearing it, you will forget what we just said."

Attempting not to compromise, Richard answered, "Let me decide what to do later."

Crossing his leg, Jacob said that the first video Gwen showed them was about how she had met Susan and together formed the company they named as INPOWER. In the same video were listed the statutes that formed their organization. The second video demonstrated techniques they employed to select their potential nominees and to increase their numbers. The third video demonstrated different ways they defended women's rights and struggled against the discrimination and abuse of men. The fourth video showed the various methods they applied to accumulate income and on what that income was expended.

Richard said, "What you are saying is that Gwen is a true defender of women's rights."

"Perhaps you are right, Richard. However, allow me to tell you who Gwen is in real life. Gwen is a very attractive and intelligent woman, but overall she is astute and cruel. Showing us the videos, she started to speak on different themes of politics and religion, leaving us surprised at her knowledge. Gwen considers the fundamentalism of state and religious principles of former times to be discriminatory acts against women, saying that many of them still continue today. To understand better her statements, she gives the example of birth control, by which governments, in order to stop population growth, imposed coercive measures on women that later resulted in prohibited practices by most religions as they rejected the acceptance for these methods.

Interrupting Jacob, Richard asked what religion they professed. "Mohammed is Islamic, and I follow Judaism. According to Gwen, seventy-five percent of the whole world is concentrated in five religions, with Christianity having the most followers." Richard smiled and agreed with her presumption.

Richard asked Jacob if he thought their different religions was the reason Gwen chose them as members of their organization. Before Jacob could answer, he was stopped by Mohammed, who said, "Jacob, you talk too much and promised me you wouldn't do it. I remind you we need to arrive early at the airport as the confirmation of our return is still pending. Please forgive Jacob, but when he starts to speak of religions, nothing can halt him, as he is able to repeat every word of the Torah by memory.

Jacob asked Mohammed not to exaggerate, though as he said, "Sometimes I forget the commas." His comment broke the ice momentarily and made the three men laugh.

Understanding Mohammed's message, Jacob stopped talking, as they needed to follow his father's instructions to keep Richard out of the matter. Hearing Jacob's words, Richard felt strong frustration, blaming himself for allowing them to read his father's letter. Maybe if he had not shared the letter, at this moment he would have had more helpful information to find his father's murderer. Despite his frustration, Richard had to admit their reasons were valid.

With his visitors refusing to give further information, Richard called the waiter and requested the check. Jacob intended to pay for it, taking out a ten-dollar bill from his pocket, which the waiter declined, saying he was not allowed to receive foreign currency. His answer made Jacob frown. Richard accepted the check and paid for it, giving Jacob his ten-dollar bill back.

Jacob was hesitant to ask Richard for another favor. Instead, Mohammed spoke up and asked Richard to call the waiter and tell him they needed a cab to take them to the airport. Richard replied he would be honored to take them personally to the airport and continue their chat. Jacob said they did not want to bother him, knowing how busy he was. "Don't say that," Richard said. "As for me, it is a pleasure to speak to friends who knew my father well."

At Richard's insistence, Jacob was unable to turn away the offer. During the journey to the airport, Richard again brought up his father, asking Jacob how they became aware of his father's death. Jacob responded that a person traveling from Israel had told him. Richard knew to whom Jacob was referring, but instead of getting into further details, he preferred to renew the conversation by asking about the other two people who were present that night in his father's condo.

Jacob's face became pale, and Mohammed said, "Hemant per Rai Shah died when a car bomb detonated in New Delhi, and Liu Wong Yen seems to have disappeared, although we fear he may be the victim of another car bomb that blew up in Shanghai, China."

Jacob faced Richard to see if he had caught the significance of Mohammed's words. Richard recalled at that instant what he had seen days before in his office on the employee TV screen when the reporter mentioned the two terrorist attacks, one in New Delhi and the other in Shanghai, where two car bombs had exploded, killing and injuring several innocent people. Of course at that moment, Richard would never have imagined the victims of those attacks were people he knew. He froze when he realized the date of these deaths coincided with that of his father's.

Seeing Richard's affliction, Jacob intervened to say, "Maybe now you can see the reason your father recommended you forget everything. Indeed, we are aware that our own lives are in danger too, so take my advice and leave us at the airport. Please forget we ever existed."

Upon arriving at the airport, Richard stopped his car and opened the trunk so Jacob and Mohammed could take their luggage out. Thanking Richard for taking them to the airport, they said goodbye, returning a salute as Richard lowered his window to shake hands and thank them for their allegiance to his father. Departing, Richard saw them in the rearview mirror hauling their luggage. He wondered if he would one day see them again.

CHAPTER 14

Before arriving at his office, Richard made an abruptly stop in his vehicle to reflect. His sixth sense kept telling him to forget everything and not to get involved in the events. But some other voice, the one of his conscience, encouraged him to go forward with the investigation. After pondering for several minutes, he decided to go for the second choice, even if it involved a higher risk to him and his family. It was the right decision to make because as a man and a son, his duty was to capture his father's murderer. Satisfied with his decision, he took out from the pocket of his suit the small recording machine that he had used to record their conversation. He pressed the key to play. After hearing their voices distinctly, he knew it had worked properly and turned it off.

In his office, Richard dialed Sam's private phone number. His responsibility was to keep the detective posted on recent events. When Lewis answered the telephone, Richard quickly reported on his meeting, expressing his frustration as he had expected to collect more valuable information for the investigation. Nevertheless, he said he had recorded the whole conversation, which he thought was worthwhile. Richard asked Sam what he should do to send it to him. Sam replied he would have an answer in one hour, and he also remembered to ask him to hold on to his father's letter. Richard seemed glad to see Sam remembered his father's letter and agreed with him.

While awaiting Sam's call, Richard thought about listening to the recording he made of their conversation. Everything appeared to be working well until Mohammed and Jacob moved to the other table and interpreted his father's letter. At that moment, their voices lowered and almost melted away. Even after turning up the volume to its maximum intensity, Richard could not hear what they were saying. Supposedly they were speaking in a foreign language, but he was not certain. Discouraged with his efforts, he chose to hear the remainder of the tape.

The tape hadn't finished when the intercom rang, Alice said she had Lieutenant Lewis on line two.

Sam quickly explained to Richard that he had talked with the director of the TIPA office. They drew together a plan in which his return to the United States was eminent. His presence was required for a meeting. This time the location was the city of Lexington, Virginia. Sam said to Richard that he was aware there were no direct flights from Mexico to Virginia, so he recommended he fly first to Washington and then shift to another plane to Richmond, where Sam would wait for him at the airport restaurant. Later, a van would come to pick them up and take them to Lexington. Richard had no questions and said he would go immediately to make the arrangements for his trip.

Rising from his seat, Richard asked Alice to make reservations for his two flights. In less than fifteen minutes, Richard was informed that both reservations were made. His departure to Washington was scheduled for 7:30 in the morning; therefore, he should be at the airport before 5 o'clock. Regarding his other flight to Richmond, Alice said was to leave Washington at 1:15 p.m., giving him enough time to catch the other flight without rushing in spite of the time difference in Mexico.

Asking Richard how he intended to pay for his tickets, Alice said one choice was to pay for them online with his credit card, and the other was to send Joseph to the travel agency and sign for them. Richard chose to pay for them online, so he drew out from his wallet his credit card and handed it to Alice, reminding her not to forget his boarding passes for the two flights.

Carrying out his instructions, Alice walked in Richard's office to leave on his desk the two reserved airline tickets and the boarding passes, saying both flights were reserved in first class. After thanking Alice, Richard dismissed her.

Richard proceeded to write a list of his pending tasks that, once they were accomplished, he check-marked and put into his briefcase the later closed with key. When he was finished with his work, Richard called Sam to inform him of his flight itinerary.

Arriving home, Richard was received by Evelyn with hugs and kisses, saying she was glad to see him home early because he looked tired and should go to bed early. Richard told Evelyn he had to travel early the next day to Virginia because his presence was required at a meeting. Evelyn was silent, then expressed her anger at Richard by saying he should recall what happened to his father. Her recommendation was to let the police perform their work and for him to stay out of it.

Richard furiously raised his voice and reminded Evelyn they were talking about his father, and no matter what he had done, he would always be his dearest father to him, and it was his obligation to cooperate with the police and see the killer properly punished and in jail. Evelyn started to sob and said to Richard he had never talked to her in that tone. Apologizing for raising his voice, Richard said he was extremely nervous about all the things that were going on. Sensing her husband's feelings, Evelyn also apologized, saying she would never mention it again, but what she had said was because she cared for him. Richard understood and thanked her.

Changing the topic, Richard asked about the children. He wanted to say goodbye to them before going to bed. Evelyn answered they were playing in the backyard, but she could call them. Richard stopped Evelyn and said he would go and look for them himself. In the meantime, she could prepare something to eat for him as his day at the office had been so busy that he had completely forgotten to eat.

After playing ball with his kids for twenty minutes, Richard said goodbye to them. Going to the kitchen, he found Evelyn preparing his food. While he ate, they talked about various topics, avoiding the subject of his father. When finished, Richard went to the bedroom, followed by Evelyn.

Setting his alarm clock for two a.m., Richard said to Evelyn it was not necessary for her to get up as he preferred to take a light breakfast at the airport. Instead, he asked her to pack clean clothes for him and put some toiletries in his handbag. Richard requested Evelyn to close the door and stop the kids from making noise. Showing his love to Evelyn, he gave her a kiss and thanked for her understanding. Evelyn responded that she loved him as well and the kids, and she wanted him alive. Leaving the room, Evelyn turned the lights off.

CHAPTER 15

The recurring dream had become a nightmare for Richard. Each time he closed his eyes and tried go to sleep, the same questions arose in him. Being unable to sleep and without finding answers to his questions, Richard rose from the bed and quickly reviewed the documents he would take to the meeting. Finding everything was complete and in order, he returned to bed and tried go to sleep. At two o'clock, his alarm clock rang, waking him up.

After his stop in Washington, Richard finally landed in the Richmond airport with a one-hour delay. Full runways at Washington Dulles Airport were making takeoffs late. During his flight, Richard recalled his recent discussion with Evelyn. Fortunately it had been a controlled conflict, but it still made him feel bad, as he had never yelled at her before. What was comforting was that she had understood he was living under a stressful situation with everything that was occurring in recent days. Richard thought it would be a good idea to invite Evelyn to dine out when everything was over.

Landing at the Richmond airport, Richard went to see Sam, who, having arrived early, was waiting for him. He was seated in the restaurant reading a book and sipping a cup of coffee. After the greetings, Sam offered Richard a seat. Richard apologized for his delay while Sam sipped his coffee and in reply said, "It's common in those types of domestic flights. However, relax. We still have half an hour before they come to pick us up."

Half an hour later, a driver arrived, ready to take them to Lexington. On their way, Richard began to talk while the van moved slowly through the noontime traffic. Sam stopped Richard, who said he preferred to talk when everybody was present. Understanding, Richard led the conversation to other topics.

When they arrived in Lexington, Raymond Sullivan was waiting for them at the entrance of a tall white building. The driver alerted him by radio of their arrival. Stepping out of the van, Richard saw an elegant man dressed in a dark blue suit and yellow tie approaching to greet them. When he saw Sam, Raymond said, "Oh my gosh, Sam! You look younger than the last time I saw you. Give me the prescription. I bet if you had come to work for me, your hair would be as gray as mine." Both men looked at each other and smiled.

Sam thanked Raymond for receiving them so soon, then introduced Richard, who had stayed some steps behind. Sam said Richard was the son of Gerald Solaris, whose case was under investigation. "Mr. Solaris has traveled a long way just to bring us important information about his father's death that he says will be of great help to our investigation."

"Welcome to Lexington, Mr. Solaris," Raymond said. "Sam has said many good things about you." Walking inside the building, he asked them to follow him as someone in his office was anxiously waiting for them.

Raymond's office was located on the fourth floor of the building and was divided into two sections. The foremost one was furnished with a gigantic desk with lots of papers on top, three armchairs facing the front the desk, and behind it a bookcase full of books from top to bottom. Separated by a panel screen was the second part, which was furnished with a three-seat leather sofa, and four armchairs. At the center was a huge rectangular table with tons of magazines on it. In the left-hand corner was a little refrigerator where cold food and beverages were kept. In one armchair was seated a man whose rude features showed he was not too cordial.

Raymond approached the man, who, seeing them, rose out of his seat to show respect for his boss. Introducing the man, Raymond said he was Detective Albert Colliere, who held a special position in their organization. Many of the most difficult cases were under his command.

He had previously worked for Interpol. For many years, Albert had been recognized as the best detective of the year. If the decision to choose his successor was his, without question Raymond would designate Albert. Albert was the person responsible for their case. Thanking Sullivan for his words, Albert said he did not deserve the award as it was his obligation to perform his work efficiently.

Sullivan asked to leave the pleasantries aside and instead proceed to work, as Mr. Solaris had come a long way merely to bring them important information for their investigation. "So let's examine what he's brought to us." Leaning forward, Richard opened his briefcase and pulled out the documents that he thought would be helpful to their investigation. Apologizing, he said his information seemed scarce and was hard for him to understand.

Pointing to the tape recorder that was set at the center of the table, Sullivan suggested that in order not to miss anything, he would record the conversation. Without receiving objections, Sullivan turned the recording machine on. However, Richard reconsidered and said it was best to hold the information strictly confidential and off the record. Sullivan turned the recorder off, relieving Richard.

Reading aloud the report he have written in the plane, he described briefly the facts since his father's death. When Richard was finished reading, Colliere said he was incorrect to think his information was minimal. On the contrary, it sounded to him as if it would be helpful to their investigation. Lewis stopped Colliere, saying he should let Richard finish sharing his information. Colliere apologized for the interruption and encouraged Richard to continue.

When the time came to read his father's letter, Richard said it was written in Spanish, but if they allowed him, he would translate it. Raymond said that was not necessary as Albert had served for many years as a translator for their organization's conferences. Colliere had mastered German and Spanish, which he had learned when he lived in Argentina for four years.

Without objection, Richard handed Colliere the envelope containing his father's letter and the recording of Jacob and Mohammed's conversation. Leaving the tape on top of the table, Colliere took the letter and, clearing his throat, started to read it aloud, making a simultaneous translation. Richard was amazed and admitted his translation was impeccable. His French accent disappeared completely when he spoke in both languages. When he finished, he put the letter on top of the table and picked up the recording. As Richard had anticipated, their voices disappeared when they moved to the other table to read his father's letter. Richard apologized, stating that he even had turned the recorder to its maximum volume, but in spite of his efforts, he was unable to clearly hear their conversation. He thought they spoke in a foreign language he did not understand, but he was not certain. Richard said he could fast-forward the tape until their voices come back. Colliere jumped up and growled at Richard, saying he wanted to hear the complete recording. When they finished hearing the tape, Raymond proposed they exchange opinions. Colliere said he preferred to study the information before giving his opinion. Sullivan understood and agreed.

Shortly, Raymond rose from his seat and asked Richard if had known of Gwen's existence and his father's bank accounts before reading his father's letter. Richard responded he had never heard his father say Gwen's name, so he was ignorant of her existence until he read the letter. And in regard to the bank accounts, he was never aware of them until he examined the contents of the envelope while on the plane travel from Los Angeles to Mexico.

Sullivan walked behind his desk and, finding his reading glasses, smiled, saying how he now needed them to read, whereas earlier he could read anything, even if was written on a bean.

Taking a breath, Sullivan asked Richard if he knew offshore accounts were forbidden to American citizens and residents because most of those accounts served to launder money or to hide illicit businesses. Their yields in general were not declared to the IRS. In response, Richard said he will accept returned the funds if the source was money laundering or dirty businesses. However, if the proceedings were proven to be legal, that money belonged to his father and he should keep it. Raymond said that the matter would be discussed later. Now their priority was finding his father's killer.

Opening the fridge, Raymond grabbed several bottles of water and passed them around. Facing Richard, he then said every comment made in that room was strictly confidential and should never leave those four walls. Not even his wife or sister should know anything about this conversation, as it was part of their responsibility to provide for the safety of his family.

Promising to keep his mouth shut, Richard thanked Sullivan for his concern for his family.

Colliere rose from his seat and took the papers that were on the table. Rudely, he said he would make copies of the documents, as he was sure Richard had forgotten to make copies for them. Richard had to admit Colliere was right in his assumption and apologized, saying his day had been so busy that he had totally forgotten to make copies for them. Mumbling and without offering an apology, Colliere took the documents and left the room, leaving everybody surprised at his bad behavior. To excuse his bad mood, Sullivan said, "Sometimes Colliere is rude, and when something goes wrong or gets out of control, he loses his temper. Colliere is a perfectionist. The words 'excuse me' or 'I'm sorry' are not in his vocabulary. Still, we must accept that for this job, he is the right man, don't you think?" Sam and Richard looked at each other and, recognizing Sullivan was right, answered they had no doubt about that.

It took Colliere less than twenty minutes to make copies. He returned the originals to Richard. Going to his seat, he said he was ready to hear the next item on the agenda.

Changing topics, Lewis mentioned he know the person Gerald Solaris had monitored in his calendar for the month of May eight days previous to his demise. He reminded Richard that when he was asked in his interrogation if he knew if his father had monitored the illness of a friend or family member, Richard said no. "Well, now we know who that someone was. Yes, Richard, your father was monitoring the illness of Pope Leon XVII. Several pieces of evidence were collected before we arrived at this determination. Looking in your father's bedroom, we found in the pocket of his suit an airplane ticket to Rome for May 16 at nine a.m. This fact led us to realize his clothes were in his suitcase not because he had not unpacked but because he was preparing to travel. In that same pocket we found a fax from an anonymous sender dated May 13, requesting your father travel urgently to Rome because the Pope's health was getting worse than expected. The sender encouraged your father to meet with the liberal cardinals before the conclave in order to convince the other cardinals who remained hesitant to vote in favor of the Argentine cardinal Alejandro Villavicencio, who in the last polls seemed to be losing popularity to the Italian cardinal Leonardo Ponti. Also, the sender emphasized that if

Cardinal Leonardo Ponti was appointed Pope, the policies of the Church would remain the same as his predecessor's, which always refused the acceptance of women in the priesthood, the elimination of the celibacy of priests, and the use of contraceptives for birth control. He was also invited to take part in the Pope's funeral at the Basilica de San Pedro if his death were to occur.

Colliere commented how clearly he could see the excellent relations his father had with the Vatican. Richard responded he was correct, even though the new generation of his family no longer held that tight relationship.

The silence in the room made Richard suppose the meeting was over. Standing, he invited them all to dine at a good restaurant. Colliere was the first to refuse his invitation, saying he had work to do. Sullivan followed, saying he had unfinished tasks to solve. Discouraged by their rejections, Richard turned to face Sam, who, smiling, in bad Spanish said, "*Yo contigo voy, mi amigo.*"

Before exiting the room, Colliere addressed Richard, saying he needed to meet with him early the next morning before he returned to Mexico, as he had received some information from Mexico that he wanted to share and get his opinion on. The meeting would take about two hours, so he was open to a time that Richard chose. In the meantime, Captain Sullivan and Lieutenant Lewis could chat. Richard responded that seven o'clock was good for him, giving him enough time to catch his flight at one. Colliere agreed and said the time was perfect for him.

The restaurant that Sullivan recommended was located in the downtown area. Their famous barbecue ribs required that people make reservations several days ahead of time. Luckily, Sullivan knew the maître d', so he called to make sure a good table was reserved for them.

Richard, whose last meal had been a sandwich at the Washington airport, was starved and gladly accepted Raymond's suggestion. On departing, Sullivan handed to Sam a pair of keys, saying they belonged to his wife's van, but he could use it tonight and return it tomorrow, as she did not need it and he was going to stay late to work that night. Sam thanked Raymond for his offer but said they preferred to get a cab. Annoyed at his refusal, Sullivan insisted Sam take the keys. Sam accepted them, saying he was indebted to him, and he would return favor when he traveled to Los Angeles.

Straightening his tie, Sullivan asked Sam if they had a hotel reservation for that night. Sam responded they did not, so Sullivan suggested the downtown Holiday Plaza, which provided full service at a reasonable cost. If they agreed, he could ask his secretary to reserve two rooms for them. Richard thanked Raymond, saying he would surely appreciate it if he could assist them with that.

The maître d' had chosen a nice table for Sam and Richard, next to the stage where a singer played guitar. The restaurant served ribs on heavy aluminum foil plates to capture the grease. Included with the slab of dry ribs sprinkled heavily with BBQ sauce were sides of fried beans and a salad. Sam stripped his whole ribs and ate half of Richard's. Looking at Richard watching him, Sam said, "I thought you were hungry,"

"I was," Richard responded, "but suddenly I don't feel too well. I guess it must be the tension I have been under these past few days that have made me lose my appetite." He asked Sam if they could leave. Richard paid the check. While they drove to the hotel, Richard thought of his meeting with Colliere, wondering what he wanted to talk with him about regarding his father.

Having dismissed his visitors, Sullivan went into his office, where he found Colliere seated, waiting for him. Raymond asked Albert for his impressions of Mr. Solaris and if he agreed his visit was helpful to their investigation. Albert admitted it was a great idea to talk with him, and Mr. Solaris had given him a good impression. He thought Mr. Solaris was discouraged by his father's behavior, as many facts of his life appeared to prove he was a dishonorable man. Raymond agreed with Albert's assessment.

Colliere crossed his legs and expressed his desire to make a plan of action with Richard's information. If he were authorized, he could analyze the collected information that night and by tomorrow morning have a summary that included the relevant facts of their investigation, which he could later use to draw up a plan of action. Accepting his proposition, Sullivan requested that Albert keep him posted on his findings. Albert promised his boss he would.

After they checked in at the hotel, Richard's neck muscles and shoulders hurt. The strain of the day had made him tense. A throbbing headache was starting beneath his temples. Taking two aspirin would help relieve his pain and make the night more bearable. Nevertheless, Richard did not take anything and just tried go to sleep, thinking that tomorrow he would feel better.

Shut up in his office, Colliere turned off his cellular phone in order to stop incoming calls that would distract him from his work. Gathering all the documents, he proceeded to properly organize them according to his needs. Searching on his computer, he found the Gerald Solaris file. Looking back at his previous information, he added the recent ones he had received. With his information complete, he prepared to summarize the relevant facts of the case. When he finished writing the report, it was nearly three o'clock in the morning. He shut down his computer and tried go to sleep, waking up at 6:15 a.m. Washing and shaving quickly, Colliere was ready to receive Richard at seven as scheduled.

When Richard arrived at seven, Colliere's secretary informed his boss was waiting for him in the conference room. Going into the room, Colliere greeted Richard courteously and invited him to a seat. To begin the conversation, Colliere informed Richard he had worked all night attempting to summarize the relevant facts of the case. Opening his briefcase, Colliere extracted the report and handed it to Richard for his critique and judgment.

When Richard ended reading the report, Colliere said he was free to tell him if something was missing or if he wanted to add anything else. Richard responded that the report was fine as it covered the most relevant points of their investigation. He also thought it was a useful tool for anyone who needed to know more about the case. Thanking Richard for his comment, Colliere said the purpose of the report was exactly as he had described.

Colliere explained to Richard that yesterday he had received a report from Mexico that he wanted to share with him and know his opinion on. But before he proceeded, Colliere wanted to ask Richard what attributes a person should possess to be promoted to a higher position. Surprised at his question, Richard answered he would consider skills, experience, punctuality, integrity, dignity, honesty, discipline, and efficiency, among others. "Did I miss something?" Richard asked.

"No, Richard, your answer is correct. However, it is sad to recognize these attributes do not count for the Mexican government, as they prefer to promote a person based on personal relations rather than skills and experience. To demonstrate what I mean, I found a clear lesson in your father, who once performed work for the Mexican government. To complete your father's file, I requested the Mexican government send me a report on your father's work history. The report said that your father began work in 1977 as an assistant in the Legal Department of the Ministry of Foreign Affairs and was ultimately promoted to be the undersecretary of the branch in 2004. In one part of this report, I found that when your father was Director of the Legal Department, he had as assistants two women by the names of Josephine Payro and Elizabeth Fangio.

When in June of 2002 the architect Louis Petrelini resigned his position as Secretary of Foreign Affairs for health reasons, the President of Mexico nominated Josephine Payro as his successor, who put her friend Elizabeth Fangio in the post of undersecretary of the branch, passing over your father, who stayed in his same situation. Then, in July of 2004, another event happened—the death of the Secretary of Finance in a plane crash. This time, the President of Mexico appointed Josephine Payro as his replacement and placed Elizabeth Fangio in the position of Secretary of Foreign Affairs, previously held by Josephine Payro. This time he did not forget your father, who climbed to the position of undersecretary of the branch, a position in which he remained until his retirement in July of 2007. Today there are rumors that Josephine Payro could be nominated by her party as the candidate for the next presidency of Mexico, with a great possibility of winning."

Colliere swallowed his glass of water before asking Richard if he had heard his father express discontent over these facts, because "knowing your father's background, I would never have hesitated to nominate your father as secretary of the branch before his two assistants."

Richard didn't know how to answer. His father had always been a discreet person who hated to discuss business matters with his family. Yet in private with his mother, he was not so hesitant. Suddenly Richard recalled the story that had been disseminated in the media stating the President of Mexico was having a love affair with Josephine Payro. Making Colliere aware of that fact, he said that is what women do to men, which had been reason enough for him to stay single. Looking at his watch, Colliere said he had promised their meeting would not last more than two hours, as he knew Richard was in a hurry to depart. He supposed that before the left, Richard intended talk to Mr. Sullivan and Lewis, so he could feel free to go, as their meeting was over. Richard thanked Colliere for his help. They shook hands and said goodbye.

When Colliere was left alone in the conference room, he was reminded of the only case in his long career as a detective that he had been unable to solve. It was the plane crash in which the Secretary of State of France, Jacques Depardieu, had died. Jacques Depardieu had been a steadfast enemy of feminism in France. During his term, the activist Turkish woman named Roselyn Taffish had led protests in the streets, burning buses and breaking windows in shops. Jacques Depardieu demanded she stop her disruption or he would send her to jail. Disobeying his commands, Roselyn went to prison. Several of her followers protested in the streets, calling for her release. Jacques Depardieu never yielded to their demands, and eight days after his refusal to free Roselyn, he died in an airplane crash when traveling with other members of his staff to a meeting of the European Union. The coincidence seemed strange as Jacques Depardieu was replaced by a woman who immediately granted Roselyn her freedom. These facts made Colliere wonder if the death of Jacques Depardieu was related to Gerald Solaris's assassination.

Raymond's secretary informed her boss, who was in the conference room, that Richard wanted to see him. Knocking at the door, they were invited to enter. Raymond and Sam were comfortably seated on a sofa, watching the news on a gigantic TV screen. They offered Richard a seat. Sam glanced at him and said they were about to experience a historical moment, as the Vatican press had officially declared the next Pope. In two hours, he was to give his inaugural speech to the public. Raymond smiled and asked Richard if he could guess who the newly appointed Pope was. Richard had no doubt and said that he bet it was Cardinal Alejandro Villavicencio. Lewis smiled, and said, "Good guess, buddy."

Sullivan sipped a glass of water and asked Richard if he thought his father would be pleased with that nomination. Richard did not answer and instead asked if anything more was known about the disappearance of Cardinal Leonardo Ponti and the two bishops. Lewis responded there was nothing yet, and everything remained a mystery, although the facts seemed to show they had been kidnapped. Richard thought a moment, then said he believed it must have been hard for the cardinals to vote in favor of Cardinal Alejandro Villavicencio and not Cardinal Leonardo Ponti, as was their desire. Lewis looked at Raymond, and they both agreed with Richard.

Richard apologized for leaving but said his plane departed in three hours, and he had to make it on time. Sullivan stood up and offered Richard his driver to take him to the airport. Richard expressed his desire to visit them again but under other circumstances. Facing Sam, Richard said he was aware his plane did not leave until seven o'clock at night and maybe he wanted to stay longer. Sam agreed and said he intended to chat with Raymond about other matters of the case. Thanking Richard for coming, they rose from their seats, shook hands, and said goodbye.

After Richard left, Raymond went to the minibar and extracted a bottle of red wine with a couple of glasses. After pouring the wine, Sam and Raymond toasted each other, promising to work together until they found Gerald Solaris's killer. Sipping his wine, Sam shared his frustration at ignoring the real activities Gerald Solaris performed for the organization, saying they must have been important for him to receive such a high payment.

Raymond patted Sam on the shoulders and said they should leave Albert to do his work. "Albert's skills and experience have led us to solve many difficult cases. Still, if for some reason he fails, we will summon Jacob and Mohammed in court, who under oath will have to tell us everything they know about Gerald Solaris's activities." Lewis agreed and said that would be a great idea.

At five o'clock, a driver picked up Sam to take him to the airport. Shaking hands, the two friends said goodbye. After Sam left, Raymond took the elevator and walked to his office. He found Colliere standing outside the door waiting for him. "Albert," Raymond said, "why didn't you go inside?"

"Sorry for the interruption," Colliere apologized, "but I wanted to discuss with you some matters of the case." In reply, Raymond asked Albert to close the door so no one could bother them.

Once he was seated, Albert handed the report to Raymond. Before taking it, he asked Albert if Richard was aware of it. Albert said Mr. Solaris had read the report in the morning, giving his approval. Seeing that

Raymond hesitated to take his report, Albert said that if at that moment he was too busy, he could come back later to get his opinion.

Without uttering a word, Sullivan puts his glasses on, took the report, and started to read it. Finishing it, Raymond asked Albert what Richard thought of it. "He said it covered the relevant points of the investigation and served as a guide to any person who would like to know more about the case," said Albert.

"I will second his comments," Raymond said.

Leaving his glasses on the desk, Raymond asked Albert if he was aware that the Argentine cardinal Alejandro Villavicencio had been appointed Pope. The announcement made Albert frown. He immediately expressed his desire to infiltrate a spy into Gwen's organization. Raymond laughed and replied he would second that idea, but could he tell him how he meant to do it, since in his report he stated the impossibility of getting there either by air or ground. What he understood was that their air defenses included a forward-looking radar system that detected a plane several miles away, making it impossible for any pilot to land unless he received the authorization of the flight controllers. And by ground, he mentioned the necessity to have an identity tag, know a password, and have one's voice recognized by a machine; otherwise, their alarms would sound, alerting the guards posted in towers, who would shoot the intruder.

"Then tell me, Albert, how do you intend to infiltrate that spy?" asked Raymond. Colliere looked at his boss and calmly said his spy would walk inside with their total acceptance. Raymond could not believe Albert's words and said, "You either are joking or are sick or are a wizard. Which are you?"

Annoyed, Albert answered, "None of them, sir." He began to explain how he planned to introduce the spy inside their organization when Raymond interrupted to ask which spy he was thinking about. Albert paused before responding that his spy did not belong to their institution.

"Then, to what organization does he or she belong?" Raymond asked.

"To a different organization we normally use."

"I assume this spy has the skills and experience to perform this kind of work?" Raymond asked.

"I am sorry to disappoint you, sir, but the undercover agent has never executed work like this."

Albert's response caused Raymond to lose control. Clearing his throat, in a rude tone of voice he asked Albert how much the spy would charge, Albert's response surprised Raymond when he said the spy did not expect a payment. He might only need them to cover minor expenses.

Raymond could not believe what he was hearing and said to Albert, "Are you joshing me?" Colliere got angry and replied he was completely serious, and every word he said was true. He would never dare to joke with his boss in these matters. Raymond apologized and said he promised to take Albert's plan under serious consideration.

Holding in his bad temper, Colliere solicited Raymond before to approve the spy's to work for them, three conditions. First, Raymond would give him total authority to control the mission, Second, no one would be involved in the case unless they had received his approval. Third, no one else could know about his plans. Accepting without objection the three conditions, Raymond promised Albert he would have the airline tickets ready by the next day.

CHAPTER 16

No one else knew of her existence. Albert had kept it top secret, but the real name of the nun Sister Marguerite was Ivonne Colliere, his sister. Despite being two years younger than Albert, they loved to play cops and robbers in their youth. Albert played the role of policeman and Ivonne of burglar. Their parents reproached them for their games, as they said they created violence. Who really enjoyed their games was their neighbor Jean Paul, a retired detective who once worked for a private investigator agency in Paris. Albert and Ivonne never passed up the opportunity go to his house and hear about the dangerous situations in which he said had participated. Jean Paul was the owner of an extensive library of books on criminology that he lent to Albert and Ivonne. Every day after finishing his school tasks, Albert found the time to learn his criminology lessons that he later practiced in games with his sister. Jean Paul was proud of his disciples, describing Albert as the brain executor, able to solve difficult cases, and Ivonne as better at handiwork, as she could easily open safe boxes, detect or install bugs, intercept phone lines, or hide cameras in unsuspected places. Jean Paul was sure both of them could make the perfect handcuff.

One night after dining at Albert's home, Jean Paul felt sick. His symptoms were a significant chill in his body and strong pain in his chest. Noticing the gravity of the case, Albert's father called an ambulance. Unfortunately, when the paramedics arrived, they found Jean Paul suffering a heart attack. Applying respiratory techniques, they tried to resuscitate him. When he did not respond, they decided to take him to the closest hospital. Lying on the stretcher Jean Paul recovered consciousness and knew he would die, so he asked Albert to approach and whispered in his ear, "God is coming for me. You know I never was rich. My only wealth lies in my criminology books that I collected during my lifetime. Knowing you will take full care of them, I impart them to you. Share their experience with your sister, Ivonne, as I know one day both of you will work together for the police in France." Saying these last words, Jean Paul died. His two sons, who lived in Marseilles and rarely visited his father, attended the funeral. When Albert told them his father's last wish, they had no objection, so late that afternoon after Jean Paul's burial, Albert received several boxes with the books inside them. Every time Albert and Ivonne opened and read his books, they remembered with nostalgia the valuable lessons they had gotten from Jean Paul, who besides being a great teacher, allowed them to live many happy moments together.

When Ivonne was eighteen, Albert made her promise that when she turned twenty-one, they would both apply to work for the French police. In spite of that promise, when Ivonne reached nineteen, she decided to go to a convent in Paris and become a nun. Albert tried to dissuade her, saying she could not break the promise she had made when she was eighteen. Even acknowledging the harm inflicted on her brother, Ivonne confirmed her decision to become a nun, saying she had had a dream in which she saw Jesus Christ demanding her to be a preacher of his doctrine in places of the African continent and countries like, China, and India. She acknowledged some of them would be dangerous sites where could put into practice the survival lessons learned from Jean Paul. Albert's mother saw how he was badgering his sister, so she intervened, warning Albert to let his sister enter her new vocation. Albert always reproached her decision, as he had always dreamed about working for the French police with his sister.

When Albert's parents took Ivonne to the convent, Albert refused to go with them. His resentment made him affirm he would never see his sister again. He kept that promise for nineteen years, breaking it only for the necessity of telling his sister of their father's death. At that time, when Albert visited the convent, Ivonne was on a mission in Africa. Nine years later, Albert made his second visit, this time to inform his sister of their dearest mother's death, but again he failed to see her when he was informed Ivonne was performing an assignment in China and India. On his third attempt, Albert was visiting Paris for work and decided to visit his sister. This time luck was on his side, and he found her there.

His characteristic sobriety disappeared when Albert saw his sister for the first time after twenty-seven years. Her youthful expression remained the same, just as when she had left home to go into the convent. They recalled happy moments together in their childhood. When Albert told Ivonne of their parents' deaths, she cried for a minute but recovered after knowing they both had a calm death in bed. Saying aloud a prayer, she said now they were both with Jesus Christ in Eden.

Continuing with their chat, they remembered the lessons learned from Jean Paul and the punishments they received from their parents for bad behavior. They did not notice the time passing quickly, and Albert realized night had fallen. Promising his return soon, Albert asked his sister for her pardon for his prior reluctance about her life choice. Going outside into the street, Albert understood the reason his sister became a nun. The peaceful air that he had breathed during his stay in the convent was now lost when he returned to the real world. However, he would forever remember the unforgettable afternoon he had passed with her.

To make his final destination untraceable, Albert requested Raymond buy for him an airplane ticket via Madrid, Spain, from where the next day he would take the train to Paris. Arriving in Paris, Albert took some safety measures to be sure no one had followed him. Touring Paris for several hours, he visited different places. Finally he got a cab and gave the address of the convent to the cab driver.

Albert rang the doorbell, and a young nun responded. Opening a peephole, she asked Albert to identify himself. After he proved he was Sister Marguerite's brother, the nun made a signal with her fingers asking him to wait. When the peephole closed, Albert wondered what would happen if Ivonne were not in the convent at that moment. However, his doubts disappeared when the nun announced his sister was in the chapel saying her prayers, but she would be glad to receive him in ten minutes. Opening the door, she let Albert inside the convent. Walking through a long corridor, they came to a room furnished with a large rectangular table with twenty chairs surrounding it. After inviting Albert to sit, the nun disappeared.

Ten minutes later, Ivonne made her appearance. In her nun's attire, she looked magnificent. Rising out of his chair, Albert intended to hug her, but stopped and only shook her hand. Ivonne smiled and said it was perfectly normal for a sister to hug her brother.

Asking him to be seated, Ivonne expressed her happiness at seeing him again. Albert smiled and in return said he missed her very much. The visit went on, touching on several things. Albert suddenly stopped the conversation and got to the point. He told his sister the reason for his visit. When Ivonne was aware of his story, she commented on how hard it was to conceive that people in this world could be so cruel.

"Don't consider my assertion as true, although my experience as a detective for several years makes me to think I am not mistaken," Albert responded. "Now that you know the reason I'm here, you can see how desperately I need your help, as you are the only person in the world we can trust to go inside in this organization as a spy without raising suspicion. I drew up a plan that can work safely for you." Ivonne paused before saying no one knew better than he she was totally out of practice and her skills could be forgotten. Facing his sister, Albert responded that part of his job was to show that was not true.

She could feel the despair in her brother's eyes. Wondering to herself, Ivonne thought about how Albert could be so sure she had not forgotten her skills in handiwork, even saying they had been granted to her since she was born. Albert promised to help her recover her skills if they had been lost, saying she would never perform a task unless she was properly trained. Ivonne felt excited but also stated her worry. Helping her brother was a priority. Nevertheless, she needed to receive the approval of the Mother Superior. Understanding her need for approval, Albert said they should not waste any more time, and she should let him go to speak with the Mother Superior.

Albert was prepared to face the moment. Without hiding any details, he told the Mother Superior his whole story. When he finished, the Mother Superior expressed her concern, saying that the job was too risky for his sister, suggesting he choose an experienced spy. Albert responded he could not agree more with her proposition. Nevertheless, she should believe him that after much effort, he could find no better person than his sister.

Looking at Ivonne, who had remained silent, the Mother Superior asked her what her thinking was, saying she would support her if she decided to continue with this new adventure in her life. Notwithstanding, before giving her approval, she wanted Ivonne to promise she would always keep present the principles that God taught them.

Promising to do so, Ivonne expressed her desire to accept her brother's offer as she still had remorse that at age eighteen she had promised him she would work for the French police but instead entered the convent. "Don't get me the wrong, Mother Superior. I will never regret this decision. Today, after twenty-eight years of being in the convent, God has offered me the opportunity to heal the hurt I inflicted on my brother when I became a nun."

Albert stayed mute. Hearing his sister's words, he wanted to intervene in his sister's favor, but he desisted, preferring to remain silent.

Before the Mother Superior dismissed them, she told Albert about his sister's success in her missionary work. Her work was profoundly valued by the archbishop of France, who was planning to take Ivonne on his visit to Rome next month. Albert said they had no time to talk about their current occupations. "Perhaps you should in the near future," suggested the Mother Superior. "However, in the meantime, promise me you will take good care of your sister." Albert promised he would with his own life, and he would bring his sister safely back when they finished their work. Smiling at Albert, the Mother Superior blessed them and wished them luck.

On the first day of her training, Ivonne was provided with material to study about the whole case. She was to read every paragraph carefully, interpreting and feeling the emotions and reactions that caused every word in each person. Afterwards, she would hear the recordings of conversations among several people involved in the case. Suggesting she take notes and write down her questions, Albert said he would come the next day to discuss them with her.

When Albert arrived the next day, Ivonne was ready to discuss the different issues with her brother. Albert asked Ivonne about her progress. She said she first could sense the fear of Gerald Solaris when he knew they bugged his phones from home and office and placed cameras to monitor his family activities. Second, the message of having monitored his family life was shocking and taken by Gerald Solaris as a warning to accept the offer to belong to Gwen's organization. To Ivonne, the service that Gerald Solaris rendered that organization had religious or political purposes. Third, the death of his wife, Claudia, was not accidental but was caused intentionally and with a defined purpose. Gerald Solaris knew the reason for his wife's death, making him blame himself and fall into a deep depression. Fourth, she supposed his wife's death was revenge against him, perhaps because he refused to do some kind of work or was intending to abandon the organization, and they thought he would expose them. Fifth, in Ivonne's opinion, he was the same Gerald Solaris who helped his subordinates climb to higher positions even when knowing he deserved them. Sixth, the deaths of three people on the same day was an act of revenge, a demonstration of power, or a warning about obedience to the survivors. Albert seemed pleased and agreed with his sister's conclusions.

To find Gwen's office location, Albert bought an aerial photo of Frankfurt City and its surroundings. Extending the picture over the table, Albert drew with a compass a radius of 200 kilometers from Frankfurt City. Paying attention to what his brother was doing, Ivonne asked what the purpose of the radius was. He reminded his sister that Gerald Solaris had mentioned in his letter that Gwen drove her car at a speed of 200 kilometers per hour. "Well, Ivonne, the radius shows the maximum distance anyone could achieve driving a car at a speed of 200 kilometers in just sixty minutes." Ivonne smiled and agreed with her brother.

The following step was to come up in the aerial photo of a local road on a surface surrounded by tall trees that led to an esplanade where could be found an airport with two runways and various buildings. Examining different sites scrupulously, Albert excluded the ones that were in his opinion inappropriate for that role. Finally he arrived at two sites, choosing the one that in his opinion better exhibited the conditions he was looking for. The locale of the site was eight miles from Offenbach City. Satisfied with his selection, he circled the site with a red crayon and said to his sister, "Ivonne, I guess we've finally found the location of Gwen's organization."

On her third day of training, Ivonne received a parcel from her brother Albert. The message inquired if she would ask for the Mother Superior's permission to put on the enclosed outfit the next day. If that would be allowed, he would pick her up at ten a.m.

Five minutes before ten, Albert was ringing the bell of the convent. Instantly Ivonne appeared wearing the outfit that her brother had had delivered the day before. The attire was simple and consisted of a white nurse's uniform with a long skirt, elastic stockings covering her knees, and a cap over her head. Delighted to see her wearing the outfit, Albert opened the door of the cab so Ivonne could step inside. While fastening her seat belt, Ivonne saw her brother was dressed in white trousers with a doctor's gown. Albert told the cab driver they were heading to Lafayette Galleries downtown. Without asking the reason they were dressed as they were and knowing her brother's mood, Ivonne remained silent, making no further inquiries. When they arrived at Lafayette Galleries, Albert paid the cab driver and walked inside the store, followed by Ivonne. Walking at a fast pace, they went through several areas without stopping to buy anything. Finally by the back door, they left the store. Crossing the street, Albert walked toward a store that advertised the sale of safe boxes.

Within the shop, they were met by an amiable man who approached them to offer his help. In reply, Albert said he desired to talk with the store owner. "The owner is not here at the moment, but I am the manager. My name is René Beauregard, and I will gladly assist you," he said. Albert thanked René and said he was a doctor and the lady at his side was his assistant. He said they both worked for a hospital that offered their patients a secure safe box. René responded he would gladly help them to choose the correct one in accordance with their needs. Albert asked René if he was the person who could make decisions in the store. After assuring he was that person, Albert smiled at him.

Being sure no one else was in the store, Albert approached and whispered in René's ear that he wanted to invite him to participate in a game. His role was simple, and for him it was a win-win opportunity and he couldn't lose. "Does this game sound interesting to you?" Albert asked. René could not understand what Albert meant and asked him to be more specific. Albert paused, then asked René how many models of safe boxes he carried in the shop. René responded they had eleven different models. "Are they all safe and difficult for a burglar to open?" Albert asked.

René was losing his temper and answered, "Yes sir, we have the best safe boxes on the market."

Albert agreed and explained to René what the game consisted of. "Your role, René, is to close the eleven models of safe boxes and grant me three hours to open them. If at the end of that time any safe boxes remain closed, I promise to buy every one that is not open." Looking at his watch, René said there was only one problem. "What problem is that?" Albert asked.

They must have lunch at 12:30 p.m. on the owner's orders. No one could remain in the store, so he was unable to stay after that time. Mumbling, Albert said he would take the challenge to open the safe boxes before René's departure for lunch.

After shutting the eleven models of safe boxes, René left the showroom. Thirty minutes passed, and Ivonne had opened three safe boxes just by placing her ear next to the boxes and listening to the clicks. But when she tried to open the fourth, she failed in three attempts. Showing despair, Ivonne asked Albert what would happen if she was unable to open the other safe boxes. She said they were more complicated and secure than the ones they used to open in her youth. To calm his sister, Albert responded there was nothing to worry about. The worst that could happen was that he would have to buy the remaining eight safe boxes. "Just so you know, Ivonne, those expenses are handled by my institution, which considers them part of the investigation. TIPA spends billions of dollars yearly for these kinds of expenses and in protection of witnesses. So relax and continue trying to open the boxes. I am certain you can do it."

Feeling better, Ivonne continued her efforts. Anticipating the difficulty she might face, Albert handed his sister a stethoscope to better hear the clicks when she moved the combination dial.

His watch showing 12:15 p.m., Albert called René, who had stayed in his office calculating a quotation for the eleven models of secure boxes that he was sure to sell. When René went into the showroom, he found Albert with a baffled face. On seeing René, Albert said he felt deceived, as he had promised all his safe boxes were impossible to open unless the combination was known. "Can you explain why all of them are open?" asked Albert. Incredulously, René hurried to confirm Albert's statement. René could not believe that all the safe boxes were open. In order to excuse himself, he said their supplier had assured them that no one could open the safe boxes unless he or she knew the combination, but now he could see they had lied to them.

Albert said it was impossible for him to buy the safe boxes as he did not want to imagine what would happen if the hospital patients' valuables were stolen from a safe box. "So please excuse us. We must find another provider who can sell us real safe boxes," said Albert, signaling Ivonne to follow him.

Back in the convent, Ivonne reproached Albert for his attitude, saying he would never change and remained the same unbearable person who once played with her in their youth. "Poor René," Ivonne said. "You left him perplexed without knowing what really happened. I can't imagine what he might be going through at this moment." Ivonne smiled.

And Ivonne was right. When René was left alone in the store, he did not know how to react. He thought he might confess to his boss what really had happened, but after thinking better, he decided to keep his mouth shut because for sure would lose his job when his boss blamed him for leaving strangers handling their safe boxes, placing at risk the prestige of their brand.

The following day, Ivonne learned how to install bugs, tap phones, and connect hidden cameras in strategic positions without leaving a trace. Albert also trained his sister to correctly use secret codes and to edit or transfer messages by using private lines.

Albert asked his sister if she knew how to use the Internet. Ivonne responded that in the convent there were two computers. One was old and no one used it anymore, but the other was bought recently. It was a laptop loaded with updated software such as Word, Excel, and PowerPoint, also the Internet was available. To protect their systems, they used the Norton antivirus system. "The Mother Superior was aware that I was a fan of these devices, so she made me responsible for their operation."

Albert mumbled, then said he was going to tell her something that was strictly confidential. "Do you promise to keep it a secret?" asked Albert.

Ivonne promised. Albert said they needed to take control of another computer. As the police, they were permitted to do so; however, this practice was for anyone else punishable with jail time. "This technique is commonly used by us to intercept messages from terrorists and criminal gangs," said Albert.

Albert asked Ivonne if she knew who those hackers were. "I recognize they are geniuses and malicious computer experts who remotely take control of another computer."

"Excellent response," Albert admitted, "but do you know how hackers take control of a computer?" Thinking for a moment, Ivonne answered that she honestly did not know exactly how that was done. "Hackers do their work by breaking security lines and deforming web servers in the computer they want to master. In their first step, they take control of the system they want to monitor. Then they proceed to wipe every trace that can detect them. They finally introduce their own programs such as sniffing, spoofing, or jamming programs that can modify or even erase all the information on a data processor. Hackers make their attempts in two ways. The first one consists of visualizing and memorizing the secret codes when the operator types them on the keyboard. The second, commonly known as a Trojan horse, consists of removing the keyboard and putting in a microchip with their own programs."

Ivonne frowned, then asked Albert if he was proposing she perform the hacker's role. Albert admitted she was right and told her of his need to capture the secret codes that would allow them to access their files, documents, and messages. "Sometimes this process is easy to accomplish, but in most cases it gets complicated and will involve the use of certain techniques. But don't worry; you will be trained and will practice until you can conquer the tasks. TIPA uses specialized dictionaries that will decipher most of these coded messages. Your task is to capture their passwords and send them to us.

"Ivonne, let's begin by instructing you on how to encipher a message. You know that encryption makes it impossible for anyone to record a message unless they know the secret code to open it. Many procedures have been designed to encrypt a message. The use of algorithms of symmetrical keys is one of them. Nevertheless, it becomes more important to protect the password than the algorithm itself. To be honest with you, I don't see possible to get the passwords by memorizing them when the operator digits the codes. Therefore, is more reliable to use the Trojan horse system, which allows us to capture the passwords that open the concealed information. In this scheme, you'll have to remove the keyboard and install a microchip in it, taking good care not to leave tracks of the installation. Once the chip is installed, we will have the access to their information when the operator types the passwords. The data will be transferred later to mine computer. Any questions?" Albert asked.

"But don't worry, Ivonne. In your training, you will learn how to place and install the microchip without being detected, so be careful and avoid making mistakes." Ivonne looked at her brother and said she understood.

Albert extracted from the pocket of his suit a minicomputer that handed to Ivonne, saying it was an important tool for her to keep working all the time. "This minicomputer was manufactured with special features for TIPA, such as its batteries lasting for eight consecutive days without needing a charge. It has a 1000-gig hard drive memory and is loaded with a camera, a recorder with hidden microphone that records conversations at a distance of thirty-five feet, as well as a wireless cubical radio able to receive magnetic and electromagnetic transmissions with reduced ELF that range from 1 Hertz to 10 Hertz, making any conversation undetectable. If by any circumstance you need help, all you have to do is press the red button hidden at the back and an alarm system will sound in my computer, making it easier to find you wherever you are. It's operation is similar to any computer. The voice adapter was designed so that while you speak the computer type the words, making a simultaneous translation to English."

Facing his sister, Albert asked her to open her hand. He handed Ivonne six mini-bugs that could easily be stuck on a flat surface in any room, allowing her to hear conversations. Finally, Albert mentioned that in her luggage was installed a false bottom to hide tools needed to perform her tasks. To access it, she simply had to release the knob place on the right corner of the luggage.

Ivonne admitted that she had forgotten many of the topics her brother tried to teach her. So with the help of notes, she practiced until she learned them. Going through several tests, Albert finally exclaimed, "Ivonne, with this last test, I can end your preparation. I feel really comfortable with the results. The article we've been waiting for will appear tomorrow in the morning paper. If I am not mistaken, they will attempt to contact you, so be prepared to move to the Pierre Dumont Asylum." Thanking Ivonne, Albert expressed his gratitude, as nothing would be possible without her help. He prayed to God to keep her safe and under His constant protection. She knew the love that he always professed to her since their childhood.

The awaited article appeared in the local morning newspaper. The upper left box of the cover page showed the headline, "ACTIVIST NUN EXPELLED FROM CONVENT." The inner section never explained the reason for her expulsion. Rather, it just stated that the nun, Sister

Marguerite, belonging to the Carmelite order, was a genuine protector of women's rights and a tireless fighter against the mistreatment and discrimination of women by men. Women of places such as China, India, and Africa were extremely grateful for her deeds. Still, much of her work seemed to be spurned by her convent. Sister Marguerite had moved her to the Pierre Dumont Asylum to await a fair trial by the ecclesiastical authorities. At this moment, radio and TV reporters had gathered at the entrance of the asylum, waiting to interview her. Their efforts failed as Sister Marguerite refused to talk with them.

CHAPTER 17

The Baron Pierre Dumont on his seventy-fifth anniversary decided to donate part of his vast fortune to a trust, which would assume the responsibility to build an asylum with his name. His sons, who depended on him financially, saw their inheritance diminished and hired a lawyer who maliciously declared their father incompetent of mental faculties, forcing him by law to go to a psychiatric hospital. The nuns being aware of the baron's condition, they went to his rescue and hired a prominent attorney to protect him. The lawyer proved in court that the baron's mental faculties were excellent, so he was released and allowed to come back to his home. Nevertheless, when returning home, the baron felt sad and lonely. Therefore, he requested that the nuns build for him a small room with a private bathroom on the second floor of the asylum. Following his instructions, a small room was constructed, and he moved from his magnificent residence to the asylum. The baron lived there for eleven years, where he was taken care of as he deserved. When he passed away at the age of eighty-six years, he was surrounded by the people who genuinely loved him. The baron never fought against his sons, but he disinherited them, appointing as his sole heirs the nuns of the convent. Among those was the Mother Superior, who at that time was thirty-six years old and who had always professed a special love and affection for the baron. Since the baron's death, no one had occupied his room, but now under the circumstances, the Mother Superior authorized that place for the use of Sister Marguerite.

The size of the baron's room was less than 320 square feet and furnished with an old bed, two night tables on the side, and a closet where the baron hung the few clothes he had. In this room, Albert and Ivonne waited impatiently to be contacted to put their plan into action. Two days passed, and nothing happened. They began to feel discouraged. On the night of the third day, while Ivonne slept deeply, two hooded people went inside the room. One stood at the door holding an Uzi machine gun while the other approached Ivonne's bed and whispered into her ear, demanding she wake up and dress because someone wanted to meet with her.

"Who are you, and what do you want from me?" asked Ivonne, taken by surprise.

The hooded person answered, "Sorry, but we can't say anymore, only that you have exactly fifteen minutes to prepare your luggage for three days."

Following orders, Ivonne packed her luggage in less than the allotted time. Asking to go to the bathroom, she extracted from the pocket of her dress the list previously written with her brother, and she compared what she already packed. Confirming she had thought of everything, she texted her brother to inform him on what was going on. Exiting the bathroom and taken by surprise she was hand tied and blindfolded. To prevent her from stumbling, one of the men took her by the arm and helped walk her downstairs while the other took her luggage. Outside on the street was a third person waiting patiently, seated at the wheel of a van.

Albert had left his car parked at a discreet distance and watched all her movements. He saw Ivonne enter the rear of the vehicle and be seated between her two custodians, while the third person at the wheel started the engine. Following the vehicle, Albert was led to a private airport outside of Paris. With his binoculars, Albert saw them abandon the car and board a plane that was ready to depart.

Fifteen minutes after takeoff, Ivonne was offered cookies and beverages, which she declined, saying she was tired and preferred to sleep. Reclining her seat, she went to sleep, waking up when she heard the voices of her custodians announcing to put their seats in a vertical position as they were ready to land. When the plane finally stopped, the person seated at Ivonne's left side said she did not need to worry about her luggage, as they would take care of it. Resigned, Ivonne accepted the offer.

Still gaged and blindfolded, Ivonne was put into a vehicle. During the journey, she tried to memorize the noises she heard, such as when a door closed or what she heard when the car stopped. At one moment, she felt she had entered an elevator and walked through a long corridor, arriving in a room. After Ivonne was released from her gag and blindfold, the hooded person showed her the room where she was to stay When her luggage arrived she could rest, as tomorrow morning at 7:30 a.m., someone was coming to pick her up and take her to the founder of their organization, who wanted to meet with her. Apologizing for having to lock her room, her captors wished Ivonne a pleasant stay and left. Mocking them, she thanked them for their kind greetings.

Five minutes later, Ivonne heard a knock on her door. Someone said they had brought her luggage. Ivonne said they could enter. She heard the door being unlocked. The person who entered the room said her name was Elysee, and she was the person responsible for taking care of her during her stay. Asking where she should place Ivonne's luggage, on the bed or leave it on the floor.? Then, said that if at any time she needed assistance, she could ring the bell placed on top of the bed and someone would come to help. Ivonne thanked Elysee and said she preferred it if she put the luggage on the bed and at the moment did not need anything else.

Picking up her accent, Ivonne asked Elysee if she was French. Elysee confirmed she is. "And so you must speak French?" asked Ivonne.

"I do. However, since my arrival here, I speak only English. That is the language everybody speaks here," answered Elysee with a crispy voice. Excusing herself and apologizing for having to lock her room again, she left. Locked in her room, Ivonne realized Elysee was the first person who had shown her face.

Alone in the room and not knowing how long she would be staying there, Ivonne decided to act fast. Her first step was to study the door lock that kept her imprisoned. Going to her luggage, she extracted from the false bottom screwdrivers and tweezers. With these tools, she dismantled the doorknob and, giving a hard push, released the lock. To impede the door from closing again she slip a cardboard. Leaving the door partially open, she carefully looked in the corridor to be sure no one was there. Walking the hallway from side to side, she verified the lack of any guards before returning to her room. Removing the cardboard, she remounted the doorknob as it had been before.

Ivonne decided to make a thorough inspection of her room. She first recognized that she had never had been in one so big and luxurious before. The base and head of the king-size bed were made of finely wrought wood.

The bedspread hung till it touched the floor and matched perfectly the pink color of the cushions and pillows. The dresser was outfitted with a six-foot mirror, and it had drawers of different sizes on both sides. In the left-hand corner of the room was a round table with two leather armchairs and a reading lamp. The room was nicely decorated with paintings by famous artists, although none of them showed religious images. The dressing room was located between the bedroom and bathroom, which to Ivonne seemed unnecessary, as in her mind she never imagined someone wearing so many clothes and shoes. The bathroom was spectacular, with an enormous bathtub, shower, and Jacuzzi, similar to the ones used by the Romans of olden times.

Finished with her inspection, Ivonne proceeded to unpack her things. When she finished, it was almost three o'clock in the morning, so she decided to go to sleep. She woke up at six o'clock. Rising out of bed, she intended to shower but was discouraged when was unable to operate the shower system, so she took a quick bath tub and then dressed and started saying her prayers. Half an hour later, she was ready to receive on time whoever came to pick her up.

At 7:25 a.m., Ivonne heard someone knocking at her door. Authorizing her enter Elysee walk inside the room. On the previous night, Ivonne did not have time to analyze Elysee's features. She was tall, young, and beautiful, no more than thirty-five years of age. Her face showed spectacular green eyes with blond hair. The military uniform she wore, consisting of dark green pants, a loose shirt, and brown boots, made her lose her feminine features. Her expression was sad, probably caused by past suffering. Without loosing time Elysee told Ivonne their founder desired to meet with her, so she requested to follow her.

While they walked through the building, Ivonne confirmed the lack of guards. Taking the elevator, they arrived at the sixth floor, where Elysee led her visitor to a spacious room with chairs placed in rows. Offering Ivonne a seat, she left to find the person with whom Ivonne was supposed to meet. Returning, Elysee came with a woman, who in spite of her age, perhaps close to sixty, showed an indubitable beauty. Her looks were unusual and exotic, probably a mixture of various nationalities. Her colored hair was perfectly combed, making her slim figure look splendid. Her attire was different from that of Elysee, as she wore a blue, pale fashionable dress of fine linen that matched perfectly with the blue navy color of her sandals. Shaking hands with Ivonne, she introduced herself saying was Gwen Swayze, founder of that organization and apologizing for not saying it in French, since even having taken French lessons at school, lack of practice made her forget it. And even when her father spoke to them in German, she had preferred to speak English, understandable to everybody. In response, Ivonne said that was not a problem for her as even though French was her native language at school, she had learned English as a second language.

Facing Ivonne, Gwen asked if she had been treated as she deserved. Ivonne got angry and replied, "You must be joking. If being kidnapped, blindfolded, and kept locked in a room like a prisoner is fair treatment for you, then I have no complaints." Gwen apologized, saying it was never her intention to harm her, but under the circumstances, she had no alternative. Ivonne disagreed with her statement, and Gwen laughed sarcastically.

After a minute of silence, Gwen renewed the conversation. To show courtesy to her guest, she said she had prepared breakfast in her private dining room and asked Ivonne if she liked cereal, juice, sugar, and milk. "Whatever you take is good for me," Ivonne responded.

Going into the dining room, Ivonne saw no one was to join them. The size of the dining room was approximately 360 square feet. It was furnished with a round table with eight chairs surrounding it, and at the back below the window was a large buffet that Ivonne supposed was used to keep the silverware. The table was set for two people. Each place was set with individual handmade cloths, linen napkins, silver plates of fine porcelain, and lead crystal glasses. On top of the buffet were placed two silver trays containing different kinds of fruits, several bowls of cereal, and jars of juices and milk. Gwen brought one tray to the table so Ivonne could choose what she wanted to eat.

Gwen started the conversation by asking Ivonne how she preferred to be addressed. "Do you prefer to be called Sister Marguerite or by some other name?" Gwen asked.

Showing humbleness, Ivonne replied, "Simply call me Marguerite."

"If that is your wish, I will call you Marguerite," Gwen replied.

Suddenly, Ivonne realized she had never told Gwen her name, so she asked how she knew it. Gwen said her name had appeared in an article in a local newspaper, where they said Sister Marguerite was a defender of women's rights and a tireless fighter against the discrimination of women in places such as China, India, and Africa. "So that was the way you found me. Now, tell me, what do you want from me?" Ivonne asked.

Gwen mumbled, then said before she could answer her question, she was interested to know how she became a nun. Ivonne answered she had found that her real vocation was to become a nun in a dream when was nineteen years old. The decision was not well received by her family, who always attempted to dissuade her. Nevertheless, her decision was made, and she entered the convent. In the convent, she earned a master's in education. She went on missionary work to preach the doctrine of Christ in places such as India, China, and Africa, and to contend against the mistreatment and discrimination that women suffered in those locations.

"How wonderful it is to discover that we both have the same goals, as my organization fights for the same objectives," said Gwen. "In fact, those goals led me to form a partnership with a North American researcher, with whom I started an organization called INPOWER."

"Pardon my interruption, but I am concerned to know what made you bring me here," Ivonne asked, intrigued.

"We believe your collaboration will be of great value to us in our organization," Gwen replied.

"But why did you choose me?" Ivonne asked again.

"At this moment, I feel I cannot answer your question. But I promise that before you leave here, you'll know."

Gwen waited patiently until Ivonne finished her milk. She then took the tray and laid it where it had been before. Going back to her seat, she approached Ivonne and asked how she thought women's discrimination began. Ivonne thought a minute and replied it was hard to know exactly how discrimination started. Historians said it was several centuries ago when a matriarchal culture existed. In this culture woman was worshiped, respected, and adored and her tasks were appreciated by most men of the clan. The meaning of war, weapons, hierarchies, and even the possession of property was ignored by them. This civilization lived in total accordance with nature, from where they got the nourishment they needed to survive.

Nevertheless, women gradually lost their freedom and superior position. Unfortunately, this matriarchal culture did not endure over time and soon was replaced by another one called the patriarchal cultural, in which men learned to fight, defend themselves from animals, and protect their territory. Ownership of property and animals became a symbol of their power. The head of a tribe became the desired position for many, as it demonstrated power and strength. Was in this culture, where the stronger beat the weaker.

They said in this culture was where appeared the first division of work. Men selected the activities of hunting and fishing as well as the support of his family, while women instead chose the tasks of home and field. Unfortunately, for women, the activities performed by men gave them more strength, and in fights, women were defeated. The force of men gave them the power to make women submit to their desires. Women fought back by looking for protection in other women and in their sons, becoming discouraged when they discovered their sons, when growing up, prefer to chose the doctrine of his fathers, that was fight in wars, defend their territory and possessions, and force women to submit to their desires— instead of the lessons they had learned as children from their mothers— respect, dignity, and adoration of females. The force and power of men gradually stripped women of their rights, yet even in today's world, in some places many of those discrimination and mistreatments still remained.

"And so, in your opinion, were men responsible for women's discrimination?" asked Gwen.

Ivonne agreed, explaining how cruel boys were instructed since childhood to exclude girls from their games, show respect to other men, and treat women as sexual objects. Married men receive respect from his family. As head of the household, men enjoy many privileges at home, such as being served food first, followed by their sons, and leaving for last the daughters and mother. Who if there is not enough food, they have less to eat."

Gwen expressed anger, saying this was unjust and unfair. Holding back her temper, Gwen asked Ivonne why at the present time and even when men and women performed similar activities, the superiority of men still was manifested. "For instance, when lifting weights, men beat women easily. In races, men run faster. Playing golf, in spite of the handicap that women have, men's shots reach a longer distance. In boxing and wrestling, they always defeat us. I bet if a sports competition were organized in which the best of each sex was chosen, the losers would be the women. Incomprehensible to me is the fact that most famous musicians, painters, artists, lawyers, doctors, and inventors in history were men also, leading me to believe they lived in a world of males in which females were made to stand in a second place."

Ivonne stayed mute for a moment before answering that maybe she was right, although women today presented a different view of life, fighting for their rights and being less submissive to men. The strength of men still was manifested. However, women had proven to be excellent entrepreneurs. Today's women were replacing men in many lines of work.

Gwen interrupted Ivonne to ask what she thought made men superior for these activities. "Perhaps ancestral genes remain in their bodies, making them stronger," Ivonne responded.

"Marguerite, what would happen if those genes were transplanted into women? Do you think their abilities would improve?" asked Gwen.

"Are you suggesting cloning their organs?"

"Sort of," Gwen responded.

"I must tell you that in spite of the advances in science, I am against the cloning of animals and, worse, of human beings. To me, God is the only creator of life, and every procedure against his law is unacceptable and reproachable," Ivonne answered.

"I guess you are right, and you should forget what I just said," Gwen said. "Marguerite, I've learned that fundamentalists of state and religious principles have been the cause of women's discrimination. Do you agree?" Gwen asked.

"Before I answer your question, I'd like to cite some passages in the Bible that show God's personality. For God, every human being is equal in His kingdom. In the chapter of Genesis, the Bible states how God on the sixth day of the world's creation made man in his image, and then in his image and likeness God made male and female. So worshiping the Father and admitting He is eternal, the Mother also is. To God, both sexes have equal and similar rights. However, women haters allude to God as male, basing their claim on the fact that when the Son of God was incarnated on Earth, God made Him male, and when Christ prayed to God, He called him Father. Fortunately, those statements are easy to refute, as God is not a male or female person. The real personage and nature of God remain unknown to us. So when it's mentioned that the incarnation of God is like men on Earth, it does not necessarily mean that God is a male. Even when Christ prayed and called him Father, that does not necessarily refer to the sex of God but to the way that His Son prayed to his Father."

Gwen smiled and said she could not agree more with Ivonne's statements. "Now to answer your question, I would say that every religion should profess an equal treatment for men and women, without considering to what ethnic group, sex, or educational level they belonged. However, the truth is that even in those civilized societies of the Old World such as the Greeks and Romans, with advanced laws and governments, they disregarded human rights and the equality of men and women. Their legislation and policies were ruled by despotism and brute force, ignoring every principle of equality, freedom, and dignity that should exist between men and women. The Hebrew religion changed some of these beliefs. The Mosaic Law and the Ten Commandments, preach an equal treatment for men and women. Prophets such as Jesus and Mohammad always offer to women a special treatment. And although some other religions tried to follow those principles, they failed when were stopped by changes that overcame in the world that made them have to accept the subordination of women."

"Yes, I must agree that the fanaticism of state and religious principles has caused much suffering and discrimination for women," Ivonne said. "The principles of God once allowed men to commit outrageous acts, violations, discrimination, and inequalities over women. To blame only religion is unfair as many of these acts originated from social and political factors, from which men took advantage of women's ignorance, to make changes in laws and principles to his benefit, depriving her of rights. It is lamentable and hard to believe that some of those changes remain today."

"What principles rule the predominant religions in the world" asked Gwen.

Ivonne saw Gwen's interest in religions, which could have been the reason she was brought there, so she tried to answer as best she could. "Christianity and Islam were born from Judaism. These three religions are ruled by the same principles, as they are monotheism and worshipped only one God who they considered creator of the universe. Heaven and hell are real entities, where at the end of the world God will send them. Each of these religions preaches brotherhood and considers their religion the sole path to redemption. Priests represent God on earth. Sacred books are the Bible for Christians, the Koran and Mul Mantra for Islam, and the Torah and Talmud for Jews. Every practitioner should follow the prophets teachings like Jesus Christ for Christians, Muhammad for Islam, and Moses for Jews. Hinduism's rules are different. Being polytheists, they worship several idols and images. Hindus believe in reincarnation and the incarnation of gods in animals and humans. Karma regulates the migration of their souls. Sanskrit is their sacred language and the Vedas their holy books. Different castes of priests and people exist for them, who, reaching perfection one day, will separate from the rest of humans. Buddhism lacks a caste system and of sacred language. They considered the life on earth of suffering, until they reach Nirvana, where they will be enlightened to enjoy the life forever."

"Thanks, Marguerite for your explanation. That clarifies many of my doubts," Gwen said.

Gwen stayed silent for a moment, then asked Ivonne if she was aware that although Christianity had continued to grow, Catholics showed a considerable decrease in their number of followers. "Don't you think the reason for this drop comes from the disapproval of your Church for the use of contraceptive methods for birth control?" Facing Gwen, Ivonne responded that perhaps she was right since today young couples resisted getting married.

Gwen could no longer wait and asked Marguerite if she could ask her something about her own religion. "Certainly. Go ahead," Ivonne replied. "What do you want to know?"

"I would like to hear from you what you think about celibacy in priests."

Ivonne thought a minute before answering. The Catholic Church considered celibacy as an obligatory mandate and perfect status for the priest. Even Jesus stayed unmarried, though He never established celibacy as an obligation for His followers.

Gwen interrupted to ask Ivonne if it was her understanding that some priests of former times were married. "Even a Pope was too, wasn't he?"

Ivonne, answered she was right, as many testimonies existed of married priests in history. One example was Peter, Jesus's main disciple, who was a married man before becoming the first Pope of the Catholic Church. Other apostles who followed Jesus were married men too. In the year 385 AD, Pope Siricio left his wife to become Pope. Others followed his example until Pope Calixto II in the twelfth century stopped the practice when he published a decree forbidding clerical marriage.

Gwen interrupted Ivonne again to ask if Pope Alexander VI was a married man with children. "No, Gwen, this time you are wrong. Pope Alexander VI, whose real name was Rodrigo Borgia, was born in Valencia, Spain. His uncle, Pope Calixto, helped him to climb first to cardinal and then to Pope, becoming Pope number 214 in history, who ruled from the year 1492 to 1503. His term is considered abominable and full of scandals. Pope Alexander never married but had as a lover a woman named Vannozza Cattanei, with whom he had four children, named Lucrezia, Caesar, John, and Godofredo. Lucrezia Borgia became famous for her beauty and Caesar Borgia for his cruelty. The Pope also had love affairs with another woman named Julia Farnesio, who later accused him of having two children that the Pope never recognized as his."

"Marguerite, why does the Catholic Church disapprove of the marriage of priests?" asked Gwen.

Ivonne answered that it was based on the incompatibility of the two vocations. "As they say, a priest needs to be a person totally committed to the Church, and if he were married would be distracted. Also, the Church assumes the life of a priest is one of reflection, isolation, sacrifice, and separation from pleasures of the world. Furthermore, when the priest is ordained, he makes a commitment to pursue his profession with care, discipline, and dedication, elements impossible to accomplish as a married man. Today the Church admits married men as priests if their wife dies before his clerical ordination. However, is then prohibited from marrying again for life."

"Marguerite, don't you think celibacy has become a major factor in the scandals among priests?" asked Gwen.

"Do you mean by scandals acts of homosexuality and pederasty?" asked Ivonne.

"Exactly. What do you think about that?"

"This question is a hard to answer," responded Ivonne. "It is my opinion that celibacy is not the primary cause for acts of homosexuality and pederasty in priests. To me, the real reason comes from the freedom God grants men to select their ways of living. That instead of following His principles, some priests take the way of evil to satisfy their sexual desires with people of the same gender or in abusing children in their care. Furthermore, those bad priests believe the freedom that God granted them means to follow their impulses and instincts, forgetting the lessons Jesus Christ taught them and that they promised to follow when were ordained. Freedom is an inalienable and fundamental human right. So when those bad priests are led by their impulses and choose the way of evil, they not only impoverish the notion of freedom, but also get separated from the teachings of Christ. Acts that being shameful, abominable, and reproachful, discredit the Church."

"Don't you think those bad priests should be severely punished? Yet in some cases they are forgiven of their sins and restored to their same position when they show repentance. Is that a practice acceptable to you?"

Ivonne thought before she answered. "I don't have the power to judge. Only God holds that power. Even the priests who represent God on earth lack the ability to judge. The role of a priest is circumscribed only to the forgiveness of sins when the sinner shows a sincere repentance. No matter how grave their sins are, the confessor will pardon them. And once they execute the penance and take Holy Communion, the sinner is saved from sin and able to be restored to his same position. However, we know by God's words that at the end of the world, He will come to judge us again, the moment in which we will be truly forgiven of sins and go to heaven or be sentenced to hell forever."

"Marguerite, don't you think that celibacy has been a major contributor to the reduction in the number of priests?" asked Gwen.

"Before I answer, I would like to ask you, do you think a married priest would be led to a more orderly and sanctified life, leaving aside his sexual pathologies and corruptions that invade the world of today? And would his marriage help to give married couples better advice, as he would be experiencing the same problems as they?"

"I can see by your responses that you are for celibacy, or I am mistaken?" asked Gwen.

"I think my responses clearly indicate my opinion," Ivonne replied.

Leaving the cup of coffee on the table, Gwen mentioned her understanding the reason for stopping the practice of married priests was that in the old times, they bequeathed their personal property and belongings to their families instead of leaving them to the Church. Celibacy stopped this practice, and now priests' resources no longer belong to their families but to the Church. "What can you tell me about this?" Gwen asked.

"Hmm," replied Ivonne. "Now that I remember, Pope Pelagio in the sixth century prevented attacks on married priests who donated their property and goods to the Church instead of giving them back to their spouses and children," said Ivonne.

"So the practice of celibacy was favorable to the Church, don't you think?" Gwen asked.

"I suppose it was," Ivonne responded.

Resting her elbows on the armchair, Gwen faced Marguerite to direct her next question about what she thought of marriage for nuns. Ivonne quickly answered that the life of a nun was different from that of a priest. It was more common to find a woman living alone than men. The task of a nun was similar to the performance of a wife in her home, the difference being that their husband was Christ, who demanded from them constant assistance. Their missionary work required them to travel frequently all over the world, preaching His doctrine and taking care of children and patients in hospitals. "If we got married, our husbands would require attention and act like spouses, taking charge of their children, leaving aside our other obligations that we accepted when we entered the convent."

"I understand exactly what you mean," Gwen said. "But what would you say about the acceptance of women into the priesthood?" Gwen asked immediately without giving Marguerite the opportunity to change the topic.

"All right, I will refer to you what I lived through in one of my missions in Africa six years ago when I was asked to help the father, Jeremy. Father Jeremy was a missionary belonging to the Benedictine order who resided in a small town in Zambia called Kala-ko-ba and preached the Catholic religion. When he first arrived in Kala-ko-ba, Zambia, forty years ago, the population of the town was two hundred people, but due to his commendable work to catechize other indigenous tribes from different communities, its population increased to almost three thousand.

The excessive work made Father Jeremy unable to perform his duties diligently as a priest, so he requested from his order an assistant to help him. Unfortunately, at that time, his order lacked available priests, so they recurred to our convent, who sent me to Kala-ko-ba to help Father Jeremy in his tasks.

"When Father Jeremy learned a nun was being sent instead of a priest, he accepted my assignment with resignation. I recall with joy the day of my arrival to Kala-ko-ba. Father Jeremy waited for me at the wharf with some other natives. When I disembarked my boat, they all came to greet me, the natives taking care of my luggage while Father Jeremy led me to the village where I would stay. Walking toward the village, Father Jeremy abruptly stopped to say, 'Sister, the cottage is set up for two people. Each room has separate walls, but there is only one bathroom, so we will have to schedule times for its use. The room on the right side is mine, and the one on the left will be yours, which I hope will suit you." Thanking him, I said everything sounded perfect to me.

"Tall, slim, and seventy-five years of age with abundant white hair, Father Jeremy had gained the sympathy and respect of the majority of the town's population except the wizard, who distrusted and hated him. Every day ending of his priestly duties, Father Jeremy spent three hours teaching me the Kala-ko-ba language, which after three months of practice allowed me to speak with the villagers. The language included short phrases but with many meanings, so to interpret them correctly, I had to use my hands.

"Every Sunday and holiday, Father Jeremy offered mass in a small parish he had built. Most parishioners stayed outside to hear the homily in the heat of the sun. Masses started at six a.m. and ended at two p.m., giving a fifteen-minute interval to rest or go to the restroom. In the afternoon, masses began at four p.m. and ended at six p.m. Finishing the masses, Father Jeremy would change out of his priest's attire for shorts and a T-shirt to instruct the children of the village in how to play soccer. The winning team received prizes such as cookies and candies, which Father Jeremy bought with the small alms he received from the mass.

"Unfortunately, my collaboration with Father Jeremy lasted only six months, as one dawn, I was unexpectedly awakened by two young natives who told me Father Jeremy was severely ill, and they thought that during the night he had suffered a heart attack. Dressing as fast as I could, I ran to his room to corroborate the terrible news. The priest lay inert on his bed, breathing slowly and with difficulty. The redness had drained from his face, making him look drawn, pale, and utterly spent. Concerned, I approached to check his pulse. He declined, saying there was nothing more to do as God had called him, and he needed to obey His commands. But before he went, I had to promise him I would take good care of his parishioners, entitling me to perform every role of a priest. He begged me not to lose his work of forty years. Once I made the promise, Father Jeremy expired."

"And what happened next?" Gwen asked, intrigued.

"Taken by surprise and without knowing what to do, I sent a telegram to Father Jeremy's priestly order requesting a replacement. But four weeks passed by, and there was no response. One day while I rested in my room, the chief of the tribe appeared with some other natives, demanding that I should perform the duties I had promised Father Jeremy to do. Driven by the circumstances, I offered mass the following Sunday, skipping the Eucharist, which should be conducted only by a male priest."

"Pardon me for a minute, Marguerite, but my cell is ringing," Gwen said. Hanging up, she said it was Elysee requesting them to come to the main dining room in twenty minutes. "Sorry for the interruption, but please continue. You were saying you were forced to perform the priestly functions."

"Well, time passed and my replacement still did not arrive, so on another morning, the chief of the tribe appeared again with a group of natives, saying some parishioners wanted to make confession and receive Holy Communion. He reminded me again of the promise I had made to Father Jeremy, who authorized me to act as a priest. In the first instance, I refused, telling them a nun in the Catholic religion is not allowed to conduct ministerial functions. He was interested to know the reason, so I explained that the canonical function is a sacrament, meaning the Church follows Christ's principles. Therefore, the priest leaves his own desires in order to accept what Christ has conferred on them in the sacraments. And although the Church admits that every human in the eyes of Christ is equal, when speaking of divine rights, they say God only concedes the privilege of representing the body of Christ in the Eucharistic act to the male priest."

"Marguerite, don't you think the exclusion of women from the ministerial function is discriminatory toward women? Is the idea that Christ and his disciples never called women the reason for discrimination against them? We all know that women in the former times meant nothing to men. History shows the dissatisfaction of Jews when they receive the announcement they will conceive a daughter instead of a son. Or when they preach in the Mishna that they would prefer to see the Torah burned with fire than be taught to a woman. Or in their daily prayers when singing the song, 'Blessed be to God that made me no pagan; blessed be to God that made me no woman, blessed be to God that made me no slave.'"

Ivonne could not believe Gwen's words and replied that in her opinion, Jesus Christ never followed the beliefs of the Jewish time. "The Bible shows the preferential treatment that Christ gave to women, proven when talked to the Samaritan at the well even was a sinner or grant pardon to the adulteress women when refused to judge her or in the Mosaic Law that promulgated equal rights for males and females in the bonds of marriage. Also, were women who first gave the paschal message announcing to his disciples Jesus's resurrection?"

"All right, Marguerite, end of the story. Please continue what you were saying," said Gwen with an angry expression on her face.

"I must tell you, Gwen, that despite my explanations, the natives never understood my prohibitions, so on the next Sunday morning, requesting God's pardon, I offered confessions and gave the Holy Communion to the parishioners. At the end of mass I thought I would feel guilty, but instead I felt relaxed and calm, as if God had granted me His forgiveness.

"Fortunately, the next week, my replacement arrived. Confessing to the priest my sin, I was surprised to hear from him that even though what I had done was bad even under the circumstances, it was better than leaving them to return to their original faith. Granting me his pardon, he absolved me of my sins, saying a lack of priests was becoming a big problem for the Catholic Church, and a possible solution would be the acceptance of women into the priesthood, as was starting to happen in other Christian religions.

"Three days after his arrival, I received orders from my convent to return to Paris. Despite the insistence of many villagers clamoring for my stay, with tears in eyes I said goodbye to them. With these last words, I left behind the wonderful experience of living in Kala-ku-ba," said Ivonne.

"Marguerite, before we leave, let me ask you this last question. Do you honestly believe everything the Bible states is true?"

"Of course I do," Ivonne answered promptly.

"Then in your belief, Jonah survived inside a whale for three days and nights? Who provided him with food?"

Without delay, Marguerite responded, "God moves mountains. Who provided Moses with the resources to survive in the desert for forty days, feeding thousands of people who followed him?"

Gwen was disgusted with Ivonne's answer and decided to end the conversation by saying her directors were gathered in the dining room awaiting their arrival.

CHAPTER 18

Walking toward the dining room, Ivonne remembered the discussion that had taken place with her brother in the days before her coming. Her brother had mentioned that his boss wanted her out of the operation because he thought it was becoming more risky and complicated than they expected. His opinion was based on her inexperience as a spy. "Do you agree with his statement?" Albert asked.

"No, I don't," she answered firmly. "I know the real reason he wants to replace me," Ivonne said.

"If you know, tell me," said Albert, displaying a sarcastic smile.

"His rejection comes because he thinks I am incapable of handling Gerald Solaris's murder and the recent disappearance of Cardinal Ponti and two bishops, which you think were kidnapped by Gwen's organization. Am I wrong, Albert?" Ivonne asked.

"My gosh, Ivonne, you surprise me. There is no doubt you inherited Dad's intelligence," Albert responded.

"Albert," Ivonne said, "now more than ever I want to be involved in this case. I don't care if I die in this venture."

Seeing his sister's decision to go forward, Albert promised to talk again with his boss to see if he could change his opinion on her removal. When dismissing his sister, Albert said, "If you're back on the case by tomorrow morning, we will start your training, so be prepared."

"Thanks, Albert. I look forward to seeing you tomorrow," Ivonne answered with a smile.

That same afternoon, Albert arrived with the news that Ivonne had been accepted on the case again. Her training was to begin right away. Albert was excited to see his sister working with him again. "To start," he said, "feel free to reject my plans if they interfere with your religious principles. But once you accept them, don't blame me that I pushed you to do something you will regret later. I've made a plan to introduce you as a spy in their organization without waking their suspicions. For this commitment, you need to be careful about whom you speak with and what you say. Don't lie or deny your religious principles. Just try to be more flexible with your answers. Your mission consists of finding the motive that led them to kill Gerard Solaris and where the cardinal and two bishops are being kept hidden. Only one condition is required of you—that is, do not compromise our institution at any time. Ivonne, be aware that your intervention will save many lives, making it unnecessary to perform a frontal attack that would cause many deaths."

Promising to follow his brother's instructions, Ivonne said she was ready to start with her training the next morning.

When Gwen opened the door to the dining room, Ivonne saw several women eating. Their attire looked like what Elysee wore. Greeting their guests, they stood up, leaving Gwen and Ivonne space to walk toward the stage. Climbing the three steps, they reached the podium, where Ivonne saw a row of chairs facing the audience. A woman was seated in the last one. Her wrinkles on her face showed she was close to sixty. Her expression was not that of a friendly person.

Gwen walked toward the seated women to introduce Marguerite. Dr. Susan Myers, has been my partner since we started the organization. "Susan graduated with honors from Stanford University. Her studies in biotechnology made the university award her the medal of merit." Without showing emotion, Susan extended her hand to show Ivonne where to sit. Once Ivonne was seated, Susan started the conversation, saying Gwen had told them that morning that a special guest was visiting them. Ivonne was about to respond when Gwen interrupted them, as she had taken control of the microphone and claimed for silence.

To introduce Marguerite, Gwen described the relevant facts of her life, saying Marguerite was a tireless protector of women's rights who had fought against the mistreatment of and discrimination toward women in places such as China, India, and Africa, where the governments imposed several limitations on women. Later, she referred to the subjects previously touched on the talk with her, finishing by saying her own organization followed that same principles. "The similarity with what we do is astonishing, as we both defend women's rights against the humiliations and mistreatment inflicted by men, Marguerite, every woman in this room has suffered at least one of these humiliations or abuses by men. That's why after being rescued by our organization, we're trained to defend ourselves. Outstanding members are hired as personal trainers of tae kwon do, others in martial arts or wrestling and boxing, while those who we consider more intellectual are directed to roles such as lawyers, defending women in divorce cases where the husband is found guilty of causing her physical injury." Ending her speech, Gwen received applause from the audience. To thank them, she made a slight bow.

Unexpectedly, a young woman with Asian features rose from her seat, and climbing the podium took the microphone to say, "My name is Soony Lee, and I left China as a small girl when I was able to escape the torments inflicted by my father. When I returned to China two years ago, I found another China. However, to my dissatisfaction, I found that Chinese women still suffer much discrimination. Hence, today, knowing Sister Marguerite's background included being in China, I would like to see if she agrees with my impression.

"In my understanding, population growth has brought China many discrimination problems. For centuries, the world's population remained below one billion inhabitants. But reaching that number, its growth became unstoppable. The world population today exceeds seven billion inhabitants and foreseen that in the next ten years, an increase to nine or ten billion will occur. This spectacular growth makes us seriously consider the Malthusian theory that says nourishment grows arithmetically while population grows geometrically. This implies that if we don't stop this population growth immediately, many countries will soon lack food, and their governments will be forced to implement emergency measures to stop their citizens from dying of hunger and thirst.

"This vertiginous growth in population is not due to an increase in births but to the reduction of mortality, in which fewer men die in wars, people living longer lives, and the effectiveness of combating diseases of malnutrition and hygiene. This is the reason that countries such as Japan, the United States, and some countries of Europe show an increase in the number of females in their population, in contrast to other nations such as

China, India, and countries in Africa, where women are deprived of food and lack adequate medical help.

"Education goes hand in hand with moderate growth in population. Better education means fewer discriminatory problems. China gives women a poor education. Therefore, discriminatory problems are greater.

"Women live longer than men, frequently reaching the age of seventy-five or even ninety, yet the world population shows fewer numbers of them. The reason is the disappearance of females. Lack of records, in some cases, but in others they were killed by their parents before they were born. Today, the number of disappeared women exceeds one billion. It is overwhelming to know that half of this amount belongs to China, followed by India, Pakistan, and other countries of the Asian and African continents. These numbers become less for the North American continent. To determine this number were used complicated and actuarial equations. By these means was found that in India, 5,000 women are killed every year by their displeased husbands when receiving their dowries. Asia sees more than 250,000 women die every year from venereal diseases from practicing prostitution while they were younger. Africa is not an exception, where more than 6,000 women die every year from their genitals being mutilated.

"In China, girls are detested by their parents since their conception. Married couples receive with disappointment the announcement of a girl's birth in. Thousands of them have died by abortion or homicide by their parents when were deprived of adequate medical aid.

"Taking Mao Tze Tung the power in China, he promised to enhance the condition of women. At the beginning of his reign, his promise seemed to be real, as he started to eliminate some degrading practices such as foot binding in women, forced prostitution, and marriages of convenience, giving women for the first time the opportunity to be incorporated into the labor force. However, when Mao was notified that China had reached one billion inhabitants, was forced by those circumstances to impose measures to stop the growth, implementing policies such as the preference for only sons and marriage of women at a certain age. His actions caused in one year the birth of one million more boys than girls. Abortions became a common practice when daughters were conceived. Married couples who conceived a girl were allowed to try again and see if they could conceive a son, but failing that, they were not allowed to try once more.

These facts demonstrate clearly the poor value that women have in China. Despite government efforts to fight gender inequality, results continue to be unsatisfactory and will not stop being so until they eliminate the policy of the preference for an only son.

"The differences in number between the sexes has brought serious problems to men. As today the deficit of females makes it difficult for males to find a mate. Furthermore, the trading of women is overwhelming, as many see it as a profitable business. The number of single males is problematic, bringing about as a consequence the kidnapping of thousands of teenage girls who are sold like merchandise every year to wealthy Chinese men, who now prefer to pay excellent prices for them than to face the expense of a wedding. Therefore, for the next generations, millions of males in China will lack a wife.

"Chinese women suffer from discrimination, mistreatment, and humiliation in their homes. Fathers, brothers, and husbands abuse of her sexually and physically. The fear to denounce them makes her submit to their desires, as was taught since childhood that woman is inferior to man. To defend their rights, the government has issued decrees that only increased the number of divorces, in which the woman always loses.

"Finding work for a woman in China is not an easy task. Men enjoy preference, and even when a woman finds a job, her pay will always be less than a man's. Furthermore, constantly is being harassed by her boss who to increase her salary demands her sexual favors. Likewise, in personnel adjustments, females are first to be fired and last to be hired.

"Recently the government implemented mandatory retirement for women at age fifty and men at sixty. At first look seems fair to women. However, the truth is it works against her, as in the early retirement makes less money in the long run. Furthermore, employers are less likely to hire women knowing about their earlier retirement. And even worse, an early pension benefits the preference for an only son, as parents getting older depend economically of their children salary, who prefer to give the opportunity to their male son than to their daughters, thinking they will in a long run earn a better salary.

"A woman's poor education makes her parents prefer she remain to do domestic work at home and in the fields like her mother did. Her education will rarely reach higher levels as parents prefer to give such opportunities to the son.

"The Chinese government neglects providing health care and nursing services; therefore, parents are responsible for the health of their children. Lack of funding from the government has made women unable to assume their role of reproduction correctly.

"The Chinese constitution proclaims the same rights for men and women in politics, economics, and family matters, establishing punishments to those who violate, mistreat, or humiliate women or children. Attempting to protect women through international legal frameworks, the government has issued laws that in most cases are unfavorable conditions for women. And although international authorities have the duty to protect the female rights, they neglect this area and concentrate on other issues to them more relevant, such as the liberation of the market in China and its integration into the global capitalistic system than to protect women in the labor force. So despite such efforts, women continue to suffer discrimination in her work. Her opportunities to climb to better positions and receive better payment still look remote. Experiencing humiliation, oppression, and discrimination in her home, school, and at work becomes an easy reason for women to commit suicide. Not surprisingly, China is the nation with the most female deaths in the world."

Leading her eyes to where Sister Marguerite was seated, Soony Lee asked Ivonne for her opinion. "If you find something is false, feel free to tell me," said Soony Lee.

"No, I must admit your version is accurate and shows real life in China today. However, the adverse conditions under which Chinese women live today will change for the next generations of women. The emancipation and liberation of the high-class woman is a reality. Today, high-tech transnational companies hire women, seeking to lower their production costs. The exporting of Chinese products is recognized worldwide. Chinese companies need low prices to compete in international markets. High production volumes have forced Chinese employers to employ females, looking to reduce their payment, but soon those companies will find that if their wages are not raised, they will lose them. Trends are leading women to a different scenario. The increase in wages will help to improve her standard of living and be less economically dependent on men. Furthermore, gathering with other women, will start to fight the discriminatory measures over her. The strength of her union with other women will make the government understand those discriminatory actions need to change or be suspended."

"I also have to agree with your comments," said Soony Lee, interrupting Ivonne in her exposition. "Wait to hear what comes next. Women get tired of being submissive to men for many years. Our organization is preparing to help these women in their fight to establish a democratic and secular government in their countries, eliminating the discrimination where it exists and creating a true separation between church and state. Also, we will support the issuance of laws that not only respect women's rights but that also forbid religious and cultural practices that harm, mistreat, or discriminate against women, and to severely punish any men who violate them. Our task consists of printing illustrative pamphlets and publishing ads in newspapers, radio, and television, that serving as training centers at the local and national level will promote among the general public and governmental and nongovernmental authorities lessons of defense in women's rights. Complementing our work, we will issue laws and rules that, without concern for religion, sex, or ethnic group, etc., will reduce or reject any act or attempt against women, granting her the privilege to denounce these acts among the international authorities, which will have as their duty the protection of her rights, letting her freely choose her lifestyle, have the number of children she wants, and establish her personal relation with whom she desire.

"What do you think of our work, Sister Marguerite?" asked Soony Lee.

"Everything sounds good to me, Soony Lee. However, you must admit many of those propositions go against the principles of many religions, don't you think?" asked Ivonne.

"Yes, Sister, we are aware of that; however, our organization intends to continue the fight, no matter what the cost would be," answered Soony Lee with firmness in her voice.

Seeing the conversation was taking longer than expected, Gwen rose from her seat to stop the discussion, saying, "Even the presence of Sister Marguerite has been of great value to us. We will need to ask her to leave us in ten minutes because we will hold a meeting in this room with the directors, at which for the moment her presence is unnecessary."

Understanding the meaning of her words, Ivonne rose from her seat but was stopped by Gwen, who said before she left, she was free to request anything she wanted. Ivonne answered nothing came to her mind at that moment, so rising again from her seat, she started to walk toward the exit. Following her steps, Gwen stood up, but not Susan, who had stayed seated and only extended her hand to say goodbye. At that moment, Ivonne understood the reason of why Susan did not stand up, as under her chair lay a pair of crutches she used to walk with, as Susan was a disabled person.

While Ivonne walked toward the exit door, several directors approached to dismiss her. Suddenly Elysee's figure emerged from the hallway, making a signal and requesting her to follow her.

Ivonne felt disappointed with her day. Gwen's conversation with her directors had not led her to know the real reason for her visit, although a supposition had crossed her mind that, if real, was frightening.

CHAPTER 19

W hile walking with Elysee toward her room and not knowing the time she had left in that place, Ivonne drew up a plan of action. Starting her plan, she asked Elysee what religion she professed. Elysee responded that during her childhood, she was educated under the Catholic religion, but marrying an Arab, she converted to Islam. Since then, which was four years ago, she had professed none other.

Going into the room alone with Elysee, Ivonne saw her disposition to continuing their chat, so she requested Elysee to close the door and sit down. To start their conversation, Ivonne thought first to gain Elysee's trust, so she asked her if she knew if there were hidden cameras in that room that could trace them. Shaking her head, Elysee mentioned the existing ones had been removed to respect her privacy. Thanking Elysee for her answer, Ivonne replied that that was exactly what she expected to hear.

Facing Elysee, Ivonne said that when she first met her, she saw in her expression a certain sadness and distress. "Perhaps I am mistaken, but my sixth sense that never betrays me keeps telling me you hide many things inside you, but you fear to express them freely. Elysee, trust me, I promise to listen to what you want to tell me, and if you need our protection, count on it." Ivonne said.

Looking at Ivonne, Elysee said, "Sister, you are right, and I will tell you the reason that took me to this sadness and distress." Not really convincing and with a low voice, Elysee started by saying, "Everything began when, at the end of my biology career, I decided to take a vacation trip to Abu Dhabi with my friend Louise. Touring the city, we met an Arab man named Emille Salim, who followed us to all the places we went. Emille seemed shy to speak with us, and Louise frequently mocked him in front

131

of him. Eight days passed, and he never dared to approach us. However, on our last night's stay in Abu Dhabi, while we dined in our hotel, the waiter came to our table, bringing us a bottle of French wine. Rejecting the bottle, we told the waiter we had not ordered one. Smiling, the waiter signaled to a man seated opposite our table and said he was the one who had sent the wine. Turning around, we found the man was the same one who had followed us all these days. Showing our gratitude, we told the waiter he could invite the gentleman to join us at our table. Accepting the invitation, he left his table to join us.

"Tall, slender, with a strong complexion, abundant black hair and sparkling green eyes, Emille turned out to be handsome a likable, respectful, and intelligent man. During our conversation, we became aware he had lived in the United States for ten years, a time he spent as a student until he graduated as an engineer from MIT in Boston, Massachusetts. While he talked, I wondered which of us he was trying to engage. I can assure you, Sister, since that first encounter, my heart pounded for that man as it never before had for another man. When we finished our meals, he insisted on paying our check and expressed his desire to see us again tomorrow. Being aware this was our last night in Abu Dhabi, he showed frustration in his face, but rising from his seat, he respectfully parted from us, saying he had passed a wonderful evening in our company. In response, we thanked him for paying our check and for the bottle of wine. Also, we said we had enjoyed the evening with him.

"The next morning, as we paid our hotel bill, the clerk told us our account was settled and there was no balance due. Asking the clerk who had paid for it, he said that he did not know who had done it, but he was sure the account was totally settled. Turning around and ready to take our luggage, we saw Emille standing next to a column. His smile showed he was the one who had paid our bill. We told him it was not fair, but he smiled, assuring us he had nothing to do with it and that maybe it was a courtesy of the hotel. Changing the subject, he mentioned that at the entry of the hotel was a vehicle ready to take us to the airport, and signaled a porter, who approached to help us with our luggage. Outside in the street, we found the car parked at the entrance of the hotel. It was a black limousine. The driver inside wore a frock coat. When he saw us, he stepped down to receive our luggage and open the rear doors. Abruptly,

Emille stopped the driver and helped us to climb into the vehicle, then he jumped inside the limousine and seated himself between us.

"During our journey to the airport, Emille offered us drinks that he took from a minibar. Choosing glasses of similar size, Emille made an excellent bartender. Mixing drinks, he prepared a martini for us. While we toasted the success of our trip, Emille requested our flight number, airline, and destination. Being aware we were flying to Paris, he requested our telephone numbers, which he wrote in his electronic agenda. He promised to see us in fifteen days since he had to make a business trip to Paris. When we asked him how he made a living, he smiled and responded that at that moment he was involved in the leisure industry.

"When we arrived in Paris, my mind could not stop thinking about Emille. Day and night I waited for his call. Recognizing everything could be a dream and it was possible I would never see him again, I tried to concentrate on my work. However, one Thursday evening, when I was to leave my apartment and meet with Louise, my phone rang. Answering the call, I immediately recognized Emille's voice. He was inviting me to dine with him next Saturday night at the restaurant Le Tour D' Argent. When Emille arrived to pick me up that Saturday night, he was driving a luxury convertible sports car, which he said he had rented. We enjoyed a very pleasant evening without mentioning Louise at all. Arriving back at my apartment, he stepped out of his vehicle to open the door for me. After admitting we had a great deal of fun together, he proposed to repeat the experience in two weeks. As he departed, he courteously kissed my cheek, and although I closed my eyes, he never made any move to kiss me more passionately.

"During the next six months, everything became the same. Every fourteen days at noon on Thursday, I received a call from Emille inviting me to dine the next Saturday night in different places. His schedule consisted of taking a plane from Abu Dhabi on Friday, flying all night to arrive early Saturday morning in Paris, where he attended to business matters to be free at night and dine with me. Early on Sunday morning, he would take a plane back to Abu Dhabi.

"One Thursday at noon, I received his invitation to dine on Saturday night at seven at Pie D'couchon. This time he requested I join him directly in the restaurant. That Saturday before our date, I stopped to buy some things, thinking I had time enough to be there at seven for my date with Emille. Walking into the restaurant, I saw Emille had not arrived yet, so I ordered a martini to calm my nerves. After two hours of waiting and having several drinks, I paid my check. Thinking something bad had happened to Emille, I hailed a taxi, giving the driver the address of the hotel where Emille said he was staying. When I arrived at the hotel, a porter approached to receive me. When I asked if he knew Emille Salim, he emitted a big smile. Seeing the anger in my face, he apologized, saying he had smiled because Mr. Salim was the owner of that hotel and of many others in Paris. Surprised at his response, I walked into the hotel to repeat the same question to the front desk clerk. The clerk answered that Mr. Salim's plane was delayed due to the bad weather that had been plaguing Abu Dhabi since two days ago. After writing a note to Emille, I requested the clerk to deliver the message to Mr. Salim. I wrote how worried I was, and no matter what time he arrived, he could call me.

"As I prepared to leave and hail a cab back to my house, I saw at the back door of the hotel the driver who had taken us to the airport in Abu Dhabi. Approaching him, I asked if he was waiting for Mr. Salim. He said he had to pick up Mr. Salim at the airport in one hour, and inviting me to go with him. But thinking it was improper to join him, I mentioned the message that I had left with the clerk requesting Mr. Salim to call me on his arrival. Noticing my nervousness, he tried to calm me, saying everything was fine, and soon I was to receive the good news of Mr. Salim's arrival.

"One hour before midnight, my phone rang. It was Emille, apologizing for being unable attend our date and explaining his delay was due to bad weather. But in return for his sin, he was inviting me to dine at seven at Maxim's the next night. When Emille picked me up that night, he was wearing a finely cut, elegant black suit with a smooth gray tie. Flattering me, he praised my dress, saying I looked gorgeous. Helped by Emille, I climbed into the limousine, finding at the wheel the driver I had met before, who, showing satisfaction, said to us we made the perfect couple. Seeing my face blush, Emille emitted a big smile.

"Going inside the restaurant, I was struck by its elegance. On the way to our table, I saw several people who recognized and greeted Emille. Our table was reserved in a private room out of the reach of regular customers. The table was set for two, with a fine linen tablecloth, gold silverware, fine porcelain plates, and glasses of Czechoslovakian cut crystal. In the middle of the table were set a pair of vases with flowers of different colors. Assisted by the maître d', we sat. Emille received two menus, one that included the meals and the other for wine. Emille rejected both, saying he preferred to order first the best champagne they had. The maître d' left, ten minutes later bringing the best champagne I'd ever tasted in my life. Pouring several glasses, we made several toasts.

"When the bottle was half empty, I chided Emille for not telling me that he was the owner of the hotel chain. In response, he said everything served to test me, as many women approached him only for his money. However, the test proved my real love for him when I showed how worried I was before his arrival. Promising not to lie to me again, Emille took my hand and asked me to close my eyes and not open them until he said to. Following his instructions, I closed my eyes, sensing something was put onto my finger. Finally he said I could open my eyes. When I opened them, I saw on my finger the most beautiful, brilliant ring I had ever seen in my life. Intrigued, I asked him what this gift was for. Smiling, he said he was crazy in love with me and that gift was his formal proposal of marriage. Without delay, I accepted his proposal, replying I was also crazy in love with him. He stated we would have two marriage ceremonies performed in conformity with both our beliefs. Mine was to take place in Paris according to the Catholic religion. I was to select the church of my preference and invite about three hundred guests. Later, his ceremony was to take place in Turkey in accordance with Islamic tradition, attended by only our families and friends as witnesses. Also, he stated we would live in Abu Dhabi, where he had his main business activities. Accepting all his terms and conditions, I said that what mattered for me was being with him without considering where we were.

"Thus, on October 5, 2005, I was married to Emille in the Sacre Couer Church. Three hundred guests attended our wedding as was previously agreed. My father was worried about my marrying an Arab who would take me to live with him in Abu Dhabi, reminding me about the way they treated women in such places. To reassure him, I mentioned Emille had been educated in the Western hemisphere, far away from the Islamic culture. Our second wedding took place fifteen days later in Turkey, following the Islamic tradition. At that wedding were present only our families and of course Louise, who signed as my witness and whose trip expenses were paid by Emille.

"After our wedding, we traveled in Emille's private plane to Hawaii, where we enjoyed an idyllic honeymoon. Our marriage had happened so quickly that every day we found out new things about each other. I was intensely in love with Emille, and he seemed to feel exactly the same for me. Something I noticed about Emille was that he never said loving things about his mother; instead, he frequently mentioned good things about his father. Back at Abu Dhabi and after one month of a wonderful honeymoon, I felt nauseous and dizzy. Emille took me to see his family doctor, who told us I was pregnant. Emille received the news with happiness and immediately hired a private nurse to take care of me. One night while we were alone in our bedroom, he suggested that I convert to the Islamic faith so our son could be raised under his beliefs. I agreed without objection. So the next day in his temple, we started the process of converting me to the Islamic religion.

"Lamentably, my pregnancy lasted only five months, as in the fifth month, I miscarried. According to the doctor, the baby was a boy. When the doctor told Emille I had lost the child, he showed frustration, but after knowing I was prevented from giving him birth to another son as my entire uterus was removed in surgery, he became so angry that he tried to hit the doctor. If he had not been stopped by the nurses in time, the doctor would have been seriously injured. Since that moment, Emille's behavior changed completely from being a joyful and enthusiastic man to being sad and bitter, scolding the domestic servants constantly. When I challenged his behavior, he answered I was the cause of his disgrace, as not only had I lost his son, but I could not give him another one.

"From that moment on, he said I would be treated like a regular Muslim woman, dressing in the hijab to cover my whole body with a veil over my face to prevent showing my beauty to others. He also prohibited me to leave the house or drive a vehicle without his authorization. The Islamic tradition allows a man to receive several women into his house, and if one of those women becomes pregnant and gives him a son, he is allowed to wed her. Also, he reminded me that if the idea crossed my mind of taking revenge on him, he would accuse me of committing adultery, the penalty for which was the death, as he plainly could prove that when we got married I was no longer a virgin. Also, Muslims considered their home a sacred place of seclusion and imprisonment for women, so if I intended to abandon him, my disobedience would be considered acts of disgrace, punishable, like infidelity, with a death sentence. And if by chance I filed for divorce and went to court, they would laugh at me, as women lacked freedom and human rights there.

"His mocking laugh increased my anger to the extent that without thinking, I started to strike his chest, forgetting his strength would be superior to mine. To stop my blows, he held both of my hands in one of his hands and with the other started to beat me furiously, leaving me semiconscious on the floor. In my last effort to stop his blows, I raised myself off the floor, took the flower vase on the table, and smashed it on his head. Blood immediately flowed from his head. Frightened at his bleeding, I ran desperately, trying to reach the stairs that led to the exit. Unfortunately, I tripped on the stairs, lost my balance, and tumbled downstairs, leaving me completely unconscious when I hit my head on the floor. When I recovered, I was in the hospital with a nurse at my side, who implored me not to move because my body was injured and in complete pain. Without paying attention to her warning, I raised my head off the bed to be sure Emille was not in that room. When I saw Emille was not present, I calmed down and took the pills the nurse offered to me.

"After several weeks in the hospital and intensive rehab treatment, I one day received a letter that said if I wished to take revenge against Emille, I should call that number. Without thinking twice, I dialed the number. A woman answered who said she was a lawyer who could make arrange documents for me to leave the country immediately, if I desired. Two days later, I received in the hospital my passport and plane tickets that would take me to Frankfurt, Germany, where Gwen and other members of her staff would be waiting for me. And since then, I have belonged to Gwen's organization."

"Did you ever try to divorce Emille?" Ivonne asked.

"I never did, although by now I might be a widow," answered Elysee.

"Do you mean you are not sure you are a widow?" Ivonne asked, intrigued.

"Exactly, as no one has found evidence of his death," said Elysee. Ivonne asked Elysee to be more explicit. Breathing deeply, Elysee explained why nobody was certain of Emille's death.

"One night while watching the ten o'clock news, I heard the reporter mention a plane crash in Turkey. Without paying further attention and being on the verge of turning the television off, I heard the name Emille Salim. Immediately my attention returned to what was being said. The reporter commented that the hotel tycoon Emille Salim was traveling in his private plane to attend the opening of a new hotel in Turkey, when unexpectedly the plane crashed five minutes after takeoff, killing everybody on the plane. Hit by the news, I called Emille's father, who sadly confirmed the terrible news, although he said he had hope his son was still alive. I asked his father to be more specific. He explained to me that it was true that four persons had boarded the plane, although it seemed none of them was his son because when identification of the bodies took place, they belonged to the pilot, copilot, flight attendant, and a fourth passenger not yet identified. The police still did not know who the fourth passenger was who had replaced his son on the plane. Since that moment, I have regularly called Emille's father. On my last call, he informed me he was seriously ill and likely would die soon, but in respect to his son's disappearance, everything remained the same. Now you see why I say might be a widow."

Ivonne paused a second, then asked Elysee if Susan had been disabled all her life or had been in an accident. Elysee said Susan was born in Los Angeles, California, fifty-six years ago. She belonged to a poor family, and her father was a drunkard who worked as an independent perfume vendor. His clients were close friends who forgave his frequent absences and missed product deliveries. Susan's mother was a self-employed woman who, with resignation, suffered her father's insults, blows, and mistreatment. She cleaned houses for rich people.

When Susan reached the age of thirteen, she started suffering from sexual abuse by her father. Despite this painful situation, Susan kept studying, receiving at nineteen the award for her excellent work in biotechnology and a scholarship to study at Stanford University. Her father attempted to dissuade her, saying as a biologist she would starve. Her father's intention was to marry Susan to his friend Harry, an old millionaire deeply in love with her, who promised that if he married her, the whole family's money worries would be solved. Nevertheless, Susan refused his offer, receiving in return threats and beatings by her father.

Helped by a friend, Susan was able to buy a bus ticket and travel to Stanford University. Six months later, after leaving her home and being in the classroom, Susan was told to immediately call a hospital in Los Angeles because her mother had been badly beaten by her father and remained unconscious. Requesting permission to leave, Susan left the university and rented a car. Unfortunately, Susan never reached her destination as her little experience driving was not enough to stop the accident. Her tires skidded on spilled oil on the highway. Susan thought her best option was to push hard on the brake, but instead of stopping, the car started to spin out, ending in a crash against the highway guardrail. The impact of the crash was so great that it caused severe injuries to Susan's spine, leaving her paralyzed from the waist down.

Despite her handicap, Susan continued with her studies, graduating with honors as a biologist in just four years when normally it took five to finish her program. Susan was a bitter but strong woman who, after her accident, was forced to use a wheelchair. The university paid an assistant to help Susan with her daily duties. However, Susan never resigned herself to her misfortune. With great tenacity, she submitted herself to interminable surgeries and rehabilitation treatments, although what really helped in her recovery of movement in her muscles and body was the insertion of motility genes that Susan discovered in her experiments. Susan limped and still required the use of crutches, but she had promised herself she would abandon them in less than a year.

Ivonne asked Elysee about Susan's mother. Elysee responded that she never recovered and died two weeks after Susan's accident. Susan blamed her father for her mother's death. When Susan recovered from the accident, she went to court and accused her father of mistreatment and sexual abuse of her mother and her, suffered when they lived together in the house. Finding her father guilty, the court sentenced him to five years in prison. Lamentably, his sentence lasted only two years, as one day he was found hanged in his own cell. Later it became known he suffered from liver cancer due to his constant alcoholism.

Without giving Elysee the opportunity to stop, Ivonne next asked how Susan and Gwen had met

"Don't take my answer as true, but they say when Susan finished her postgraduate studies, she was hired to work for a transnational laboratory company. Her genetic work made her the winner of the Gruber Foundation Prize. Gwen was also invited to the award ceremony. One week after this event, Gwen had invited Susan to be her partner in the company she was starting. Finding they had similar goals, both seeking revenge against the mistreatment and discrimination of women by men, Susan immediately accepted the offer."

Ivonne was about to ask Elysee what she meant by "insertion of motility genes in her body." But she skipped that question and preferred instead to know if Elysee, as a biologist, had worked with Susan. Elysee responded she did once, although she was replaced later by Doctor Hollander. "What kind of work did you perform for Susan?" asked Ivonne.

"Mostly it was in biotechnology and genetics. What do you know about genetics, Sister?" Elysee asked.

"Only the basic principles that I learned when studying biology at school. I'm sure I've forgotten them."

"Would you like me to remind you of some of them briefly so you can understand what I will tell you later?" Elysee asked.

"I sure would appreciate that," Ivonne replied.

Briefly, Elysee explained to Ivonne how the human body is made and how the cells work in reproduction when they divide and form a cellular egg called a zygote that, when activated, produces an embryonic genome and the first component of DNA. Am I going too fast?" asked Elysee.

"No, please continue. I am really interested in more," Ivonne responded.

Elysee stood up and walked toward the window. Looking outside, she said, "What I will tell you next probably will hit you, Sister. Susan led her experiments to decipher the language of life. Using her vast knowledge, she started to manipulate the characteristics of one individual to another. To reach her target, Susan had to master several techniques of genetic manipulation, starting first with vegetables and then animals. In vegetables, Susan enhanced several dominant and recessive characteristics, creating high resistance to certain diseases and reducing the time of growth to harvest maturation. While focusing her experiments on the animal sector, Susan obtained better cattle breeds. The manipulation techniques also helped in the reproduction of dogs and cats.

"Sister, I loved my work and would stay long hours in Susan's laboratory, on many occasions forgetting to eat and even sleep. Susan abruptly stopped me from working with her and substituted Doctor Hollander when her experiments moved on to manipulate the genes in human beings. Her goal consisted to transfer a zygote with chromosome genes to another zygote that later insert it in a woman's embryo. Susan studied several methods of gene replacement, not stopping until she was able to recognize with certainty the location of the chromosome in which was the gene she intended to manipulate. Susan built several scenarios of chromosome genes, drawing real maps allowing her to identify if the genetic characteristics of that individual were compatible with their genetic structures, to later determine if they belonged or not to that same individual. With that objective, Susan drew graphics of genetic unions to ensure that the original hereditary characters were compatible with its chromosomal regions or if they deviated from the genetic characteristics that were required for her manipulation.

"Looking for solutions, Susan found the attended techniques of reproduction filled in part her expectations as they exhibited a similar technology of what pretended to use, that was to insert in the feminine ovule the masculine chromosomes with the replaced genes of individuals with outstanding characteristics—physical, neurological, psychological and pathological."

Suddenly, Ivonne rose from her seat and, excusing her interruption, said she needed to go to the bathroom urgently. In the bathroom, Ivonne left the door partially open. Extracting the minicomputer from the pocket of her dress, she tested the recording machine to be sure it had worked properly. Hearing their voices clearly and waiting for the right moment, Ivonne took several pictures of Elysee with her digital camera. Finishing her task, she returned the minicomputer to her pocket and walked back to sit where Elysee waited for her.

"As I was mentioning before the interruption," Elysee said, "Susan chose as her best option the attended techniques of manipulation. To perform these tasks, Susan needed several collaborators. So she selected from five women who had never been pregnant and five who were mothers. The tenth women would be instructed in artificial insemination techniques and in the test-tube fertilization process. Warning them that no matter which method of ovulation was chosen, the first step was to apply hormones that stimulated the production of their zygotes.

"Giving them lessons in artificial insemination techniques, Susan instructed them that the selected spermatozoids would be inserted into their uterus to later lead to a more natural fertilization process. In regard to the test-tube fertilization process, they were taught that their ovules would be extracted and fertilized externally in a laboratory, to later be embedded as pre-embryos in their maternal uterus. After examining both procedures, Susan preferred to chose artificial insemination, thinking that besides minimizing the risk when male spermatozoids with replaced genes were introduced into their uterine cavities, it would later lead to easier natural fertilization. First Susan had to collect the sperm from several men, which was kept frozen in a refrigerator to prevent decomposition. Then, helped by powerful microscopes, Susan extracted the semen of several men that mixed to make only one element. In her first attempt, Susan failed to do it, as the semen deteriorated at the moment the chromosomes with replaced genes were mixed. Without despairing, Susan found new procedures to preserve the semen, so after several attempts, she was able to transplant the cells containing the spermatozoids with replaced genes without their suffering decomposition.

"Satisfied with her results, Susan called the women who were selected to receive the manipulated spermatozoids in their uterine cavities. Her tests showed that the tenth women got pregnant. However, only three of them arrived at gestation; the seven others failed when their fetuses presented deformations, which Susan immediately destroyed. Going further in her experiments, Susan cloned the embryos of the three pregnant women by using the artificial division technique in a fertilized ovule. Today in Susan's laboratory, multiple samples of these cloned embryos with replaced characteristics exist, which are kept frozen until the results of the original characters are known.

"Four weeks ago, something unexpected happened to these three pregnant women, as they started to suffer from constant bleeding. Worried about their health, Susan sent them to the hospital, but despite the doctor's efforts, the three women died ten days ago. According to Susan, their unborn children were girls with a high IQ, able to run long distances without getting fatigued, able to solve mathematical formulas of great complexity, learn a language by merely trying it once, and having the strength to defeat any adversary of a greater age. Sister Marguerite, I am glad those babies did not survive; otherwise, Susan would encourage them in evil ways, only to demonstrate the new generations of men what these empowered women would be able to do.

"But guess what, Sister? Her experiments did not stop there, and now Susan has applied her knowledge of biotech to life in microbes. As we all know, the world is full of multiple microbes, most of them benign, but others are highly dangerous and powerful transmitters of infectious diseases, as when they are applied to the manufacture of microbiological weapons. Today, Susan keeps multiple samples of these microbes in her laboratory. Most of them are harmful transmitters of contagious diseases that, if shot into a human being, would gradually lead to death."

"Tell me, Elysee, how do you know this information if you no longer work for Susan?" Ivonne asked.

Elysee laughed before she answered. "Susan writes a daily report detailing the findings of her experiments that she keeps in a safe box in her office. Cleaning her office one night, I found the upper drawer of her desk unlocked. I opened it, and inside was a piece of paper. A quick review was enough for me to know Susan had written the combination of her safe box on it. After memorizing it, I left the office in a hurry. Several weeks later, one night when I had stayed to work late, I decided to pay a visit to Susan's office. Opening the door carefully, I went inside. With the combination in hand, I opened the safe box and extracted a bunch of documents, finding under those the reports detailing all her experiments. Reading them quickly, I tried to memorize must of them. As I had been involved in some of those experiments, it was easy for me to interpret the reports."

"How reliable and accurate do think your information is?" Ivonne asked.

"I would say it is one hundred percent reliable," answered Elysee.

"Why didn't you take pictures of these reports?" asked Ivonne.

"I had no time, and it was too dangerous for me to stay in the office because a guard might have seen me."

"Elysee, who else besides you knows of these reports?"

"I believe only Gwen, Susan, and probably Dr. Hollander, who sometimes works with Susan. Besides them, no one else," Elysee responded.

For a moment, both stayed silent. Ivonne then asked Elysee how Susan got the men's sperm for her experiments. "Oh, Sister! Please don't ask me that question. I think I've loosened my tongue too much," Elysee responded in a sobbing voice.

Holding her breath for an instant and invoking God to not let her make a mistake, Ivonne said, "Elysee, what you said to me about your organization has been of great value. So to return the favor, I would like to compensate you for your information by confession to you the real purpose that has brought me here. My life depends on the actions you can undertake. Even so, I am ready to confront the risk."

"What are you talking about?" Elysee asked.

"Listen to me carefully, Elysee," said Ivonne. "First you need to know the real purpose that brought me here. Indeed, it is absolutely true that I am a nun. However, at this moment my duty is something other than being a nun. A TIPA officer asked me to act as a spy, entrusting me with the mission of finding out what goes on inside your organization."

"Sister, you are scaring me," said Elysee, a nervous tone in her voice.

"Please calm down and keep listening," Ivonne asked. Quickly Ivonne told her whole story. Elysee listened with mouth wide open and a pale color in her face. Finishing Ivonne asked Elysee if at any time Gwen had mentioned the names of those five men who worked in their organization. She answered she had no idea there were five men working for their organization. Gwen and Susan were extremely cautious about sharing information. "Maybe their closest collaborators knew about them, but others like me are completely ignorant of what goes on inside the organization."

"Elysee, now that you know the purpose of my real mission, would you consider exposing me?" Ivonne asked. "You have the right to do it, and I promise to face the consequences without resentment."

"Don't ever think that, Sister," Elysee replied. "I also have told you many things I detest about our organization, so if you need my help, count on me."

Thanking Elysee for her offer, Ivonne said that before she accepted her help, she would promise that in the event her mission was discovered, she would never expose her. This time Elysee was the one who thanked Ivonne.

"Now, that our agreement has been settled, tell me, Elysee how did Susan get the sperm of those men?"

Thinking for a moment, Elysee responded, "It is my understanding that Susan kidnapped several men whose aptitudes seemed to fill the expectations she had for manipulation in her experiments. One of those men probably was my former husband, Emille Salim."

Ivonne was surprised at her answer, so she asked, "What makes you suppose that?"

"It was by randomness that I became aware of it," Elysee responded.

"Could you be more explicit?" Ivonne asked.

"It was almost two months ago, when Susan and Gwen were chatting in the library and I was called to bring them coffee. Usually I knock at the door before going inside, but this time, finding the door partially open, I went inside without being noticed. I heard Susan tell Gwen about the success of her experiments, that she was able to gather the sperm of several men into one mixture without it suffering decomposition. Congratulating Susan, Gwen asked if among those sperm was Emille Salim's. Susan said it had been a real pain in the ass to get his sperm as he had refused to give it, and only with threats that I would be tortured did he consent to give his sperm. Then both laughed and agreed Emille was the perfect specimen for their objectives. Without listening to the end of the conversation, I left the room in a rush. When returned I made noises so they would be aware of my presence. Seeing me coming into the room, they both laughed and stopped their conversation immediately."

Ivonne was terrified of what she had heard. Taking a breath, she asked Elysee if she knew where those men were being kept hidden. "I guess they are kept in a small room of a two-story building located on the northeast side of the development. This site has two guards all day and night who prevent anyone from going inside besides Gwen or Susan."

Lowering her voice, Ivonne asked Elysee, "Who else besides your former husband could be there?"

"I don't have the slightest idea who else might be there," Elysee responded.

Noticing Ivonne's interest, Elysee said the building they presently were in had undergone several modifications. The auditorium that once was on the third level was moved down to the first level to expand its capacity. The small meeting rooms located on the third level where Gwen showed Gerald Solaris the videos had disappeared to be replaced by more rooms. Under those were Gwen and Susan's rooms. "Now I remember seeing the Rembrandt picture you mention in Gwen's room," she said.

"Oh my! These changes could make my work more difficult," Ivonne said.

"Were you planning to take from the safe box those videos?" Elysee asked.

"That idea still remains in my mind," Ivonne replied.

"I can see the frustration on your face," Elysee said. "Maybe what I am going to tell you can help to facilitate your work. Every night before going to sleep, Gwen takes pills to calm her nerves. They put her in a deep sleep from eight o'clock, when she goes to bed, until five o'clock, when she wakes up to go to the gym, where she exercises until six. Returning to her room, she bathes and prepares to confront her daily duties that start at seven."

Thanking Elysee, Ivonne said her information was encouraging. "Elysee, where do you sleep?" Ivonne asked.

"My room is on the fourth level of this building, number 410," Elysee responded.

"Do you share the room with anyone?"

"I did until two weeks ago, when my roommate, a reddish-haired Czechoslovakian woman named Howie, left to go see her mother in a hospital in Los Angeles."

"So right now you sleep alone in the room?" asked Ivonne.

"That is correct," Elysee answered.

"What kind of work did Howie do for the organization?"

"She was the kitchen chef's assistant. Why are you asking so many questions about my roommate? Is there something bad about her?"

"Oh, no, no, I was just curious," Ivonne responded. "What are Gwen and Susan's room numbers?" Ivonne asked.

"Susan has room 301 and Gwen has 310. Both of them are the most spacious and luxurious in the development."

"Where can I find Susan's laboratory?" Ivonne asked.

Elysee walked to the window and opened the curtains to show Ivonne a huge circular building about 120 feet in height with a large transparent dome. "That huge building is Susan's laboratory," Elysee said. "The walls are protected with polarized crystals that are able to resist not only solar rays but also the impact of bullets from a plane. Her laboratory is equipped with an ionization system that constantly works twenty-four hours a day to capture every minuscule particle of dust. The security system is high-tech, making it impossible for anyone to go inside without the proper identification authorized by Susan," Elysee said, "Sister, maybe you would like to know the layout of our whole development," Elysee asked.

"Yes, I would like that," Ivonne responded.

"The land covers a surface of 1,550 acres without considering the airport area. At the south are found Building A, Susan's laboratory, and the hospital. Building A is used as a headquarters for the offices of our main directors. The auditorium, as I said, has been transferred to the first level, expanding its capacity to seat comfortably more than 1,100 people. The second, third, and fourth levels are used as dorms, and the fifth, sixth and seven levels as offices, dining, and conference rooms. To the west are buildings B and C, where most sports and cultural activities take place. These buildings have gyms, a stadium, and other amenities, including a library. This section covers the largest part of the development. To the east we find seven buildings, used to lodge the second-level personnel who work in the development. Finally, to the northeast is found the two-story building in which I believe those men are kept hidden. This building appears to be a warehouse due to its cement structure and steel laminated roof. The building also connects by a bridge to the airport, where Gwen and Susan keep their private planes."

"Thank you, Elysee. Your information is of great value to me," Ivonne said. "Elysee, where can I find evidence of Susan's experiments?"

Elysee thought a moment, then replied that everything should be found in Susan's computer. "How can I get that information?" Ivonne asked. Elysee was annoyed at so many questions but answered that no one was allowed to go inside her laboratory without showing the proper identification tag.

Taking a deep breath, Ivonne explained to Elysee that part of her assignment was to install a chip in Susan's computer to access passwords and information, so in a tone of despair, she asked Elysee to help her. Thinking fast, Elysee replied that maybe there was a way. "What comes to mind, Elysee? Please tell me," Ivonne asked.

Seeing her desperation, Elysee explained her plan by saying Susan's secretary was her close friend. "Her name is Samantha, and she often invites me to take coffee with her. If I ask her to have coffee with me, she needs to go to the basement to prepare it, giving me enough time to perform your assignment. What do you think of my plan?" asked Elysee.

"It's awesome. We will put it into action tomorrow," said Ivonne with excitement. "Elysee, let's not waste more time. I will show you what I have learned to prevent you from making mistakes. Using a screwdriver, you need to dismantle the keyboard. When the keyboard is dismantled, insert the chip in an undetectable place, leaving a free space for the operator when she uses the keyboard. After connecting the keyboard again, be careful to leave the computer as it was before. Any trace we leave can lead to terrible consequences. Nothing will go wrong if you follow my instructions."

"I don't foresee any difficulties in performing that task," Elysee said.

Suddenly, Elysee's cell phone rang. Answering the call, she listened to Gwen's voice instructing her to tell Sister Marguerite of their desire to meet with her tomorrow morning at seven. Asking Elysee where Sister Marguerite was at that moment. Elysee responded was in her room since had been locked in there two hours ago. Hanging up, Elysee's face looked pale. "I am sorry, Sister," she apologized, "but for a moment I got scared thinking Gwen could be aware of our conversation. Fortunately, I was wrong, and Gwen just called to say she wants to meet with you tomorrow morning at seven. I will come to pick you up before that time. I don't have the slightest idea what she intends to speak with you about. I only hope it won't interfere with our plans."

To calm Elysee, Ivonne mentioned that if it was God's desire, they would be executing their plan tomorrow. At the end of the day, they could meet to talk about the results. Ivonne asked Elysee to provide her phone number in case she needed to call her.

After writing her cell phone number on a piece of paper, Elysee gave it to Ivonne. Then, hurrying to leave the room, she said their chat had taken longer than expected, and before someone saw them, she had to leave and lock the room. Before she said goodbye, Elysee asked Ivonne if the executions of Gerald Solaris and the other people were made by their organization. "We need more evidence to prove it. That is why I am here," Ivonne responded.

"It makes me feel sad just to think it was my organization that killed those people," Elysee said, shutting Ivonne in the room as she left.

Alone in the room, Ivonne extracted her rosary from the pocket of the dress. Lifting her eyes to the sky, she thanked God for His guidance and forgiveness. When her prayers ended, she placed the rosary back in the pocket of her dress and took her minicomputer out. She entered the password that gave access to the main menu. Searching through several files, she found the command that said, "Attach information." When she press that key, the program requested the password of who intended to send the information. Typing Albert's password, the screen displayed "Proceed with your sending." Attaching the recording made of the conversation with Elysee and the pictures taken of her, Ivonne sent them. Returning to the main menu, she found the command "To chat." After pressing the key, she was asked to type her brother's password again. Once the screen started to flash, she knew she was connected and ready to speak.

After greeting her brother, Ivonne mentioned she had sent information that she thought was urgent for him to review. Albert said he would look at it later. Ivonne then informed Albert of her intention to get the videos. Knowing that they were kept in Gwen's room, Albert tried to dissuade her, saying it was too risky for her. However, at Ivonne's insistence, Albert had to agree with his sister's plan. "Just be careful. Remember that any failure can end our mission and maybe your own life," said Albert.

At six o'clock at night, Ivonne heard a knock on her door. Someone from the outside said she was bringing her food. Hurrying, Ivonne put the computer inside the pocket of her dress and collected the papers on the desk. After giving permission to enter, she was surprised to find Elysee coming in, hastily pushing a cart. On top of the cart was a silver tray filled with plates of different foods. Without considering Ivonne's opinion, Elysee had selected several fruits, a big piece of salami pizza, and a cup of tea that was placed separately on a different plate. Ivonne was willing to have Elysee stay and chat, but she refused, saying she had other things to do. Appreciating her nervousness, Ivonne did not press her more. Elysee had placed the plates not used by Ivonne on the silver tray and started to push the cart hastily, where promptly she disappeared without uttering another word. Locking the door with a key she left. Ivonne was astounded, thinking something bad had happened to Elysee.

At eleven o'clock that night, someone ran quickly through the darkness in the hallway of the third level toward the stairs to the fourth level.

CHAPTER 20

While Elysee chatted with Ivonne in her room, in the dining room Gwen held a special meeting with the main officers of her organization. After listening to Gwen's proposals, Soony Lee rose from her seat and went to the podium to say, "With the rights conferred to me as secretary of the meeting, I request the audience to cast their vote either accepting or rejecting Gwen's proposals. Therefore, I ask members of the audience to lift their right hand if their vote is in favor or keep their hand down if it's in disfavor." After counting the votes of each person who lifted her right hand, Soony Lee reported to the assembly, "As an examiner and with the powers conferred to me by our statutes, I state the present attendance was thirty-three members. From that, thirty-two voted in favor and only one in disfavor."

Gwen, who was seated at the front the audience, did not see who the person was who had voted in disfavor of her proposals. She was surprised when Soony Lee stated that person was Susan. Turning her head around, she saw that Susan was seated with her hand down. Concerned about her reaction, Gwen asked Susan her reason for voting against her proposals. "I just don't agree with them," answered Susan calmly.

"What do you dislike about them?" asked Gwen with anger in her voice.

"To be honest, there is nothing wrong with your proposals. It is Sister Marguerite whom I dislike and don't trust," responded Susan. Gwen asked Susan what the basis of her distrust was. Susan said at that moment she had no evidence, but her sixth sense kept telling her she was not to be trusted.

"Oh, come on, Susan," Gwen said. "Leave that pessimism behind. Sister Marguerite is only a nun. What harm can she do to us?"

"I don't know what it is exactly, but her expression makes me think she lies to us. Anyway, to end with the discussion, my vote in disfavor does not stop you from putting your proposals in action, so why do you need my vote?"

Disliking her answer, Gwen asked Susan to change her vote, noting that since they had started the organization, their decisions were always made by mutual consent. Susan was not really convinced but agreed with Gwen, saying she would change her vote. She raised her right hand in the sign of approval.

"All right, Soony Lee, let's call again for a new vote," Gwen demanded. This time Gwen's proposals were unanimously approved, and her plans were to be put into action immediately.

Seeing that everybody agreed with her proposals, Gwen repeated that Sister Marguerite would be notified of their desire to meet with her tomorrow at seven. "Her decision is fundamental to continuing with our plan. Otherwise, if we can't convince her, the plan could suffer a disruption. Is that understood?" Gwen asked, raising her voice.

The audience applauded and agreed, so Soony Lee declared the assembly ended.

CHAPTER 21

Ivonne had slept barely two hours when she was awakened by the sound of her alarm clock, set to ring at twelve midnight. Her decision to get the videos from Gwen's room still persisted. Rising from her bed, she saw her computer vibrating, announcing a new message was received. The message was from her brother, Albert, who demanded she abort her plan to get the videos. The reason would be explained to her later. Surprised and frustrated, Ivonne tried to call her brother. A voice mail answered, saying that the phone at the moment was out of service. Annoyed but used to obeying orders Ivonne, returned to bed with resignation. Minutes later, she was in a deep sleep again.

When Ivonne woke up, it was almost five o'clock in the morning. After saying her prayers, she showered and dressed before calling her brother, who this time answered her call. Chiding her brother for stopping her decision to get the videos, Albert responded he was terribly sorry, but at that moment could not give her an explanation. Furthermore, he was glad he had stopped her in time and she had followed his instructions. Telling her to pay close attention, Albert instructed Ivonne to distrust any person in the organization, including Elysee. Later she would know his reasons for saying that. She asked Albert if she could attend her appointment with Gwen. Albert replied she could, but as soon as she discovered the real reason why Gwen was bringing her there, she should faint. A doctor named Simone would be coming to her rescue. Simone was part of their team and should follow her instructions exactly. Ivonne nodded her head affirmatively and said she had understood.

As Ivonne expected, someone knocked on her door at seven. After permitting the person to enter, Ivonne saw an unknown person coming in. Surprised at not seeing Elysee, Ivonne asked for her

"My name is Christine Momeck, and I am instructed to take you to Gwen," she answered.

"Pardon my curiosity, but can you tell me where Elysee is?" Ivonne repeated her question.

"Sorry, but I am not allowed to say anything else. So if you would please follow me," Christine responded in a rude tone of voice.

Without uttering another word, they walked quickly through the hallway to take the elevator that led to the sixth level. When the doors of the elevator opened, they walked toward the conference room, where Ivonne found several of the faces that she had seen on the previous day in the dining room. Now they were all seated around a splendid rectangular table. Seeing her guest come in, Gwen rose from her seat to greet Ivonne and place her in the seat next to her. At that moment, Ivonne felt an uncommon nervousness in her. Everything in the environment seemed normal, but her sixth sense was advising her something was going wrong. Wondering what the reason could be, she made a quick examination of her audience. On the other side of the table was a vacant seat. Ivonne immediately understood to whom it belonged, as Susan's absence was obvious.

Gwen requested silence and thanked Marguerite for spending the day with them. Then she said Marguerite must be curious why they had brought her there. "For your relief, I will tell you that we have no other intention than to defend women against the mistreatment and discrimination of men. So to have a better idea of their work, I've invited some people to briefly describe the different discriminations that women suffer in their daily lives and what measures we're implementing in trying to stop them. But before listening to them, I propose we have a light breakfast in the dining room. We would be pleased if you could join us."

After finishing breakfast, everybody followed Gwen to the private elevator. When they arrived at the first level, the doors opened, revealing a splendid auditorium where more than a thousand people were seated, waiting patiently for their arrival. With strict military discipline and in perfect silence, Gwen began seated her directors in their respective places. The front rows were reserved for directors of higher rank, while the second and third rows were for those lower in the hierarchy. Every row started to quickly fill, leaving only one seat empty, which Ivonne supposed belonged to Susan.

When everybody was seated and in perfect silence, a woman climbed the stage to take control of the microphone and said, "My name is Annika, and I will expose the discrimination of women in the labor force.

"No one knows for certain how the different activities of men and women start to develop. Some historians assume they come from the different behaviors, capabilities, assumptions, and prejudices that each sex performs independently of the political, economic, or geographical environment in which they live. For others, the divisions come from the work each sex chooses, where men select to support his family and women the activities of home and field. These functions worked in harmony for several generations until today, when the woman needs to add to her old tasks, the support of her family, as her husband's salary becomes insufficient to give the family a way of living with dignity. The world crisis and inflation in prices have diminished the economic purchasing power of families, making it impossible to sustain families with only one salary. To counteract this situation, women are searching for part-time jobs or work in the informal market. However, they soon recognize that this kind of job is not enough to help sustain her family. So they are forced by circumstances to find full-time jobs. The woman gets discouraged when finds her salary is less than a man's even when she performs similar works. And even worse, she is often harassed by her boss, who promises to increase her salary in exchange of sexual favors. It is sad to see that in personnel adjustments, women are the first to be fired and last to be hired. Not even in her own home can a woman enjoy freedom, as her husband is who disposes and distributes the income of the whole family in accordance with his wishes.

"Equal positions at work should pay similar wages and salaries for both men and women. Unfortunately, in real life this does not currently happen, as the payment of women is always less than for men. The needs, opportunities and limitations are different for men and women. Works can be similar for both sexes, but the opportunities and limitations become different. Several stages of life for women give testimony to this statement. Works are compensated by responsibility and time. A clear example is the unmarried or divorced woman without children who enjoys a greater opportunity to climb into high positions with better salaries. Their bosses seem pleased with this kind of woman, who is more liberal and disposed to stay for more hours at work. In contrast is the married or divorced women with children who need to worry about the care of their husband and children, facts that undoubtedly cut her aspirations to climb into higher positions with better salaries that will require more responsibility and extended hours at work. The discrimination toward widowed women starts from the day of hire, since employers aware of her older age abused of her by offering starvation salaries that these women need to accept in order to survive with dignity. The pregnant woman is under severe limitations. Employers are displeased with her condition because they know in advance the absences and incapacities that will have to overcome at the time she gives birth to the child. And what to say of the woman who is infected with AIDS or other venereal diseases due to her husband's infidelities and becomes practically unacceptable to work in companies when doctors detect her illness in blood tests and employers became aware of them. Many of these women become an easy target for prostitution or to commit suicide.

"Looking for solutions, our organization has implemented several strategies. Some are directly designed to compensate women, offering them the same opportunities with similar payment as men. To achieve our target, we offer free courses in which professional and technical advisors teach these women how to compete favorably against men. The learning will serve them to optimize their traditional skills and capabilities toward the horizon of their new enterprise activity, demonstrating to these men with their success what the new generation of women is able to do. Following our purpose we invited several women to participate in this kind of work, entrusting them with the task to go and speak with competent authorities so that together we can issue laws and rules that penalize any discriminatory act that might befall these women."

Gwen made a sign, and Annika hurried to end her speech. Following Gwen, Ivonne stood up and started to clap, as did many others of the audience. To thank the audience for their applause, Annika made a slight reverence.

Ending the applause, Gwen climbed the stage and, taking control of the microphone, announced the next speaker. "Valeria is going to tell us about the discrimination of women in several religions," she said.

An elderly woman approached the podium and, taking control of the microphone, said, "As Gwen said before, my name is Valeria, and I am the eldest person in this organization. I came here due to the mistreatment I received from my ex-husband for many years. Gwen and Susan rescued me, and I am extremely grateful to them. At this moment, my mission is to prove the poor development of women in several religions of today's world as well as to find solutions that will improve their way of living. During my speech, I don't intend to blame any religion or recriminate against any religion in particular. My speech is intended just to show how men unwarrantedly have manipulated religious concepts to their benefit, to deprive women of their rights and force on them discriminatory practices. To make my argument more understandable, I will show some examples of how men have manipulated religion to their benefit.

"Before we start with a specific religion, I would like to explain the discrimination women suffer in matters of reproduction. Today, most religions in the world still fight against the use of contraceptive methods of birth control, which they consider to be abortive. The only accepted method of birth control for them is the natural one once used by their ancestors. Refusal to use these new methods of birth control have led countries such as China, India, and others to lose control of their population growth. To control this population growth, governments today have imposed measures that have become discriminatory against women, such as the one-child policy and marriage of women at a certain age, measures that have led women to multiple abortions and ruptures of marriages.

"After this brief introduction, I will proceed to mention the discrimination of women in several religions. We know that Islamic women of older times enjoyed a better life than those of today. They were adored and respected by men, not like today, when woman's image is unworthy and completely devaluated. Men of those countries have used diverse ways and techniques to manipulate women and make them submit to their desires. To show their superiority and power, men have forced women to undergo degrading practices, such as the wearing of a tunic that covers her whole body and a veil over her face. The garments represent for these men a religious identity and not a repressive tool as everybody thinks, being to them an indispensable attire to prevent women from falling into adultery or misbehavior, which in those countries are penalized with the sentence of death.

"Fortunately, wars in those countries have helped in her liberation, as Western immigrants who now live in the Islamic world have started movements to fight the discrimination of traditional Islamic society. These movements are intended to eliminate the stereotypes that for decades have been perpetuated in that nation. Their work has reached outside communities, letting them know what is happening inside Islam and inviting them to participate in defense of these women. This relationship between the people living in the country and outside communities has helped to exterminate many instances of segregation for these women by issuing laws that prohibit the use of religious cultural customs such as covering the body with a tunic and using a veil over the face, practices that are without doubt considered insane, repulsive, and harmful to women. These anti-Islamic movements have made extraordinary progress for women, leading them to access better education and awareness of birth control methods to stop population growth, as well as to find jobs, among others. Nevertheless, advances are slow, as some of these women still resist changing their attitudes, making the work more difficult. But despite these difficulties, every year these women's movements show a significant increase in followers. Our organization has decided to join some of these movements and make significant monetary donations, expecting to see in the near future these women completely liberated from these discriminatory practices.

"It is overwhelming to find that Islamic women who have left Islam and come to live in the Western Hemisphere also suffer from discrimination. Many schools prohibit their attendance when wearing their traditional garments. Bullying of these girls has become a common practice. Who need resist the mocking and laughter of other students and even teachers for wearing their chosen attire. Parents refuse to send their daughters to school, alluding to the bad treatment they receive from other students and teachers. To confront this problem, school directors have met and determined this practice is completely unacceptable in a democratic world. Seeking solutions, they concluded these girls should be accepted in their schools even while wearing their traditional garments. Only one condition is required from them—the girls' acceptance of being taught in the new ways of life. The expectation in the long term is that these girls will voluntarily accept leaving their traditional garments and instead begin to dress in the Western style. These lessons should also be beneficial for their families, who, if they change their lifestyle, can stop discrimination against them.

"Buddhism is recognized as a religion of peace and kindness. Its founder, Siddhartha Gautama, later known as the Buddha, lived 2,500 years ago. Despite coming from a royal family, he never intended to be a god or prophet. Buddha was addicted to meditation, basing his beliefs that one can free the spirit by denying the flesh. Buddha denied the principles of equality in human beings, even he respect and treat women well, always thought the Buddha could reborn only in men. His theory of transmigration believed humans were entrapped in this world in an endless cycles of rebirth after death. The soul was reborned into a new physical identity, depending on the ethical quality of deeds from its preceding life, to later culminate in a transcendental, mystical experience of its own enlightenment and spiritual salvation called Nirvana, which Buddha considered was the spiritual illumination and release of human beings from suffering, lust, and anger.

"Buddha rejected from the beginning the acceptance of women as nuns. For him, monks were superior to nuns. This unequal relationship between nun and monk orders forced nuns to receive orders from monks. The admonition of a nun to monks was strictly forbidden. Proclaiming equality in his monastery orders, Buddha granted men and women the same number of votes and similar rights. Nevertheless, were monks who revoked this equality, alluding that for disciplinary reasons, the monastic female orders never reached the same number of votes as men. As the female orders suffered an interruption when the lineage of transmission for a succesor in teachers and disciples took place. While in the monastic orders of men never suffered an interruption and the transmission was always properly made. By following these principles, a nun who reached enlightenment for her religious dedication would never have authority over a male monk, even if he stood at an inferior level and had not reached the illumination yet. With these simple examples is shown, even Buddha granted the same rights and votes to monks and nuns, the monks, using manipulation techniques, deprived nuns of their rights. Seeing these practices of discrimination unfair to women, we encourage the nuns to fight against them, starting with a separation of orders to avoid any contact with monks," said Valeria with anger.

"The acceptance of a true separation between church and state looks distant for the Orthodox Jews. In reward for their political votes, governments grant men several privileges, like leaving untouched many of their laws in their marriage system, in which a woman remains tied to her husband until his desire. In divorce laws, women are always the victims of their husbands, even she is the one to receive the bad treatment and abuse from them. Sinful for a Jewish is a divorced woman who marries again. Her sons of a second marriage will be considered bastards and prevented for life to marry a woman from the same religious community, only able to do so with a woman in his same condition. Women's menstruation is a symbol of impurity; therefore, daughters from an early age are relegated to perform the duties of home.

"Most Jewish synagogues excluded women from participating in the Minyan quorum or from reading the Torah, although nothing is written in the Torah forbidden women from participating in this service. The priesthood is strictly forbidden for women. Expectations for change still look distant; therefore, some take the risk and escape from the yoke of their parents and husbands, knowing that if they get caught, will be severely punished. Nothing of this would happen if a true separation between church and state really existed.

"Opposed to the Orthodox religion a liberal Jewish doctrine has arisen. In which the Jewish women is able to perform many of the activities until now reserved for men only. For them, women's menstruation is a normal function and not a symbol of purity or impurity used to discriminate her. This doctrine is focused primarily on protecting women's rights at her work as well as in education, health, reproduction, and religious matters, among others.

"Christianity presents similar characteristics to the Jewish religion. Their traditional principles are based on the attitudes of Jesus Christ and

His disciples. Rejection of abortion, no matter in what stage the women is, has become fundamental to Christians, as the life of a child is sacred and starts before conception, and no one but God has the right to end it. Therefore, the use of any contraceptive method for birth control other than the natural one is strictly forbidden.

"These conservative principles has lead new generations of women to abandon their religion, and be shielded by others considered more liberal. Therefore, countries that once were Catholic such as Spain and Italy today have experienced a significant reduction in marriages as women consider a wedding as unnecessary to make a family. The reason should be attributed not only to campaigns that promote the use of contraceptive methods for birth control, but also to women's voluntary distancing from the Church. Many consider the privilege Christ gave to the male priest to represent His body in the Eucharistic act, which is still denied to women, an unfair practice that denigrates women. A new generation of Catholic women today have begged for the elimination of celibacy in priests as some of them are in love with priests, but the Church forbids their marriage, forcing some of these priests to desert their vocation or be involved in sinful relations with these women. The practice of celibacy has become a major factor in desertion by priests. This reduction in the number of priests is becoming a great problem for the Catholic Church. One possible solution would be to accept women into the priesthood, as is happening in other religions of the world today. A married priest and a mixed priesthood would help to better carry the hard work missionaries need to perform, as couples would assume their responsibilities more happily being together. However, it is sad to say this acceptance looks distant, and we will continue to fight until we achieve satisfactory results," said Valeria.

"We know some liberal Protestant churches are today allowing women into their ministry. Furthermore, they also are open to women in high positions in their hierarchies and to letting them make significant decisions in their churches. The ministry of women has started and will not stop until they are highly recognized and respected by leaders of their communities. Religions with strict traditional and fundamental principles will take more time to accept women, but despite their resistance, the day will come when the discrimination of women in the ecclesiastic sector will end.

"To conclude my speech, I would say the exclusion of women in priesthoods is a misogynistic act of gynophobia and sexism, in which men want to keep women tied to them and ignorant to prove their superiority and to deprive women of their rights. Abusing of her ignorance, men have manipulated, mistreated, and discriminated women. Therefore, we foresee for the next generation a renewed concept of women in which we will fight to recover their rights that have been lost."

Standing from her seat Ivonne said to Valeria, "Not everything you said is true. The Catholic religion has also made important reforms. For example, when I was a child, women had to cover their faces with a veil to go inside a church; now this practice is obsolete. The fast to profess Communion used to be twelve hours; now it is reduced to one hour. Priests were the only persons authorized by the Church to touch the host and give Communion; now the ministers of Communion are allowed to perform these functions. Masses were offered in the Latin language with the priest's back to the audience, causing a distraction for their parishioners. Today, masses are given in native languages, and the priest faces his audience. Earlier, fasts were more rigorous. Every Friday of the week and every day during Lent, it was forbidden to eat meat; now the fast is mandatory only on certain days and on Thursday and Friday of Holy Week. Music played at church was sacred and sung only by the authorized choir, priest, or cantor. Today the music is not just sacred, and the parishioners can sing together with the choir. Torments of priests and nuns were eliminated, making their lives more benevolent. The isolation of priests is not as strict as before, as priests are allowed now to have closer contact with his parishioners," Ivonne said.

"I must admit your statements are also true. But for me, these changes are irrelevant compared to the ones of major importance, such as the elimination of celibacy in priests, acceptance of women into the priesthood, and the use of contraceptive methods for birth control, which are still rejected by the high authorities of your Church," said Valeria with an angry tone of voice.

Disliking the way Valeria responded, Gwen went to Ivonne's defense, ordering Valeria to step down the podium and go to her seat. Showing resignation, Valeria obeyed her orders and returned to her seat.

Apologizing for the incident, Gwen climbed the stage and announced the next speaker, who would illustrate the discrimination of women in education and health. Gwen's reaction made Ivonne wonder if the reason for bringing her here was linked with religious purposes. Leaving her thoughts aside, she tried to concentrate and listen to the next speaker.

A young lady of approximately twenty-eight years named Sharon stood from her seat and climbed the stairs to the podium, where Gwen transferred the microphone to her. To start, she said. "One of the most severe discriminations that women suffer today is related to educational matters. Ignorance of women has served men in deprive them of their rights. It is sad to hear that women in educational matters are considered inferior to men, evidence for which can be found in their frequent absence from school. A big difference exists in the attendance of boys and girls. Girls exhibit less than three-quarters of the attendance of boys. The underdeveloped countries and countryside also showed more absences of girls. To blame these girls is unfair because their absences are not their fault, as they need to assist their mothers in their home duties of taking care of their brothers, as her father's salary has become insufficient to support the family, requiring the mother to work. Boys are rarely requested to help with these activities.

"Another reason for women's absences is the high educational costs that parents confront. And although in many cases the education is free, parents still spend money on materials and uniforms. These expenses have made parents give the education they can afford to their sons, thinking that when they are grown, they will find the best jobs with better salaries than their daughters. The idea also persists that daughters will marry one day and leave their parents, and if they become pregnant, they will be expelled from school. Another fact of their absence from school is the corporal punishments they receive from their teachers.

"Efficiency and talent are factors in being well paid for work. A lack of them and deficient preparation relegate girls to performing home and field duties or, as their best choice, being hired in minor, unimportant jobs. Traditional culture is another impediment to school attendance, such as in Muslim societies, in which forbid their daughters to have a male teacher, and need to find a female professor who offers to teach girls. These teachers lack preparation and center their knowledge on subjects traditional to women such as weaving, decorating, and cooking, among others, activities that never will help women to climb into higher positions with better salaries.

"In spite of these unfortunate factors, a new generation of women is foreseen. Today, many countries of the world offer a mixed education in which women receive the same preparation as boys, making them capable of competing at work with men. Men need women to work, as their salary is not enough to support a family with dignity. Women mostly leave their traditional work in the home and fields and find work that will really help their husbands to support the family. Their better preparation and education will open a wide field of opportunities, different from the ones their ancestors had. Women's incorporation into the labor force not only allows them to leave the manual work they did before, but also to perform professional, technical, and scientific activities that before were reserved only for men.

"Health and fertility go together with education. A better knowledge of family planning allows a woman to choose freely the man she wants and the number of children she will have. Her education allows for knowing the kinds of services rendered by health institutions they need during pregnancy, as well as medical attention for their children, who can receive vaccinations that will prevent them from contracting mortal diseases. Also, a woman will be aware that many governmental institutions provide free nursery services, allowing her to leave the care of her children to trained personnel while finding work to earn more money or continuing her studies.

"Education also makes daughters, mothers, and wives more responsible and conscious of their duties, as well as able to demand from their parents, and then later from their husband and bosses, respect, dignity, and integrity. Women's new preparation will allow them to participate in important decisions at home and work. Once free from other obligations and with better preparation, women will be ready to fight for their liberation, leaving behind the oppression back they suffered for centuries and demanding from men respect for their rights and fair treatment.

"Our organization will propel and economically support this new generation of women, offering them a better education and way of living that will allow them to compete against men with courage and intelligence in technical, professional, and scientific activities. They will demonstrate to men what they are able to do in terms of work, leaving them with no reason to reject them and helping them climb to higher positions with better salaries. Furthermore, they will gradually eliminate the prejudices and discriminatory practices that have weighed over them for centuries."

Finishing her speech, Sharon stepped down from the stage. While going to her seat, she heard several audience members applaud, and she thanked them with a nod of her head.

Gwen waited patiently until the applause ended, then standing, she took the microphone and directed her sights to Ivonne, saying she would talk about a relevant discrimination that women suffered and about which men had preferred to remain silent. "Yes, Marguerite, I am referring to the discrimination of women in politics." Frowning, Gwen said, "It is overwhelming to find that despite the efforts women have made to obtain the right to vote and run for office, her performance in politics has been discouraging. Even though some women have been able to achieve presidencies and ministries, women's permanence in politics has failed, as these women were replaced by men. Furthermore, their teams were formed mostly of men, who were the ones who made the important decisions, leaving the woman leader out and with no other option than to obey their instructions. Unfortunately, and although it sounds strange, women themselves discriminated against them when they thought the woman leaders' performance was more by her feelings than her brain.

"Our organization has the purpose of placing those women into higher positions. To reach our goal, we started a massive advertising campaign, showing to the public a different view of women, highlighting work achievements that would help dismiss the bad image that could lie over them. At this moment, countries of the American, European, and Asian continents have women candidates for their presidencies and ministries. If they win these elections, they will form their teams exclusively of women to prove to men what they can achieve in politics.

"Marguerite, it was approximately five years ago when we started actions that would eliminate some discrimination women undergo in their daily lives. Advances in our work still show poor results. Gender inequality and lack of respect for women's dignity still prevail, being more intense in underdeveloped countries and countryside, making our work more difficult. Women for centuries have been relegated to perform duties at home and in the fields, laborious indeed but rather appreciated by men. The women of today demand to leave her other activities and find instead external work that without a doubt will place them in a better position socially, politically, economically, culturally, and religiously, which, although requiring greater responsibility, will be more rewarding for them.

"Looking for solutions, we approved in our annual assembly to invite twenty-two women experts in different fields, who will join us in the defense of women rights. Following our objectives, we selected women of different nationalities, leasing a complete floor in Madrid, Spain, that will serve us as lodge and offices. On the first day of our meeting, we defined strategies that lead to reduce violence and corruption, diminished illiteracy and poverty, and increased participation by women in higher positions of governmental, private, and ecclesiastical sectors.

"Our work was divided into two phases. The first phase included listing the main actions to take, that in accordance with a new legal order will consider equal rights for men and women and reduce discrimination against women. The second phase was the execution of actions listed in the first phase. Finishing our plan, we saw with satisfaction the fairness of our work, making us think that if the war between the sexes were to be overcome in the next generation, the winner would be the one who showed better preparation in social, political, economic, cultural, and religious matters. Based on these actions, we have formulated a plan that not only will improve women's superiority but will establish goals to impel them into better preparation."

When Gwen pronounced this last phrase, the room fell into complete darkness. Behind the opening curtains, a huge screen with a wall projector operated by remote control from a computer started to descend from the ceiling. Ivonne was amazed at the change of scenery, as in her mind it seemed difficult to assimilate all this new technology.

Once the computer was loaded with a DVD, the title *Gwen's Trip to Madrid, Spain, September 25, 2008* appeared on the screen. The projection showed Gwen with other women visiting different places in Madrid such as the Cibeles Fountain, the Real Palace, the Prado Museum, and the Door of

Alcala, among others. Ending the film were the names of the women who had joined Gwen on the trip, listing their work that each performed for their institutions, such as the Commission of Legal and Social Conditions of Women, Economic and Social Advice for Women, the Development Fund of the United Nations for Women, and other nongovernmental organizations of the United Nations such as the Economic International Center and the Committee for the Elimination of Women Discrimination, among others. From the twenty-five names listed, Ivonne recognized three at the end representing INPOWER: Gwen Swayze, Susan Myers, and Soony Lee.

The DVD automatically advanced and suddenly started to show Gwen's performance in a committee meeting. Having been designated the Coordinator Manager, her functions consisted of executing the listed actions. The committee give Gwen a five-year term to see preliminary results, requiring her to present a detailed report for each task when it was ended.

Gwen could build her team as she wanted, even selecting women of different nationalities and specialties. However, each woman hired had to provide proof of her level of academics and experience to perform that kind of work. Each group consisted of six women; the supervisor was responsible for coordinating the work of her group. Each group should include at least an international lawyer, economist or accountant, engineer or architect, and a doctor. The international lawyers were committed to the study of laws and regulations in different nations and to the issue of new laws and rules eliminating discrimination against women. Economists and accountants had the mission to set up new companies and to manage and review their financial statements. Engineers and architects were entrusted to supervise the remodeling of buildings, which would serve as schools and health clinics. Finally, doctors had the commitment to supervise the purchase of hospital equipment and to see if health clinics and nurseries were properly installed.

In order to explain each task, Gwen took the microphone to say, "Equality is the cornerstone of human rights. Discrimination is the violation of human rights that takes form in violence. Violence generates prejudice and hatred among persons from different races, ethnicities, religious beliefs, sexual orientations, and genders. To help eliminate some of these, we have joined the anti-Islamic, anti-Orthodox Jewish, and other movements that have started to fight the degrading practices that have lain over the women of today's world. The fight requires constant monitoring and statistical reports showing every incident and crime that leads us to provide the means of defense to combat them. Official authorities today have important roles to ensure the accuracy and effectiveness of this monitoring and to find out if the implemented policies are working properly. Our strategy includes speaking with officials of diverse governments to convince them to eliminate the violence that surrounds those countries. Our international lawyers' group has spent many hours studying the inequality of the sexes, finding in countries such as China and India where population growth is most dramatic, and which governments have imposed mandatory measures to stop it by implementing coercive policies for women such as the preference for an only son and marriage for women at a certain age. Measures, without a doubt, unfair and discriminatory to women. That to China for example brought women to an increase in abortions and disgrace to mothers, who feeling guilty of killing their daughters, have become a common path to committing suicide.

"In India, sex inequality is more complicated, as it involves religious matters. Different religions in India have contributed to keep women in a state of backwardness, considering them an impediment to the path of salvation. For them, women are unworthy of receiving the highest religious goals of salvation unless they are reborn in men to be released from the cycle of birth and death.

"Speaking with governments of China and India we have proposed changes in the measures that have imposed against women, that without losing the goal of reducing population growth would be fairer to women. Discussing these issues for several days, they finally recognized that their present measures not only had increased the supremacy of men but also discriminated the women. As a remedy to their damages, they did consent to provide women with better education and open new schools and health institutions. Teachers in those schools should give family planning courses that explaining new methods of birth control will prevent women from becoming pregnant. These courses should fulfill the commitment of reducing population growth but with fair practices for women, as well as helped to mitigate the trade of women, reduce prostitution and suicides in women.

"The proposed plan of action included three steps. The first step was directly designed to combat violence and threats in the world due to negligent and corrupt authorities who have openly declared being incapable to stop them. The second step was lead to eliminate the stigma that for centuries has considered women inferior to men as well as to mitigate her illiteracy and poverty. The third step consisted of increasing women's participation in high positions in the governmental, private, and ecclesiastical sectors.

"Once out steps were set, we started to work with different authorities of the government, issuing laws, norms, and policies that typify violence as a major crime, as well as penalize with prison or large fines any violation of a woman, either physical, sexual, or psychological, whether was performed in her home, school, work, church, or any other place, understanding that a violation includes any act of sexual abuse, torture, forced prostitution, kidnapping, or sexual harassment that harms women.

"To stop the abuse and mistreatment that women undergo in different stages of their life, we made the following propositions:

"= For women who work in the labor force, we offer changes and amendments in their labor laws not only to eliminate discrimination and provide equal rights, but also to encourage forming unions and launching strikes when their work conditions differ from those of men.

"= For women who practice prostitution, we offer monthly checkups to prevent them from contracting venereal diseases, as well as monetary aid to use for rehabilitation if they decide to leave prostitution.

"= For women submitted to trade, we offer to make laws in their favor that will combat this degrading practice, penalizing any corrupt officer who dares to authorize this practice in exchange for receiving money with ten to thirty years in prison.

"= For women who are in prison, we affirm that no matter their present status, they have the right to denounce any act of sexual abuse, violence, or harassment against them, penalizing anyone who dares commit these violations with severe corporal sanctions.

"= For women who belong to the army or similar institutions, we exhort them to demand from their superiors equal treatment and similar hygienic conditions as men, denouncing any act of abuse or sexual harassment against their integrity or personal security and penalizing anyone who dares attack them with jail.

"– For any older women who suffer the abandonment of their family and become potentially suicidal, we offer to speak with their governments and see if they will provide them with social security services in case of disability, granting them also a small pension to survive when they reach the age of sixty-seven.

"= For women who live in the countryside, we offer to speak with their governments and find out if they can grant financing to buy a decent home, to purchase tools for work in the fields, or simply to start a small family business, warning them that the property title should be under their name no matter in what civil status she was.

"= For women who suffer gender discrimination, we offer to make laws in their favor, eliminating the discrimination that lies over them. That helped by legal advisers would have the right to denounce these acts, requesting to restore the damages that were made to her.

"=For women who lack health services, we offer to speak with their governments and see if they agree to open more health clinics and nurseries. To give the example, we have invested from our own resources in remodeling some buildings that will serve as health clinics to provide these women with basic medical services and day care nurseries. Trained personnel will take care of children while the mother goes to perform other activities.

"To find the disproportion that exists between the births of boys and girls, we requested from the Chinese government to provide us with information about numbers of abortions and infanticides of females that appear in their records, making them aware the disproportion is due to the preference for an only son policy. As a remedy to damages for these women, we proposed them to consider in their next cycle of reforms respect for women and elimination of any coercive or restrictive measures that lie over her, warning their rejection would be reported to international authorities who have the power to impose severe sanctions.

"In order to decrease population growth and eliminate coercive measures against women, we proposed to implement courses on sexuality and family planning in which women learn to use methods of birth control that besides preventing pregnancy will prevent them from undergoing dangerous surgeries such as tubal ligations or abortions, making women aware that the responsibility of fertility lies over her, as men have eluded the practice of vasectomy, claiming they would lose their virility.

"To help give jobs to unemployed women, we formed several companies of a different nature, hiring only women to work in them and paying them besides her salary a reward of forty percent in company stock. In order to finance these companies, we requested loans from foreign banks, giving them as collateral the same contracts we signed with our international clients.

"According to our accountants, in a term not to exceed five years, these companies will generate enough profits to pay us the remaining sixty percent of the company stock, which will be sold to them at market price or at cost, whichever becomes less. Once the selling of the company is completed, will leave them as absolute owners of the company, so with a proper management of these women, they will show to the world what they are capable of doing. If their success comes to be as expected, we will continue to open more companies following this same procedure.

"To fight girls' illiteracy and guarantee them the same education as boys, we granted scholarships to the best girl students, allowing them to conclude their elementary education and to continue in superior grades free of cost to their parents when they are unable to afford it. Following this objective, we elaborated a budget plan in which for each dollar spent by their governments, our organization will contribute the same amount. These funds should be used to open more schools for these girls, with experienced professors who will teach important subjects that will allow them to compete with men later in their work. Also, we invited them to participate in scholastic programs to help them eliminate the stigma that considers women inferior to men.

"To increase the participation of women in high positions in the governmental, private, and ecclesiastical sectors, we selected several résumés of women with outstanding capabilities who were proposed as candidates for these positions. Warning those who received them that their rejection of our candidates would be submitted to judgment among international authorities, that if they considered their rejection a discriminatory act, not only would they have to reverse the rejection but also restore economically the damages caused to our candidates."

Ending her speech, Gwen looked to Ivonne and said. "The progress we have made to fight some of the existing inequalities is unquestionable, but spite of our efforts, equality with men looks distant. Probably at this moment, you are asking yourself, *What does everything you have said have to do with me?* As I promised yesterday, I will explain our purpose in bringing you here. Going back five years, we invited five men to participate in our organization. All were of different nationalities and religions, and all had excellent relations with their governmental, private, and ecclesiastical sectors. Unfortunately, all of them failed in their tasks, especially the one who professed the Catholic religion and in whom our organization had great expectations of success."

Gwen took a breath, then asked Ivonne the question if she thought modernization would be of benefit to the Catholic Church. "Depends on what you mean by 'modernization,'" Ivonne responded.

"What do you know about the new Pope?" asked Gwen, changing the subject.

"Not much, as I never have had contact with him, although I've heard from others he is a hard worker and a true believer in change in the Church."

"Marguerite," Gwen said, "I have known the Pope since he was a bishop and always admired his discipline and way of working. Our organization is willing to support him because he has promised to fight with us in the defense of women. Nevertheless, we know there are some cardinals who are against him. One of them is Cardinal Leonardo Ponti, now missing. Therefore, we think that you as a nun can work with him to try to convince the other cardinals to accept his new policies of change in the Church."

Ivonne was shocked when she heard Gwen's words, so thinking fast, she answered, "But first I will need to get permission from the Mother Superior of my convent, but now, being expelled, I am unable to request her authorization."

"That should not be a problem," Gwen replied. "If your wish is to help us in this task, I will talk with the Pope, who will send the Mother Superior of your convent instructions to reverse the order for your expulsion. What do you say, Marguerite?" Gwen asked.

Ivonne was astounded to hear Gwen's response. She never imagined Cardinal Alejandro Villavicencio, now Pope, could be involved in the kidnapping of Cardinal Leonardo Ponti and the two bishops in exchange for receiving Gwen's contribution. But hearing what Gwen had said, that possibility existed. At that moment in Ivonne's mind came the thought of what would happen to Cardinal Ponti and the two bishops if she rejected Gwen's proposal. Maybe they would be killed. So with no other option, she decided to play the same game as Gwen. Suddenly she remembered her brother's words when he said, "As soon as you are aware of the purpose they brought you here for, faint." So now that she knew what brought her there, she should follow her brother's instructions.

CHAPTER 22

While Ivonne listened to Gwen's speech in the auditorium, something unexpected was happening in Susan's bedroom. Seated in one chair, Elysee, with tears in her eyes, begged for mercy, while in another chair, Susan shouted loudly, demanding answers to her questions.

"Elysee, don't make fun of me. I am not stupid, and I know well the kind of bitch you sometimes can be. Instead of being grateful when I rescued you from your husband, Emille, you betrayed me by killing my embryos. Now my patience is gone, and I demand from you truthful answers to my questions.

"Tell me, Elysee, why did you stay so long yesterday in Sister Marguerite's room? What were you talking about?" asked Susan with a tone of anger in her voice.

"We talked about several topics of our lives," Elysee responded.

"During the conversation, did you find out if Sister Marguerite is really a nun?" asked Susan, intrigued.

"Yes, I did. She assured me has been a nun since she was nineteen years old."

"Elysee, I really hope during that conversation you never mentioned anything that could compromise our organization," Susan said.

"Oh no, I would never dare to do that," answered Elysee promptly.

Susan stayed mute for a moment, then renewed her interrogation, asking Elysee where she thought she had left her identity tag. "I swear that last night before going to bed, it was attached to my uniform. However, when I woke up this morning, it was missing," replied Elysee, showing her sincerity and concern.

"So that makes you think someone stole it while you slept, or I am wrong?" asked Susan. Elysee was not really convinced but answered it was quite possible someone stole it while she was sleeping.

"Would you blame Sister Marguerite for stealing it?" asked Susan with a crispy voice.

Elysee thought quickly and answered, "I don't see any real reason to suspect her."

Lifting her shoulders, Susan expressed to Elysee her distrust for Sister Marguerite, saying she felt uncomfortable with her, as her sixth sense kept telling her she was not a person to be trusted. However, as she had no evidence to blame her for stealing her ID tag, she was giving Elysee the day off to find it. But if by tomorrow it was still missing, she should come to her office so she could authorize another one that would allow her to go inside the lab. Also, and this was a warning to Elysee, if by chance she came to see something strange in Sister Marguerite's behavior, she was to come and tell Susan immediately. Finally, Susan said, "If I discover you have lied to me, beware of the consequences. Is that clear, Elysee?"

Promising to follow all her instructions and seeing that Susan was dismissing her, Elysee felt a great relief.

CHAPTER 23

I n preparation for her fainting, Ivonne decided to catch the attention of Rachel, the woman seated at her left side. The noise Ivonne made while she deeply inhaled and exhaled air was enough for her neighbor to ask if she was feeling well. Ivonne responded she felt a strong pain in her chest, and her eyes were blurring as if she were going to faint. Seeing the gravity of the situation, Rachel rose from her seat and asked Ivonne not to move. Climbing the stairs to the podium she found Gwen was speaking with Soony Lee. Being Gwen aware of what was happening, she immediately called the infirmary on her cell phone. Whoever answered the call said the ambulance should arrive in five minutes with a doctor inside.

The ambulance arrived before the expected time. The doctor was a woman of no more thirty years, who stepped out of the ambulance hauling a stretcher. Followed by others, the doctor arrived at where Ivonne was lying. Seeing the numerous people surrounding her, the doctor expressed her need to be alone with the sick person, as such a crowd only restricted the patient's breathing.

The doctor instructed Gwen to obey her orders, but Gwen approached to ask, "I don't remember seeing you before, Doctor. Who are you, and why didn't Doctor Sarah Hollander come?"

"Oh, I apologize. My name is Doctor Simone Blake, and I was sent by Doctor Hollander, who at the moment is unable to come as she is assisting another patient," answered Simone.

Seeing Simone dressed in a white coat with a stethoscope hanging around her neck, Gwen accepted the excuse and took a step backward, leaving Ivonne alone with the doctor. But she stopped at a prudent distance to watch what Simone was doing.

Using the stethoscope, Simone examined Ivonne's heart. After listening for a while, she exclaimed with alarm, "This woman is suffering an infarction to the myocardium. Her life is in real danger, so if we don't take her to the hospital soon, she will die. I will need two women to help me place her on the stretcher," Simone announced.

Immediately two women appeared to help her place Ivonne on the stretcher. One held her shoulders while the other pulled her feet up. Once Ivonne was on the stretcher, they hauled it into the ambulance. Simone climbed in the back of the ambulance to prepare and connect the resuscitation equipment. Testing the equipment to be sure it worked properly, she told her helpers to step out and close the back doors of the ambulance. Obeying her orders, they both stepped down. At that moment, Simone jumped to the front, took control of the wheel, and started the engine. Lowering her window, Simone thanked her helpers and, accelerating, disappeared with Ivonne inside, leaving them perplexed and stunned because they thought they would go with her.

Simone Blake's real name was Simone Eckberg. She was born in Lausanne, Switzerland, thirty years ago. Tall, blond, with intense blue eyes, Simone belonged to the upper class of Swiss society. Her father was a recognized banker. He became a widower when his wife died of breast cancer when Simone was barely four years old. Simone was educated in the best Swiss schools. Being an excellent student but exceptionally exemplary in sports, was accepted to be part of the Swiss Olympic team when was twelve years old, winning two silver medals in the high jump and pole vault competitions at age fourteen.

When Simone reached the age of fifteen, her father took her to climb the Swiss Alps with him, like the Jungfrau and Mount Pilates. On her twentieth birthday, as a gift, her father gave her permission to climb the tallest mountain in Switzerland with him, the Finsteraarhorn, whose height exceeded 14,032 feet. When they reached the top and started to descend the mountain, they were surprised by an avalanche, which thanks to her ability Simone avoided, but lamentably her father was hit and dragged down the hill, leaving him completely motionless and with severe bone fractures. Displaying her strength, Simone loaded her father over her shoulders and continued the descent.

When they arrived at the emergency clinic, her father was submitted to a thorough examination. After the doctor finished his examination, Simone was notified her father would be not be able to climb a mountain again in his life. Wiping tears from her eyes, Simone swore never to climb a mountain again in her life, a promise she kept for four years until she broke it at her father's insistence when friends invited her to climb Mount Everest, considered the tallest mountain in the world at 29,028 feet. That was a dream she had always had, so Simone accepted the challenge.

To be properly trained, Simone ran ten miles every day and swam other three hours without stopping. Feeling satisfied with her physical condition, she started to climb mountains again, such as the Finsteraarhorn, Viescherhorn, and Aletschhorn, whose heights were half that of Mount Everest but good enough to practice alternative breathing techniques for use when she lacked oxygen. After two years of practice, Simone was ready to do the climb. Saying goodbye to her father and other friends, Simone traveled to Nepal in the Himalayas, where she was to meet her friends for the expedition. Their climb turned out to be successful, as everybody in the expedition reached the top of the mountain. The success of her climb led her to be invited to participate in the mountain's rescue squad, where she learned advanced techniques of medical aid. Unfortunately, this work lasted only one year.

One day, Simone was invited by another friend to join the TIPA. Used to dangerous challenges, she accepted the offer, so before reaching the age of twenty-seven, she was admitted to participate in the institution. Albert Colliere soon heard about her merit and her feats, and he immediately invited her to be part of his team. Now Simone had to face the most important challenge of her life, the rescue of her boss's sister.

Having driven a prudent distance and looking to make sure no one had followed them, Simone stopped the ambulance abruptly. Exhibiting her sports ability, she jumped to the back of the ambulance where Ivonne remained lying. Seeing her eyes were closed, Simone approached to ask her, "Are you OK, Sister?"

"Oh yes, I feel great," Ivonne replied. "Do you think we were able to fool them?"

"I hope we did, Sister. I must confess I felt nervous when Gwen questioned me. For a moment I thought she suspected something, but fortunately, when she saw me dressed like a doctor with the stethoscope hanging around my neck, she believed all my answers. Nevertheless, we need to take action and try to alleviate any doubts that could come to her mind," Simone said.

"How did you arrive here, and who told you about my fainting?" asked Ivonne, intrigued. "I will answer your question quickly. Last night I climbed the wall, helped by a rope and a pulley, without being noticed by the tower guards. By the way, my name is Simone, and if I am not mistaken, your brother told you something about me, didn't he?"

At that moment Ivonne remembered her brother's instructions when he said a person named Simone would come to her rescue, and to just follow her instructions.

Simone moved closer to Ivonne and said, "Now that you're aware of who I am, I will tell you that everything was performed in accordance with your brother's plans, who entrusted me with the mission to rescue you. I need your cooperation and for you to follow my instructions without any further questions." Ivonne faced Simone and said she was sorry, but she refused to go with her because she first needed to accomplish her own mission. Furthermore, she had made a promise to a woman named Elysee to take her out of that place if someone came to her rescue. "And as she's relying on my promise, it would be ungrateful to leave her without her knowing I had left."

Simone showed her consent by saying they would take Elysee with them, even though her instructions were to bring Ivonne alone. Nevertheless, she figured her brother would not mind if they arrived with Elysee also. "Now, in regard to your mission, I will tell you it was diligently accomplished, as all the information you gathered and sent to your brother was of great value for us to formulate his plan of action. But at this moment, I beg you to forget everything regarding what happened and try to concentrate on the next steps to follow."

"I thought I had failed in my mission," Ivonne replied.

"Don't ever think that. Your intervention was of great value to accomplish our plan of action. When we have more time, I will explain to you everything that happened in detail," Simone answered.

Not really convinced by Simone's words, Ivonne really hoped she had not lied to her. Briefly and without interruption, Simone explained to

Ivonne the plan they had drawn up for her rescue. Being aware under her religious principles that violence was not to be contemplated, she promised, when possible, to avoid it. However, even thought she would try to prevent violent incidents, it was hard to know ahead of time that they would not have to face any, so to be prepared, she was going to hand her a gun in case they needed to defend themselves.

Ivonne immediately rejected the gun, that without even touching it, she said she never had used a gun before in her life and was not expecting to learn how to use one now. Simone understood her reasoning and without uttering a word put the gun inside her pocket.

CHAPTER 24

The infirmary's location was on the basement level, close to the elevator doors. Stepping out of the ambulance, Simone and Ivonne walked through a desolated corridor until they arrived at a door whose sign said, "For Authorized Personnel Only." Opening the door with caution, Simone walked inside, followed by Ivonne.

The infirmary was divided into two sections. The right side was used to treat serious cases and emergencies; therefore, it had several beds and the best equipment. In contrast, the left side had only two cubicles in which doctors treated patients with minor illnesses. Doctors Sarah Hollander and Nadia Hessler, both graduates of Duke University, were responsible for the two sections. Simone led her to the right side, where Ivonne saw two people lying on the floor. Their bodies seemed motionless as if they were dead; however, Ivonne saw their feet and hands tied and gags in their mouths, so immediately realized who they were.

Striking her cheeks softly and applying a shot to her right arm, Simone commanded Hollander to wake up. Still remaining in a sleepless state due to the previous shot, she had no idea what really was happening. "Doctor Hollander," Simone said, "we need your cooperation. Your refusal will make me kill your assistant, which I know you don't want to happen. Are you understanding me?" Simone asked.

Disturbed but understanding Simone's words, Hollander nodded her head affirmatively.

Seeing the doctor's disposition to cooperate, Simone removed the gag from her mouth and untied one of her hands. Simone requested her obedience and reminded her she would kill her assistant if she did not follow her instructions thoroughly. Understanding the meaning of

Simone's words, Doctor Hollander nodded her head affirmatively several times.

Feeling her mouth free of the gag, Doctor Hollander asked how they had gotten in there. Responding in a rude tone, Simone said that was not her concern, but now she should pay attention as she did not intend to repeat the instructions twice. All she had to do was dial the auditorium extension and request to speak to Gwen. When Gwen answered, Hollander was to read exactly what was written on a piece of paper. "Don't leave anything from this script out at any moment. If you start to say improper things, I will kill your assistant instantly. For your information, I will be listening to your conversation on another extension, and my gun will be pointed at the temple of your assistant all the time. Is that understood?"

Ivonne decides to intervene in the doctor's defense, saying that as she was willing to cooperate, it was unnecessary to keep pointing the gun at her assistant. Simone put down the gun and yielded to her request, saying this time she won, but if at any moment something went wrong, even with her pleading, she would have to kill her assistant. Ivonne did not respond but was pleased when she saw Simone lower her gun.

Following instructions, Doctor Hollander dialed the auditorium extension. A woman answered who said Gwen had left the auditorium with her companions five minutes ago. They could probably be found eating in the dining room. Doctor Hollander dialed the dining extension and told the person who answered of her need to speak with Gwen. In response, her interlocutor said Gwen was eating and hated to be disturbed, but after knowing it was Doctor Hollander who was calling and who said it was an emergency, she paged Gwen, who, when hearing her name, rose from her seat to take the call.

After apologizing to Gwen for interrupting her meal, Sarah Hollander expressed her worry over the nun's condition. Saying they had done everything that was possible to revive her, but they had failed as her vital signs did not respond. Her suggestion was taken her immediately to the hospital in Offenbach City. Previously she had talked with the doctor of that hospital, who, knowing the case, offered to have ready on their arrival a heart specialist to examine her immediately. She was also invited to join them if wanted. Also, expressing her need for another favor, she asked if she could warn the tower guards of their departure to prevent them from shooting. Their estimated time of departure was in approximately two hours, as they first needed to make arrangements for her transportation. Also, she said Doctor Blake was going with her so she could drive the ambulance while she, Doctor Hollander, took care of the patient. Nadia was staying as she had offered to take care of the patients while she was out. "Do you agree with my plans, Gwen?" Hollander asked.

Without any objections, Gwen consented to her demands, saying she would take care to warn the tower guards of their departure, but regarding her invitation to join them, she preferred to stay out of the matter. She advised Sarah not to forget to take her identity tag and use the password to the open the doors and deactivate the alarm systems. Gwen also reminded Hollander that if Sister Marguerite came to a fatal ending, not to compromise their organization. With that in mind, she was authorized to take from the hospital funds the cash she needed to pay the bills, avoiding the use of credit cards that could track them. If she needed more money, she should just call Gwen, and she would find a way to send it immediately. With a promise to follow her instructions, Hollander thanked Gwen and hung up.

When the conversation was over, Ivonne, alarmed, asked Simone what they were going to do if they lacked their identity tag and did not know the password that would open the doors and deactivate the alarm system. Simone patted Ivonne on the shoulder and said she did not have to worry as everything had been thought of in her brother's plan. Then, whispering in her ear, Simone confessed to Ivonne that she had extracted from Elysee's uniform her identity tag while she slept the previous night in her bedroom. For sure she did not know who took it, thinking someone had stolen it during her sleep. As was mentioned by her brother, Ivonne had Elysee's phone number, so she asked to call her and tell her they had her identity tag.

Searching her dress, Ivonne found the piece of paper where Elysee had written her phone number. While she dialed, she hoped Elysee would be available. Luck was on her side, as Elysee immediately answered.

Saying it was Sister Marguerite who was calling, she reminded Elysee of their conversation yesterday, when she promised if someone came to her rescue, she would take her with them. "Well, last night, that person arrived, and I convinced her to take you with us. I just want to know if your wish still holds true. If so, you should pay attention to my instructions. If you have questions, ask them now, as we are running against time, and if Gwen suspects something unusual is going on, we will be in deep trouble."

After Elysee expressed her desire to go with them, she was notified they had her identity tag. Elysee mentioned Susan had scolded her that morning, questioning and blaming her for losing her tag, giving her the day off to find it. Ivonne requested of Elysee a favor—if she could please pick up her luggage from her room. Elysee said she would try, not promising anything as she thought it would be dangerous for her to hide from cameras while walking through the hallway with a suitcase in hand. Taking the phone, Simone said in a rude tone of voice she did not care about her complaints but demanded she bring Ivonne's luggage.

Requesting a safe place where they could meet, Elysee suggested the basement of Building C. For her, that place was safe and easy to reach. Elysee knew they were located in the infirmary; so she gave instructions on how to get to Building C.

Free of ties, Doctor Hollander stood up and stretched her legs. Simone waited patiently until she finished, then she told the doctor of their desire to leave this place. As she was willing to cooperate, they did not intend to harm her. All they needed of her was to help them open the exit doors and deactivate the alarm systems by using her identity tag, password, and voice recognition. Hollander expressed her desire to cooperate but first wanted to know what their plans were for Doctor Hessler. Simone responded she was to give her another shot, making her sleep for several hours more, then free her of her bindings. She would be seated at her desk, and when she woke up, probably wouldn't remember anything that had happened. Agreeing with her terms, they walked toward the ambulance, where, following instructions, Hollander took control of the wheel while Sister Marguerite and Simone stayed at the back, watching her movements.

Arriving at the site, they found Elysee waiting for them. Climbing into the ambulance via the back doors, Elysee saw Ivonne and Simone seated in there. Suddenly a strange affection emerged between Simone and Elysee, as if they were old friends who had not seen each other in a long time. Elysee recognized the person at the wheel. She preferred not to ask questions and just said she had brought Sister Marguerite's suitcase as requested. Pleased with Elysee for accomplishing her assignment, Simone lowered her voice and, preventing Doctor Hollander from hearing, asked if anyone had seen her leaving.

Assuming she had taken good care to hide from the cameras, she thought no one had seen her figure walking with the suitcase. She suggested hurrying before someone could review the film. Simone agreed and immediately handed her a piece of paper on which she had made a transcription of the letter Gerald Solaris had given to his son describing the procedure to get inside Gwen's organization. Elysee was to read that paragraph and say if she agreed with that procedure. Reading the letter, Elysee said what it said was true; however, the procedures had changed, and now the security system was more accurate and complicated than before.

Simone demanded Elysee explain what changes she was referring to. The old system needed two doors opened before they could exit; the present one needed them to cross three doors. The old system required the driver to put her identity card and password into a machine, which, once verified, opened the first door. In the new system, the identity card was not an only a simple card with the driver's data as before, but it also had an electronic chip that, once placed in the windshield, took a picture of the vehicle and corroborated the driver's data. In both systems, after passing through it, the first door would close, leaving the driver trapped in a room in complete darkness. To continue to exit and light the room again, the driver needed to be properly recognized by voice. The old system required from the driver only the voice recognition to open the second door that led the driver through a dark tunnel that, when illuminated, disconnected the alarm system and allowed the vehicle to exit. Now the new system was different, as it required not only the driver's voice recognition to open the second door that closed immediately, but the driver also needed to set the vehicle on top of a sensor placed on the floor that, besides illuminating the tunnel, also disconnected the alarm system. Finally, the third door opened only when the vehicle approached, leaving it free access to exit.

"Oh my God!" Simone exclaimed loudly. Seeing Ivonne's expression, she apologized "Sorry, Sister, but the new security system prevents us from performing our previous exit plan. I will tell you why it won't work anymore. I received the instructions from my superiors that at the same time we exit the place in the ambulance, a group of commands needs to be introduced inside. The previous system allowed us to keep both doors open simultaneously. Now in the new system, it is impossible to practice this maneuver, as the second door closes immediately after passing through it. To open it again, it is not only necessary to have the driver's voice recognition, but the vehicle also has to hit a sensor located on the floor, which is placed at a far distance from the third door, making it impossible to keep the three doors simultaneously opened."

Elysee agreed with Simone's assumptions, saying in the new system, it was impossible to perform that maneuver, as the new system simply blocked the opening of a new door unless the other door was properly closed. Furthermore, she was afraid that if someone intended to keep the three doors opened simultaneously, the alarms would sound, alerting the tower guards. Also, in her belief, the time for the commanders to cross the whole entrance was too short, and they easily could be trapped without the opportunity to exit if one door closed before they could reach the next door.

Simone sounded desperate and said they had to think of another solution. Suddenly, she asked Elysee if when they needed to introduce several vehicles at the same time, did they use that same procedure? Elysee replied that for those cases, they had it programmed to open the three doors simultaneously, and to last longer, to disconnect the alarm system and prevent the alarms from sounding. Immediately Simone asked where those control systems were. Elysee did not know. Without wasting time, Simone turned around and faced Doctor Hollander to repeat the question. The doctor apologized for not understanding the meaning of her question, which made Simone lose control. With an angry voice, she repeated the question once more, warning the doctor to not make a fool of her or she would be killed. To make the doctor aware she was not playing, she unhooked her gun and pointed it at her temple.

Feeling the coolness of the gun on her temple, Doctor Hollander gave up, saying they had won, and she would take them where those systems were. She warned them the place was well protected and the systems were kept inside a vault that no one could open unless they knew the combination, which only Gwen, Susan, and maybe the guard knew. Furthermore, to open the vault, they needed to be experts in electrical systems, and if they thought she could help, they were wrong, as she was a doctor but not an electrician, so she suggested they should find another solution.

Without considering Doctor Hollander's words, Simone turned around and faced Ivonne, saying she knew by her brother's words she was good in such matters, so she needed her help to open the vault. With her characteristic humility, Ivonne responded she would make her best effort to help her. Thanking Ivonne, Simone shared her new plan of action.

"Doctor Hollander, take us where those systems are," Simone demanded, lowering her weapon and reestablishing the doctor's breathing.

Simone made Elysee responsible for Dr. Hollander's care, so she handed her the Beretta gun that once had been given to Sister Marguerite and which she had rejected. Elysee thanked Simone but said she preferred to use her own gun, which was a Ruger 22 mm caliber. After a brief discussion, Simone convinced Elysee to keep her gun and use the Beretta instead, which would be more impressive to the doctor.

Taking the Beretta, Elysee inspected and released the safety, saying the gun was familiar to her, as she had once used a similar one, which brought her sad memories. Simone preferred not to question Elysee and kept silent.

Doctor Hollander drove the ambulance, and they arrived at the site. As they were warned, a security guard came to them. Saluting the security guard on duty, Doctor Hollander said, "Good afternoon, Annette. The last I remember, you were on the morning shift." Annette responded she was correct, but she had come to replace Laurene, who was committed to another assignment. Also, she recalled Annette had gone to the infirmary looking for a remedy for her headaches and asked if the medication had worked well for her. Annette responded that her headaches had completely disappeared.

Sensing the nervousness in Dr. Hollander's voice, Annette asked what had brought her there. Doctor Hollander asked Annette if Gwen had not notified her of their coming. Facing the doctor, Annette answered she had never been notified someone was coming. "Maybe Laurene forgot to report the message to you," Hollander said. Annette responded it was difficult for that to happen because every time they received a message, it was written in a notebook so the next guard on duty could be informed.

Stretching her neck, Annette looked inside the ambulance and found the doctor was not alone, that other people were with her. Asking who those people were, Doctor Hollander responded they were two doctors and a sick person who needed immediate assistance and had been confined to a hospital in Offenbach City. Annette saw it was an emergency, so she asked what they needed from her. "We need you to extend the timing of the doors opening and to disconnect the alarm systems," Hollander replied.

"I guess I can help with that. However, I need to first get Gwen or Susan's authorizations. Without them, I am unable to help you," said Annette.

Seeing Annette walking toward the guard booth, Simone stepped out of the ambulance and calling Annette by name, she requested her to stop walking and put her hands over her head. Annette stopped but disobeying Simone's command to put her hands over her head, she unhooked her gun and turned around, ready to shoot whoever would dared to attack her. Seeing her reaction, Simone fired a bullet into the air, requesting Annette to throw her gun on the ground. Instead of proceeding as Simone asked, Annette started to fire her gun, forcing Simone to throw hers on the ground and avoid being hit by a bullet. Simone found a safe place to hide, and demanded Annette drop her gun and surrender. She refused Simone's order, and Annette continued shooting. The gunfire went on for several minutes until Annette, preparing to shoot, showed her head, and before she could fire, Simone hit her head with a bullet. Annette instantly collapsed on the ground. Cautiously and still with gun in hand, Simone approached to inspect her body lying inert and lifeless on the ground. Dragging the body inside the booth, Simone closed the door and walked toward her spectators in the ambulance. When she was ready to climb in the rear door, Ivonne stepped down and, horrified, chided Simone, saying she had promised to avoid violence. "Isn't the killing of a person a violent act for you?" Ivonne asked.

Simone tried to calm Sister Marguerite down, saying she had warned Annette several times, demanding she throw the gun to the ground before she started to shoot her. Disobeying her orders, had started to fire on her, forcing to hide to defend herself or otherwise she would be the one killed. "Would that be a better option for you?"

In a trembling voice, Ivonne answered, "Of course not. Don't ever say that."

"Then you have to believe that I did everything possible to stop the gunfire. I never had any intention of killing her, as I always thought Annette would be a helpful person when we needed to change the programs in the control systems. However, I could not let Annette call Gwen, who would immediately send more guards to trap us." Simone asked Ivonne to try to forget the horrible incident and instead concentrate on following her plan.

Ivonne could not believe her answer and asked Simone if she had any feelings. Simone replied she did, but during her training, they learned to leave their feelings behind and continue on with their assignment. Ivonne responded she had to differ from her opinion and requested God for forgiveness. Simone said she would be grateful if she was considered in Ivonne's prayers too.

Hollander, who was aware of what had happened, asked Simone why she had killed Annette, who was a good person. "Her disobedience led to her death. So take note, Doctor Hollander," Simone answered.

Simone was not about to lose more time and asked Doctor Hollander how far they were from the control systems. She said they were close, so she suggested to leave the ambulance parked there and walk.

Opening her suitcase, Ivonne extracted the tools she thought they would need to open the vault and put them inside the pocket of her dress. Stepping down from the ambulance, she ran to join the other women, who had walked ahead.

Forming a single line with Doctor Hollander leading the four women, they started to walk through an illuminated tunnel. After a walk of approximately ten minutes, Hollander stopped and with a sarcastic smile showed the site of the vault, saying now she would like to see them open it. In front of their eyes was an enormous vault manufactured of indestructible steel in the form of a cube. The dimensions of the vault seemed to be seven feet in width, seven feet in height, and seven feet in depth. At the front was a dark gray metal door with a silver handle, where the mechanism to open it seemed to be.

Simone ordered the doctor to take a step backward. She approached Elysee and whispered in her ear, saying was going with Sister Marguerite to examine the vault, and she should keep an eye on the doctor, warning her not to let the doctor do anything stupid. Therefore, should point the gun at her at all times, and if she needed to shoot her, was allowed to do it.

Once giving Elysee her instructions, she approached Ivonne, saying both would make a quick inspection of the vault.

From the pocket of her dress, Ivonne selected the stethoscope. Moving the opening mechanism slowly, she listened carefully to every click while moving the combination system from left to right and right to left several times. After failing at three attempts, she started to get desperate. Remembering her brother's lessons, she breathed deeply, trying to calm down. Leaving the stethoscope to one side, like a common burglar she stuck her ear to the safe, moving the dial slowly but accurately and listening carefully to every click that it made. Suddenly she felt the lock yield and the handle move. Being sure she had reached her objective, she pulled the handle to open the door slowly and carefully, fearing that opening it would make the alarms sound. Noticing nothing happened, Ivonne decided to step inside the vault.

Going inside the vault, Ivonne found it was perfectly illuminated. Making the first inspection, she stepped to her left, where found a board full of wires with different colors. Directing her sight to her right side, Ivonne saw several metal drawers with locks, resembling bank safe deposit boxes. For a moment her face showed frustration; however, leaving it aside, she made an effort to study the multiple wires of the control system. Luckily, raising her eyes, she saw hanging on the wall a diagram explaining in detail each section of the operational system.

Giving thanks to God, she proceeded to study and interpret the diagram. The alarm system was divided into sections, so after reviewing the drawing, she found the one that corresponded to the exit doors. Apparently, the mechanism was rather simple. All she had to do to disconnect the alarm was cut the red-colored wires.

Excited by her findings, Ivonne stepped out of the vault to update Simone on what had found. Simone proposed that both she and Ivonne cut the wires to save time. Agreeing with her, Ivonne said she would show Simone how to cut the wires, while she, Ivonne, would study the mechanism that opened the doors. That would save time. Agreeing with her, Simone asked for the clippers so she could start cutting the wires.

With renewed enthusiasm, both walked inside the vault. After explaining to Simone which wires to cut, Ivonne walked directly to the system that controlled the programming to open the doors. Inspecting the system, she found the program was controlled by a clock. Without wasting time, Ivonne proceeded to change the time to open the doors. She then moved the clock hands in order to keep the doors open not for the usual thirty seconds but to last three minutes, enough time for the commanders to go inside while they exited in the ambulance. Looking at her watch, Ivonne programmed the exit for 5:15 p.m., thinking thirty minutes was enough time to reach the ambulance and find the entrance. Completing her assignment to change the timing of the opening, Ivonne ran to help Simone, who was finishing cutting the final wires of the alarm system. Aware of the time left, they closed the vault and followed Elysee and Doctor Hollander to the ambulance. Doctor Hollander was at the wheel and was ordered her to drive them directly to the exit door.

On their way, Doctor Hollander laughed and asked if they were able to open the vault. Simone said that not only had Sister Marguerite opened the vault, but she also had disconnected the alarm systems and changed the time of the program that opened the doors. With great surprise, Doctor Hollander said she never could have imagined a nun performing that kind of job, but now she could see she had a gift granted by God.

Ivonne agreed and with humility said she was right, that God was who had granted her that gift.

In the ambulance, Simone approached Elysee, asking for her suggestion for a safe place where the commandos could hide. Thinking fast, Elysee suggested a place that immediately received Simone's approval. Now she needed to contact the main commander of their mission. For that she needed a radio to transmit the message.

Simone asked Doctor Hollander to pass her the ambulance radio. The doctor laughed, saying that radio had been out of service for a long time, and she had left hers in the infirmary. Simone turned to Elysee, who said using hers was too risky because Gwen could intercept her call at any time. Showing despair, Simone said she needed to make the transmission right away because Captain Midway the main commander of the group of commandos was expecting her call at any moment. Interrupting Simone, Ivonne said she had a radio on her computer that could be used for that purpose.

Simone ordered Ivonne to reset the radio at its lowest possible frequency so no one could detect them. Ivonne proceeded to do that. Her brother had taught her how to do it, so she lowered the frequency to five Hertz.

Elysee observed Ivonne's movements and said that at that frequency, no one could hear a message. Simone immediately shut Elysee up, saying nobody was asking for her opinion. When the radio was set to the lowest frequency, Ivonne passed it to Simone, explaining what to do to listen and speak.

Dialing the secret code, Simone said, "Rachel to Midway, do you read me? Over."

"Yes, we do. Over," responded the voice.

"Our expected time to exit the ambulance is in ten minutes. Alarms were disconnected and the time of the program to keep the doors open was changed to three minutes. Once you go inside, you'll find a circle with three paths. Take the right one and walk straight until you find in approximately 1,000 feet a two-story building with no windows. Surround the place, and in back is a black door. Push it and go inside. No smoking as the site is full of explosive chemical materials. Remain in there until darkness falls. Over and out," Simone said.

"Understood. Over and out," Midway responded.

At 5:35 p.m. sharp, the ambulance drove out. Doctor Hollander left the place without further complications, while the group of commandos stayed outside hidden behind the trees, waiting impatiently for instructions from the commander to begin their entry plan.

Seeing the ambulance depart, Midway lowered his hand and immediately, with indescribable discipline and efficiency, the commandos ran to the entrance, trying to avoid being seen by the tower guards, who once having notified Gwen of the ambulance's departure did not pay much attention to what has happening below.

At 5:37, the group of commandos had concluded their entrance. Following Simone's instructions, Midway directed his small group of twenty men to the right-hand path. Walking straight, they found the two-story building with no windows previously mentioned to them. To be sure they were at the right site, Midway surrounded the place until he found the black door at the back. Without wasting time, Midway pushed the door, discovering a padlock was impeding its opening. Without showing despair, he called over his sergeant, Jeff, saying they needed to open the door. They looked the padlock, and with his characteristic calm, Jeff Hoffman, after having examined it, gave such a tremendous kick that the lock broke into pieces.

Going inside, they found a dark room. A cold and humid breeze invaded the interior, making difficult to breathe. Remembering Simone's words, Midway mentioned the room was full of explosive chemical materials, so it was strictly forbidden to light any cigarettes or matches. After congratulating his commandos for the success of their entrance, he said they should remain in that room until darkness fell. In the meantime, they could rest or sleep, as he would take care of waking them up when the time came to start their mission.

CHAPTER 25

G wen was reading a book in her room when her cell phone rang. Answering, she heard Susan's voice, who, alarmed, asked for Elysee, saying she had been looking for her all day. She had called her cell phone, but no one answered. "Were you aware that Elysee lost her identity tag last night? She believes someone stole it from her uniform," said Susan. She had interrogated her that morning but denied she knew who stole it. No one could go inside her laboratory without an identity tag. So if by tomorrow she was unable to find it, she would have to authorize a replacement for her. And even worse, she could not find Sister Marguerite either. They had inspected her room and found no luggage in there. "Do you know where she can be?" Susan asked.

Trying to calm Susan, Gwen said that unfortunately, Sister Marguerite had suffered a heart attack while was in the auditorium and was urgently taken to the hospital in Offenbach. Doctor Hollander was in charge of her medical attention. Surely it was she who took Sister Marguerite's luggage from her room. Also, she had warned Doctor Hollander to keep them out from that matter, if Sister Marguerite have a fatal ending. It was she who had personally authorized their departure in the ambulance, and had notified the tower guards so they would not shoot at them. But in regard to Elysee, she did not know where she could be. She supposed she was still looking for her identity tag and promised to keep Susan posted if had news from Elysee.

Susan was not really convinced and expressed to Gwen her distrust of Sister Marguerite, saying many strange things had happened since her arrival. Meanwhile, she promised to follow Gwen's advice and try to stay calm. Then she said would be working in her laboratory until midnight, as she had to finish some experiments with her microbes that started a week ago. Early in the morning, Gwen would find on her desk a full report with more details. Thanking Susan, Gwen promised to examine the report and send her comments in brief. Ending the conversation, Susan said goodbye to Gwen and hung up.

Ten minutes after their departure, Simone ordered Doctor Hollander to stop the ambulance. They were to make some changes. She would go to the back with Elysee while Sister Marguerite came to the front and served as copilot. "Sorry, but for security reasons, we have to blindfold you and tie your hands again," said Simone. Elysee would be taking care of her, so she should behave as Elysee was authorized to shoot her if necessary.

Taking control of the wheel, Simone showed Ivonne a map of Frankfurt City. She was to find a small airport circled in red. That was their destination. They needed to arrive there in less than an hour as a plane was waiting for them. She should try to travel on rural roads, avoiding the main highways when possible, as besides being less safe, they were more traceable.

Speeding the ambulance, Simone drove across local roads. Following instructions, Ivonne directed her, avoiding the main highways when possible and going on rural roads. Arriving at an intersection where several highways divided, Ivonne asked Simone to lower her speed, as she had found a shortcut on the map that would lead them directly to their final destination.

Approving her route, Simone said the shortcut would save them fifteen minutes of driving. While Simone drove the shortcut road, something unexpected happened at the back of the ambulance. A discussion between Doctor Hollander and Elysee took place. Doctor Hollander was expressing her understanding of Elysee's hated toward her. "Believe me, Elysee, it was not my fault. Your own failures led Susan to the decision to replace you with me," Hollander said. Elysee replied she had no interest in being reminded of the incident again.

"Elysee," Hollander said, "I bet you don't know the history of my arrival to Gwen's organization. Now that we have time, I will tell you.

"Everything started when I finished my doctorate at Stanford University. I was hired to work in a small hospital close to Chicago. My companions at work considered me a nerd, as I never dated men, and my work was the only important thing in my life. However, one night while I was still working in my office, a female doctor came in, inviting me to a wrestling match. I first rejected her invitation, but at her insistence, I ended up accepting. The show did not attract me at all, but after the fight, my companion invited me to go to the dressing room of a fighter named Rolando, who was the big star of the show. Born in Puerto Rico, he was twenty-seven years old and a handsome man, to whom I must admit I immediately felt an attraction I had never before experienced with another man. That same night, Rolando invited us to dine in an elegant restaurant. To my surprise, Rolando was not only a wrestler six foot six inches tall and weighing two hundred and thirty pounds, but he was also an educated and intelligent man, who for economic reasons had become a wrestler. His real vocation was as an archeologist.

"The next morning at our meeting, I received from Rolando a beautiful bouquet of roses. Since that moment, his invitations became more frequent. One night after giving me a passionate kiss, he proposed I move into his place. At first I resisted, but after his insistence, I accepted, moving all my things to his apartment the next day. Six months passed without complaint. However, one night while I was working in the hospital, I felt sick. Asking my superiors permission to leave the hospital, I arrived home early and found Rolando completely naked and drunk with two prostitutes, one on each side of him lying in our bed. When the two prostitutes saw me, they took their clothes and left. After I chided Rolando, he rose out of bed and, without even covering his nudity, threatened me, saying, 'I am a man, and no one can stop me from doing what I want. For your information, you'll never satisfy my sexual needs completely, so I looked for someone else besides you, finding my total satisfaction in the two poor prostitutes that you chased away. Furthermore, I was feeling sad tonight since I lost my last opportunity to compete for the world championship, which I have to blame you for. I did not train well enough because of being with you.'

"'How can you blame me for what happened to you tonight, when everything I've made since I met you was to love and take care of you' I said. Approaching him, I tried to console him, but I received in response a hard punch to my face that threw me straight to the wall. In his anger, he started to throw everything at hand at me. Frightened, I ran, trying to reach the door, and found that his body impeded my exit. Then, grabbing my hair, he smashed my face on the door, breaking my nose. In complete desperation, I kicked his balls, knocking him down, and then I took a chair and smashed it over his head. Blood spilled and stained the floor. After he touched his wound with one hand, he emitted a strident guttural noise before continuing to hit me savagely. With my last strength, I took a bottle of wine that was on the dining table and, breaking it into pieces, thrust the glass into his stomach. He fell to the floor, gasping for air, saying he never thought I would kill him in such a way. Our neighbors heard the loud noises and had called the police, who shortly arrived with an ambulance and paramedics. Seeing my wounds I was immediately taken to the nearest hospital. Unfortunately, Rolando was not that lucky, and he died on his way to the hospital.

"After several weeks in the hospital I recover from my wounds. Later was submitted to trial. An incompetent defense lawyer and a jury of only men found me guilty of committing murder in the first degree, with a sentence of twenty years in prison. During my stay in prison, I was submitted to all kinds of sexual abuse and mistreatment from the male guards. Even the director of the prison had sexual relations with me in exchange for granting me some privileges. My hatred for men increased every day. I swore that if one day I was left free again, I would take revenge against them. I believe my prayers were heard, as one day after being in prison for three years, I finally was freed when a female lawyer proved I had killed Roland in self-defense while he was hitting me savagely. Later I knew it was Susan who had sent that lawyer, and since then I have been extremely grateful to her. Furthermore, two years ago, Susan helped me to pay for my studies to be a doctor of nuclear medicine. My contribution was of great value to her experiments. Now, confidentially, I can tell you we are really close to reaching revenge against men. The success of her experiments will be a key factor in ending women's discrimination in the world.

"All right, Sarah, now that I've heard your version, what do you need from me?" Elysee asked.

"I want to ask of you a big favor."

"What favor is that?" asked Elysee, intrigued.

"I need for you to kill me."

"Why should I kill you?" Elysee asked

"Because I prefer to die than betray Susan". Hollander said to Elysee while she drove the ambulance she had thought about her future, coming to the conclusion that all they wanted from her was to tell them everything she knew about their organization. "Once getting my confession, they will surely torture or even kill me. If that happens, everything I know about Susan's experiments will be uncovered, putting at risk her whole project of taking revenge against men." Betraying Susan would be awful to her, so she begged to be killed. Knowing Elysee's hate she always professed for her, it was a great opportunity to take revenge and kill her.

Understanding what the doctor meant, Elysee agreed to her request and, pointing the gun at her temple, she prepared to pull the trigger. Suddenly, the doctor stopped her and said before she was killed, she needed another favor from her. Elysee asked what that favor was. Hollander said she wanted her hands untied and blindfold removed so she could see the moment was shot.

To fulfill her request, Elysee proceeded to remove the blindfold and untie the doctor's hands. She now begged Elysee to shoot her straight in her heart so she would die sooner and with less pain. "Do it promptly before I back out of my decision" Hollander demanded. Elysee pointed the gun at her chest but then lowered it, saying she was sorry but she was unable to do it.

Doctor Hollander insisted she shoot her, reminding Elysee when she belonged to the D Squad and had killed so many people. Elysee said that was different, as she never had to kill someone face to face. Hollander asked Elysee to hand her the gun so she could kill herself. Without thinking of the consequences, Elysee handed the gun to her. Once it was in the doctor's hand, Hollander loudly insulted her, asking how she could be so innocent and such a bloody bitch at the same time. "Don't tell me you are not guilty of killing the embryos of those poor pregnant women."

"Susan thought I was stupid when I failed to mix the semen from several men into one element. But were you aware that when I performed the autopsy on those pregnant women, I found in their ovaries semen contaminated with a substance I never used? Elysee, you were the only person with the experience and knowledge to know what would cause that contaminated semen in those women. I believe your purpose in doing that was to discredit me in Susan's eyes, thinking that my failure would make Susan replace me with you again. I must admit your plan worked well, as Susan began to mistrust me. She never again kept me at her side in her experiments as she had before. Now tell me, Elysee, was that your real purpose, or were you planning something else?" asked Hollander. "Never mind. You don't need to answer my question. The reason is in the past. Now it is more important for me to know what the mission of those commandos is. Who went inside when we departed in the ambulance?" Hollander asked.

Elysee threatened the doctor, saying even if she knew, she would never tell her. Doctor Hollander was not pleased with her answer and said, "Don't tease me, bad girl. Instead, try to cooperate." Elysee spit on her face. Doctor Hollander lost her temper, saying nothing would stop her now from killing her and her companions.

To prove how brave she was, Elysee threatened Sarah, saying she demand her to shoot straight to her heart. Hollander was so angry that she answered, "Is that a threat or a suggestion?"

"You can take it as you want, but just proceed to shoot me, Sarah," Elysee demanded.

Reacting with anger, Doctor Hollander released the trigger and furiously cut cartridge before saying, "All right, Elysee, before to kill you everyone has the right to request a favor. What will be yours?"

Quickly Elysee answered she wanted to know if her former husband, Emille Salim, was among Susan's prisoners. Hollander replied she did not know the names, although Susan had informed her that some were very important people. Without providing an opportunity to end the conversation, Elysee asked what Susan's purpose was in keeping them imprisoned. "She said some would be used in her experiments, but others would be used to deal with in negotiations."

Annoyed at her questions, Doctor Hollander said Elysee's time was up and she needed to kill her. Doctor Hollander was preparing to shoot when Elysee noticed her hand trembling. With a quick movement, Elysee rose from her seat to give a tremendous kick to Hollander's stomach, who fell to the ground in pain but without losing possession of her gun. Seeing the doctor could hardly breathe, Elysee threw herself on her body, intending to disarm her. During the struggle, Elysee shot a bullet in the air to warn her companions something bad was happening in the back of the ambulance. The doctor's strength beat Elysee, who regaining possession of the gun demand Elysee return to her seat

Hearing the shot, Simone stopped the ambulance immediately. Asking Ivonne to remain seated, she stepped out of the ambulance and, unhooking her gun carefully, approached the back to find out what was happening. When Simone approached to open the back doors of the ambulance, she was surprised by a tremendous slam in the face, making her fall and hit her head on the paved ground, leaving her momentarily semi-conscious. Seeing Doctor Hollander that Simone could not move and was lying inert. She jumped on her body and pointed the gun at her temple.

Having remained seated in the ambulance on Simone's orders, Ivonne felt her sixth sense and decided to take her minicomputer out of the pocket of her dress. Finding the red button hidden at the back that her brother had advised her to press if she felt was in danger, she pressed it, hoping someone would get her message and come to help. Then, disobeying Simone's orders, Ivonne stepped out of the ambulance and found Doctor Hollander pointing a gun at both Simone's and Elysee's bodies.

Without feeling fear, Ivonne approached the doctor, reminding her that on one occasion, Simone had saved her life and that now was the time to return that favor. She hoped her words would stop the doctor from killing them. When the doctor saw Ivonne coming closer, she commanded her to stop, saying if she wanted to see her companions alive, she would have to cooperate with her. Ivonne promised she would do what she demanded in exchange for her promise not to kill the two other women. Hollander agreed to those terms. The doctor told Ivonne to help her tie Simone and Elysee around the trunk of a tree. Both hands should remain tied at the back and with strong knots. When she finished with that task, she was to hand Hollander the rope so she could tie Ivonne also around the same tree. The task was performed according to her instructions.

When the doctor saw them perfectly tied around the tree, she said she would go in the ambulance to tell Susan what the commandos were intending to do. She also said she hoped that Ivonne had contemplated their rescue in her prayers; otherwise, the crows would take care of their bodies, which in that case wouldn't be her fault. She expressed her desire to blindfold them and put gags in their mouths, but she desisted after thinking it would be better and more impactful for them to see when the hungry crows would fly around their bodies looking for food. Furthermore, that would help Sister Marguerite say her prayers aloud to God. Hollander honestly thought only a miracle would save them. Feeling sorry to leave them in such a precarious condition, she mentioned her time was running out, and she had to notify Susan what to expect from the commandos. Maybe the next time they met would be in heaven, or probably in hell, who knew? With a mocking laugh, Hollander left them.

Seeing Doctor Hollander leaving and wishing them luck, Elysee asked how they could ask for help if they were tied up. Recovering her strength and speaking for the first time, Simone said they had to stop Doctor Hollander from telling Susan what the commandos intended to do. Seeing her recovered, Ivonne asked how she was feeling. Replying with a smile, Simone said she felt dizzy and maybe had a bump on her head, but otherwise she was OK.

To calm Elysee, Ivonne mentioned that before everything happened, she was able to send a message requesting her brother's help. She trusted he had heard her message and soon would send someone to their rescue.

Ivonne said she still feel guilty for her failure to get the information off of Susan's computer. Simone replied she did not have to worry since that information should by now be in her brother's hand. "How can that be if I failed to get it?"

"Because the information you sent to your brother was of great value to elaborate the plans for our mission." Ivonne asked Simone to be more specific. Breathing deeply, Simone said that the previous night, she had climbed the wall to go inside Gwen's organization. Walking into Building A and specifically Elysee's bedroom, she found her deep asleep. "With extreme care, I detached the identity tag from her uniform, which allowed me later to go inside Susan's laboratory. Helped by some pictures you sent from Elysee to your brother, they tailored for me a wig exactly like Elysees hair and a uniform the same as the one Elysee wears. With a similar appearance and using the identity tag, I was able to deceive the guard who was in charge of the entrance to Susan's laboratory. Walking inside the laboratory found Susan's office, unlocking the door I found the computer on her desk. Without wasting time, I dismantled the keyboard and introduced the chip that is to give us access to passwords and information. Making sure not to leave a trace of my work, I closed the office. Fortunately, the guard did not pay further attention when I left the laboratory. So it everything goes well, all the information from Susan's computer should by now be in your brother's hands."

Elysee could not believe what she was hearing and repeated her understanding that Susan's experiments were now in the hands of Sister Marguerite's brother. "Exactly, Elysee, or at least that is my hope," Simone said. Ivonne now understood why her brother had stopped her from getting the videos from Gwen's room.

"Sorry for interrupting your conversation, but something keeps bothering me," Elysee said

"What is that?" Simone asked, holding back her anger at being interrupted from her previous conversation.

"I would like to know what I can expect of my future." Thinking fast, Simone responded if they were lucky to be rescued alive, they would fly in a private airplane to Barajas Airport in Madrid, Spain. There, another plane would be waiting to take them directly to Lexington, Virginia, where they would gather with her director and other people that wanted to meet them.

"And after that meeting takes place, what can I expect?" Elysee asked again.

"Then you will be free to go wherever you choose," Simone replied, annoyed to answer so many questions.

"Sister Marguerite, do you think one day I will meet again with my ex-husband, Emille?" Elysee asked.

"No one rather than God can answer your question, Elysee," Ivonne replied with sincerity.

In the meantime, while the three women chatted, Doctor Hollander drove the ambulance, taking the same way Simone had before, hoping to soon find a highway that she recognized. Being in an excellent mood, she began to sing a song that she used to sing in her youth. The noise of her singing prevented her from hearing a helicopter that approached, flying above the ambulance. When at last she heard the sound, she sped up, trying to evade it. Seeing her efforts were useless, she lowered the window and shouted at the pilot to stop following her. Without paying attention to her warnings, the helicopter continued to follow. Annoyed, she began shouting to the pilot, who in return this time took a megaphone to demand the doctor stop driving. Instead of obeying his orders, she sped up her vehicle faster. Suddenly a person in the helicopter pointed a rifle and began shooting the ambulance's tires, deflating them and forcing the doctor to stop. Seeing the impossibility of continuing with her driving, Doctor Hollander jumped out of the ambulance and, using the front door as a shield, started to shoot her gun at the helicopter. The person in the helicopter pointed his rifle again and shot the doctor, who collapsed to the ground. Descending from a ladder hanging off the helicopter, the man touched ground and, approaching with care, went to where the doctor's body seemed to lie inert. When he approached to examine the doctor's body, Dr. Hollander took her gun and shoot to the intruder, who this time responded to its firing without contemplation of hitting the body and causing her immediate death.

Concluding his mission, the man on the ground heard a voice calling from the megaphone in the helicopter. "Karl, try to clear the road and move the ambulance to one side. See if you can find a place to bury the doctor's body. Meanwhile, I'll go see if can find Detective Colliere's sister and her companions."

CHAPTER 26

"Jeff, wake up. Darkness has fallen. The time has arrived to begin our mission," Midway said, trying to illuminate the sergeant's face with his small flashlight.

"I'm glad the moment has arrived as I was starting to get bored," Jeff replied.

"According to my watch, by now it should be dark outside. Jeff, don't you think it would be a good idea if we briefly reviewed our strategy of attack before going into the field?" Midway suggested.

To follow his captain's instructions, Jeff woke up his commandos, saying the moment they were waiting for had arrived, but before going to the field, Captain Midway was suggesting briefly reviewing their strategy of attack. If during his review questions arose, they should keep them to the end, that there would be time to answer them late. "Is that clear?"

Understanding, the commandos in a unison voice answered, "Yes sir."

While Jeff was speaking, Midway stayed at his right side, illuminating the sergeant's face with his lantern. Breathing deeply, Jeff started by saying, "Commandos, our mission is based on a fast operational displacement and the infiltration method of attack. Speed and discipline in movement are key factors for the success of this technique. As we are aware, this organization has implemented several security measures, making our maneuver more difficult to perform. Therefore, be careful and follow every step diligently, as any failure can put in the guards of the towers on alert, which would force us to change our strategy of attack. For that reason, be careful when you establish distances in your attacks and select the infiltration methods to use.

"This operation is classified as high risk, so be extremely cautious with your movements. Always do them with fast speed and visualize every opportunity. When you feel sure, attack. Just a last recommendation: try, when possible, to prevent any direct confrontation with your enemy, as our failure in this ground attack can later lead to a failure in the aerial attack.

"When every group ends their mission, find the best way to exit. When you exit, do so accurately, on time, and in the right place. At your departure, keep in constant communication with your companions, warning the other groups if you face a problem.

"Also, pay attention to your companions' signals when it is time to advance, and always have your machine gun prepared to fire. Don't ever take unnecessary risks, and always walk or run in a straight line. Keep a reasonable distance from your companion to prevent one shot, can kill both of you. I suggest it is reasonable to leave at least sixty feet of distance from your other companion. This way both of you will be protected. Kneel down if the enemy comes close to you. Immediately find a safe place to hide. Let the enemy approach, and when it becomes an easy target, attack. If you have to jump your enemy, put your knife in the throat and cover the mouth with your hand to impede their shouting. Always walk in dark places, that way your risk is minimized. If you hold someone prisoner, keep watch over them and do not harm until were properly questioned.

"When departing, use a different path than your entrance to prevent falling into an ambush. When you have finished your mission, contact the other groups to see if they did not face problems. Use your radio at its lowest possible frequency to avoid being detected. Also, don't forget to inform the aerial commandos of your position to avoid being fired on by them.

"Finally, take my advice on several matters that have worked well for me, saving my life. Always keep relaxed and unstressed because fear can take you make mistakes. Also, keep in mind that our worst enemy is time. So if you need to hide to be saved, put into practice the survival techniques you have learned. Use your radio and call the others, telling them your position. Find the right place to hide while you wait to be rescued. If unfortunately that rescue does not come soon, stay hidden in that place, and don't move until you can be sure no one has seen you. Don't ever estimate the place where you are hiding as the best because there is no safe place unless it is completely undetectable to the enemy, even at short distances. With this brief review, I have finished my comments."

Thanking Jeff for his remarks, Midway admitted It was of great value to them. However, he wanted to add a suggestion because he knew everybody in the room had families waiting for their return. His suggestion was never to take unnecessary risks unless completely necessary. "Feel confident, as all of you were properly trained to accomplish the mission. The success depends on you and not on luck." He wished them all the best and a safe return, promising on their return to have for them a bottle of wine to celebrate their success in their mission. Making a military salute, the commandos promised to be cautious in their attack and to make a safe return for the benefit of their families.

When Midway finished, Jeff said he would need eight volunteers to go with him and make the area recon. "Whoever wants to volunteer can take a step forward," Midway said. Everybody in the group gave a step forward, confronting Midway with the dilemma of choosing only eight of them.

Once his small battalion was made, Midway asked Jeff if he agreed. "Indeed, all my men are good to me," Jeff responded.

After receiving his acceptance, Midway reminded Jeff not to forget Rosco. Rosco was a tiny robot guided by remote control from a computer. Outfitted with a periscope and powerful camera with a zoom lens, Rosco was able to reach unbelievable places and avoid the vigilance of hidden cameras. Guided by remote control at a distance that exceeded 500 feet, it monitored every image that went to the computer, which could later be reproduced as pictures when needed. Rosco's creator was a German named Fritz Rosco, who sold his invention to TIPA for more than nine million dollars.

"Of course not! I would never forget Rosco. It is our key element and the first to go in our plan of action," Jeff responded with a smile.

Jeff and his small troop of commandos abandoned the place where they had to stay hidden for several hours. Following his commander's instructions, Jeff walked directly toward Building A, which he was informed was the headquarters of the main officers. At a prudent distance, Jeff stopped and watched the building. He saw some lights still on in the bedrooms. Extracting Rosco from his backpack, he started his plan of action.

With outstanding skills, Jeff guided Rosco directly to the air conditioning vent, which he knew crossed the whole building. Rosco took images of corridors, stairways, conference rooms, hallways, offices, dining rooms, and even bedrooms where doors remained open. After a survey of thirty-five minutes, Rosco returned to its base. Reviewing the pictures, Jeff gave his approval before returning Rosco to his backpack.

For the next step of his mission, Jeff guided his commandos directly to the airport, where two guards watched the entrance. Signaling to stop, Jeff said maybe he could fool those ladies with the airplane trick. He extracted from his backpack several pieces of a dismantled plane that, once assembled, he put into flight. Operated by remote control, the plane flew. Once he was sure the guards were following its flight, Jeff abruptly stopped the engine, making the plane crash to the ground. Surprised, the two guards ran to see the plane where it had crashed. When both kneeled down to examine the plane, two of the commandos jump them, covered their mouths, and cut their throats with knives. Concluding their task, the commandos returned to Jeff to receive instructions for their next assignment.

The next assignment was to take control of the plane flights. Jeff explained that the mission required three commandos to join him. Going to the upper level, they walked toward the flight control tower. Two women were in charge of flight. When they saw four armed commandos coming into the room, they raised their hands in a sign of surrender. With the commandos pointing at them with machine guns, Jeff looked for a place where he could lock them up. Finding the closet doors open, he pushed the women into it. Hands tied and gags in mouths, the two women received instructions to remain quite or otherwise be killed. Once those women were locked up, Jeff went to examine the keyboard that controlled the flights. Calling one commando, he gave orders to disconnect the panels that controlled the radar in order to lose detection of foreign planes that could approach. In the meantime, he was to go and meet Midway to receive instructions for the next step of their mission.

Having examined the pictures Rosco had taken, Midway discussed with Jeff where the commandos should be placed to prevent anyone from escaping. Four commandos would have to stay outside and block every possible exit. Each commando had to be prepared to point their weapons and request immediate surrender, and if anyone showed resistance, they were allowed to shoot them. The other four commandos were to go inside Building A. Their attack needed to be executed with extreme speed and discipline, each commando using an oxygen mask. Smoke bombs would be thrown into corridors, hallways, bedrooms, dining rooms, and even the auditorium to flush out anyone who had stayed inside when the attacks were finished.

Overcome by the smoke bombs, these women would desperately try to find a way to escape. The commandos should never trust anyone, and if someone came close, they were to point their weapons until the women surrendered and then to hold them as prisoners. "Remember," said Jeff, "our objective is not to kill but to hold them as prisoners and later get their confessions. But if they resist, shoot to kill, and their deaths will serve as a warning to the others."

Bill and the other three commandos were given another assignment. They would be responsible for setting bombs around Susan's laboratory. The bombs had a time set and would explode five minutes after being deactivated. Bill was the responsible person for the group with the assignment to press the red button that started the clock's countdown. He had to run fast and find a place to hide before the bombs exploded. If the bombs did not cause the expected destruction to Susan's laboratory, an aerial attack was scheduled for later.

Midway said he had reserved for himself the task of rescuing the prisoners, whom Susan kept hidden in a small building located on the northwest side of the development. Those prisoners had to be brought alive and safe to their own countries. Three of them were very important people but older than the others. These persons would probably need special help to walk and climb into the helicopter that would be waiting for them to take them to place unknown. The others were younger and probably could walk by themselves, "but remember, all of them must be rescued and taken safely to their homes." Their mission in both cases consisted of leading them and seeing them climb safely into the two helicopters. In the event the commandos saw someone firing at the helicopters, they were to shoot to kill with their machine guns. They could not take the risk of letting the rescued prisoners being injured.

For this mission, Jeff needed four commandos to join him. Two of them were to take care of the guards while the other two went inside with him to rescue the prisoners. At the time they saw them coming out with the prisoners, the two commandos who had stayed outside would take the responsibility of leading them to their respective helicopters. Jeff reminded them that the three elderly persons were to climb in the black helicopter while the others were to go in the green one. While this maneuver took place, everyone needed to be alert and help the other team when possible, but overall, they were to keep in mind that nothing bad must happen to any of the rescued prisoners. Their mission would end when all of the rescued prisoners were safely in the helicopters and sent to their own countries.

Once the attack plan was understood and the respective commandos selected for each mission, they left the place where had stayed hidden for several hours, promising to regather soon but in after their mission.

CHAPTER 27

Simone was getting worried. Soon night would fall, and the place where they were standing did not offer safe protection. It seemed almost impossible for someone to pass by them on the road and save them. Furthermore, if they didn't take immediate measures to protect themselves, such as making a good bonfire that would frighten the coyotes and wolves away, they would die by being eaten by them. The crows that flew in the sky increased in number, searching for their bodies. The situation was turning desperate and required a plan of action, as they could no longer stay waiting for someone to come to their rescue. They needed to take immediate measures to defend themselves; otherwise, an attack by those wild animals would be inevitable.

Simone moved to one side and tried to free herself from the tied rope. Seeing it was impossible, she asked her companions if they saw any possibility of free themselves from their bindings. Elysee answered that her ropes were tight and the knots strong, so she doubted she could get free. Ivonne made an effort to get free of her bonds, but seeing the impossibility, she responded she was in the same situation as Elysee.

Simone thought a moment, then said, "We have no other option and need to put an emergency plan into action; otherwise, we will all die. The plan won't work without your help, so pay attention to what I am about to say. On the count of three, both of you will push hard with your legs, trying to get closer to me. This maneuver will help me to loosen my ties. Once loosened, I'll make my best effort to twist my wrist, trying to get one hand free. If we can reach this objective, what follows would be a lot easier. For your information, when I belonged to the Mount Everest rescue squad, during my training we learned escape lessons, so now is the time to put them into practice."

Following Simone's instructions, on the count of three, Elysee and Ivonne pushed hard with their legs, trying to get closer to Simone. After repeating this several times, Elysee gave up, saying it was impossible for her to get any closer. Evaluating their efforts, Simone said her task was to prove if she was able to release her right hand first. With great effort and pain, Simone made several twists of her right wrist, which, after several attempts, she was able to free. Shouting with excitement, she showed them her right hand completely released. Sharing in Simone's success, the three women began to laugh incessantly. What followed was rather simple as Simone, once released, proceeded to untie her other companions.

Free of their bonds, the three women, at Simone's instance, started to collect dry branches, which they needed to make a good fire that, besides frightening the wild animals away, would serve as a signal if someone came to their rescue.

Finishing their tasks, Simone and Elysee went to sleep. Ivonne stayed awake to say her prayers. Suddenly Ivonne felt a strong vibration in her body. The computer was announcing a message was being sent. Reading the message, she knew it came from her brother. He was advising them not to move from there as he had sent a helicopter to their rescue. Waking up Simone, Ivonne showed her the message. After reading it, Simone returned to her sleep.

The night was getting cooler. A strong breeze blew in their faces, making them move closer to the fire. With the lack of food and water, Elysee started to complain, saying she could no longer resist surviving, and if someone did not come to their rescue soon, for sure they would all die. In order to console Elysee, Ivonne invited them all to pray. Elysee and Simone, who had not practiced any religion for several years, under the circumstances accepted Ivonne's proposition. Kneeling down and raising their eyes to the sky, they prayed to God, saying. "Dear God, if your will is to send somebody to our rescue, please do it promptly; otherwise, we will die of hunger and thirst."

While they prayed, they heard in the sky the sound of a helicopter approaching. Simone was the first to hear the noise and stopped her prayers. Standing up, she started to wave her hands wildly so the pilot could be aware of their presence. Following Simone's example, Elysee and Ivonne stood up and waved their hands. They started to shout loudly so the men in the helicopter could hear them. "We are here! Help, help! Please come to pick us up!"

The two men in the helicopter saw a campfire and the three female figures jumping wildly and waving their hands. Larry focused his binoculars on the point behind the trees and finally said with excitement, "Herman, I think at last we've found them."

Herman took the binoculars and focused on the point Larry had mentioned. Once he saw clearly the three women waving their hands, he said to Larry, "I think you are right, pal. Let's go get them."

With outstanding skill, Herman guided the helicopter to the indicated point, maneuvering around multiple trees that stood above the women. Larry, who kept focusing on the site, said to Herman, "Now I am sure these are the women we're looking for, as one seems to be dressed like a nun and the other like a doctor."

Herman made a plan for Larry, saying that while he kept the helicopter stable, once on the ground, Larry should wait for his instructions. Without further complications, Larry descended the ladder. Immediately after touching ground, he joined the three women, who, after greeting him, related the horrible experience they had lived through. Simone told Larry of the escape of Doctor Hollander in the ambulance and her intent to inform Gwen of what she knew about the commandos' mission. To calm Simone down, Larry mentioned how the doctor had been stopped. She had to believe their intention was never to harm her, but because she disobeyed their order to stop the ambulance, they had no other option but to shoot and kill her. Knowing of the doctor's death, Ivonne said a prayer to God, requesting His pardon.

Suddenly a voice came from the helicopter. Using a megaphone, Herman shouted loudly to Larry, saying they had no time to waste, as they needed to pick up Karl and take the ladies to the airport.

"This is what Herman wants us to do. With my help, you will climb into the helicopter," Larry said.

Simone proposed a plan to climb. She would go first because her experience climbing mountains would be helpful for this kind of job.

Sister Marguerite would be next and would be helped by Simone. Last would be Elysee. Larry would help her, staying on the ground and holding the ladder to keep it steady while the women climbed it because the air blowing from the helicopter move the ladder violently, making climbing more difficult. Seeing them safely seated in the helicopter, Larry would do his own climbing. Luckily, the maneuver was successfully performed according to Simone's instructions.

After picking up Karl, Herman flew to the airport. As they expected, a plane was waiting to take them to Madrid. Being escorted by six uniformed men to the plane, the three women were welcomed by the pilot and flight attendant. When they were properly seated with fastened seat belts, the plane doors were closed. Twenty minutes after takeoff, the flight attendant brought them on a tray several glasses of wine and different delicious cheeses. Rejecting the glass of wine, Ivonne showed her hunger by cutting a big piece of Swiss cheese. Both Elysee and Simone accepted the glass of wine and also cut a big piece of Roquefort cheese. After they finished their appetizers, the flight attendant removed their plates and brought for each a big plate with a delicious Parmesan chicken breast, with spinach a la cream as the side. Finally for dessert, they ate a big piece of chocolate pie with vanilla ice cream on top. When the women finished their meals, the flight attendant fold their tables and closed the curtains so they could sleep. In a moment, the three women were falling into a deep sleep.

The landing in Madrid was at a private airport, far from the regular terminals used by the commercial lines. Escorted by four uniformed men, the three women were led to a Falcon jet of eighteen seats. Once aboard, they received the pilot's welcome, offering them a pleasant flight. The interior of the plane displayed extreme luxury. It had been recently remodeled with a light gray-colored carpet that matched perfectly the color of the seats, which were in genuine leather and allowed the passenger to recline comfortably until they reached a completely horizontal position. Many U. S. congressmen had traveled in that plane. The eleven-hour flight proceeded without complications. The stress they had lived through before made them sleep profoundly, waking up only when they heard the flight attendant's voice announcing they were landing at the Lexington airport in Virginia.

CHAPTER 28

Standing at the bottom of the ladder of the plane, Albert waited impatiently for his sister to come down. In his right hand he was carrying a bouquet of roses. Seeing his sister stepping down the ladder, Albert approached to instruct Ivonne that when she received the bouquet of roses, she should put her minicomputer into the pocket of his suit. Following instructions, Ivonne did what her brother asked. After greeting Ivonne, Albert saluted Elysee and Simone, who stood separately from the rest of the group.

Addressing Elysee gently, Albert said it was a pleasure to meet her. Then going to Simone, he thanked her for bringing his sister back home safely. He said they would find time to talk later, but now he believed they were tired and wanted to rest, so he had made arrangements with his assistant to take them to a hotel. They would be picked up in three hours for a meeting scheduled with his general director and others who would join them. "Oh! I almost forgot to tell you that in the closet of your hotel room, you'll each find clean clothes that I personally selected and hope will fit your needs."

While Albert spoke, Elysee did not pay attention to his words, as she was waiting for just the right moment to ask him if among the prisoners they had rescued was Emille Salim, her former husband. Albert knew what Elysee wanted from him, so he innocently asked Elysee to what prisoners was she referring to. Surprised at his question, she answered, "The men Susan held prisoner in our organization." Apologizing, he said no one had revealed to him the names of prisoners; furthermore, he did not know if they had been safely rescued. In the afternoon, he was expecting to receive another report. Maybe in there he would find the answer to her question.

Thanking Colliere, Elysee said she would appreciate any information he could provide.

Excusing himself, Albert left, saying he still had work to do, but his assistant was to take care of them. After Albert left, a black limousine approached, ready to take them to their hotel. The driver, was dressed in a blue suit with a red tie. He opened the rear doors of the limousine. Helping the ladies to climb in and seeing them comfortably seated, Jonathan introduced himself and returned to his wheel and, without uttering a word, drove to the hotel. On their arrival, the general manager of the hotel was waiting for them to welcome the guests. At his signal, a bellboy approached to give them keys to their respective rooms. Jonathan stayed to watch the execution of his boss's orders, then left the hotel when he saw the women take the elevator after saying he would be back in three hours to take them to the office.

Alone in her room, Ivonne took her rosary from the pocket of her dress and prayed, thanking God for his help and mercy. Ending her prayers, she opened the closet, finding to her surprise clothes appropriate for a nun. Taking out the wool nightgown, she placed it under her pillow. Then she decided to take a quick shower and dress in her clean clothes. The new attire fit perfectly. Seeing she still had one hour remaining, she sat at the desk and started to write down the experiences she had lived through in Gwen's organization. When she finished, it was time to go down to the lobby and gather with Simone and Elysee. Finding a comfortable seat in the lobby, she waited for the arrival of her companions. To her surprise, when the elevator doors opened, she saw them both wearing similar apparel but in different colors. Their similar anatomy made them look like twin sisters. Ivonne immediately recognized how easy it had been for Simone to deceive the guard when she went into Susan's laboratory pretending to be Elysee.

Elysee confessed she felt weird wearing that attire that for years had not use a dress and just the military uniform. For a moment she had refused to put it on, but when she saw her uniform so dirty, she decided to wear it.

While the three women chatted, Jonathan made his appearance in the lobby, saying he was ready to take them back to the office. At their arrival,

Albert was waiting for them at the entrance of the building. Signaling his assistant, he ordered the three women to follow Jonathan.

Taking the private elevator, they arrived at the fourth level, where the conference room was located. Raymond Sullivan was chatting with two other people, but seeing the three women come in, he immediately interrupted his chat to approach and greet his guests, saying. "Ladies, Albert has not arrived yet. He must be present at our meeting. In the meantime, let me introduce myself to you. My name is Raymond Sullivan, and I am the director of this institution. My guess is you must be Sister Marguerite, and you, Elysee. As for Simone, I know her very well. I am really honored to have you all joining us in our meeting. I am aware of the important roles each one of you has played in our mission, so congratulations to you all," Sullivan said.

Simone wanted to give credit to his boss, so she said the brains was Detective Colliere. They only executed his plan, so he was the one who deserved the congratulations. Sullivan decided to end the conversation and, turning around, invited the two people with whom he was talking earlier to join them.

Introducing them, Sullivan said one was Lieutenant Samuel Lewis of the homicide squad of the Los Angeles Police Department. The other was Richard Solaris, son of Gerald Solaris, whose case was under investigation. Both of them had traveled from faraway places just to join them at their meeting. Extending hands, they greeted each other. Without wasting time, Sullivan invited them to eat lunch in the next room. Sandwiches, salads, soft drinks, and coffee were available. "Feel free to take whatever you want. Our meeting is scheduled to start in exactly twenty minutes, so if someone needs to use the restroom, do so now. After the meeting begins, no one will be allowed to leave the room."

Finishing their meals, the women went into the conference room. Each seat had a label with their names. With everybody seated and in complete silence, Albert made his appearance and walked to the podium. He took the microphone and said, "We are gathered today for the purpose of finding out who murdered Gerald Solaris and others. I might say that we have collected important information that will be shared with you in time. But before we start this meeting, everyone in this room must follow two rules. First, no one is allowed to use a cell phone, so please put yours in this envelope. Second, we all need to sign a nondisclosure agreement, promising never to reveal to anyone what will be said here today. The violation of this agreement will be punished by jail time. Do I make myself clear?" Albert announced in a demanding voice.

When his rules were agreed to and everything was set in accordance with his instructions, Albert proceeded to introduce Ivonne, who was to relate her experiences while she was in Gwen's organization. Then Elysee turn came who briefly related her marriage with Emille Salim and how she had met with Sister Marguerite, who later invited her to leave the organization with her.

The last to speak was Simone, who mentioned the way she had climbed the wall to go inside Gwen's organization and how she deceived the guard to go inside Susan's lab and stole the information from her computer.

After the remarks, Albert declared a ten-minute recess for people to stretch their legs and go to the restroom. When everybody was back and in perfect silence, Albert mentioned the next item on the agenda would be the behaviors of feminist groups and what they pretended to do. "As is well known, feminists base their principals on their hatred of men. The stigma that considered men superior to women is no longer valid in their vocabulary. The strength of men once used to subjugate women is totally unacceptable for them. Feminists follow principles that they only consider favorable to women. Feminists have developed actions and behaviors to defend women's rights against the mistreatment of men. Their protests have surpassed limits as they have manifested in streets, burning buses, breaking windows in shops, and even committing murder.

"To understand what feminists want, we will go back in history to when women claimed their freedom for the first time. France was the first country to have feminist groups. The French Revolution of 1789 made some isolated groups of women emerge, who started to protest against inequality with men. The French Revolution worked in their favor when they claimed they wanted justice through the same rights of freedom, equality, and fraternity as men. However, their movement never progressed, as it was stopped abruptly by the Napoleonic Code, which nullified the equal rights of men and women.

"The Industrial Revolution of 1840 brought to women their first acceptance as workers in the labor force. Even though their pay was less than that for men, the advances seemed favorable to her. However, this movement was later dissolved when Communism in Russia arose and the Catholic Church promised to give women a better way of life, something that never happened. The true liberation of women was due to the economic crisis and the inflation of prices throughout the world, which brought men unemployment and brought women to be accepted in the labor force. Even though her salary was less than that of men, she became a great support to her family. The salary earned from her work cut her dependence on and support of her husband. Once feeling free and independent of her husband, she started to demand divorce for her bad treatment. Birth control campaigns also helped. Besides stopping the increase in population, they worked to the benefit of women, improving her way of living.

"Women continue to fight. Today, their efforts are geared to conquering governmental positions. To reach her goals, she gathers with associations and institutions that offer to help in her fight against the aggressions of men. Most feminists considered religions their enemies, such as the Islamic religion, in which women are said to be treated worse than animals. Or even the Catholic religion, in which they refuse to accept a God who protects only men. Blaming God for the discrimination in the Catholic Church is unfair because it was the high hierarchs of the Church who manipulated the religion's concepts to their benefit, preventing women from entering the priesthood or climbing to high clerical positions in the Vatican, practices unacceptable to them. As with every religion, the Church should preach God's equality for men and women.

"Feminists believe women's weakness comes from giving birth to a child. Undesirable pregnancies are frequent; therefore, to abort a child has become a common practice. To stop relations with men, they prefer the acceptance of lesbian relationships. Feminists preach in schools and educational centers that every man is a potential violator who wants to harm them.

"For feminists, the practice of a woman serving her husband is unacceptable. For them, this practice is a sign of weakness that should be eliminated. In her new identity, a woman breaks the rules of the family role. Sons now see the father as prevented from asserting his power and the mother assuming decision-making in their home. Most feminists decide to keep the same gender but assume the role of men. For them, the woman's role as mother and wife has come to an end. The new division in activities makes men behave differently with women, as now his attitude should be of love and understanding; otherwise, he will lose her. Her knowledge and better education work in her favor, helping her to climb into higher positions in the governmental and business sectors. However, many men still resist letting women work. Their masculine tendency refuses to accept women exerting power, as many still think that women were better when performing the duties of home and fields.

"Feminists have ensured that the men of today are less masculine than before, as they have adopted feminine features such as wearing long hair, using earrings, and even putting makeup on their face. In contrast, women of today have adopted masculine features, such as wearing short hair, wearing pants, and even eliminating the use of makeup and jewelry. These changes have helped women to be better accepted in social, cultural, economic, and political sectors, but not in the ecclesiastical, in which her equality to men still looks distant. Men rely on their strength to defeat women, minimizing her intelligence and better preparation, which in a short time will be used to displace him from the pedestal in which he still stands today.

"Now that you are aware of what feminists wish to do, I will refer to a file found on Susan's computer that was classified as personal and confidential. The file describes Gwen and Susan joining Roselyn Taffish, an activist woman accused of causing serious problems to the French government as she frequently starts protests in the streets, burning buses and breaking shop windows. Jacques Depardieu, French Secretary of State, demanded that Roselyn stop her protests or he would take her to prison. Disobeying his orders, Roselyn went to prison. Her followers gathered, blocking several streets in Paris and demanding her freedom. Nevertheless, Jacques Depardieu never yielded to her petitions of freedom. One week after his refusal, Jacques Depardieu died in a plane crash when traveling with other members of his staff to a meeting of the European Union. The plane crashed into a mountain at low altitude. The pilot flying the plane belonged to the French air force of France, and two years before had receive the Medal of Merit for his outstanding flight skills. Now please, ask yourself this question: Do you think the plane crash was accidental or premeditated?" Albert asked.

"The next item on the agenda is explaining what led us to perform a surprise attack on Gwen installations," Albert pronounced

Albert said had broken out in a sweat when he heard the tape recording with Elysee's conversation his sister had sent him. "My detective's sixth sense made me feel something had gone wrong and my sister was in real danger. Without thinking twice, I turned to my director, Raymond Sullivan, who, after hearing the recording, shared my opinion. Without wasting time and granting me total authority, I started to elaborate a plan of action.

"Knowing Simone was in New Jersey on another assignment, I called her. Being aware of my urgency, she flew back to Lexington to receive instructions on how the rescue plan for my sister was to work. Receiving the necessary tools to perform her work, that same day Simone was flying to Frankfurt, arriving at night at Gwen's installations. Her mission consisted of rescuing my sister and bringing her safely home. Being Simone an excellent mountain climber, she scaled the wall and stole Elysee's ID tag from her room to get inside Susan's laboratory. After deceiving the guard by wearing a wig and uniform to what Elysee wore, Simone found in Susan's office her computer. Proceeding to detach the keyboard she install a chip allowing us to access her files, messages, documents, and information. However, to our surprise, when we tried to open the files with the information, we found they were encrypted with secret codes. Without wasting time, we put to work our high-tech machines, which contain innumerable dictionaries and billions of secret codes.

"It was not until three nights ago that we begin to decipher Susan's files, finding valuable information in them. In one of those files, classified by Susan as personal and confidential, we found information that I will describe later. Having opened the file, we started to read it, horrified and not believing what was written in there. Drawing an immediate plan of action that was discussed with my superiors, we all agreed it was necessary to make an immediate surprise attack on Gwen's installations specifically designed to destroy completely Susan's laboratory; otherwise, the consequences would be catastrophic.

"That same night, under Midway's command, a group of armed

commandos was traveling in a private jet to Gwen's installations. Their mission consisted of destroying all evidence of Susan's experiments and rescuing the prisoners Susan was holding.

"Most of you are probably wondering by now what was found in that file. First, I would like to mention that Susan's cruelty has no limits. Her hate and thirst for revenge against men are indescribable. Susan revealed how she and Gwen had met with Roselyn Taffish, a feminist activist leader who controlled more than 129 women's organizations in different countries. The purpose of the meeting was to sign an agreement with both organizations that will lead women into better positions in the social, cultural, political, and religious sectors and to fight against the inequality of wages with men. Also, proclaiming feminism should be taught in schools as an additional academic matter, where women would learn to defend themselves against discrimination and mistreatment by men. The agreement included first joining forces and then to eliminate the supremacy of men.

"Susan and Dr. Sarah Hollander were designated as those responsible for achieving these objectives. Their vast experience in exploring the life of microbes made them the right people to reach these objectives. Susan would be responsible for presenting her plan of action to the board of directors.

"Susan was expert in genetic manipulation techniques and in deciphering the language of life in microbes. Her experiments in genetic manipulation were concentrated on the substution of genes from an individual with outstanding skills into another who lacked of such genes. Her ability to reconstruct maps and redesign graphs with different scenarios was amazing, as she was able to identify and compare without error the characteristics of the genes of an individual and to know if they belonged or not to that same individual.

"Everything in the file seemed to be normal until we discovered the dark point unknown to us. Susan had discovered that inserting the male chromosomes of an individual with substituted genes of healthy, strong, and educated men who showed outstanding physical, neurological, psychological, and pathological characteristics into female ovaries could create a zygote with those characteristics. To perform this task, Susan needed to collect and mix the semen of several individuals to make only one element without it suffering decomposition. Susan failed in many of her attempts. Frustrated at her failures, Susan worked to find another solution, discovering that if she added a new element she called "*basal tremens*", the semen would not suffer decomposition when it was frozen. Helped by powerful microscopes, Susan discovered that the newly added element not only preserved the semen from suffering decomposition but also made the semen lose its sexual power, making it gradually grow weaker. Excited at her discovery Susan proceeded to insert the basal tremens into the feminine ovule, finding that in women, there were no side effects. Continuing with her tests, Susan found the weakness of semen not only made men lose their sexual power, but after a long time it could lead to erectile dysfunction and finally to complete impotency. To remember what she was doing, Susan wrote everything in detail on her computer, using formulas, symbols, codes, and graphics, which fortunately we were able to decipher on time, helped by our machines and experts.

"The next step for Susan was to find a way to insert the basal tremens in men without their noticing the side effects. Susan found the solution in her dreams. Despite knowing the risks she would confront, Susan decided to go on with her plan. To execute her plan, she wrote a list with the names of her feminist friends who at that time worked for prestigious international laboratories or health clinics. Susan had thought the best way to insert the basal tremens in men and women was as a vaccine injection used to combat certain contagious diseases. The dose for men would be stronger than for women. Susan knew by her tests that for women, there were no side effects. To make the vaccine, Susan needed the collaboration of international laboratories, which for her was not a big deal as many colleagues recognized her prestige. Her résumé as biologist was reliable, and nobody would doubt her discovery was no different from any other intended to combat another disease. Susan knew in advance that without the use of a powerful microscope, no one could detect the hidden element in the vaccine. Furthermore, the weakness of the semen in men would show delayed effects, so the signs of impotence would never be linked with the vaccine made the year before."

Simone could no longer hold in her anger and said that Susan was crazy and completely insane. How could she think to practice such an evil thing? Agreeing with her, Albert responded, "Just keep quiet and wait to hear what comes next.

"Susan's cruelty had no limit, and to execute her plan of inserting her vaccine with the element basal tremens, she thought first to practice it on the men she was holding prisoner in the warehouse building. Among them were important people whose names at this moment I am unable to reveal. Fortunately, with our surprise attack, we cut short her bad intentions, stopping her plan to take revenge against those poor men. The bombs thrown in her laboratory destroyed every minuscule particle of her tests. However, to be sure no evidence of her experiments was left, I ordered a thorough inspection. I expect to receive the report of these findings later tonight," said Albert.

Colliere took from the table the report Captain Midway have sent to him and read with detail their mission. Briefly he described how their attacks were performed. The one made to Gwen's hearquarters and the others to the tower of control in the airport and to Susan's lab.

Albert paused before to said, "I guess by now you are wondering what happened to Gwen and Susan when our attacks took place, or am I wrong? Let me tell you what happened to both of them. Susan was sleeping profoundly in her bedroom when the alarms sounded and woke her up. Seeing smoke inside her bedroom, Susan ran through the hallway to find out what was happening. Leaving her bedroom, she encountered in the hallway a group of armed commandos who were moving toward her room. Susan instantly realized something was going wrong, and she returned to her room and closed the door. Following her principle that it is better to die than become a prisoner, Susan took a strong dose of drugs that she used to calm her nerves. When the commandos entered her room, they found Susan lying on the floor. Seeing that she was still breathing, a commando gave her respiratory aid that failed, and Susan expired. However, before dying, she was able to say that no matter what happened to them, the empowerment of women was under way, and nothing would stop it. Gwen was luckier than Susan as she was able to escape through an emergency exit unknown to us. Nevertheless, we are confident that the confession of her companions will soon lead us to her," Albert said.

"Also, Susan mentioned in another computer file what had happened to the three women in her experiments who got pregnant. According to her, those three pregnant women were expecting the birth of girls with outstanding features in about two months more to prove to men what this new generation of women would be able to do. However, and in spite of her efforts and care, the three women unexpectedly started to suffer from constant hemorrhages. Her tests showed an abnormal growth in their embryos. Susan tried to stop these growths but failed, and the three women die two weeks later, matter that made her start taking drugs, possibly the same she used when she decided to end her own life."

Richard could no longer hold his question and, on an impulse, he asked, "By now you must know who killed my father."

Sullivan chose to respond. "Not yet, Richard, but we are close to finding who did it. We feel confident in our findings, but we need more evidence to trap the killer. Somebody is in our mind, but for obvious reasons, we cannot at this moment reveal the name."

"Our next item on the agenda is to comment briefly on what so strongly impacted Gerald Solaris when he saw the videos," Albert interrupted. "To prevent misunderstandings, we invited Liu Wong Yen, who in his own words will tell you what he lived through together with Gerald Solaris. Liu performed an important role in Gerald Solaris's life, as they were both hired to be part of Gwen's team. Liu was present when Gerald Solaris saw the videos that so strongly impacted him. The last news we had about Liu is that he was missing, and Jacob was unable to find him, supposing he died when the car bomb exploded in Shanghai, China, killing and injuring several people. But to our surprise, Liu is not dead and appeared last night in our offices to tell us things that we did not know about Gwen's organization and that now he is disposed to share with you."

At Albert's signal, a man of approximately fifty-six years of age, a slim figure and abundant white hair, walked inside the conference room. Richard immediately recognized him to be the same person he saw was two years before that night when he visited his father in Los Angeles.

Avoiding introductions, Albert conducted Liu to the stage. Liu showed shyness, thanking the group for giving him the opportunity to share his experiences. "First, I want to tell you I met Gerald Solaris several years ago when Gwen gathered us with four other people in a small conference room at her office. After Gwen offered a light snack rejected by most of us, she walked toward a bookcase located at the back right-side corner of the room. The bookcase kept hidden a safe embedded in the wall that, when a Rembrandt painting was moved to the left, came at the sight. Opening the safe, Gwen extracted several boxes containing videos that later were put into a videocassette player and projected onto a gigantic TV screen.

"Gerald Solaris was at that moment the only person in the room who had not previously seen the videos, so Gwen advised the videos were strictly confidential, and their content should never be revealed to anyone, as they would put at risk her organization, bringing to them terrible consequences. Briefly, I will try to discuss what we saw.

"The first video described the history and status of Gwen's organization. The second video showed the procedures they followed to select their candidates for their organization. The third video showed the number of current members and what the expected increase was in the following years. The fourth video described the amount of income they collected from different sources and what they intended to do with it. If I am allowed, I can tell in detail what was found in each one," said Liu, looking at Albert, who was nodding his head, authorizing him to do it.

Inhaling air, Liu started his explanation by describing the first video in which Gwen and Susan joined forces to make a partnership agreement, with the commitment to defend women against the mistreatment and discrimination inflicted by men. Following their objective, they created an institution they named as INPOWER. In that same video, they listed and outlined the obligations, rights, and goals to follow in the future.

"In the second video were explained the methods of induction they used to select their candidates who have suffered discriminations from men, and how they trained these women to defend their rights against the abuses inflicted of parents, husbands, and bosses. The video exhibited how a woman married to a millionaire deprived her husband of his fortune in a divorce, discrediting him among the financial community, which, after knowing of his income reduction, made him fall into bankruptcy when was unable to pay his debts. In the same video was the case of an actress who, to get million-dollar contracts, was the lover of a movie producer, who in exchange for her sexual favors paid her stratospheric salaries in movies, salaries that had never been reached by other famous male actors. In another part of the video was shown a case in which a politician did not care to help her lover climbed into the first level of governmental positions in exchange for going to bed with her, and how this same woman denounced him later in public for infidelity, breaking his aspirations to be selected as the candidate for the presidency of his party. In summary, each case showed the lessons taught to women on how to use the weakness of men to work in their favor, who once glimpse by her beauty and attractiveness would concede to her demands, even sacrificing his own prestige. At the end, the video stated how these women winning their cases, would gratefully reward Gwen's organization giving a generous monetary donation.

"The third video had the most impact, as it showed the number of current members they had and the expected growth in the following years. The method the organization used to bring in candidates was called geometric progression. Its operation was simple: two women who had suffered discrimination and mistreatment by men would collaborate, each one bringing two other women who had suffered the same harm. These four women, then, were each committed to bringing two more women, adding eight women, who later should bring another two, bringing the number to sixteen women and so on. The procedure could reach an exponential growth. So if the number of members when we saw the video was two hundred, maybe by today it could exceed fifty thousand. The procedure to find candidates was different in every case, as some of these women were scattered around the world. They were found when their pictures appeared in magazines or newspapers or on radio or TV. Hospitals, police stations, and courts were also sources to finding these women. Even the army qualified as a good place to find them. Once these violated and mistreated women were contacted, they would receive monetary help from Gwen's organization for their travel expenses. Arriving at Gwen's organization, they were submitted to several tests in order to know their present physical condition and educational level. The tests were performed by expert psychologists and physiotherapists, hired by Gwen to remove their trauma and to teach them how to defend themselves when they suffered attacks from men. When their training courses were finalized, the newcomers were evaluated. Those who were outstanding might be qualified to be hired as teachers or to take care of the newcomers. Gwen was intending to open several clinics around the world with independent management by the Germany headquarters. The travel expenses during their stay were paid by Gwen's organization, which later requested a refund when they were able to provide it."

Apologizing for the interruption, Albert asked Liu if he had heard Gwen speak of the Death Squad. Liu responded he had not and had no idea what he was talking about. Albert said he would briefly explain what he had found in a file regarding the Death Squad.

"The Death Squad is a separate division of Gwen's main organization. The supreme commanders are also Gwen and Susan. The Death squad better known as D Squad is made up of 500 women, properly trained to kidnap and kill men. Their training requires a strict military discipline as their objective is to kill every man who interferes with them. The D-Squad counts among them extraordinary snipers and teachers of martial arts and war techniques. Their training goes beyond the normal aeronautical engineering or automotive mechanics, being able to set explosives in planes, cars, and other places without being detected. The equipment and weapons used by them are quite impressive. Most of them are high executives in Gwen's organization, but others are scattered around the world, whom we need to find immediately before they continue to cause further damage.

"Now, to my mind come several cases of air and land accidents that maybe were performed by the D-Squad. Even Hemant and Gerald Solaris could have been killed by someone belonging to this squad."

"How did you discover the existence of the D-Squad?" Liu asked.

Albert said everything was detailed in files from Susan's computer. Then he apologized for interrupting Liu's remarks and said could continue.

"As I was saying before the interruption, the fourth video described the different sources they used to collect money and how that money was spent later. The amount of money they had collected was impressive, exceeding thousands of millions dollars. The sources were several. Some came from Gwen's own fortune, others were donations received from grateful women for winning their cases. Extortion became a common practice to increase their income. Men paid great amounts of money to stop their infidelities or dirty businesses being exposed to their wives. Therefore, it was notorious that the outstanding figures for these procedures were women who, after using their glamour as a weapon, made men succumb to their desires. The income collected later was used to bribe authorities, to pay personnel working for the organization generously, or simply to cover their daily expenses."

Liu was starting to comment on how Gwen had threatened them to belong to the organization when Lieutenant Lewis felt a vibration on his body. His beeper was announcing he needed to answer a call immediately. Rising from his seat, he signaled Sullivan and Colliere to follow him. When the three men left the conference room, Lewis explained to them what was expected from the call. They returned to the conference room and apologized, saying they had to leave the meeting for a moment as an emergency had arisen that needed their attention immediately. Meanwhile, Liu could continue with his remarks. However, since no one was authorized to leave the room, their return was expected in thirty minutes. Seeing that everybody had understood the instructions, Albert left the room, finding Lewis and Sullivan holding the elevator doors open.

Liu paused before he continued speaking, and Richard saw the opportunity to ask him what his father's activities were in Gwen's organization. "Before I respond to your question, I would like to mention who your father was. Your father, Richard, was a tireless worker. His success at bringing women in to the ecclesiastical sector is unquestionable. None of us on the team accomplished what your father did. Helped by the Legion of Christ and the Opus Dei, your father was able to open several mixed colleges in different places, where students of both sexes received equal treatment. Using his excellent relations with the Church, he made significant improvements in favor of women, which none of us in our own religions achieved. His work to eliminate women's discrimination in the Catholic Church was fully recognized. The night you visited your father, we were working on a proposal to make changes that could bring women's participation into higher positions of the Church.

Richard remembered the moment when he had walked inside his father's apartment that night and saw a moment of panic in their faces, so he asked Liu what his father was saying to them to make everybody react in that way. Liu clearly remembered the moment and responded that Richard's father was mentioning to them his experience of eight days before in a small town of Jalisco called Atotonilco el Alto. "The Church authority of that community was a stubborn conservative, chauvinistic, and misogynist bishop who enjoyed discriminating against women. To enter his parish, women had to cover their face with a veil, and they were prevented from climbed to the altar and read the Sunday readings. Your father's mission was to convince the bishop to open mixed colleges in his jurisdiction. After several days of discussions, the bishop refused to accept your father's proposals. Five days after his rejection, the bishop traveled to Guadalajara in order to attend matters of the Church with other priests of his locality. When the bishop was about to step down from the bus, he received the fire of an AK-47 machine gun shot at a distance from a black Mercedes, killing the bishop instantly. The news mentioned the bishop was shot by mistake when he was confused with another person who belonged to a band of drug dealers. Nevertheless, we and your father knew that was not true, and the real reason was something else. Now, when Detective Colliere mentioned the Death Squad, to my mind came the idea that the bishop was killed by that squad."

"What you are trying to say, Liu, is that Gwen eliminates whichever men interfere with her plans, or I am mistaken?" Richard asked.

"I would agree with your thinking, Richard, as Gwen sends someone to kill any men who dare to interfere with her objectives. That's the reason I hid when she intended to kill me by setting a car bomb to explode in Shanghai."

Richard immediately asked Liu how the last days in his father's life were.

"Richard, I hoped you would never ask that question. However, as it comes from you, I'll do what I can to answer it, to show the great appreciation I always professed for your father when he exhibited his courage to challenge Gwen's commands, even knowing in advance that his disobedience would led to his death."

"Everything began with the illness of Pope Leon XVII, making everyone think he would die soon and a successor would need to be appointed. Gwen was in favor of appointing the Argentine cardinal Alejandro Villavicencio to be his successor, as he had promised to her his support of many important changes in the Church, such as the elimination of celibacy in priests, the acceptance of women into the priesthood, and the approval of preventive methods for birth control. Your father's commitment was to promote campaigns in his favor."

"Everything seemed to work well for your father until the traditionalist

Italian cardinal Leonardo Ponti made his appearance. The popular Cardinal Ponti started to gain followers, while the popularity of Cardinal Alejandro Villavicencio suffered a decrease. Gwen felt her hopes of climb women in the priesthood would vanish, so she sent your father an ultimatum, demanding he accept her contributions to bribe the other cardinals who seemed reticent to vote in favor of Cardinal Villavicencio. The contributions were rejected by your father, who instead worked on a PowerPoint presentation in which the main topic was the same Cardinal Villavicencio. The purpose was to explain to the cardinals, who did not believe in change, what the benefits would be if modernization in the Church took place, such as helping young couples who had abandoned the Catholic religion when they were prevented from using birth control methods. In his presentation, he demonstrated the advantages of following more liberal tendencies; otherwise, if they continued with traditional and conservative tendencies, they were likely to lose more parishioners. On another subject, the presentation discussed the celibacy of priests, who, after living in isolation, preferred to abandon their priest careers to get married, or, unfortunately, as some did, become homosexuals or pederasts. A lack of male priests was another problem for the Church, and one possible solution was the acceptance of women into the priesthood. Each day, missionary work declined. Eliminating celibacy and accepting women into the priesthood would make young married couples do this work without complaint and would support leaving their homes. The acceptance of these measures would also help return people who had abandoned the Catholic religion to find in another religion what they lacked in theirs. Furthermore, the population growth in the world had to stop. Governments imposed discriminatory measures against women. The acceptance of preventive methods of birth control would help to eliminate some of them. Your father's task was to convince two of the cardinals who disliked the liberal tendencies proposed by Cardinal Villavicencio, making them excellent promoters to convince the other cardinals to vote in favor of the cardinal they proposed."

"Unfortunately, your father ran out of time when the death of the Pope came sooner than expected, leaving your father without a weapon to face Gwen, who continued to insist on bribing the cardinals. Despite his deplorable situation, your father rejected Gwen's offer again, who by this time was unable to control her anger and sent someone to kill him. Gwen's anger did not stop there, and knowing Hemant and I had begged in your father's favor, offering our support, she decided to eliminate us also. She set bombs to explode in our cars when we stepped inside. Unfortunately, her plan worked, and Hemant died when his car exploded when he was leaving his home in New Delhi. Being luckier than Hemant, I was able to escape and survive the bomb that was set for me in Shanghai. After staying hidden for several days, I was able to talk to Jacob, who provided me the information that Detective Colliere was the person responsible for finding the killers. Without delay, I took a plane and flew to Lexington, expecting my information would help him to find the killers sooner," Liu said.

Richard could not believe what he was hearing and asked Liu what had made his father belong to Gwen's organization when his principles in life were other than hers. Liu mumbled before answering that his father had been monitored in his life, allowing Gwen to know everything about his family. "The feeling was threatening, and without another option, your father accepted membership to her organization. On one occasion, your father, disliking some things that were happening, told Gwen of his decision to leave the organization, promising not to expose her. Gwen never responded to his proposal but instead sent someone to kill your mother. Feeling guilty for her death, your father suffered from a deep depression. When he recovered, he decided to live in the United States and keep his family away from risk. In other words, your father became Gwen's bait to catch the big fish, as without complaint he promised to follow her commands. But breaking his promise, he disobeyed Gwen's orders when he refused to bribe the cardinals, even knowing this act of rebelliousness would bring him fatal consequences. Believe me, Richard, your father was not afraid to die. What scared him was that Gwen could take revenge against you and his family."

Hearing these last words, Richard felt remorse for his father. Now that he understood the great love his father professed for them, he felt sorry just thinking how difficult it must have been for him to live isolated and far from the family that he loved just to keep them out of danger.

CHAPTER 29

strong storm was to hit the small town of Colton City, California. Following his boss's instructions, Miguel Rodriguez parked his police car in front of an old building, whose façade looked deteriorated for lack of paint. It bore the sign of the community's public library. Picking up the umbrella he had placed under the seat, Miguel walked toward the glass door. Going inside, he found a desk where a young lady dressed the classic outfit of a librarian, long black skirt and wearing glasses that enhanced the beauty of her blue sparkling eyes. Seeing Miguel she asked if he was looking for a specific book. Taken by surprise but prepared to respond quickly, Miguel said he was looking for a book on criminology. Rising from her seat, the librarian made a sign to follow her. Walking through a narrow corridor, she arrived at a shelf where stood a few books properly organized.

Apologizing to Miguel, she said the library did not carry many books on criminology, although she hoped he could find what he was looking for among those. Thanking the librarian, Miguel responded he was sure those books were what he was looking for. Dismissing the librarian, Miguel went to the shelf, and taking the first book that was at hand he walked toward a round table in the center of the hallway. Seated there was a nice lady pleasantly reading a book. When she sensed Miguel, she raised her head and greeted him with a smile, then continued with her reading.

Miguel said he was sorry to interrupt her, but he needed her to come with him, as she was under arrest for the murder of Leslie Preston. She had the right to remain silent. Also, she had the right to a lawyer while she was questioned, and if she lacked one, the court could appoint one for her. Smiling, she thanked Miguel for saying so, but said it was unnecessary to call a lawyer as she knew the reason for his coming, so if was allowed, she would pick up her coat and go with him wherever he wanted. Ordering to put hands behind her back he handcuff her. When the handcuffs closed on her wrists, she shook.

When they left the library, a strong rain was falling. Opening his umbrella, Miguel invited the woman to cover herself with it and instructed her to walk straight ahead to the police car parked in front of the building. Miguel help her to climb inside the police car.

The rest of the journey occurred without any uttering another word. Arriving at the police station, Miguel helped her to step out the police car, and taking her arm, he walked her directly to the interrogation room.

The interrogation rooms were rather small, scarcely furnished with a small rectangular table and three chairs surrounding it. The people submitted to interrogation were watched through a two-way mirror to know exactly what was happening inside of each room. In one of those rooms was Detective Miguel Rodriguez attempting to get a confession from his arrestee.

She seemed extremely calm when he asked her to give her name, age, and nationality. "Before I can answer your question, Detective, I want to know what charges you have for accusing me of," she said.

"For murdering Leslie Preston," Miguel responded.

"What makes you think I am guilty of committing that crime?"

Holding his temper, Miguel answered, "We have enough evidence to prove you are the murderer."

"To what evidences do you refer?" she asked.

Miguel lost his patience and said, "You will know later, but now I need you to tell me your name, age, and nationality."

"Please don't get upset, Detective Miguel. That is not good for your health," she said.

"I won't repeat my question again, and you'd better give me an answer. What is your name, age, and nationality?" asked Miguel with a rude tone of voice.

"My name is Romy Choweski. I was born in Czechoslovakia. My age is fifty-seven," she answered in a sweet tone of voice.

"Now we are getting to understand each other better. What work did you perform for Gerald Solaris?" Miguel asked

"I was his domestic assistant," Romy answered.

"How long have you worked for the Solaris family?"

"I believe around thirty-six years, since Mrs. Solaris hired me to take care of her children."

"Is it true you have an aunt by the name of Isabel Pawa and a cousin named Leslie Preston, known better by nickname Howie?"

"Yes, I do," Romy answered. "But what do they have to do in this matter?"

Ignoring her question, Miguel continued his interrogation, asking Romy if her cousin Howie had reddish hair.

"Yes, she does, but what interest do you have in the color of her hair?" asked Romy Miguel saw Romy was getting upset, so he asked if she considered herself a good stamp collector.

"Yes, I do," Romy answered with a nervous tone in her voice. "I feel proud of my collection."

This time it was Miguel the one who tried to calm Romy, saying that getting upset was not good for her health. Taking a deep breath, Miguel asked Romy if she was responsible for killing her cousin, Leslie Preston. But before she could answer his question, he was going to show the evidence they had collected to prove she was guilty of murder.

"To what evidence do you refer?" Romy asked.

"I guess I have to be more explicit and explain in detail what we found." Facing Romy, Miguel said that while during the search of her home, they found on the pillow of her bed several reddish hairs, which they assume did not belong to her as the color of her hair was dark. "Intrigued by this fact and knowing the hate you have for men, we supposed the hair belonged to a woman."

Interrupting Miguel, Romy said, "And what makes you suppose the reddish hairs belong to my cousin Howie?"

"Good question, Romy. However, the response will come to you later. In my previous question, I asked if you considered yourself a good stamp collector. I must agree that you are an outstanding stamp collector and should be proud to be. Unfortunately, this collection will bring disgrace to you when we find the evidence to declare you guilty of performing the crime against your cousin Leslie."

"What is this evidence?" Romy asked, challenging Miguel.

Holding his temper, Miguel calmly answered, "While searching your home, we found in your stamp album, in the Germany section, three stamps with the seals of Offenbach City. The dates of the seals were July 22, 2007, and May 3 and 8 of 2010."

"Don't go further, Detective. That is easy to explain," Romy interrupted. "Mr. Solaris was the person who gave me those stamps when they were received on his letters."

"That answer sounds reasonable to me; however, after we interviewed the post office employee in Offenbach City, he remembered that the person who bought those stamps was a person with reddish hair. Examining his records, the employee found the destination of those letters was your address, Romy. Strong coincidence, don't you think?" Romy stayed mute and did not answer. "Going further with our investigation, we found your cousin Leslie had traveled to see her mother, who was confined to a hospital in Los Angeles. The immigration services office provided us the information, saying her date of arrival in Los Angeles was May 9, 2010, coming from Frankfurt on flight number 904 of Lufthansa Airlines. What can you tell me about this?" asked Miguel. Romy stayed mute and did not answer.

"Searching through several hospitals, we found your aunt Isabel Pawa had been confined to Sinai Hospital. Interviewing the hospital nurse, we found out your cousin Howie had visited her mother every day since her arrival but had been missing since May 15, the last day she visited her mother. The nurse made several calls to Leslie's phone without getting a response. Concerned about her absence, the nurse called the police, who started an investigation to find her whereabouts.

"The immigration authorities assured them that Leslie Preston had not left the country. Sadly, the body of your fifty-nine-year-old beloved cousin was found six days later by a fisherman, drowned in a lake. She had been savagely stabbed with a hunting knife. Her wrists had swelled, making us suppose she had fought against her aggressor before she died. Tell me, Romy, what led you to kill your cousin? Was it revenge or an act of self-defense?" asked Miguel. Romy showed a pale color and did not answer.

"Romy, I am going to show you three pictures, and you have to tell me the names of persons who appear in each. Is that understood?" Miguel asked. Romy moved her head in a sign of consent. "Who are the people who appear in this first picture, Romy?"

Looking at the picture, she answered they were her aunt Isabel, Howie, and her.

"Good," Miguel said. "Now, regarding this same picture, tell me the date it was taken."

"The date the picture shows is July 27, 2007."

"Perfect. By chance do you remember the date on which Mrs. Solaris died?"

"Of course," Romy said. "It was July 29, 2007."

"So we can assume this picture was taken two days before Mrs. Solaris died. Isn't that so?"

"I guess so," Romy answered.

"Romy, do you recognize who is with you in this second picture?"

"Indeed. That is my cousin Howie."

"Do you see on the left flap of your coats that you are both wearing a pin with a black butterfly?"

"Yes, I do. But tell me, Detective, where did you get this picture, because it never was in my family album?" Romy asked.

"You are right, Romy. This picture was taken from Howie's bedroom by a spy we infiltrated into Gwen's organization. Tell me, Romy, what does the black butterfly mean to you?"

"I don't know. I received this pin as a gift from my cousin Howie".

Miguel was about to explode, but controlling himself, he said to Romy, "Let me refresh your memory a little. We know the black butterfly is an award for successfully passing tests that would rank you as a member of the D-Squad. Do you want me to explain what the D-Squad is?" Miguel asked with anger.

"No, Detective Miguel, that won't be necessary."

"Romy, the Secretariat of Foreign Affairs of Mexico reported to us that your cousin Howie was in Mexico City from July 27, 2007, to July 30, 2007. Her trip was paid for by Gwen Swayze with a Visa card. We also know Mrs. Solaris was killed in the supermarket, the cashier assuring us the aggressors had women's voices with foreign accents. Just as a reminder, does your cousin Howie has a foreign accent? Furthermore, her height and anatomy seemed to coincide with the cashier's descriptions of the aggressors."

"Are you accusing me of killing Mrs. Solaris?" asked Romy.

"No, Romy, I never said that, but we believe your cousin Howie did it," Miguel said.

"I would never dare to touch Mrs. Solaris as I loved her too much," Romy said.

"We know the love she always professed for you also, accepting you as another member of her family. No, Romy, we are not blaming you for her death," Miguel replied. "Did the police ever question you about her death?" asked Miguel.

"Yes, they did, but all I could say about her death was what Mr. Solaris had told to us."

"Did you know Mr. Solaris stopped the police investigation, saying her death was an accident?"

"No, I did not," Romy replied.

"Do you know what led to Mr. Solaris's depression?"

"No, I don't," Romy said.

"It was the remorse he felt for his wife's death. Mr. Solaris was displeased with many things that happened inside Gwen's organization. He asked Gwen for permission to leave with the promise of not exposing her. Gwen never believed his promise not to expose her, so in revenge, she sent your cousin Howie with another person to kill his wife as a warning about his imprudent request. Now, tell me, Romy; what led you to kill your cousin Howie? Did you do it in self-defense because she attacked you?" asked Miguel.

Romy stayed mute for a moment, then realizing the time had come to tell Miguel the whole truth, she said, "Detective Miguel, my conscience keeps asking me to say the whole truth of what really happened, so tell me, where do you want me to start?"

Thanking Romy for her sincerity, Miguel promised to help her when he could. Miguel smiled at Romy and said, "Let's start from the beginning by telling me how you met Gwen Swayze," said Miguel.

"Everything began on the night of August 20, 1968, when the city of Prague was invaded by the Russians. After my father and brother were killed when they tried to defend us from being raped savagely, my mother and I were transported to a Russian concentration camp. Aware my aunt Isabel that lived in Mexico of our deplorable situation, she request Gwen to help us to escape. Gwen sent a group of women properly trained to help us escape. One night when our guards were sleeping deeply after having celebrated their victory and being totally drunk, we were able to escape. Arriving at Gwen's organization, my mother and I were submitted to proper training, where we learned to defend ourselves and kill a person when commanded to. After passing several tests, I graduated in martial arts and war techniques, becaming a member of the D-Squad. My cousin Howie was my teacher and was she who gave me the pin with the black butterfly, as an award for passing the tests. The picture you show me was taken on that day. When I finished the course, they made me swear under oath to obey their orders unconditionally and with loyalty. One week after finishing the course, at my aunt's request and counting on Gwen's authorization, my mother and I were sent to America.

"The trip was unbearable, so much so that my mother died during the journey. In spite of my pleading, her body was thrown out to sea when two sailors thought her body would stink and infect the whole crew. I disembarked in Veracruz, where my aunt was waiting for me. Knowing of my mother's death, she tried to console me and asking if I was ready to continue with the journey, we took the bus to Mexico City.

"Several years after my arrival at Mexico City, my aunt was able to arrange my immigration status so that I could work in her employment agency and earn a decent salary. At that moment, Mrs. Solaris was looking for someone who could take care of their home and children. After working for the Solaris family and being treated as another member of their family, my aunt asked me what kind of work Mr. Solaris performed for the Secretariat of Foreign Affairs. Aware of his excellent relations with the governmental, business, and ecclesiastical sectors and showing an interest in what he was doing, my aunt asked me to provide more details, saying Mr. Solaris would be of great help to Gwen's organization. She assigned me to get that information by monitoring his life. Setting bugs to hear conversations and placing cameras all over his house and office, I monitored his life for several months. Satisfied with the results of that monitoring, Gwen elaborated a plan to contact him. Hearing from a tape recording that Mr. Solaris needed to travel to Frankfurt to attend a dinner with the German ambassador, Gwen made her plan to meet Mr. Solaris."

"Stop, Romy. Are you telling me that you killed Mr. Solaris?" Miguel interrupted.

"Oh no, Detective Miguel. It was not me who killed Mr. Solaris. It was my cousin Howie who did it."

"How can you prove what you are saying is true?" Miguel asked.

"All right, Miguel, let me tell you how I was aware of this fact. One day after Mr. Solaris died and I was questioned by Lieutenant Lewis. Find arriving at my home my cousin Howie seated on the porch, wearing Levis pants and drinking a cold lemonade. She asked where I had been, and I told my cousin everything that had happened to Mr. Solaris. Laughing, she said to me, 'Romy, Mr. Solaris deserved to die.' Surprised at her statement, I said Mr. Solaris was a great man. There was no doubt he was handsome and rich, and many women would fall in love with him, although for me he was too old. 'Do you mean you met Mr. Solaris?' I asked.

"'Yes, cousin, I did yesterday,' Howie replied.

"'How come you never mentioned anything to me?' I asked.

"'I guess I owe you an apology,' Howie said.

"Miguel, what follows is what Howie said to me exactly in her own words. 'Cousin, do you remember yesterday when I borrowed your car and said I would go to see my mother when she said was not feeling well? Well, after seeing her at the hospital, I decided to pay a visit to Mr. Solaris. Using the remote control that I found in the glove compartment of your car, I opened the gate and went inside the complex without having to pass through security. Using the keys found in your car I took the elevator arriving at his apartment. Changing my clothes, I put on a long, black fitted dress with a low neckline that left plenty of my breasts showing. Lowering the light to give a romantic touch to the dining room, I set three places with individual tablecloths and silverware. When Mr. Solaris arrived around 8:45 p.m., he found me seated in a chair in the dining room. Surprised and quite impressed at seeing a woman whom he had never met and wearing that outfit, he stammered before he asked me how I got into his apartment. After learning I was Leslie Preston, your cousin, he began to calm down. Asking for your presence, I responded you had gone to the pharmacy to buy medicine for your cold.

"'He sat in a chair close to me, and we began to chat. To start our conversation, I mentioned the love you always professed for him. In return, he said he loved you too, like a member of his family. In reply I said the love you felt for him was different, as you got jealous each time he invited women to his apartment. "Do you mean Romy is really in love with me?" he asked.

"""Indeed she is," I replied, "but she is shy to demonstrate her love because you never considered her seriously. Mr. Solaris, do you mind if we open a bottle of wine and make a toast?" I asked.

"""Of course not. I will really enjoy making a toast with you," he answered. Going to the kitchen, he brought back a bottle of wine. After it was opened, he asked, "What will be the toast?" I responded the toast was to celebrate his failure. Without understanding, he asked what failure I was referring to.

"""The one of making Cardinal Villavicencio the next Pope," I answered. Intrigued, he asked how I was aware of that assignment. Explaining, I said, "Because I belong to Gwen's organization, and it was she who told me about your disobedience and refusal to use the funds she offered to bribe the cardinals who still remained hesitant to vote in favor of Cardinal Villavicencio. Her plans to allow women into the priesthood vanished when you failed to convince the cardinals of the benefits to modernizing the Church. Gwen is intolerant of disobedience, and your failure made her get mad. To take revenge, she sent me to kill you." Hearing her last words, Mr. Solaris was unable to control his rage and furiously stood to hit me. At that moment, I inserted the shot containing thallium nitrate into his throat. Feeling the shot, Mr. Solaris moved backward, then straggled back to me and tried to strangle me. Putting my defensive techniques into practice, I defeated him by twisting his arms and wrists. With the lack of breath and feeling a strong pain in his chest, Mr. Solaris collapsed onto the floor. Loading his body over my shoulders, I opened the dining room windows and threw his body out. The trees cushioned the sound of his fall before he crashed against the pavement of the pathway.

"""Sticking my head out of the window, I saw no one had seen me. Fortunately, the darkness of night and the solitude of the place worked in my favor. Erasing every trace that could detect me, I quickly cleaned the place and prepared everything to make everyone think Mr. Solaris had committed suicide. When I was about to climb into your car, the security guard on duty approached me. Recognizing your vehicle, he started to question me. Yes, the guard was a nice tall guy,'" she said with nostalgia.

""His name is Jack," I said.

""Who cares what his name was?" Howie answered me angrily. "He was just a stupid fellow who thought I was Mr. Solaris's lover, and even if I tried to convince him I was simply a visitor, he would never have believed me. Feeling he would expose me and with no other option, I made a plan to kill him. Approaching him, I start to flirt with him. Excited about my behavior, he tried to kiss me. At that moment, I inserted the needle containing the shot of thallium nitrates into his throat. Feeling the pain, he walked straight to face me but instantly fell to the ground. Cleaning every trace of his presence, I loaded the body over my shoulders and stuck him inside the trunk of your car. Leaving the place, I stopped at a gas station to fill the tank and buy five gallons of gasoline and a lighter to make a good bonfire. Driving the car I found a nice spot adequate for my purpose. Spreading gasoline around his body, I threw it into the flames, which after several hours burned his whole body. Collecting the ashes, I buried them in a vacant lot close to your home.'"

"Believe me, Miguel, I was completely devastated, emotionally and physically, when she finished her story. Suddenly I feared Howie had told me everything because she was intending to kill me too. Quickly I ran inside the house toward the kitchen, intending to find something to use if I needed to defend myself. Turning around, I saw Howie standing in the doorway, looking at me. Her face had a strange expression. Suddenly she ran up the stairs to the kitchen and walked toward me, I shrank. 'What are you trying to do?' I asked.

"She smiled. 'Yes, cousin, I am coming after you.' We both startled and looked at each other. Howie had a gun in her hand, and I froze when she walked toward me.

"'Howie, don't be stupid, and try to calm down,' I said.

"'I should have killed you before, but my mother's illness stopped me from doing it. I think my mother loves you more than me, her real daughter.' Her hand was firm and did not shake when handling the gun.

Cutting cartridge, she came closer to me. Suddenly her cell phone rang. The nurse from the hospital was calling, saying her mother was dying and wanted to see her. 'Tell my mom I'll be with her in half an hour,' Howie answered. Looking at her watch, she complained, 'Why did that damn nurse have to call me at this moment? I have no time to waste and need to kill you soon so I can go and see my mother,' she said. Thinking fast and before she could pull the trigger, I threw myself at her, intending to disarm her. While we struggled I remembered the hunting knife I always kept in the kitchen drawer close to the stove. Unexpectedly, Howie lost her balance and fell to the ground. Kicking her body with all my strength, I rose to grab the hunting knife. Once it was in my hand, I stabbed her several times until she was dead.

"I was dazed for a minute, and without knowing what to do, I cleaned up everything that could indicate her presence. Then, hauling her body, I put it inside the trunk of my car. Wondering what to do with her body, I decided to throw it in the lake."

Miguel remained silent while Romy told her story. When she finished, he asked Romy if the gun Howie had belonged to her. "Yes, Miguel, it was her gun." Romy answered.

"Romy we assume that gun was the one they used to kill Mrs. Solaris".

"Where is that gun now?"

Romy mumbled before answering she had buried it in the backyard of her house.

"Detective Miguel, did you think I was the other robber who killed Mrs. Solaris?"

"Yes, Romy, at some moments we did."

"No, Detective Miguel, I was not one of those robbers. I would never have dared to harm Mrs. Solaris, as she was the loveliest person I ever met in my life."

"I believe you, Romy," Miguel said. "We know for sure Howie was one of those killers; however, we still don't know who the other person was. Questioning the cashier, we know they were both tall people with foreign accents. With this last question, I am ending my interrogation. As I promised you, I'll do my best to help when you are sent to court."

Sobbing, Romy thanked Miguel, saying she regretted what had

happened with her cousin Howie. At Miguel's signal, two guards walked into the room to handcuff Romy and take her to her cell, where she was to pass the night. The guard reminded Romy she was strictly forbidden to speak to anyone except her lawyer. Romy smiled at the guard and said she wasn't expecting visitors that night. Romy suddenly stopped to ask Miguel a favor before he left. "I would like to tell Richard I regret causing him and his family so much trouble." Miguel promised he would send her message to Richard.

Minutes later, Miguel was in his office, writing the report he would send to his boss. Helped by his tape recorder, he reviewed every step of Romy's confession. After checking the report several times and being sure there were no mistakes, he finally was satisfied. The next step was to encrypt the information with a secret code that only Lieutenant Lewis and he knew. Following his boss instructions he was to send the report to Raymond Sullivan computer, where Lewis was supposed to be present.

CHAPTER 30

Three men waited impatiently in Sullivan's office for the information Miguel Rodriguez was to send with the confession by whom they thought was the person responsible for committing these crimes. The message icon began to flash on Sullivan's computer, and Lieutenant Lewis immediately entered the secret code that was to open the encrypted information.

Sullivan stood on one side of the printer, ready to receive the sheets. When the last print came out, he proceeded to organize the file to read it. Not a single word was uttered while Sullivan read the report to them. Finalizing it, Sullivan said to Albert that it was hard to believe these women with such pretty faces were able to commit such atrocities.

Lewis agreed with his statement, saying that at the beginning, her alibi worked perfectly, distracting him toward thinking Mr. Solaris had committed suicide. "The remote control Leslie used to go inside the complex without going through security was a great strategy to divert our attention to suicide. However, after searching Mr. Solaris's apartment, we found several pieces of evidence that made me think I was on the wrong track, evidence that later was confirmed when the autopsy was performed.

"My mistake was to blame Romy for committing the crime against Mr. Solaris. However, while we searched Romy's house and found several reddish hairs on her pillow in the bedroom, that led me to remember what Richard Solaris had told me in his interrogation when he was questioned about Romy's relatives. What follows is already known by us.

Knowing who was responsible for committing the crimes against Mr. and Mrs. Solaris an the other people involved in the case, Raymond Sullivan proposed to close the case. Lewis agreed with him but not Albert, who stopped them, saying they still had a dark point to verify. Surprised at his answer, Sullivan asked what dark point he was referring to. Albert replied that at that moment could not reveal it, but if they gave him ten minutes, he promised to tell them, as he still had pending some tests to support more evidence. Granting his petition, Sullivan left his office, saying he would wait for him in the conference room, where their guests expected their return. Lewis more prudently stayed to offer Albert his help, who in return thanked Lewis for staying, but he said all he needed from them was their return to the conference room and not to mention to anyone what they had talked about.

Following his instructions, Sullivan and Lewis returned to the conference room. Opening the door, they found their audience waiting impatiently and in total silence. Seeing Ivonne's her brother was not with them, she asked where he was. Sullivan responded that he was attending to a call but was to join them in a few minutes.

When Albert returned to the conference room, his face looked pale, as if something serious was worrying him. Apologizing for his delay, he took a seat at the right side of Sullivan, who, seeing his condition, asked Albert if he was feeling well. "I am fine. Just tired, as last night I could not sleep, analyzing the case in detail."

Albert rose from his seat and walked toward the stage to say they had worked on this case long enough, their investigations finally discovering who was directly responsible for committing the crimes. "Detective Miguel Rodriguez apologizes for not being present with us at this moment, but he remains in Los Angeles, preparing the confession of who we found is responsible for committing the crime against Leslie Preston. Maybe some of you will be hearing the name of Leslie Preston for the first time, so let me tell you what her role was in Mr. Gerald Solaris's life. Captain Sullivan has authorized me to read the defendant's confession, so please remain seated and silent until we have finished."

Albert paused a moment to breath and then exposed everything what they have found.

Richard exploded in anger, saying he knew Romy well, and she would never kill anyone unless it was completely necessary. "Could you see Romy stab her cousin in self-defense when Leslie was prepared to shoot her gun?"

Indeed, Richard understood it was a great mistake for her to try to hide her crime instead of calling the police. Nevertheless, he was disposed to help her by hiring a good lawyer who would demand her immediate freedom. Richard would himself act as a witness to tell everybody what he knew about Romy.

Apologizing for getting agitated, Richard said could not contain his anger when he heard in Romy's confession was Leslie Preston who had killed his father and mother. Romy worshiped and admired her cousin Leslie. The saying was that she was so strong that she could defeat four men who dared to attack her at the same time.

Albert waited patiently until Richard had recovered and calmed down. Renewing his exposition, he said he had another announcement to make. Under the roof of that very room was a traitor among them. All glances led to Liu, who, disconcerted at Albert's words, did not know what to do. Albert said they were wrong thinking Liu was the traitor. The real traitor to confront was Elysee. The statement made Ivonne jump out of her seat, saying Elysee had collaborated with them when they needed to escape or introduce the commandos into Gwen's organization.

Albert shook his head before asking Ivonne if she could remember the name of one aggressor who had killed Mrs. Solaris. "Yes, Albert, we heard in Romy's confession that one of them was Leslie Preston, her cousin."

"All right, Ivonne, now I will tell you the name of the other aggressor. Her name is Charlene Roussillon. Do you recognize that name?"

"No, Albert, tell me, who is Charlene Roussillon?" Ivonne asked.

"It is Elysee's real name," Albert responded.

"How did you find out that was her real name?"

"Because we asked the Sacre Couer Church, where she married Emille Salim on October 5, 2005. His spouse's name was Charlene Roussillon. Furthermore, when I showed the picture you sent me to the church's chaplain, he recognized Elysee as the women who had been seen several times making arrangements for her marriage. Knowing Elysee's real name is Charlene Roussillon, we requested the immigration authorities to provide us information about her, finding she had traveled to the United States on the same plane and date of July 27, 2007, as Leslie Preston. We also sent the tape recording of the conversation you had with Elysee to the cashier who worked in the supermarket where Mrs. Solaris was killed. He immediately recognized her voice and accent, saying that was the same voice as one of the robbers.

"In another file on Susan's computer, we found a list of duties Elysee had performed for the D-Squad. Under those was the bomb she set to crash the plane in which the Secretary of State of France had died with other members of his staff when they traveled to attend a meeting of the European Union. The cause of the accident was reported as pilot error. It was hard for me to believe he had crashed the plane into a mountain at such a low altitude when I saw the pilot's record, who had been awarded the Medal of Merit for his flight skills.

"Let me tell you another sign of her lies. Reviewing your tape in the minicomputer I found the conversation Elysee had with Doctor Hollander in the back of the ambulance. Listening to it, I was surprised when Dr. Hollander called Elysee a bitch and blamed her for killing three pregnant women. Intrigued by this accusation, we found the answer in another file on Susan's computer. Dr. Hollander reported to Susan that in performing the autopsy on those pregnant women, she found in their uterus semen contaminated with a weird substance unknown to her. The contamination of the semen caused those pregnant women constant bleeding and hemorrhaging that finally ended their lives. Dr. Hollander blamed Elysee for their deaths, saying she was the only one aware of her experiments. According to Dr. Hollander, Elysee's purpose was to discredit her in Susan's eyes, making her think she was stupid and that she had made a mistake when she mixed the semen of several men into one element. Discrediting her would serve Elysee in recovering her position as Susan's assistant.

"But guess what, Ivonne? Dr. Hollander was wrong in thinking Elysee's main purpose was to discredit her. She did not know her real purpose, which was found later, when we heard the tape with your conversation you had with Elysee, where she stated was prevented from getting pregnant again as her uterus was removed when she lost her child. Being Elysee aware that those women would germinate in their embryo a child probably with Emille's semen. In an attack of jealousy, she proceeded to contaminate the semen that those women were to receive in their uterus, knowing it would end their pregnancy and probably their lives. Her plan worked well, and those women died before they could give birth to their children.

"Then deaths brought Susan into a deep depression. To relieve her pain, she took drugs, as Susan had hoped those children would be women with outstanding and superhuman features never before achieved by a woman. The fatal incident made Susan distrust Dr. Hollander, whom she started to exclude from her experiments. Dr. Hollander swore to take revenge on Elysee. The opportunity came when she was alone with Elysee in the back of ambulance and decided to deceive her by asking Elysee to kill her. What follows is already known by you. Dr. Hollander is dead now, but her testimony would have been of great value to us at this moment," Albert said.

Ivonne could not believe what she was hearing from Albert. She said everything sounded awful to her. Albert smiled and answered, "Wait until you hear what comes next, which will serve as testimony to declare Elysee as the traitor.

"When Simone released you and Elysee from being tied up, Elysee used her cell phone and texted a message to Gwen, alerting her to our attack. Fortunately, her message came too late as our attack had commenced half an hour before. Nevertheless, it warned Gwen of our attack, allowing her to find emergency exits unknown to us for her escape. So when the commandos got inside her bedroom, she was no longer there."

"Why didn't Susan escape with Gwen?" Lewis asked. Albert responded that his question was excellent, but the reason was that she was never notified of the attack. As Elysee resented her displacement as Susan's assistant, and hoped that dying Susan Gwen would replace her as the substitute.

Elysee stayed silent, listening to every accusation against her. Unable to control her rage any longer, she rose from her seat and, nearly shouting, said everything Detective Colliere had said was a big lie, and he did not have evidence to blame her. Smiling, Albert responded that while inspecting her cell phone, they found the text message she had sent to Gwen. "Don't you think that is good evidence?" Albert asked.

Furious, Elysee now understood the reason Albert at the beginning of the meeting had requested them to put their cell phones inside the envelope. "Do you know, Detective Colliere, that a cell phone is considered personal property, and I can sue you for using it without my authorization?" Elysee asked.

Albert smiled again and said, "In the first place, Elysee, you voluntarily put your cell phone inside the envelope. Then, for your information, it was the telephone company that provided me the text message information on your cell phone, confirming the time and date you sent the message to Gwen."

With furious eyes and the feeling she was trapped, Elysee decided to use her last resource, and taking out of her pocket a Ruger 22 mm caliber pistol, she pointed it at them, saying, "I need everyone to put their hands up and over their heads; otherwise, I will kill you. I have to congratulate you, Detective Colliere, as everything you said about me is true. Unfortunately, it is too late, and none of you will live to use it."

Everybody obeyed her command except Albert, who calmly said, "Don't be foolish, Elysee. I always considered you a wise woman. It is much better for you to surrender. You are trapped, and the guards won't let you go unless they receive authorization from Mr. Sullivan or me. Look, Elysee, here is the deal. If you lower your gun and promise not to shoot us, I promise to be benevolent in your trial. What do you say?" Albert asked.

Elysee laughed and responded that he must think she was stupid to agree with his deal, as she knew well he would never be benevolent at her trial. "So if you don't obey my orders, you will be the first to be killed."

"And how do you intend to kill me?" asked Albert.

"What a silly question. Of course, you will be killed when I fire my gun."

"But to fire a gun and kill someone, you need real bullets, don't you think?"

"Are you insinuating, Detective Colliere, that my gun is not loaded with real bullets?"

"Let me tell you something, Elysee, that at this moment you don't know."

"What is that?" Elysee interrupted.

"Before your arrival, the lock of your room was arranged so it would not lock from the inside. Helped by the hotel manager, my assistant went into your room while you were taking a shower. Seeing your dirty uniform lying on your bed, he found your gun and replaced the real bullets with blanks, then left the room before you could see him."

"Are you insinuating, Detective Colliere, that my gun is not loaded with real bullets?"

"That is correct, Elysee. If you intend to kill us, you'll find out I do not lie," said Albert. Elysee was not really convinced by Albert's words, so she squeezed the trigger to kill Albert. Laughing, he said, "Are you convinced, Elysee?"

Elysee threw the gun to the floor and ran toward the door, finding two large policemen preventing her escape. Feeling trapped, she surrendered. Albert ordered the policemen to arrest and handcuff Elysee, but before they could send her to jail, he stopped to say he had received the report on the rescued team. Among them was her ex-husband, Emille, who seemed to be in bad condition. His mother was waiting for him at the airport in Beirut.

Thanking Albert for the information, she asked for one more favor—if he could tell Emille she regretted not being present at the time of his arrival, but business matters had prevented her going. Albert promised to deliver the message. Dismissing Elysee, Albert went to the conference room where their guests waited for him.

CHAPTER 31

lbert excused himself for the interruption, saying he had received a call from Rome. Captain Sullivan excused himself from the meeting, as he needed urgently to travel to participate in a meeting with high clerical authorities of the Catholic Church.

Cardinal Leonardo Ponti and the two bishops had been rescued and sent to Rome. Their arrival was received with joy by several cardinals of the Church. After meeting with a secret agent on the same day of their arrival, they were told everything that had happened. Finding it hard to believe that Cardinal Villavicencio was involved in a religious conspiracy with an activist leader of a women's organization led by Gwen, who had made the commitment to help the cardinal become the next Pope. Gwen's organization would give a generous contribution to the Church if the Pope in return promised to modernize the Church, eliminating celibacy, accepting women into the priesthood, and approving the use of preservative measures in birth control. Gwen had kidnapped them, promising their lives in exchange for their votes of acceptance. The deal required the signature of approval from the Pope, who pretending ignorance of everything that had happened would join with several other cardinals to sign the agreement in order to prevent the kidnapped clerics' get murder.

"Fortunately, thanks to our surprise attack, they were rescued before they could sign any agreement. Being aware of the circumstances, the cardinal and the two bishops visited the Pope and requested his resignation. The Pope, feeling trapped, said he would offer his resignation to the public in six hours, giving the excuse that his personal doctor had discovered initial symptoms of Alzheimer's in him, and before the illness advanced, he preferred to resign as Pope and retire to an isolated place known only to him. On the day after his resignation, the cardinals would be summoned in conclave to designate his successor, which without a doubt would be Cardinal Leonardo Pontl, who once was considered to be the successor of Pope Leon XVII."

Mr. Sullivan traveled to Rome to be present at the new Pope's appointment. Having departed Lexington at 5:30 p.m., he was expected to arrive in Rome at 9:30 a.m. A limousine had been arranged to pick him up at the Leonardo Da Vinci Airport and take him directly to the Vatican, where he would gather with the high authorities of the Church to assist in the sentencing Cardinal Villavicencio deserved to receive.

"Now that Susan is dead and Romy and Elysee are in prison, I might close the case of Gerald Solaris's murder, although finding Gwen and the other members of her staff who were able to escape with her is still pending," said Albert. "At this moment, every vehicle crossing the German border is being thoroughly inspected, making it difficult for Gwen leave the country. In my personal opinion, Gwen is hiding with a friend someplace in Offenbach City. Nevertheless, we are confident the inspections won't let her go too far. The media has offered us to help in our search, showing flyers with her picture and announcing in the newspapers and on TV and radio a reward of five million dollars for her capture. Without a doubt, in less than a week, we should have Gwen in prison," Albert said.

Lewis agreed with him, then asked how he knew about the bullets in Elysee's gun. Everything was recorded in my sister's minicomputer. Colliere smiled and answered that when Simone handed Elysee the Beretta, she said she could use her own gun, which was a Ruger 22 mm caliber. Knowing that, we bought blanks to fit her gun, making the exchange of bullets when Elysee took her shower."

"That was a clever strategy on your part. If not for you, some of us would be dead by now."

"Sorry to interrupt your conversation," said Richard, "but I feel really tired and want to go rest in my hotel. I need to call my wife and sister and tell them what has happened. But before I depart, I would like to express my gratitude to everyone present and absent who so diligently collaborated on this case. Thank you, Sister Marguerite and Simone, who executed Albert Colliere's plans and risked their lives to find my father's murderer and rescue the cardinal and two bishops. The mastermind of the operation was you, Detective Colliere, who was able to move every piece of the puzzle with extreme perfection. The plan to send your sister as a spy without rousing Gwen's suspicions was unbelievable, as was stopping what Susan intended to do to those men in time, as well as your discovery of Gwen's religious conspiracy to make Cardinal Villavicencio Pope."

When Richard was finished with his flattery, Albert said he did not deserve any of it as everything he did was part of his job. Many other people deserved recognition more than he, especially his father's friends who showed their loyalty to him in the last moments of his life, such as Liu and Hemant, who did not mind risking their own lives.

"Yes, Detective, you are right," said Richard, "and also to Jacob and Mohammed, victims of Gwen's demands but loyal to my father. When after reading my father's letter telling me not to get involved, they preferred to follow his commands than to say what they knew of Gwen, thinking it would put my life at risk. I also thank those absentees, such as Detective Miguel Rodriguez, who stayed to collect information leading to Romy's confession, and to Captain Raymond Sullivan, among others, all key people in the case. And what to say about you, Sam? Since that first interview, you have offered me your experience and sincere friendship. It is sad to remember Romy and Howie, who were poisoned by Gwen since their childhoods, making them promise to follow her orders and kill when she demanded. And finally, before I depart, I would like for Detective Colliere to call me a taxi that can take me to my hotel," Richard said finally. Ivonne rose from her seat to remind Richard he had forgotten to thank someone else. Richard said he was sorry, but no one else came to mind.

"It is God, whose mercy blessed us, sending to you the Holy Spirit and protecting your family and you," said Ivonne.

Richard agreed with her statement and thanked Sister Marguerite for her reminder. "Let us hold hands and make a prayer to our Lord," Richard proposed. Everybody agreed, and they held hands to pray together. Finally, Richard was informed Jonathan was in the basement waiting to pick him up and take him to his hotel.

Albert stopped Richard to say that before he left, he wanted to tell him they had reviewed his father's bank accounts, finding the money was legal, as he had never used the accounts to launder money or for dirty businesses. Furthermore, as he had paid his income taxes correctly, Richard could dispose of those funds immediately. Thanking Colliere, Richard said his father kept those funds for his and his sister's benefit.

Richard was about to take the elevator when was waylaid by Lewis, who wanted to talk privately with him. He invited Richard to have breakfast with him at the airport restaurant tomorrow. Richard agreed and asked if six in the morning was OK for him. Lewis answered that was perfect, and he would see him there.

CHAPTER 32

At six o'clock sharp, Richard found Sam drinking coffee in the restaurant and complaining about the prohibition against smoking, saying there was no place in the airport where he could smoke, and he had to leave the airport to go and smoke out in the street.

Inviting Richard to sit, Sam called the waiter to order their breakfast, saying he was really hungry because last night he was so tired that instead of dining, he preferred to go to sleep in his hotel. Richard said that last night he had eaten a good steak in his hotel before going to sleep.

To start the conversation, Lewis informed Richard that Cardinal Villavicencio had been arrested and sent to an isolated location that morning, where he was to remain the rest of his life. The news would say he was ill. Richard was not allowed to say anything. He promised he never would but said was glad to see the cardinal was paying for his sins.

Lewis mentioned that was not what he wanted to discuss, but instead he was interested to know Richard's plans for the future. Thinking for a moment, Richard said that after arriving in Mexico, he would return to his work and live the same life he always had with his wife and children. Lewis shook his head and asked permission to give him some advice, suggesting he should go on vacation with his family. Richard agreed and said he was intending to travel to Israel and then Arabia to personally express his gratitude to Jacob and Mohammed. Sam shook his head again and said, "Don't you think it would be better if you went to Hawaii or another place in the Caribbean that can make you forget the bad moments you've recently lived with the death of your father?"

Agreeing with his suggestion, Richard said that when he got to Mexico, he would tell Alice to make the arrangements for his trip.

Sipping his coffee, Richard asked Sam what his impression was of Gwen's organization. Sam said the question was tough, but he would try to answer the best he could. He said Gwen's mission was to defend women against the mistreatment and discrimination of men, which in theory he agreed. History showed that the ignorance of women from their lack of education made men submit them to their desires and to discriminate and mistreat them. Times had changed, and today the economic crisis and price inflation worked in her favor. Her husband's unemployment made her go find work to help support their families. Today, most countries in the world offer a mixed education in which men and women receive the same treatment. Women's capabilities and intelligence served to combat the ignorance in which they had lived for years. Now women performed the same work as men, although in some cases with lower pay.

What continued unchanged for women was her acceptance in the higher hierarchy of the Church. Most feminists considered this a discrimination act, and they fought to eliminate it. "Richard, I am not a Catholic, but I know many of these restrictions were originated in the time of Christ. Don't you think it is time for Catholics to be more flexible and accept in their doctrine and principles a modernization of the Church by eliminating celibacy for priests, accepting women into the priesthood, and allowing preventive methods of birth control? Don't you agree, Richard, that those changes would benefit their religion, bringing back many parishioners who had left to find in another religion what in their own was forbidden?" Richard stayed mute and did not answer.

"Richard, there is no doubt that Gwen and Susan were feminists and men haters who tried to impose several reforms in favor of women. Following their objective, they hired five men with different nationalities and religions and paid them stratospheric salaries just to convince Church authorities of the benefits of allowing women into the priesthood. Gwen selected Gerald Solaris as one candidate to perform this work. His excellent relations with the Vatican made him the right person to convince the cardinals who were still hesitant to vote in favor of Cardinal Alexander Villavicencio, who promised that if he became Pope, he would help Gwen bring women into the priesthood and into high clerical positions in the Vatican. What follows is better known by you.

"Richard, don't you think the hierarchs of the Catholic Church should eliminate celibacy in priests, accept women into the priesthood, and approve the use of contraceptive measures for birth control?"

Richard thought a minute and said, "Maybe I do, but without a doubt they won't, claiming those changes go against the teachings of Jesus Christ."

"Don't you think a modernized Church would bring in more parishioners?"

"No doubt it would; however, in the short term, I don't see Church leaders accepting these ideas."

Richard sipped his coffee and change of topic asking Sam what led him to believe a secret international organization was behind his father's murder. Lewis smiled and answered it was his sixth sense as a detective and other clues he found when he searched his father's condo that led him to know his father had not committed suicide. "The plan to murder your father was almost perfect, and only a professional would be able to carry it out. Distracting my attention by leaving clues leading me toward suicide was a great strategy. Furthermore, after listening to your interrogation, I knew the crime had political or religious purposes. So I supposed an international organization could have been behind it.

"Richard, what do you think of Susan's last words before she died, when she said the empowerment of women was under way and nothing would stop it?."

Richard said he agreed with her statement, as even that today women still lives in more poverty than men due to disparities in their payments. And their parents believed in giving a better education to boys, thinking that when they grew up, they would earn a better salary than their daughters. And the threats and types of discrimination that women faces in reproductive matters, as the Social and legal institutions do not guarantee by law the equality of women and men. "But in spite of this matters, we need to recognize women's advances. Her incorporation into the labor force has helped to improve their status in life by earning decent salaries that made them depend less on men. The men of today perform tasks that once belonged only to women, such as cleaning the house, washing dishes, and changing their children's diapers. Women's new identity has caused men to lose their masculinity, who has adopted feminine features such as wearing light-colored fitted pants, put earrings in their nose and ears, and even going to beauty parlors to color their hair and eliminate wrinkles. Maybe it is sad to recognize, but the women of today need men less. Assisted reproductive techniques such as artificial insemination and in vitro fertilization make women pregnant without the need for sexual contact with men, making some women more independent and leading them to practice lesbianism. The men who lose their masculinity and treat women badly are at risk of losing their relationships. Studies prove the brains of women have more neurons than men, making them more intelligent and capable of solving problems. The real man of today does not attract women by his strength but with care and love. Her better education has tended to eliminate many of the discriminatory practices that have been still laid on her.

Sam agreed with his statement and said to Richard, "Let's take this as a lesson to put into practice in our own life."

Changing the subject, Sam asked Richard what he intended to do with his father's condo. When he arrived in Mexico, he would speak with his sister and explain everything that had happened, and together they would make the decision of what to do with his father's condo. Maybe she would like to keep it for herself as her husband loved to take their children to Disneyland every year.

Richard promised Sam that the next time he came to Los Angeles, they would get together to talk and eat in a good restaurant. He also invited Sam to come to Mexico and visit Cancun, where his sister had a nice condo in Playa del Carmen. "You can bring your wife and children also."

"Sounds good to me. On my next vacation, I will consider your offer," Sam said.

Glancing at his watch, Richard said it was time to go, as he had forgotten the time to board his plane was 7:45 a.m. And as the line for inspection kept growing, he had better leave. Rising from his seat, Richard gave Sam a hug, saying, "I am going to miss you, buddy."

"*Yo recuerdo tu tambien, amigo mio,*" responded Sam, making an effort to speak Spanish. Richard laughed and said he could see he still remembered some Spanish words. "Not too many," Lewis answered.

Hauling his luggage, Richard walked toward the inspection line. While he waited, he waved his hand, saying his last goodbye to Sam. Sam ran to find a place where he could see the plane take off. An old lady dressed in an elegant blue suit approached him to ask if the man who had waved his hands insistently at him was his brother.

"No, Mum, he is not my brother, but he is like one to me because I am honored to be his friend," answered Sam with a smile.

END

Printed in the United States
By Bookmasters